CRY IN THE DARK

Collins looked at the drawing that little Johnny had made. It was a drawing of children—sixteen of them.

All their faces bore a look of anguish.

Collins looked up and felt something like an electric shock. Johnny's own face showed the same expression: a Greek mask of tragedy, a face of suffering.

Collins realized that Johnny was attempting to speak. For a shivering moment, he did not want to hear.

"Heh . . . heh," the boy stammered, his face reddening. He swallowed, gasped, and slapped his right hand down on the drawing. "Heh . . . help." The boy took another deep breath, and then in his aching, rusty, hoarse voice, Johnny at last forced the sentence out: *"Help us."*

CHILDREN
OF THE KNIFE

BRAD STRICKLAND

AN ONYX BOOK

ONYX
Published by the Penguin Group
Penguin Books USA Inc., 375 Hudson Street, New York,
New York 10014, U.S.A.
Penguin Books Ltd, 27 Wrights Lane, London W8 5TZ, England
Penguin Books Australia Ltd, Ringwood, Victoria, Australia
Penguin Books Canada Ltd, 2801 John Street, Markham,
Ontario, Canada L3R 1B4
Penguin Books (N.Z.) Ltd, 182-190 Wairau Road, Auckland 10, New Zealand

Penguin Books Ltd, Registered Offices:
Harmondsworth, Middlesex, England

First published by Onyx, an imprint of Penguin Books USA Inc.

First Printing, August, 1990

10 9 8 7 6 5 4 3 2 1

 REGISTERED TRADEMARK—MARCA REGISTRADA

PRINTED IN THE UNITED STATES OF AMERICA

PUBLISHER'S NOTE
This is a work of fiction. Names, characters, places, and incidents either are the product of the author's imagination or are used fictitiously, and any resemblance to actual persons, living or dead, events, or locales is entirely coincidental.

BOOKS ARE AVAILABLE AT QUANTITY DISCOUNTS WHEN USED TO PROMOTE PRODUCTS OR SERVICES. FOR INFORMATION PLEASE WRITE TO PREMIUM MARKETING DIVISION. PENGUIN BOOKS USA INC.. 375 HUDSON STREET. NEW YORK. NEW YORK 10014.

This is for Tonya Cox,
who proved worthy of her unicorn;
and for
Amy and Charles Rutledge,
who came to my aid with a party.

And they brought young children to him, that he should touch them: and his disciples rebuked those that brought them.

But when Jesus saw it, he was much displeased, and said unto them, Suffer the little children to come unto me, and forbid them not: for of such is the kingdom of God.

—The Gospel According to St. Mark

CHAPTER ONE

1

Pete Collins stepped out of the cabin into a Sunday heavy with the threat of storm. Clouds so deeply gray they were almost purple hung pendulous in the sky. The pines stirred in a fret of wind, the sweet gums fluttered and rustled.

Down the slope the gray Chanussee River showed choppy through breaks in the trees, the waters streaked white by fitful gusts. Collins took a deep breath: the air smelled of electricity, of lightning and ozone.

As if in answer to his thought, a searing bolt crackled horizontally just above the tallest trees and a second later thunder slammed into the earth, making Collins flinch. The thunder rolled away downhill, trundling and grumbling like a runaway truck on eccentric wheels, as the first rain started. It fell in huge, cold, splatting drops that hit the unpaved drive with audible *cracks* and sent up spurts of fine red dust. More rain *pinged* against the unwashed Ford Ranger, making black spots on the dirty film.

Collins felt a couple of drops strike him on forehead and arm so hard that they stung, and he retreated through the cabin door, ducking his head in a way that had become habitual for a man who had stood six feet tall twelve years ago when he was fifteen and who had topped out at six-two.

Collins closed a suddenly restive door against a burst of wind and rain. For a few seconds he stood there, hearing the clatter of rain—hail?—against the weathered clapboards. Then, feeling vaguely uneasy, he went to the side window and looked out at a day gone silver with driving, spiking rain. He stood there, a big man, not more than five or six pounds too heavy, his dark blond hair too long from neglect. He brushed it off his forehead and leaned against the wall, his face close to the window-pane. Again a close bolt of lightning lit up the north Georgia hills blue and white, and the thunder rattled the panes. There would no fishing this June day.

"Damn," Collins said, though in fact he felt mainly relief at not having to be out in the boat.

The rain came in curtains, wave after wave of it, bending the trees and sheeting across the river. It drummed so hard on the roof that it muted the thunder, though the lightning strikes were so close that the lightning and the thunder came simultaneously. Staring out the window, Collins was so caught up in the spectacle that the pounding on his door caught him by surprise, made him jump as the lightning had earlier. He opened the door and William Whitepath swung in, crouched over and partly covered by a black slicker that he had spread over his head and shoulders. "Close the door!" Whitepath bawled. Collins got a faceful of rain and a glimpse of Whitepath's battered Army-green Dodge van as he slammed the cabin door against a burst of cold rain.

"You wasted a trip," Collins said as Whitepath shed the dripping slicker, tossing it down on the hearth.

"I was on the way when it hit." Whitepath swept a palm back over his lustrous black hair. Rivulets of water ran down his ruddy face, and he swiped them away with the back of his hand. William Whitepath was a strongly built man, five feet ten and 170 pounds, mostly muscle. Whitepath claimed to be a full-blooded Cherokee, and he looked as if he probably was. He had to be at least forty, though his wide smile made him seem years younger than that, white teeth flashing in a dark face. His manner was a young man's, too, and Collins, not yet thirty, felt very much at home with this smiling brawny man. He turned the smile on Collins now. "Got anything to drink, Pete?"

"It's barely noon, Will. Too early for drinking," Collins said, picking up the slicker and hanging it from a corner of the mantel.

"So white man says. My Cherokee ancestors consid-ered it night whenever they couldn't see the sun. Sun's behind the clouds now, so it's time for a drink. Mind if I help myself?"

"Go ahead. Everything's where it usually is, in the cabinet behind you." Collins sat and watched Whitepath pour himself a drink, scotch straight up. "Want some ice?"

"Naw. Want one?"

"Too early for me. That true about the Cherokees? That it's night whenever they can't see the sun?"

"Naw, I made it up." He lifted his highball glass toward Pete. "Here's how." Lightning flashed; the electricity died; thunder rattled every loose item in the cabin. "Jesus," Whitepath said, and he knocked back half of the drink. "At least you wouldn't get sunburned on a day like today, huh?"

Collins gave a single rueful laugh. "If there's a full moon, I can get sunburned at midnight."

Whitepath squinted at him. "Guess you're right. You blue-eyed blonds just ain't made for a man's world. Oughta get a little color, like me." He sighed and glanced at the Apple computer on its stand against the wall. "Anyhow, you can get some writing done, huh?" He sank into one of the room's three chairs, a recliner that had seen better days. It was covered now with a blue-and-white diamond-patterned quilt in lieu of upholstery.

"I guess," Collins said, sitting in the armchair on the other side of the fireplace. The cabin, suddenly gone dark, seemed smaller to him, closer. "If I feel like it."

"No inspiration, Pete?" Whitepath asked, his teeth flashing white in the darkness.

"No, it's not that." Lightning photographed the front room of the cabin, spilling in through the three windows, catching Whitepath with the glass halfway to his lips. Collins waited until the thunder died down before speaking: "Hell, I did the newspaper stories. I've got all the material. Inspiration's got nothing to do with it."

"What's your problem, then?"

"Dunno. Guess I'm burned out on the whole subject of drugs."

"Maybe it's just the amount of work you gotta do. How long's this book gonna be?"

"My guess is five hundred pages, manuscript."

Whitepath whistled. "Damn. When you gotta turn it in?"

"First of January."

The lights flickered, glowed a weak orange, and decided to die again. Whitepath got up in the dark and splashed more scotch into his glass. "Five hundred pages in six months? Hell, can you do it, Pete? How much you got done now?"

"Of the book manuscript? About a hundred and twenty-five. There's the feature series, too. There's twenty, thirty thousand words in it. About seventy or eighty pages."

Whitepath sat again. "You done a hundred and twenty-five pages since you opened this place up? What's that, three weeks? I take it back. Keep goin' like that, you'll have the book finished by August."

"If I can get up the energy to do a little work. I—"

"Shhh."

Collins paused and listened. He heard only the howl of the wind, the chatter of the rain. Lightning, not as close, lit up the world outside. "What is it?"

"Dunno. Something. Where's Eightball?"

"Damn, I forgot him. He must be outdoors." Collins got up and went to the front door, a kettledrum ruffle of thunder accompanying his steps. He opened the door on steady, rattling rain, no longer a cloudburst but hard enough. "Eightball!" he shouted. "C'mon, boy!"

The black cocker with the single round white spot on his chest crept out from under the Ranger. The dog loped through liquid red mud, bounded through the door, and shook himself.

"Shit!" Whitepath covered his drink with the palm of his hand and turned his head against the spray of water and mud. "Didn't know you'd let him in or I wouldn'ta mentioned him."

Collins laughed, disappeared through a door to the back rooms of the cabin, and a moment later came back with a tattered red towel. Eightball had flopped onto the hearth, and he submitted to a rough toweling with tongue-lolling enjoyment. Finished with the dog, Collins made a few dabs at the furniture. "Can't hurt this junk, anyway," he said. "It's all crap. Judge gave Dorothy the good stuff."

"I thank God for divorce courts. They give you pale-faces some idea of how the red man felt when the law stole all his land." Whitepath raised his glass. "To the American system of jurisprudence."

"Hear, hear."

Whitepath drained his drink and stared past Collins at the window and the downpour outside. "I think it's gonna rain all day."

"Cherokee weather medicine?" Collins asked, crumpling the stained towel and dropping it on the hearth near Eightball.

"Naw. Color radar on the TV showed a line of thunderstorms all the way from here back south and west to Birmingham."

"Why'd you even bother to come out on your one day off?"

Whitepath shrugged. "Maybe white man's magic don't work all the time. Besides, you always have a pretty good selection of liquor on hand. Say, is that computer safe when it's lightning like this?"

"It's on a surge protector. Cabin's got lighting rods."

Whitepath grunted. "And you can't use it while the power's off. Typical of white man's inventions."

"I haven't thrown away my Faber-Castell American. I could still write—if I wanted to. Anyway, the computer's useful in all sorts of other ways. I don't have to leave the cabin to do my research, for instance. I just modem through to one of the information services and call up anything I want."

"Great," Whitepath said. "Just what you needed. Something else to keep you shut up here like a hermit."

Eightball got to his feet and trotted to the door. He sniffed at the crack, looked back over his shoulder at Collins, and yipped. Collins, who had sat down again, said, "Quiet! You don't want to go out, boy. Too wet."

The dog whined and scratched at the door. Then he came back to the hearth, sniffed the towel, turned around, and whined again.

"Dog senses something," Whitepath said. "Same as me."

"Bullshit," Collins said. "You don't sense anything except a chance to drink some of my booze."

Whitepath's dark face set itself in a slight frown. "Seriously, Pete. Something's building. I can feel it."

"What?" Collins asked.

"I dunno. I've had a funny feeling since last week. We were runnin' a population count on the squirrels—hey, don't laugh, it's part of a forest ranger's job—in the national forest. I was over on Claxton's Ridge—know where that is? About thirty miles from here, as the crow flies. Anyhow, the Forestry Service has a research station there, damnedest thing you ever saw. About, I'd guess, a hundred acres or maybe even more, enclosed in a double chain-link fence. I was around there, just in sight of the installation, when a helicopter took off somewhere inside—there's a line of trees not far inside the fence, you can't actually see the buildings too good—and I heard something."

Thunder, much tamer now and farther away, purred outside. After a moment, Collins asked, "Well? What did you hear?"

"I thought it was kids."

Collins frowned. "What do you mean, kids?"

"Kids," Whitepath insisted. "Buncha kids, crying. Begging. But there ain't any kids around." He leaned forward in the recliner, and Collins thought he saw him shiver. "They cried and cried. All the rest of that day, no matter where I went, they cried and cried. It was like they was in my head."

"Well." Collins grinned.

"Don't laugh at me." Whitepath's voice was level and serious. "I heard it all day long. I heard it at night. I dreamed about it. That was last Thursday. Things ain't seemed right since."

Despite himself, Collins shuddered, as if from a sudden chill. The dog looked up into his eyes and whined again. Off in the distance thunder trundled across the pine-covered hills.

2

The Delta 757 slanted down toward thickly clustered clouds. At first they were white and shining in the sun; then, as the jet nosed into them, they became thick gray mist. Looking out over the starboard wing, Ernest Fisher could see only as far as the first engine cowling. The darkness of the clouds made the Plexiglas window reflective, superimposing on the wing a ghostly image of Fisher's face, gaunt and seamed beneath its thick thatch of steely gray hair. His forty-six-year-old face. His face that looked ten years older than that damned baby face of Grade's. Fisher straightened in his seat, frowning.

After some minutes in the fog, the plane dropped through the cloud cover. Below them, its green, gray, and red colors muted by the overcast, lay the patchwork landscape around Atlanta. Glancing out the window again, Fisher spotted Stone Mountain—like a sculpted granite tit, he thought—and from its position he oriented himself. The city was off to the west, on his right, its sprawl gray with distance and light rain. The airplane banked in that direction. Hydraulics whined as the landing gear lowered and locked. Fisher sighed, adjusted the briefcase on his lap, and leaned back in his seat. He was flying tourist—he always did when on commercial flights—but the two seats next to him were, as always, unoccupied. As he had told Mr. Grade last Thursday, he was willing to appear inconspicuous, but not to the extent of having to put up with idiotic chatter. Grade had suggested that if Fisher felt that way about it, he might as well fly first class. The suggestion alone guaranteed that Fisher wouldn't.

He closed his mind to the murmured conversation, the roar of the engines, the soft chiming of the FASTEN SEAT BELT sign. Fisher had always possessed the enviable ability to shut out nonessentials and to concentrate on the important things. He was doing that now.

He was thinking about the Grade Committee.

Or, to give it its proper name, the Joint Intelligence Services Review Committee. Headed by that prick Randall Grade, who had left the unit in 1976 to work for the CIA, who had left the CIA in '88 to work for the new administration. And who now had visions of himself as, what, the nation's VP in two years' time? At any rate, Grade had it in for the Biomedical Counterespionage Unit, more familiarly known as Slow Tango.

Fisher closed his eyes and saw Grade's face again, that smarmy, sincere, schoolboy face. Smooth and pink, not a line on it. Christ, the man was fifty-two. Probably had had a few tucks taken here and there. And how easily the phrases rolled off that silken tongue of his—"temporary austerity measures . . . dynamic reevaluation of operational requirements . . . improved intelligence acquisition systems . . . impact assessment of departmental worth."

Meaningless phrases, bureaucratic gabbling. What it boiled down to was that Grade envied his, Fisher's, coup. What it amounted to was a threat to terminate the unit for good. All because Grade, who had actually initiated unit operations back in '66 when it looked as if the country was never going to get out of Vietnam, had bungled the job, had produced nothing usable in ten years of trying—nothing except his clever plan of sneaking the unit's budget in among operational expenses of three branches of the armed services. Whereas Fisher, within a year of taking over the operation, had—

The aircraft lurched as the wheels touched down. Fisher opened his eyes. The plane screamed along a wet runway, through misting rain. People were already standing up, opening the overhead compartments, rummaging for their belongings. Fisher kept his seat.

The plane taxied to position. The accordion-fold exit gate extended to kiss the hull. The door whined open. The pilot said something nearly intelligible about hoping they would all fly again. Fisher stayed put until the crush of passengers had gone by. When only a dozen or so slow movers were left behind him, he rose, briefcase in his left hand, and followed the crowd. At the door a flight attendant smiled at him. He nodded at her, his expression neutral. She didn't seem disturbed. "Your carry-on," she said, handing him his overnight case.

Fisher took it, grunting his thanks, making a mental note to check it for surreptitious entry before opening it himself. Had someone opened it, the snooper would have found nothing except three days' worth of soiled laundry; still, it was best to know if anyone was close enough to be checking up on these things.

Dougherty was waiting inside the gate. "How'd it go?" he asked, falling in step beside Fisher.

Fisher glanced around, saw only travelers. In a voice too low for anyone but Dougherty to hear, he said, "Shitty. I'm pretty certain that Grade is going to recommend a fold. We'll need ammo if we want to stay in business."

"Okay."

"Chopper ready?"

Dougherty, a compact and husky man of perhaps fifty with a gray-streaked brush haircut, shook his head. "Negative. It's storming like hell at the installation. We wait or we drive."

"Damn." Fisher sighed. "Any news?"

Dougherty waited until they were on the long escalator down to the transportation plaza, well away from anyone else, before whispering his answer: "One death. The Gamma boy."

"Shit."

Dougherty's shrug wrinkled the shoulders of his off-the-rack suit. "What the hell. He was a non, anyway."

"Yeah. Cremation?"

"Already done. Everything SOP."

"When?"

"Thursday evening. Not long after you left, in fact. Doc K. found him dead in his room. I gave the cremation order a little past four P.M. It was over that night." Dougherty paused. "Stark raised hell over it."

"What was his problem?"

They stepped off the escalator and strolled toward the shuttle dock. "He wanted a PM. But he was too late; by the time he found out about the Gamma boy, we'd already burned him."

Fisher gave Dougherty a hard sideways look. "Why no autopsy?"

"He was a non, Ernest. What's the point?"

"The point . . . Forget it. Not here. We'll talk about it later."

They crowded onto a car on the shuttle train and rode to the concourse gate set aside for helicopters. "No chance of persuading the pilot to take off?" Fisher asked. Dougherty shook his head. In his dark gray suit, white oxford shirt, and blue tie, Dougherty looked like a military man, like a hammered-down Marine colonel ill at ease in unaccustomed civvies. Or like a cop only recently promoted to the detective force. At five-ten, two inches shorter than Fisher, Dougherty was a slow-moving man, walking with a heavy, lumbering gait. He certainly didn't look like the kind of agent who was capable of pulling a top scientist out of the Soviet Union.

And yet the two of them had done just that, back in the bad days of '76, with Fisher running the operation and Dougherty the point man. And nobody, not even a prick like Grade, could say that Stark, a second-generation German scientist working for the Soviets, hadn't been worth the effort or the investment. Ignoring the fact that the geneticist could be a pain in the ass, his work was a coup that no one—at least no one with Ultra-level security clearance, and that number was small indeed—could dismiss.

But, dammit, Grade was baying at their heels now.

Dougherty brought Fisher back to the present: "Want me to arrange for a car, or should we wait for a break in the weather?"

Fisher bit his lip. "How long will we have to wait?"

"Weather service says storms will continue for another two hours, anyway."

Fisher grunted and checked his Rolex: 1:35 P.M. "What the hell," he said. "Let's have a drink."

Dougherty had a wonderful wallet. He took a card from it, put the card in a holder, and flashed it at the right people. By one-fifty the two of them sat in comfortable chairs in a small room with a window overlooking one of the runways. An airport employee, a pretty black woman, took their orders and came back within five minutes with two drinks, bourbon for Dougherty and gin and tonic for Fisher. When she left, Dougherty took out of his breast pocket something that looked like a transistor radio. He flicked a switch and put the device on the table between them. It hummed for thirty seconds before presenting a display on a small liquid-crystal screen. Dougherty checked it and nodded. "Room's clean. And even with a parabolic amplifier, the window wouldn't yield a voice trace, not with the jet noise. We can talk."

"I don't like crossing Stark." Fisher sipped his drink with fussy daintiness. "We keep him happy at all costs. You should have let him autopsy the kid."

"Stark was away, off in Atlantic City; we didn't get him on a secure line until the next morning. And anyway, how many autopsies has he done?" It was a rhetorical question, Fisher knew. "Christ, he's cut up thirteen already. Our three best positives and ten nons. What has he found?"

"Nothing," Fisher said.

"Damn right. And look at the paperwork we have to

do every time. I don't like it, Ernest. Never leave a paper trail. Never. And the Alpha girl—"

"Yes, I know."

"Jesus, he used her as a *control*. He took her apart living—"

"Charlie—"

—cut up a ten-year-old child just to check—"

"Charlie!"

Dougherty glared at him. "Hell. You know how I feel about these damn PMs."

"I know. Who authorized Stark's jaunt to Atlantic City?"

"He authorized himself. Right after you left."

"I should have guessed. He back yet?"

"Yeah. Came back that next morning, raising hell about what we'd done. Anyhow, the kid's burned now." Dougherty sipped his bourbon. "So. What are we gonna do about Grade?"

"Play for time. We have more than a hundred positive test series. I want you to pull the best twenty for me."

Dougherty shook his head. "Ernest, you can't use 'em. Hell, out of the nine committee members, only Grade and Longworth have Ultra clearance—"

"I'll go over Grade if I have to."

"Yeah? And what happens when he gets to be vice-president? Or president, even?"

Fisher smiled, a drawn smile that felt weary on his face. "I guess we just have to make sure that he never gets to be either. One way or another." With his forefinger Fisher drew together the beads of moisture clinging to the outside of his highball glass. They condensed into one drop that slid down slowly, writhing across the surface like a gentle tear.

3

Thirteen hundred miles to the west of Atlanta the morning had dawned cool, clear, and blue, the sky that rich copper sulfate hue that you see at high altitudes. Beth Engstrom glanced at it occasionally through the ranch-house windows. It was a beautiful Colorado day.

She wept as she looked at it, then threw herself furiously back into her assault on the house.

It was barely noon, and she was a small woman, but given the constraints of time and her petite body, she had accomplished miracles. Already she had stripped all four beds, the one she shared with her husband the colonel, the two in the guest rooms (one could have been a nursery, could have been, could have been), had changed them, had dusted ferociously, had vacuumed the bedrooms, had washed the bedroom windows, had scrubbed the three bathrooms so that tile gleamed and chrome shone like platinum; then she had moved on to the hallways, dusting, vacuuming, changing the burned-out bulb outside the bedroom door, had broken out the Murphy's Oil Soap, had scrubbed the doors themselves until the grain grew dark and lustrous; and now she was about to start on the kitchen.

She had stopped only for a moment, just for a cup of strong and bitter black coffee. Looking out the kitchen window had broken her down. The backyard was trim and neat, kept that way by Colonel Engstrom (we're not old, it's not too late, he's not yet forty-five, I'm only thirty-three) himself. Like a man waging war on an army of insidious irregulars, Fritz—no one who had know him for more than five minutes ever called him Frederick— buzzed the mower over hostile territory twice a week, making the lawn so uniform and green that she could imagine her husband and his buddies shooting a game of billiards in the Engstrom backyard. Their neighbors on the left, the Kelleys, were more casual, letting their yard go a little wild and shaggy before firing up the Snapper. This was their mowing day, and their boy, Colin, was manfully steering the self-propelled machine, though it was much too big for a twelve-year-old.

The Engstroms' son would have been twelve.

Beth hurled the cup of coffee from her. It smashed against the wall, making a brown splotch like a jellyfish trailing its tendrils.

She looked at it and wept, wept so hard that her throat ached. A part of her mind told her it was all right, the wallpaper was vinyl-impregnated, it wouldn't stain, Fritz would never know. Another part wanted to bring down the house, to pull everything in on her head.

To drive out the dreams.

She covered her face with her palms, smelling the sharp formic-acid odor of the soap. "Am I losing my mind?" she asked. Her hands muffled her voice, sent it back vibrating into her sinuses. She bit her teeth together hard to hold in a scream.

They had come to her occasionally in the last nine years, the dreams of a lovely little boy. He had grown, curiously, in her dreams, just as a real child would have grown. He was a toddler, indistinct, tow-headed, chubby face grave, something special about the eyes.

She remembered the first time she had dreamed of him like that, a little boy in a white shirt and red corduroy overalls with a cookie in his hand, turning it, inspecting it gravely: and she had thought, *He's mine.*

The image was a gift from God, she thought, and she treasured it in her heart, that dream of the child who never was. She couldn't tell Fritz that; he was nominally a Lutheran but practically an agnostic, and he would worry about her, she knew, if she spoke of visions from on high. Still, somehow she believed that God had pitied her barrenness, had sent her a picture of the boy they had tried so hard to have, she and Fritz, the child who had come dead into the world. God had given her a glimpse of the baby as he must be, surely, somewhere, maybe in heaven.

But that had been the first dream. Since then the baby had grown, and the dreams had darkened.

If Beth wanted, she could go to the bedroom and pull from her lingerie drawer the little blue-covered diary, the kind that twelve-year-old girls buy at the dime store (though she had bought hers at the PX at Scott AFB, back when Fritz was working in photo recon). It held a record of her dreams over the years; not all the dreams, to be sure, but the ones about the child.

She could have counted the records in the book, though she had no need: the number was etched in her memory. In nine years there had been thirty-seven of them.

As of last night, thirty-eight.

The first four were recollected long after the fact, for she had not bought the diary at once. After her first dream, half a year went by before in another restless night of fitful sleep she saw the same child, her child, squealing with delight and clutching a plush Mickey Mouse toy to his chest. Then more months passed until she dreamed of him swinging, swinging safely in a toddler's swing, but shrieking with half-happy fear at the swoop and plunge of movement. Still more time went by until she dreamed of him screaming in pain after pinching his fingers in a drawer. Weeks after that one she bought the diary and began to record her dreams, hoping to capture them, to hold them, to make them somehow more real.

They had come more frequently sometimes, had vanished for months on end at other times. Lately they had been dreams of pain, of needles, of glittering instruments, of blinding green lights and shrill head-splitting noises, of hypodermics, of nausea. Through the horrors, the child grew: his fair curly hair became the exact golden shade of her own, the quizzical tilt of his brows mirrored Fritz's habitual expression. Their child, beyond any doubt. The twelve-year-old she dreamed of now no longer laughed (he never spoke in her dreams, and his strange eyes never lost the sheen of babyhood). Now he cried or screamed. Shrieked.

And oh, God, the latest dream, the one that had awakened her at four that morning—

Beth took her hands down. The coffee had spread in a brown puddle across the kitchen's café-au-lait tile floor. She squeaked her chair back from the table and snatched a wad of paper towels from the dispenser.

The cup was in half a dozen pieces. She picked them up and tossed them into the trash. She swabbed up the spill of coffee, cold now against the tile, and with more paper towels, dampened with water, she scrubbed the wall. The stain came off easily.

She got to her feet, feeling her knees shake.

She went to the bedroom and opened her lingerie drawer. Found the book. Got a smooth white Bic pen from the cup beside the telephone.

Sat on the bed and opened the diary to a fresh page.

Dated it.

Then for a long time she sat staring at the date. She took a deep breath and wrote:

> Last night I dreamed my baby was lost. It was night, stormy. He was caught in briars, trying to climb up a

steep hill. There were trees all around. It was so dark.
Except for the lightning. There were storm clouds far
off, and they lit up inside now and again with lightning. It made the clouds turn pink and blue. And the
thunder came.

My baby was afraid.

Beth Engstrom paused. Then she added one last line
and stared at it:

I am afraid.

4

"She's frightened," Alice Weston said softly.

Dr. Karl Stark nodded in his absent way. "I know that,
Nurse. But we must have the test," he said in English so
flawlessly unaccented that it could not be his native language. The scientist, heavily built (though not actually
fat, Alice thought, not like me), gazed unemotionally at
his subject. Only his hands betrayed an inner excitement:
clumsy-looking, blunt, they picked at each other with a
harried, almost insectile insistence as they always did
when Stark was hiding his feelings. His fingers were
rarely still even in the lab: if he wasn't methodically
ripping apart a paper cup, he was drumming them on the
computer consoles, as he did now.

The Beta girl lay in her form-fitting body mold, her
head, shoulders, torso, arms, and legs immobilized by
straps. Her eyes rolled wildly. Guttural gasps escaped her
lips.

She was not one of the better-looking ones, Stark had
offhandedly told the nurse once. It was true: Kathy Beta's
head was too large for her body, her eyes too widely
separated, her reddish hair too sparse, her ears somehow
misplaced, low on her skull. Then of course there were her
hands. They had thumbs but no separate fingers; they
were brown mittens of flesh, clenched now in terror.

The nurse said, "If I could explain it to her—"

"Miss Weston. No explanation is possible. She would
not understand you in any case, even if she responded to
language. It is too complex for this child's mind to com-

prehend. The scanner is ready. Insert the catheter, if you please."

Alice murmured, "Yes, Doctor," carefully keeping her face neutral. This series of PET scans used technetium-99w as the tracer, suspended in glucose and injected directly into the carotid artery. Kathy's teeth clenched tight as her eyes rolled to the side, fixing on the broad expanse of Alice's white uniform. Softly, so that Dr. Stark could not hear, Alice said, "It's all right, baby. It won't really hurt."

But the girl's neck strained when Alice swabbed the antiseptic on, and when the needle pierced the artery, Alice heard in her head the scream the girl would have made had she not been mute. Stark activated the platform, and it slipped the girl back so that her head rested inside the great white doughnut of the scanner. Motors hummed and whirred; hydraulics hissed; the immobilized girl whimpered, not with her useless larynx but with her teeth and lips, a keening hiss of air breathed out. The computers went to work, quickly, silently putting together a cross section of Kathy Beta's brain.

God, Alice thought, let me not scream today. Let me stick it out until tomorrow. If I can make it through tomorrow, I can make it through the rest of the tour.

The scans tomorrow were scheduled to use oxygen-15 as the tracer, an isotope with a half-life of only two minutes. It was inhaled through a mask, not injected; the compact cyclotron in the room next door piped the atomically tagged gas directly into the scanner room. The children tomorrow would be frightened, too, but their terror would not be as great as Kathy's, and it would be unaccompanied by pain as the scanner did its work.

"Twenty-seven in the entire United States," Dr. Stark had boasted of the device on her orientation tour six months earlier. "Not counting ours, of course." Of course. Who would count a clandestine nuclear-medicine installation placed in the middle of the wilderness somewhere in the Southeast, an installation serving a most limited clientele of seventeen children between the ages of eight and thirteen?

No. Not even seventeen children. Of sixteen children now. As of last week. Last Thursday.

Dr. Stark had little to do while the computers made

their pictures. As if he could look into her own skull without benefit of tomography, as if he could read her mind, he said, "Did you get a chance to see the dead boy last week?"

"No, Doctor. I was on the evening shift last week." *You know that.*

"Mm. A gross evaluation would be worthless, anyway. Still, I should have been called."

"Mr. Fisher was away," Alice said. "And we understood you were in New York."

"Atlantic City." Stark smiled. He had a broad face, bluff Teutonic features, hair that once had been somewhere between red and blond, strawberry blond as they used to call it, but now was frosted with gray. It was a quintessentially German face, blue-eyed, strong-jawed. "They say the Soviet Union is becoming more and more capitalist, but Russia has no casinos that I know of. That is one of the benefits of the West. I was experimenting with a system for blackjack. You know blackjack?"

"Twenty-one," Alice said, feeling the flesh of her arms pucker into gooseflesh. Surely Stark was not supposed to refer to his homeland; that surely should have been secret. And Stark was the sort of man who kept his secrets by making sure that those who shared them could not talk.

"Twenty-one, yes. The French call it *vingt-et-un.*"

"I know the game, Dr. Stark." The scanner had rotated around Kathy through half a circle. It edged microscopically forward and began to rock back in the other direction. "I've never played it in a casino, though."

"It is one of the few games of chance that I care to play. The others . . ." Stark made a throw-away gesture. "They are truly games of chance, of luck. But blackjack may have an element of skill in it, for someone who knows what he is about. I came out a winner. Two thousand seven hundred and fifty dollars to the good, as they say. It's all in the system. Still . . ." The smile gave way to a dour look, corners of the mouth turned quickly down. "Still, I should have been called. Specimens and samples should have been taken."

"Yes, Doctor."

Stark's nervous fingers caressed a computer keyboard without pressing the keys. "I would have expected the staff to do that for me, even in my absence." Genial tone, reproachful words, and so neutral in vocabulary: specimens. Samples.

Brain samples, nervous-system samples. Gland biopsies. Smears of blood on glass slides. Bits of bone marrow. Even, she had heard from some of the other nurses, snippets of hair.

But Stark didn't get you, Johnny, Alice thought to herself. And she added, *Good for you!*

"I have to content myself with these examinations instead," Stark was saying, emphasizing his words with a doleful shake of his head. "It is like closing the barn door after the horse has been stolen. But perhaps we may come to an understanding of why the boy died. Perhaps we may protect the other poor children from the threat."

"Yes, Doctor," Alice said again, though inside she was shrieking.

"Series over," an electronically generated voice announced.

Stark turned away. "Get her back to the quarters," he said without looking around.

Alice removed the catheter, trying not to hear Kathy's gurgling breath, trying not to smell the urine she had voided in her panic. "Here," she said, unstrapping Kathy's torso. A cart of towels stood nearby. She took one and cleaned Kathy as well as she could, trying to keep her broad body between the little girl and the two men in the room.

She wrapped Kathy in a terry robe and helped her down. The girl clung to her, buried her face in Alice's large bosom.

"She's ready to leave, Doctor," Alice said in a loud voice.

Stark, intent on a color monitor, waved a dismissive hand. Jerry, the guard at the door, entered a code on the keypad and the lock clacked. "Come on, honey," Alice said softly. "Let's go to your room."

Jerry, tight-lipped, shook his head at Alice as the two left. Jerry had very little use for Stark, Alice thought. But she would never speak to Jerry about the doctor; not here at Paranoia Palace.

Alice had to support Kathy. They turned left down the long fluorescent-lit hall, everything white tile and gleaming chrome. Another guard opened a door for them, and a third took them up two floors in the elevator to ground level. Kathy breathed a little easier when the door hissed open.

This was the nursery wing—an antique name now that all the children (all the *surviving* children, Alice thought) were approaching puberty. The walls here, as below, were of concrete block, but on this level they were painted in primary-colored murals, a panorama of a circus with red-nosed clowns, smiling orange tigers, beautiful cartoon ladies in pink tights. Kathy recognized it and unclenched, just a little.

Alice sighed. She felt like a mother to them all, felt like the mother that she would never be; not at thirty-eight, not when she was so heavy. Nothing physically wrong; but some women are destined to be barren not by the body but by the mind.

Kathy was in the third Beta room. The fourth and fifth were empty. Perhaps they had never been occupied. Perhaps their occupants, like Johnny last week, had died.

Perhaps Stark had parts of them in his collection.

5

Julie Lind had decided to be hard.

It was a job, that was all: a limited-term job. She had already put in three of her eleven months at the installation. Eight more months of work, then one of R&R, and then she'd move on to something else, something less secret, something that wouldn't drive her crazy. The trauma center in Virginia, perhaps, where they put back together the James Bonds who returned less than whole from missions they couldn't talk about; or even the recuperation facility in the Hawaiians where the burned-out, washed-up, screwed-over victims of this or that waited to die, waited in isolation enforced by their knowledge of secrets and by their psychological inability to contain them. The mentally incontinent.

Or maybe there would be another position available, a teaching position on a military base or even at an American school attached to an embassy. There was always some position open for a teacher, for a speech therapist, for a serviceable young woman; and Julie was all of those.

Attractive, too, if she did think it herself. She had not gained an ounce in the six years since college; she still wore a size seven. What's more, she had the distinct feeling that the years had improved her, for she was one of those girls who mature late, who are still awkward and gangly, nearly adolescent, at twenty but at twenty-five are suddenly graceful women. And she took care of herself, kept her jet-black hair neatly coiffed, got enough exercise to stay in tone, ate the right things in the right amounts. She had been recruited right from college in her senior year; the CIA had found use for her, had allowed her training that was easily the equivalent of a master's degree. From there she had moved to other services, and she had no doubt, absolutely none, that she could find another position easily whenever she cared to look.

Meanwhile she would be hard; she wouldn't let the children get to her.

And yet . . .

She sat in semidarkness, chin resting on her hand, looking out the front window of her apartment unit across the rain-chopped swimming pool toward the main compound. A government building, beyond all doubt: it had that look. Red brick, pinkish concrete trim, tall narrow windows, four stories for the central block, two for the west wing (hospital and testing) and two for the east (dormitory and school). A U.S. flag hung limp in the rain from the flagpole in a circular flower bed (pink and lavender impatiens; red-veined coleus; firework-orange marigolds). The drive and turnaround, black asphalt, glistened in the rain, threw up a fine haze of spray from the harder lashings.

Julie looked to the left, beyond the west wing. A cylindrical yellow-brick chimney towered there. No smoke drifted from its top. That wasn't surprising: the furnace operated at such a high temperature that no smoke ever poured from the chimney, only incredibly hot vapors that danced in heat shimmers against the blue sky. The vapors had appeared last Thursday evening.

And ever since, Johnny had haunted her dreams.

He hadn't been bad.

Some of them were. The Delta twins. Some of the others. Flippers for hands, distorted faces. But Johnny could have been taken for normal, except for his hands, those twelve fingers.

And of course the eyes.

The pale gray eyes, the irises so lacking in pigment that in dim light you usually saw only the pupils, black spots in the unbroken whites. In daylight or strong indoor light, the irises showed up, a pale, pale gray, veined with streaks of the lightest blue imaginable. But you hardly ever saw the children in full light; they didn't like it; it hurt them. When they went out to the playground, usually they wore wraparound shades. And usually they did not stay outside long. They complained of the heat.

The crematory fire burned at 2000 Fahrenheit.

"Stop thinking about it," Julie told herself aloud.

If there were only something to do, she thought. Stark had canceled classes upon his return from the outside, and she and the other two teachers, normally idle over the weekend anyway, now had no way of knowing when they would be permitted to work with the children again, had nothing to do but wait. If not for the rain, she could scare up a game of tennis with David or Sheila or Larry (or, she added mentally, if Larry were not on duty, he could think of other games); she could crash the aerobics class that was sure to be going on in the gym; she could check out a video from the BX, or a book from the library.

Or watch TV, the satellite feed carefully monitored to give the inmates of the installation the vague impression that they were within a few score miles of Washington, D.C., an impression that she already knew to be false.

Or she could take a nap.

And dream of Johnny Gamma and his pleading eyes.

Julie got up and paced the living room. She hated it, hated its institutional anonymity, its motel-modern design. She walked through to the bedroom and stood for a while at the back window, looking out over the parking lot; the vehicles standing there in the rain were all modified Yamaha golf carts, identical but for the different combinations of primary colors meant to individualize them. Past the lot was the ridiculous six-hole golf course— the director was a golf nut and insisted that the course kept the men in shape, though God only knew how much it had cost the taxpayers to design, build, and then conceal the six short holes.

After the golf course came the woods, the fence, and the hills beyond. She could, if she chose, go for a walk. If she headed north from here, she would go about a thousand yards before coming to the first fence; and then she would stop or die. South was a little better; you could head south for nearly fifteen hundred yards, almost a mile, before hitting the inner perimeter. East and west were about equal distances, say eight hundred yards each way. But bounding and binding the installation on all sides were the fences, the dogs, the guards.

The place was a posh prison for Julie as well as for the children—and after all, it was for those children that the place had been created, a decade or so ago.

Julie wondered how many had died, how many had gone up the crematory chimney in those invisible bursts of superheated gas. The dormitory had thirty rooms in all; had there ever been thirty of the children? Now there were only sixteen.

One less than last week.

She sighed and switched on the television set. She flopped onto the unmade bed and reached for the remote control. Thirty-eight channels were available on a one-hour delay, the four network feeds (though commercials were blanked out) plus thirty cable/satellite options, movies, sports, and news, and the instructional channels. Medicine, education, computer science, humanities. Just in case you needed to brush up on your own field or earn credits in the others.

Julie turned the TV to 27, a news/weather feed. Like the others, this one was denatured, indefinite in locale, though the newscasters gave the D.C./Virginia/Maryland area special coverage. But as Larry had pointed out some time ago, one could pick up clues.

Now, for instance, the national weather map showed no storms in the D.C. area. There were scattered showers over the eastern portions of the Midwest, rainfall in Maine, and thunderstorms in the Southeast. Julie's three-month hitch had already shown her enough heat and humidity to rule out Maine and Ohio. She had decided already that the installation was somewhere south of the

Mason-Dixon line. Frowning at the map now, she discarded Florida (sunny skies there) and South Carolina (the storms hadn't moved that far east). That left North Carolina, Tennessee, Georgia, and Alabama.

Not Alabama, she thought. Too hilly.

She switched off the TV and lay back, her hands linked behind her head. What good would it do to pinpoint their location? She'd never talk about it, not even with Larry. Not even to herself. What had Larry said that first afternoon, when they were out in the woods between the third hole of the golf course and the fence?

"Here the television watches you."

He might have been joking.

But she thought not.

Making love inside, in a bed, was better than creeping under a bush, like a couple of horny teenagers. She and Larry had never made love in a bed. So maybe the joke held more truth than humor: maybe Larry really thought they were watched. Certainly the red tape, the documents that she had had to sign, the monthly inventory of her apartment the quartermaster carried out, made it seem likely that someone, somehow, was watching them. No one had said that making love was forbidden, but it might be; and Larry could be afraid, she supposed, of getting caught doing something against the rules.

She lost herself in thoughts of Larry, of his curly black hair and gleaming brown eyes. He was—nice. She didn't love him. But he was nice to be with. His brown eyes.

She fell asleep at last, only to awaken with a gasp sometime late in the afternoon.

She had been dreaming of other eyes.

Eyes of palest gray.

Pleading eyes.

Silver eyes.

Dead eyes.

CHAPTER TWO

1

The storm blew itself out by four o'clock that afternoon. The rain persisted for a little while longer, transformed to cat's-paw swipes of brief showers, but the lightning had gone away. The electricity had come back on at two-thirty, and now Collins, alone—William Whitepath had left as soon as the wind and rain had let up a bit—sat at the computer and pretended to work.

It went nowhere; the story was dead on its feet. Collins scanned the monitor, which displayed in glowing green phosphor twenty-four lines of less than deathless prose. He felt frustration balling inside him, the kind of frustration that had driven him, a few days earlier, to agree to the fishing expedition that the storm had aborted.

The problem, he decided, was not in lack of inspiration; he knew what was coming next, after all. It wasn't a work of fiction that he was about, but a book illuminating the way that U.S. enforcement organizations had worked at cross-purposes for some ten years on the problem of drugs and drug smuggling. He had the material; he knew the whole sorry tale from beginning to end; he did not suffer the absence of the reportorial Muse.

He was just played out on the subject, he decided.

That happened with reporters, especially those who worked on one particular story for too long. He lacked freshness, he lacked the zeal that he had felt three years ago when he first began turning over rocks. It was old to him now, stale; and it was hard to imagine the book being fresh to any new readers.

Collins sighed and saved the last few lines of prose to disk, then switched the computer off. He pushed back from the console and made himself the drink he had put off earlier, scotch and water, mild enough. Thank God alcoholism was not working against him; he had seen enough drunken newspapermen in his time to make him appreciate his own exceedingly moderate taste for the stuff. He rarely had more than one drink, and that one he would nurse along for nearly an hour.

Eightball was restless again, scratching at the door and looking back over his curly black shoulder. "Okay, boy," Collins sighed. "Go catch a rabbit or something." He came over, opened the door, let Eightball out into the newly washed afternoon, and then followed the dog.

Eightball trotted over to the Ford Ranger, sniffed the front right tire, and then lifted his leg. "Thanks, buddy," Collins told him. "I'll remember that next time you want out." Eightball looked around, wagged his tail three times, finished his business, and scratched up a few globs of mud. Then he ran out his long, pink tongue and yawned.

Collins took a deep breath, inhaling the piny scent of the hillside. "Want to go down to the river?" he asked Eightball. The cocker wagged his tail and fell companionably into step beside Collins.

They made their way down the wooded hill, using a worn path made treacherous by the rain. The Chanussee had swollen since that morning: it more than filled its accustomed banks, and at the edge of the water green grass and weeds stood partly submerged, tugged to the right by the strong pull of the current. Collins looked across the river—it was about fifty feet wide at this point, though it widened rapidly just downstream before empty-ing into Lake Byron Reece—and saw no life on the opposite bank.

No wonder. Most of the vacation homes were to the south and east, on the shores of the artificial lake. Only a few scattered cabins ran this far upstream, chiefly older structures, mementos from fifty years ago and more, a time when the Chanussee flowed in a narrower channel, when those who came here were mainly fishermen in quest of mountain trout. Collins's Uncle Joseph had been one of that brotherhood, and he had built the cabin for himself back in the tight years of the Depression, when he was still young.

Collins had hardly known his Uncle Joe, who had been

twenty years senior to Pete's father. He remembered the old man chiefly from holidays, from Christmases when the white-haired, bloated copy of his dad would come roaring into the family home, breath strong with whiskey, pockets full of surprises for Pete and for Pete's brother and sister. Joe had been like a homegrown Santa to the kids, more like a grandfather than an uncle. Collins smiled to himself in recalling the old man. Not until he was in college did he begin to suspect that Joe Collins might have a good reason for being a bachelor at age sixty-five. By then Pete, in his sophomore year, had read a little Freud, a little Jung, and words like "latent homosexual" came easily and glibly to him.

But be that as it may, no one was more surprised than Pete when his uncle died and passed along his fishing cabin to his oldest nephew. Pete had married by that time, was in the throes of his first disastrous year as a teacher of political science at Fulton Community College; he had talked himself, if not Dorothy, into believing that the mountain retreat might be just the thing to let him unwind during the summer vacation.

But his life had unwound instead, beginning that year. Dorothy had postponed having the child they had spoken of because she had just completed her business degree and had a good offer from an Atlanta public-relations firm. Their weeks at the cabin were acrimonious, not loving; and by the time they returned to Atlanta, their marriage had been fractured if not broken.

Pete had left teaching that year at Christmas. He was too soft, he realized, too easy a mark for the students with sob stories of family emergencies, of suddenly deceased grandmothers, and his grades reflected it. His bell curve was skewed too much toward the high side. Word had gotten around that Mr. Collins's Pol Sci 101 was a crip course. He left before the dean could speak to him about the problem.

And he found another job almost immediately, writing for the *Atlanta Alternative*, a small independent daily that had grown up since the sixties, since the day when it had catered to the hippie community of Tenth and Fourteenth Street and Piedmont Park. Now it was a David facing the twin Goliath of the *Atlanta Journal-Constitution*, and like the biblical David, it had a few rocks up its sleeve.

It was just the place for Pete. Frank Hamill, a college buddy, had found a place there as opinion editor, and Frank had persuaded the management to hire Pete, a dogged researcher and a talented writer. At first he did pretty tame stuff, but when he nosed out tales of corruption in certain county commission offices, backed his stories with fact, and broke them in the paper, his star rose. He became an investigative reporter. He remained one for five years, both for the *Alternative* and then later as a regional stringer for *National News Weekly*.

He made a good living.

But as his star rose, so did Dorothy's. And it outglittered his.

She progressed rapidly in her own career: she was handling her own string of clients at age twenty-three, was a vice-president at twenty-five, and just last year, at twenty-seven, she got the chance to head a new branch of the company in Orlando. She brought home first a salary matching Pete's, then half again as much, finally twice as much. And her money paid for the condo in Atlanta, for her designer clothing, for her BMW.

There had been no question of her passing up the Orlando opportunity. She handled the divorce as she had come to handle her business affairs: directly, efficiently, thoroughly. She had told him her decision at breakfast one morning, had the papers in his hands by dinnertime that evening.

Pete had no reason not to sign them. He had lost her long ago, cuckolded not by another man but by a career. "Thank you," she had said as he put his name on the lines. "I wish you the best, Pete."

"And you," he had said, meaning it. Before the divorce was final he had published the first story in the drug series; by the time Dorothy had moved to Orlando he was being mentioned as a Pulitzer possible; and by the time the prize had been announced he had resigned from the paper—though Frank, now managing editor, insisted on calling his move a sabbatical—and had moved permanently to the cabin in the hills. To write a book, he told everyone.

Well, that was a laugh.

He had come to the cabin because now he identified with Uncle Joe Collins more than ever before; because he had begun to see himself as the jolly uncle who would show up at his brother Donny's house with presents in his pockets for Tammy and Misty, or who would visit his sister Tracey with a fielder's glove for the eighteen-month-old Scott. Bachelor uncle. Childless man.

Pete sipped his scotch and hunkered down to tickle Eightball's ears. "If I was really going nuts," he told the dog, "I'd probably be talking to you. Right?"

Eightball, his nose quivering as he tested the air on the riverbank, did not even look up.

Collins stood and went to the boat dock. It was a ramshackle affair that cried out for hammer and saw and fresh timber, but he had been neglecting it for years and it had not yet collapsed. The canoe was snugged to it, half full of rain. Collins took off his shoes, rolled up his jeans legs, and stepped down into the boat. Using a rusty Maxwell House coffee can, he bailed until most of the water was out. Then he climbed back to the dock, feeling its aged timbers shudder from the heavier current of the rain-swollen Chanussee, and hauled the aluminum canoe out of the water, his muscles straining.

He tilted the last of the rainwater from the boat, inverted it over the dock pilings, and lashed it down. Then he slipped his damp feet back into the Nike walking shoes and stood up for a last survey of the river.

Afternoon was waning. Overhead the clouds had begun to break up into ragged gray patches, with fragmented lines of clear blue showing between. A patch of sunlight glinted on the river, moved off to the farther shore, and lost itself in dark pines. Collins dusted his hands and looked around for Eightball, but the dog had disappeared.

He retrieved his glass from the piling—he had made the drink forty minutes ago, but it was still half full—took a sip, and arched his back, working out a kink.

He had just finished the drink, fifteen minutes later, when he heard Eightball up at the cabin. The dog was barking frantically up and down the canine scale. Collins set off up the slope at a run, not taking the path but dodging between the trees, wincing at the lash of a blackberry vine across the front of his bare ankle, blinking away tears at the switch of a pine bough across his open left eye.

When Collins was halfway to the cabin, the dog's barking stopped as if a tape recorder had been shut off. Collins yelled, "Eightball! Here, boy!" as he stumbled up the steeper part of the climb, but the dog did not respond.

He broke out of the underbrush at the edge of the drive. Eightball was there, sitting in the mud beside the Ranger. He looked—odd.

"Eightball?" Collins said, approaching the dog.

The cocker spaniel did not look around. He was facing the car, his head moving from side to side in something like a slow palsy, something like the movement of a snake charmed by a fakir.

Collins, frowning, stooped and put a hand on the dog's head. The muscles were tense: he could feel them tremble against each other, as if Eightball had gone into some sort of seizure, as if a spasm had locked his sinews in place. The dog still did not look at him.

Collins, grunting, lifted Eightball and turned him over, as if he were holding a baby. The mud-splattered coat left red streaks on Collins's old gray shirt, and more red mud dripped off the lax paws to spatter on the white toes of his walking shoes. The dog's eyes were abnormally wide, showing some dingy, capillary-streaked white all around the iris, and the pupils were dilated as far as they could go, two depthless pools of glossy black rimmed by the merest suggestion of brown iris. The dog trembled in his arms.

Collins carried him into the cabin, wrapped him in a couple of bath towels, and got down the telephone book to find the vet's number. But then Eightball whimpered, crawled out of the nest of peach and blue towels, and looked at him quizzically.

"You okay now?" Collins asked, realizing how shaky his own voice was, how his heart pounded.

Eightball whimpered and looked around as if dazed. He tottered over to Collins on unsure legs—he had behaved just that drugged way when coming home after the vet had castrated him three years before—and sat, his head cocked, looking up. The eyes were still odd, the pupils still enormous, but they showed more iris than they had.

"Let's see if you're hungry," Collins said. He went to the kitchen, Eightball tack-tacking along behind, his claws keeping a steadier rhythm now on the oak floor. Collins opened the cabinet and got out a box of Milk-Bones. He fished one out and held it toward the dog. "Hungry, boy?"

Eightball took the dog biscuit gravely and sat for a moment with it sticking from his mouth as if waiting for a light. Then he chewed, broke it in half, swallowed, and picked up the other half. When he had finished licking up stray crumbs, the dog thumped his tail and looked up for more.

"I guess you're okay," Collins said, exhaling. He looked at his watch. It was almost five-thirty, too late for anything but an emergency call to the vet. "But you're going to town tomorrow to see Doc Akers. You scared me, boy."

They went back to the living room. Eightball lay stretched out on the hearth for a few minutes, got up, snuffled in a corner, turned around to look at Collins, and then padded back to his place and collapsed again. Collins grunted to himself. The dog stared off into the distance with the bemused air of a stroke victim, he thought to himself; there was that remote, hopeless, pondering, puzzled look to his face.

But whatever had happened seemed to be passing. That evening Eightball ate his usual hearty supper of Alpo beef-and-liver chunks; then he lay beside Collins's chair while Pete read, another part of their comfortable routine. Nothing more happened, at least not until Pete, ready to turn in, opened the door to let the dog out.

Eightball looked at the oblong of night and shivered. He turned and ran into the bedroom.

Frowning, Collins went after him, finding him cowering in a corner. He picked up the dog and carried him outside. Eightball went around the corner of the house and did his business; then he darted past Collins and back into the cabin.

Collins, following Eightball inside, closed the door. After a moment he bolted it, an unusual precaution.

He found Eightball back in the bedroom, this time under the big bed. "You smell something out there, boy?" he asked.

The dog crept out into the light, tail wagging. Collins slapped his hand on the red Georgia Bulldog blanket covering the bed. "Okay. For tonight, since you're under the weather."

Collins fell asleep with the dog at his feet, down at the end of the bed. He half-woke once, feeling Eightball shifting his weight uneasily; then he fell asleep again.

But at three-seventeen the next morning Collins woke again, woke to the raging barks and desperate snarls of the dog, woke to hear Eightball throwing his body hard against the window.

And with that waking the nightmare really began.

2

Ernest Fisher was far too tired to sleep. But that didn't stop him from resenting Karl Stark, a self-proclaimed night person. Stark seemed right in his element, alert and composed as he sat across from Fisher. Fisher, his eyes aching from the fluorescent overhead lights, grew irritated with Stark. Reprimanding him was like punching a shapeless mass of dough. And the man waited so calmly before speaking back, waited until, as now, Fisher had run out of things to say himself.

"I want to register the complaint with you," Stark said for the third or fourth time that night. His voice sounded louder than it usually did, as most noises do in buildings emptied for the night. "And if necessary with higher powers."

Fisher nodded, leaning back in his swivel chair. The back of his head brushed the closed vertical blinds that kept the night outside the room's one window. "I've noted your complaint. But what about my point? In my absence you are the highest authority here. What possessed you to run off that way?"

Stark was a paper shredder. He sat working at his pastime in his shirtsleeves, a loosened dark-blue Cardin tie hanging from his collar. Stark sat across the desk in Fisher's office and tore a blank piece of typing paper into thin strips, then tore the strips to confetti. Fisher could tell how agitated the man was by the amount of paper he got through. Tomorrow the cleaning staff would be hard

pressed to remove all of the tiny bits of paper he showered on the carpet. "I did not come to you to be made a
prisoner," he said.

"You haven't been." Fisher opened his arms in a gesture that took in the office, and by implication the rest of
the world as well. "Does this look like a prison?"

It was not the best thing to ask, for Fisher's office in
fact did have about it some of the bleak anonymity of a
prisoner's cell—or a monk's. No photographs, paintings,
or citations decorated the plain cream-colored walls. The
furnishings were equally Spartan: the discreetly deep-
piled gray carpet, the two brown leather-covered visitors'
chairs, two wall-filling bookshelves, the desk, Fisher's
swivel chair, a wastepaper basket, and in one corner a
vast gray safe nearly man-high. But the scientist did not
glance up to take in Fisher's gesture. Stark's eyes were
downcast, fixed on the paper between his fingers. "When
I was still a little child—"

"I asked for your reasons, not your autobiography."

Stark ignored the interruption: "When I was a child,
my father told me of the life in the West. Before the war
he traveled to Monte Carlo every year, did you know
that? He loved the glamour. The glitter." The word
"glitter" rolled off Stark's tongue in a peculiar way,
accented with a guttural *gl* sound, the *r* almost gargled.
The way he pronounced "glitter" made it by far the most
Germanic-sounding word in his vocabulary. "My father
was a wealthy man in Germany, son of a powerful family, in his own right a greatly respected man."

"And a smart man," Fisher said. "He joined the Nazi
Party early."

Stark's shrug dismissed twenty years of European history in a moment. "He was really an apolitical man. He
joined only because he knew that being a Nazi would
enable him to prolong his romance with his real love.
With science."

Fisher nodded, although he knew that Stark's father
had joined the Hitler Youth when only fourteen, a long
time before any strong signs of his "love affair" had
become evident.

"He was never really with them," Stark said, stripping
a ribbon of paper only a couple of millimeters wide from

the plain white stationery he held in his pink, well-manicured hands. "Not in his heart."

"Perhaps not," Fisher said without enthusiasm. Half-hearted Nazis did not receive the perks and rewards that the old man had. On the other hand, it was hard to imagine a whole-hearted Nazi, wife and infant son in tow, fleeing *toward* the Soviets, a clutch of rocketry secrets incubating in his skull. Fisher had once heard a man say that if the United States had had Stark's father instead of von Braun, there would have been no Cold War, no Korea—because the United States would have been the supreme power on the face of the earth by 1950.

Stark was silent for several seconds, apparently lost in reverie. He sighed before speaking again: "I was bewitched by his stories. You must remember I was only three when my family fled Germany. I share with my father a love for the rich life." He permitted himself a rueful shake of the head. "Sometimes I think my Lysenko-believing colleagues on the project were correct; I feel my expensive taste is inherited." His full lips quirked up at the corners to show Fisher it was only a joke.

"Yes," Fisher said dryly. "You defected because you wanted to live the life of a decadent capitalist."

"Look at it from my point of view. Here I am with thousands of dollars accruing every month in my bank accounts. I have exactly two opportunities every twenty-eight days to confer with my stockbroker; otherwise, it is work, work, work, with no company except the subjects or the support group. And I cannot allow myself to get close to them, for obvious reasons. So every once in a while, yes, I leave the compound to enjoy a little life."

Fisher's voice was quiet, its fury barely contained: "You jeopardized our entire mission for a gambling jaunt."

"You are scolding me." Stark pursed his mouth in a parody of prim apology while his clumsy-looking fingers nipped several torn strips of paper into nearly precise squares, very tiny ones. "You wouldn't if you understood. You can't imagine what sort of life I had in the Soviet Union. They don't trust Germans there. Not since the Great Patriotic War, at any rate." His tone mocked the Russian name for World War II, exactly reversed its meaning. "There is a good-sized German minority in all the cities of the European USSR. But only another German could find them. They have learned the value of concealment."

Fisher shook his head. "This is completely beside the point."

A small blizzard snowed from Stark's hands to the gray carpet and he began to rip more paper from the large sheet. "Is it? I think not. You asked for an explanation of my actions—"

"For only one action."

"—and I am giving it. You must understand that under the circumstances it was very difficult for me to receive my university training. An outsider, one of a distrusted underclass. You have no idea. And then, when I had received my degree and joined the project, it was even more oppressive. You may sneer at me, but the maniac Lysenko has not been dead so very long, my friend. So much of my training in genetics and heredity I had to unlearn. So much of Soviet science I had to disregard."

Fisher began, "I only want—"

"Please. Let me continue. All of us were that way, all of us on the project. We had to be politically immaculate, and so in public we assented to whatever the officially approved line on biology might have been. In private we struggled to unlock the real secrets; and even then we hardly shared them for fear of being thought disloyal. It was too absurd. Even then I took what opportunities I could for travel, for a break from routine. It was because of my yearning for variety that I came to the conference in Berlin. Otherwise you would not have been able to enroll me."

Fisher grunted, his anger buried beneath his own weariness and Stark's volubility. "I suppose you've been taking off every time I've been away from the installation."

The room was so quiet in the depths of night that the razorlike sound of Stark's fingernails on the paper came through clearly. "Not every time. Only when work was slow, when there was little to keep me here." He stared into Fisher's eyes with insolent brashness.

"How much did you drop at the tables?"

The eyes did not waver, and the lips quirked up in a smile. "I was winning."

Fisher, looking into those ice-blue eyes, felt his stomach tighten. He had come back to a mess, to a carnival of recrimination. He had spent all afternoon and most of the evening trying to resolve some of the antagonism that was almost a palpable force, and he had put off talking with Stark—who had been busy all afternoon with tests, anyway—until late that night.

But he could not let Stark escape without a reprimand. Nor could he find a ready method of putting the fear of God into the man. After all, the entire twenty-million-dollar project rode on Stark's shoulders, and the man knew it; Fisher couldn't fire him. The eyes said that now, said it with a cool insolence. "It isn't the way you should show gratitude, Karl," Fisher said at last. "We've given you an excellent cover, an undetectable second identity. But the KGB is full of very patient men. And what if one of them should recognize you? It's far too dangerous. I can't guarantee your safety if you leave with no warning like that."

"I will take my chances. I doubt if the KGB are looking for me anymore. I know the project was too secret for them to be involved directly."

"It isn't only them," Fisher said. "You know how tightly we've run the unit. You know what measures we've taken to keep it secret. There are some of our own people who'd give a lot to find out exactly what we've been doing with our appropriations."

"The CIA, you mean."

"And the NSA, and the INR. Not to mention military intelligence. You obviously don't appreciate how few friends we have. And how many powerful enemies."

"Indeed. It seems the entire alphabet is against us." Stark was almost through with his sheet of paper. "But it will work out. I trust you to take care of such matters."

"I'm not sure I can take care of Randall Grade."

The scientist, his eyes on his fingers and his paper, smiled to himself. "Causing trouble for you, is he?"

"Not yet. I don't think you know how powerful his committee has become since the joint services shakeup, since the downgrading of the CDI office. He's in a position to do us lots of damage now. But if there is trouble, it's yours, too." Fisher picked up a capped Pilot ballpoint pen, tapped the desk with it three times, and put it back on the blotter. "Grade knows too much and not enough. He's got the outlines of the unit pretty firmly in hand. If he found out we've been experimenting with nonconsenting subjects—"

"You will not let him learn this. I have a great deal of faith in you. And we do have certain—allies. The military services might like to know more about just what we are accomplishing here, but they do value us; surely the DDI is on our side." Stark looked as if he were about to add something, but he evidently thought better of it and closed his mouth again.

"It's late," Fisher said with a glance at his Rolex. "Finish what you have to say."

"I was going to say that we have closer enemies to worry about. Some here in the compound, for instance; the medical staff who allowed the cremation on Friday."

"That's an internal matter."

"It was wrong to destroy the Gamma cadaver without an autopsy," Stark asserted. "True, he had never demonstrated any clear psi ability; but we know from the Epsilon girl last year that some very interesting alterations in the target area of the brain come with puberty. Perhaps he was a latent; perhaps the developing portions of his brain contributed to his death."

Fisher picked up a death form, its spaces neatly filled out in the Prestige Elite typeface used on all the unit's printers. "He died of heart failure."

Stark flicked the fingers of his right hand, sending up a little burst of confetti into the air. "I have spoken to Dr. Kornbluth about his imprecise documentation. Heart failure. That is not a proper term. Not a scientific term. His heart stopped beating and he died. But what made his heart stop beating, hm? That is the question an autopsy might have answered."

Fisher suppressed a yawn. "I suppose you have a theory."

Stark smiled again, still without showing his teeth. "Of course. You have to remember that in working with human genes we are doing something like using a power shovel to pick up and align single marbles, one at a time. Our tools are that clumsy, the molecules that small. The sets of genes that control the development of the nervous system are not a completely distinct cluster; changing one of them will almost invariably—and inadvertently—change another. In a fantastically complex way, genes are linked.

That is the reason for the eyes, no doubt; for what has eye color to do with intelligence or with psi talents? Nothing? Yet the eyes are the giveaway—"

Fisher snapped, "That and birth defects. And idiocy."

"Not so!" Stark tensed, bunching his shoulders. His suppressed accent, verging on German with overtones of Russian, broke out in his voice: "At the very beginning I warned you. I said the risks were very great, not so? I told you a twenty-year survival rate might be only twenty percent, only fifteen. And of those five or six, perhaps only two—"

"Dr. Stark," Fisher said. Now that Stark's anger was aroused, Fisher became contrastingly cool. "Calm yourself."

Stark clamped his mouth shut. His icy eyes narrowed. Then tension slowly drained from his face, from his jaw. The German shrugged. "All I am saying is that altering the psi gene may well have altered the genes controlling the involuntary nervous system. Then the further changes of puberty could cause a damaged medulla oblongata to send faulty signals to the heart. It is a possibility. If it exists, we should try to compensate for it in the rest of the children."

"Compensate?"

"Pacemakers, perhaps. A way to control the heart."

"None of the other children have shown any weakness of the heart."

Stark had finished his last rectangle of paper. He dusted a few stray white particles off the knees of his dark blue trousers. "No. But it is something to watch for."

"Then tell your staff to watch for it."

Stark nodded and stood. "I have done so already, of course. If that is all—"

"No. sit down."

Stark looked longingly at the paper on Fisher's desk, but he sat down without picking up a sheet. His pink, blunt-fingered hands wrestled with themselves on the midnight-blue field of his thighs. "What else?"

Fisher swiveled gently back and forth in his chair. "Have you gone through the printouts I asked you to review?"

"Of course. On the plane there, and again on the way back." Stark gave him a grin. "I know, I know, I was a bad boy to take classified documents with me like that.

But to an outsider they would have meant nothing; and I was careful not to let them out of my immediate possession."

Fisher picked up the matte-black ballpoint pen and tapped it on his desk as if preparing to conduct the New York Philharmonic. "Were you able to come to any judgment regarding the Soviet team's progress?"

Stark pursed his lips and frowned. "It has been twenty-five years. They have had time," he said very slowly, all trace of accent now vanished, "to force-breed only three generations of psi-enhanced subjects. But the most recent generation would still be infants. And our people did not project significant success and replicability for five generations, at least. Forty to fifty years, according to our best projections."

"But the computer estimates?" Fisher leaned forward in his seat, making the swivel chair squeak. "Given the data, wouldn't you say there is a fair chance that the Soviet Union has a psychic force in place already?"

Stark's face was impassive, but now that Fisher had made clear what he was looking for, the scientist nodded. "It is very possible that there is a cadre of passive ESP agents working for the USSR. Clearly the Soviet Union has impressively expanded its ability to project what key Western leaders will do. I would say there is at least a fifty-fifty chance that their people are telepathically eavesdropping on selected targets already. Is that what you wanted me to say?"

Fisher leaned back. "I need that in writing. Someone has to tell that to the Grade Committee," he said. "Someone has to scare them into backing away from the unit. Otherwise we could find ourselves out, Karl. We could see fourteen years of work go down the drain. We could find ourselves branded as madmen, as renegades—"

"As murderers," Stark suggested with a deprecating smile.

Fisher looked at him for a long moment. "As worse," he said in a tone that ended the interview.

3

Anthony and Andrew had a little night game.

The White Lady had gone away a long time ago, and now the bedroom was almost dark, illuminated only by the fugitive light that could leak in through the barred windows, around the edges of the closed blinds, through the crack under the locked door. Anthony, lying in his bed, could just make out the clown picture on the wall opposite, over the light-making thing, beside the locked door. It was almost a monochrome in the dim filtered light, though he knew it well: a sad-faced hobo clown in a battered round hat and ragged black clothes holding five balloons in his gloved hand.

But when he closed his eyes he could see

(the lion picture, onetwothreefourfivesix lions in a triangle)

the picture in Andrew's room next door, equally dim, equally well-known. So Andrew was awake, too, with his eyes open. It was hard for any of the children to sleep now that Johnny's reassuring warm yellow light was gone. It had burned brightest, had been the most comforting. His eyes still closed, Anthony concentrated on Andrew's light, a pale blue light, like the moon seen through thin cloud. Anthony could not really *see* his brother's body, could not visualize clearly the macrocephalic head, the stubby arms, but he could perceive the glow, the aura, that surrounded Andrew and made him a whole and complete being. Some of the other children glowed a little brighter than the two boys, some a little dimmer. Most of the adults hardly glowed at all. How did they make it through a black night with no reassurance?

Anthony squinched himself up tight inside and as hard as he could sent

-1!-

and in a moment Andrew returned with

(-2-).

It was nearly their oldest game. Anthony sent back 4, received 8; returned 16, got 32. They ran the numbers higher, doubling every time. Before long Anthony sent 8,388,608 and received nothing in response. Andrew was tired of the doubling game. It was an almost-worn-out game, too well known to delight anymore.

Anthony tossed in bed, trying to make his heavy head more comfortable on the pillows. He was a little upset with Andrew, for the day had been a frightening one. He had been taken to the Cold Place where the Big White Man had done the Pain Things. And afterward there had been the Light Thing and the Noise Thing from outside, terrifying the boy.

His brother, though, had not been to the Cold Place today. A White Lady had been with him during the lightning and thunder, keeping him safe. With the dispassion of childhood, Andrew felt no sympathy for his brother's distress. Andrew was sleepy and uninterested in the old game of doubling, though usually he could get in the last number, the one that would finally baffle Anthony.

The last time it had been a number of more than three thousand digits.

Anthony thought of numbers a lot. Many things were not clear to him: the marks on paper that the Different-Color Ladies wanted him to "read" were not. Sometimes he could hold them in mind for a little while, could grunt out "A-ee, Buh-ee, See, Duh-ee," all the way up to "Zuh-ee"and be told that he was a Good Boy and that he was Doing Well, but the names of the marks would slip away from him over the next few days and when he saw them again, he could not tell the Different-Color Lady the name of even one.

Sometimes he could listen in as the Different-Color Ladies talked about him and Andrew. He did not know what *severe developmental retardation* meant, but he sensed it was a Bad Thing and somehow his fault. He had no working definition of *Down's syndrome*, but he knew somehow that the phrase applied to him and to Andrew. Andrew, whose light was not quite the same as Anthony's, never listened in to the Big People's thoughts. Anthony could not tell if this was because he was indifferent to them or because he was incapable of doing the trick. Andrew was better than Anthony at remembering the names of the marks on paper. He was not as good at remembering the names of different colors or at recalling how to use the potty.

But for both brothers, numbers were different. In Anthony's mind, numbers were clean and bright, glowing with their own light, as the children glowed. Numbers were clear, individual, they almost had personalities. Anthony saw *1* as a stiff-backed soldier, *2* as a swimmer coming up for air, *3* as a kindly old lady with a big pillowy bosom. It was easy to know the numbers.

The Different-Color Ladies would not play number

games with him, though. They wanted him to *count* onetwothreefourfivesix, a silly thing to do. There was no skill in it, no reward from it. Since he was not interested in *counting* he did not do it, and they tried no more interesting games with him. But Andrew, his brother, understood. They were not often in class together, for the Different-Color Ladies found the two *disruptive* and *distracting* when they put their heads close together and chanted numbers that had *no significance*. So usually the two of them had to play their games this way, after dark, when their minds could touch even with a wall between them.

In Anthony's lonely reverie the numbers began to align themselves in a new way. No longer individual lights, they formed constellations now; beautiful wholes, individual, complete, self-contained. Anthony caught his breath. He spent a few moments alone with them to make sure he was seeing them correctly. Then he closed his eyes to darkness. In the next room over, Andrew was asleep or at least had closed his eyes. Anthony felt for him, reached into the darkness. He found his brother's pale blue glow and sent, as hard as he could,

-1!!!-

There came no response. Andrew, though still wakeful, was no longer in the mood to play the doubling game, and he was not aware of the wonderful new concept that the numbers had given Anthony. Anthony realized that this time he was in the lead and had to help his brother along. He sent

-2!!!-3!!!-

and felt a sluggish stir, a flicker of interest. He waited, but when nothing came back, Anthony provided another clue:

-5!!!-

This time there was no mistake. Anthony felt slow glee from Andrew as the new idea took root, burgeoned. From Andrew he got back a tentative

(7-?) (-11-?)

and so he confirmed with a definite

-13!!!-

and Andrew immediately, confidently replied

(-17!-).

The new game was on. Anthony had intuited the principle of prime numbers, of numbers that could be divided evenly only by themselves or by 1. Within a minute they had run through more than twenty prime numbers each. They slowed then, but the game went on for a long time, went on until nearly dawn. By the time they were both tired enough to fall asleep, they were exchanging primes that a mathematician would have required a mainframe computer and weeks of computation to produce.

The Delta twins were not quite twelve years old.

4

The Engstroms sat at their dinner table. Beth had her hands together, holding on tight, waiting for Fritz's verdict. Her husband, his face still boyish beneath his military haircut, was bent over her diary. The overhead light shone through his clipped hair to illuminate a round pink spot of scalp at the crown of his head. He had changed from his uniform to jeans and T-shirt, the clothes looking awkward and out of place on him even to Beth, who had first seen her future husband when she was eighteen and he thirty; even then the uniform of an Air Force officer (not yet a captain then) had seemed the most natural thing for him to wear.

She could not stop weeping, and through her tears she saw a blur of their life together: their first time in bed, in a cheap motel room a few miles from the base. He had undressed her first, and she was already beneath the sheets when he began to take off his own clothes. He had paused, fingers at his belt, to warn her. He had been married once already, and his wife had not liked the military life. He was not a good man to love.

But she had loved him then, had loved him all that summer, had loved him to the altar and ever since. She loved him now, even as she feared his verdict on her dream diary.

He looked up from the book at last, his blue eyes haunted. "It's been going on for that long?" he asked.

She nodded. "But the dreams are getting worse now," she said, her voice trembling.

His face was troubled. He had one of those faces some men are blessed, or cursed, with: he would forever look like a high school senior, his nose seeming not quite formed, his eyes clear and bright, his forehead smooth. He would be an old man, she thought, with the face of a boy. He was quiet for a long time before speaking: "Is it just the dreams, hon? Is there something else?"

"I don't know." She clenched her hands together, tight enough for her nails to bite into her palms. "Fritz, it just seems so *real* to me. I can't explain it."

He reached for her hands, rested his big warm palm on her balled fists. "You know it isn't possible."

Beth would have screamed had her throat not been clogged with pain. "I don't know that," she said, her voice dry and harsh and rushed. "I don't know that at all."

"Hon . . ." He paused, his eyes puzzled as they always were when he groped for words. "Hon, we—we saw our baby. And he was dead."

"We saw a body," Beth corrected him. "A little tiny body. We don't know if it was ours."

"But they warned you before you went into labor—"

"He wasn't dead! I felt him moving in my stomach, even after that doctor said there was no heartbeat. I *know* he wasn't dead!" She gulped. Then, trying to keep her voice even, quiet, she began again: "Fritz, wasn't it suspicious to you? I had to spend the last three months at the clinic, and they kept telling me the pregnancy was difficult, but it wasn't. It wasn't. I would have known. I felt fine, Fritz, just fine. And he was moving like a little demon inside of me, kicking and somersaulting."

His smile was tender. "Hon, you're not a doctor. And they said—"

"Damn the doctors. I know, Fritz." She took a deep, trembling breath. "Why didn't they let you in the delivery room? We'd been through the course. And why did they knock me out with anesthetic? We'd agreed on a saddle block—"

"Hon, they said the delivery—"

"It was not a difficult birth! Fritz, it was all over in under two hours. Two hours, Fritz, for a first child. You remember all the men's stories at the officers' club that night when they got started on how the first kid takes its own sweet time? The Baileys, seven hours. The Duponts, a day and a half. But it took our baby less than two hours to be born, Fritz, and I was up and around in three days."

Colonel Engstrom looked back down at the diary. When he raised his blue eyes to her again, she saw with a shock that they brimmed with unshed tears. "Hon," he said brokenly, "we have to trust the doctors. They—"

"I don't trust them. I shouldn't have trusted them then."

He was quiet for a long time. Night had fallen outside their house, the soft cool night of early summer in Colorado. The streetlights had come on, and from out front, faintly, came the sounds of some of the neighborhood boys playing underneath them, a night baseball game. The crack of bat against ball punctuated their yells, their laughter. It was late, but they were free, out of school, and as boys will, they would hold on to the day until their parents took it out of their hands, put it away with their bats and gloves, and sent it along to bed as they sent their children. Fritz, his head cocked, seemed to be listening to the sounds. Finally he said, "Suppose we wanted to be sure, hon. What could we do?"

"I don't know," she said. She managed a weak smile. "I thought that would be your department."

He rubbed his eyes with the thumb and forefinger of his right hand. "I suppose I could call some of the intelligence guys in D.C. and ask them to check the place out. Some of them would do me a favor like that."

"And what if they find something funny?"

"Let's wait until they find it before we decide to do anything about it, okay?" He opened the diary again. "My God," he said. "You've been having these dreams all this time?"

"Uh-huh. I didn't want to tell you about it because . . ."

"Because I'd think you were crazy?"

"Yes."

He smiled at her again. "Hon, I've always said you were crazy. From the moment you told me you'd marry me, I've known you were crazy. Only a crazy woman would do that."

"You're a liar, Fritz Engstrom," she said, returning his smile through her tears.

In a serious voice, he said, "You're stronger than I thought, hon. Dreaming this all these years, not ever telling me—you're a lot stronger than I thought you were. Stronger than I would be."

This time she reached across the table for his hand. "Fritz, you—you've never had any dreams like mine, have you?"

He shook his head. She saw real regret in the movement. "No, hon, I never have. My spookiness lies in the other directions."

She knew what he meant. They had been in Germany when, early one morning, she had awakened to find him dialing the telephone. "What is it?" she had asked. He had said, "My mother's sick." He had sensed the stroke the moment his mother had fallen to the floor half a world away. Later that day he had known the exact moment of her death. That was Fritz's spookiness.

He gave her hand a squeeze. "Hon? Could I—would you tell me something?"

"What?"

"Nothing. I'll make some calls tomorrow. I promise you."

She squeezed his hand. "Fritz. What did you want to ask? We've never had secrets from each other."

He nodded, but still he wouldn't quite meet her gaze. He cleared his throat and spoke with an uncharacteristic hesitancy: "When you dream about the—about our son—what does he look like?"

"Why, Fritz," she said, surprised that he had not guessed it already from her dream descriptions, "he looks like you."

And only then did his tears spill.

5

The boy was on the edge of giving up.

He was growing very weak. He lived more in his mind than in his body anyway, but now the body threatened to desert him, to fall away from spirit in a dead and exhausted lump, no more aware than the mud he had struggled through. For the most part he traveled during the night hours, when the hurtful sun was gone, but for the last many hours he had gone on through the day; and even with the sun up, it seemed to him that he walked in darkness, in gloom.

But not wholly in darkness. A Milky Way of minds surrounded him. They were stronger when he closed his weary eyes and saw only with his own mind, pinpoints of light above, below, around him: he was like an astronaut spacewalking in the center of a brilliant galaxy.

But the minds were minute, mere flickers of blue or grayish-white; that's why they seemed like stars, faint and faraway. Consciousness they had, in a dim sort of way, but no self-awareness. He caught the neural activity but no thoughts, for these minds held no thoughts for him to read. They were the minds of bugs, of worms, of an occasional overhead bat (a bright white shooting star across the night sky of his awareness), and now that he had found a bridge to creep across, of the fish underwater. These were dim and greenish-yellow, like fireflies, darting here and there, chasing each other or schooling together, like living constellations. But they were cold lights, knowing only the drives to eat and to reproduce; they were not the warmer, more complex lights of mammals.

Indeed, those were few. He had sensed some, the ruddy smears of prowling foxes like burning torches glimpsed through the trees, the jaunty red will-o'-the-wisp that was a stray cat, the paler, cooler glimmers of sleeping squirrels and rabbits, the darting red-hot coals of mice and voles in the rustling grass. And once a great horned owl had swooped low over him like a passing comet, setting his awareness ablaze with a hot yellow lust to kill.

Oh, his mind burned with life, nearly overflowed with the awareness of it all around. The one thing he could not sense accurately was his own mind-light, though he knew it was warm and yellow; that much he had sensed from the others back at the Place, the children who knew. Now, he thought, his light probably burned even brighter, now that it was so tenuously connected to the living body. That body was weak, hungry, shaking with cold and wet.

He had been traveling Away from the Place for a long time and had missed many meals, until his stomach was a growling hollow cavity within him. At first he traveled by repulsion, seeking only to leave the inimical grown-up minds of the Place behind. He had run through the forest that first night, keeping almost to a straight line, and behind him the unbearable clatter and yammer of thought had at last paled, had vanished entirely. Only then did he become aware of his surroundings, aware of his lostness.

That first dawn he had crept into the hollow of a fallen tree. It was full of termites—pinpricks of blue—but he surrounded himself with his own light, his yellow light, and the insects were frightened by it and swarmed to another part of the log. He slept with the rich odor of decaying wood in his nostrils, and he woke hungry and thirsty.

He had found a stream to quench his thirst. He drank deeply from the water that rushed chuckling over smooth rounded stones, grateful for the taste of it, but there was nothing to be done with the hunger. The sun was low and red (it burned his eyes cruelly, though it was to his right as he walked, and he was shaded by trees) when he started away again, this time guided by the warning flares of mind somewhere far to his left. Once in deep twilight he toiled to the top of a tree and saw from there a ribbon of gray, traveled by speeding cars. That was where the people were: that was the origin of the thoughts. He saw a car come and felt in his head the driver's awareness: *gonna be dark when I (two green lights a possum's eyes) get home wonder if the kids'd like to see a movie (foot on brake, curve approaching {tires nearly bald damn have to afford new ones} little gas there) maybe something good's on TV . . .*

The thoughts made his head hurt, and it was an effort to put himself in tune with them. The boy let go, feeling a rush of relief as the jumble faded to only a soft background murmur inside his skull, then to quiet. He had learned that trick early, when he was only four or five: how to think away from the minds of others, how to insulate himself so that he did not go mad from the cacophony in his head. Now, however, he used a great deal of energy to keep himself alert, to stay open to thought: his talent might be the only thing to save him. Clambering down from the tree, he turned his path a little more westward and soon left the speeding grown-up minds of motorists behind. Then there were only the idiot lights of the animals and insects.

And now, days later, as he plodded across the bridge,

he brought it all back in memory. Should he, after all, have turned toward the road, not away? He felt himself on the edge of an abyss and dimly knew that it must be the final drop of death. He paused midway across the bridge, feeling the fish below him in the water, glimmering like sparks flying from a submerged bonfire. It was madness to stop there, where a car would be sure to fix him in its lights, where the only place to go was over the rail and into the dark fearful water, but he was too tired to care. His jeans had been ripped and torn. Through the fabric he felt coarse sand and gravel. He almost passed out, concentrated on a twirling blue hungry point of light to his left; a spider, spinning her web in the dark. Her mind was a little pinwheel, the shape of her web, an instinct millions of years old. The spider had come a long way to meet him there above the river.

He too had traveled far. He knew that. Along the way he had had some food, not much: once he sensed people ahead, a man and woman and a child. He had come close enough to see and hear them, but kept within a thicket of fern. The girl was older than he, perhaps fourteen or fifteen. They were a FAMILY with a MAMA and DADDY and DAUGHTER. They had come out on a HIKE and were having a PICNIC.

The words meant almost nothing to him, but the thoughts that accompanied them carried meaning—and feeling. He wept a little, silently, to feel their fondness for one another, to feel himself left out of such emotions. Had the feeling been a little stronger, had he felt their love not a closed circle but one open to possibility, he would have made himself known. But his differentness kept him aloof, even through his need, even through his hunger. Drooling, he hunkered on his butt in the undergrowth as they ate, and a half hour after they had gone he had crept out to dig up their leavings from where the DADDY had covered them with last year's soft moist leaves. He found a crumpled paper bag with nearly a whole packet of potato chips, some crusts of baloney sandwich, and three browning apple cores inside it. He wolfed it all down. That had been his only meal, and he had eaten it the day before yesterday.

But hunger was only a gnawing annoyance. The aloneness was much worse than that, and the very worst of the journey came with the storms, late at night. He had been terrified, had crouched in a thicket of blackberry vines, scratching his neck and arms cruelly on the thorns, while the sky racketed and exploded. The rain was hard, sharp on him even through the canopy of leaves, and when he set forth again the rain still fell. It slacked off with dawn, hung in the sky overhead until noon, and then broke again with even greater fury. He was soon chilled and soaked through. Somehow he kept going, though now he was casting the net of his thoughts ahead, looking for something to run to, not just away from. He would have to have people.

But not just anyone; he was too different to trust just anyone. He knew the kind of person he needed. Not someone whose mind shone cold and sharp, like Dr. Stark, but someone like Teacher or Nurse, someone with a friendly ruddy glow. Dr. Stark's thoughts were all sharp reflecting glass and edged steel, and it hurt to touch his mind, but Teacher and Nurse had minds you could warm yourself by. He searched for another like them. Several times he almost had one, but the person always moved away long before he could get there. He knew what cars were—he saw lots of them on the television back at the Place—and he knew that most of the minds he found were in moving cars, just passing through the forest on roads he never saw. That was comforting, in a way. True, he would have more trouble finding a friend, but then the people from the Place would have more trouble finding him, when they discovered the Trick.

The spider finished her web, a neat spiral strung between three rails of the bridge, two horizontal and one vertical. It exactly matched the spiral in her brain. The boy pulled himself up by one of the bridge supports and staggered on, clinging to the rail. They would discover the Trick sooner or later, he knew. The other children had helped him to play the Trick, but he was the center, the nucleus; sooner or later the others would forget to concentrate, and then it was only a matter of time. He got all the way across the bridge before he had to sit again and rest, give his trembling knees some of the respite they demanded.

He was so near now. All during the rain he had struggled ahead, until at last in the late afternoon he had paused, checked by a bigger stream than any he had found. This one, swollen and choppy from the rain, was yards and yards across, and he felt in its depths the minds of the fish. He could not swim at all, and he feared the size of the water, the underness of it.

Still, on the other side, quite near, he sensed a mind that was comfortable. Two minds, really; one very small mind that was deep red and uneasy, the other the reddish-orange of kindness. The smaller one, the red one, was an animal's mind. The other was a man's, thinking grown-up thoughts about boats and water and the weather, thoughts so unfocused that they confused the boy and hurt his head.

He could not quite connect with the man's mind. It was almost always that way with adults: their minds were spinning constructs, many-sided and complex, never still for a moment, except in sleep, and touching one in a real way, a talking way, was as difficult as walking straight after you had been turning as fast as you could go in circles. Something always veered away from you . . . .

There was, of course, MAMA. He plugged into her mind now and again, always when she was sleeping. There was something strange about the bond between MAMA and him: she was oh, far, far away, and yet he could always find her when he sought her. He could never do that with other adults—any respectable distance defeated him, and certain types of walls seemed to make it even harder—but MAMA was always close, somehow. He could touch her completely when she was asleep with her mind open, but even during her waking hours he could feel her and draw some comfort from her. When she responded in her dreams, he felt bad-good inside, knowing the love that she would have given him and bitterly missing it. But except for MAMA when she slept, he could converse with no grown-up, though he and the other children had been very talkative.

Still, though he could not exchange information with the grown-ups, he could pick it up. And lately the thoughts of those running the Place had become dark and threatening, like the clouds that brought lightning, rain, storm. Thunderous words rattled in their minds: *termination, closure, euthanasia.* The world of the Place was frighteningly insecure, and the thoughts of the grown-ups swam in waters of distrust and fear. He did not like it that way; if he could have things his way, all thoughts would be smooth, all clouds white and kindly.

The small red glow across the river moved up the hill in erratic starts and bounds, zigzagging away from the man. He decided to try to take it, to see with it, as he could see with the eyes of the other children when they were close together, when the power was strong. He closed his eyes. His teeth ground together. He strained, his heart racing, his lungs heaving for more air.

And he felt himself sliding in.

The dog was terrified, sensing itself losing control. It yelped, barked, shuddered. He saw through its eyes, heard with its ears (keen piercing sounds, sounds no human ear could hear, the screams of insects the hum of electricity in the walls of the house). Above all, he could *smell* things, things that filled his head: mud, oil, the MAN, the OTHER MAN, fish, a thousand other aromas. The boy finally locked himself in, at last stopping the larynx from its paroxysms of barking.

He could not work the unfamiliar muscles, found himself trembling and paralyzed, staring at a great black bulk. Its colors were utterly strange, its proportions wrong, but he realized that he was looking at a CAR. Something moved him. The man's face swept into his vision. He felt himself being picked up, carried, felt the man's concern; and then it was too much. He slipped back from the dog's body, found himself again, a crumpled little boy, one foot being tugged by the cold and rushing water of the river. He drew his leg out and sat panting for a long time.

Something told him to go right. He had to travel for a long way, and he made very slow progress, having to pause to rest every few hundred feet. But at last, deep into the night, he found the bridge, a wooden span across the river.

Now he gathered his strength again and rose, groaning with the effort, feeling his face flash hot and then cold. He crept along, skirting the dirt road, making for the cabin that held the man and the dog. He hunched himself over on his pain like a little old man, staggering, stepping on his own feet.

He walked listening to the squelch of water in his

sneakers, feeling the clammy hold of his shirt and pants on his body. His head spun with weariness and hunger. As his body weakened, he felt his awareness draining away, too. He drove his unwilling legs on.

He passed in and out of full consciousness, but always he kept moving. At last he was crawling, heading up a slope. All was dark before him, but a more solid darkness loomed ahead: a car, a house.

He struggled to think himself into the house. He was almost at the end of his strength. The minds were there, but pale, so pale, and both still now, both asleep. He tried to take the dog again, succeeded in touching its mind, in waking the animal. Fear flooded the creature, fear that it was once again on the edge of possession. It began to bark.

His face was in the mud. It was cool and smelled of iron.

Light burst on him—not mind-light, but real light, the electric glow of a lantern.

Words buzzed in his ears. They were too fast for him to understand, and his exhausted mind was picking up almost none of the thought behind the words. He could not answer.

Someone lifted him. He felt himself being carried, felt the cold clothes stripped away, felt the warmth of hot water. A cloth swept mud from his face—he wore a half-mask of it from the driveway—and he opened his eyes. He was in a white tub, and the water came from a hand-held shower. It splashed warm in his face, down his chest, down his back.

He went away for a while and came back to find a cup at his lips, hot milk in his mouth. He gulped eagerly.

Light was around him. The man was here. "Can you eat?" the man asked him. This time the words were slow and clear, and he understood them; from the man's mind there came, like an echo, *poor boy poor boy poor boy*. He nodded. Moments later, it seemed, he was sipping hot soup, Campbell's vegetable beef, one of his favorites. He alternated that with the milk, enjoying the white taste, the puckery feeling inside his lips and on his tongue. Vitality seeped back, but he was so sleepy.

"Son," the man said, "where did you come from?"

He could not talk. "Sleep," he begged.

"What?"

"Sleep," he said, and as hard as he could, he sent a thought with it.

"You need sleep now," the man told him, as if it had been his own idea. "We'll worry about what to do with you in the morning. Come on."

Despite his exhaustion, the boy felt a leap of joy: the man had grasped his thought. He had communicated, not just with another one of the children, but with a grown-up. He wanted to smile but sobbed instead.

The man had clothed him in an undershirt and pajama bottoms; the shirt hung off him, the legs of the pajamas had to be rolled up into huge cuffs, and the waist was so loose that they threatened to fall from his hips. But the man carried him to the bedroom, put him beneath warm covers, put out the light.

You sleep too, the boy sent.

"I'll be all right on the cot. I'll be just in the next room. You call if you need anything, okay?"

He understood the intent more than the words, but he forced his mouth to say, "Okay." In a way, the hardest part of his entire journey came in the next hour, for he had to force himself to stay awake, to make sure that this man would not betray him.

The man rummaged around in the next room for a short time, setting up a cot, finding blankets. The boy fought sleep to perceive all this. The thought was always deep in the man's mind that this was ODD, that he wasn't ACTING RIGHT, that SOMETHING HAD TO BE DONE, but with the boy's help the thought never came to the surface. Only when the man had turned off his light, only when the fire of his mind had cooled to the ruddy glow of dreaming embers, did the boy sleep at last.

And for the first time in many months, he slept with hope.

CHAPTER THREE

1

Dr. Leon Beckerman was the first inmate of the Slow Tango installation to express doubt.

Nurse Alice Weston had lunch with him on Monday in the crowded installation commissary, and in the course of small talk over his beef Stroganoff and her iceberg salad (she ate very little, really, but the pounds never seem to come off), she chanced to remark that it was a pity they had lost the Gamma boy.

Beckerman, a youngish forty, a brawny man who was trading the government a year of bondage at the installation in exchange for a guaranteed five-year research grant, paused, his fork with its load of beef and noodles poised halfway to his lips. "Lost? What do you mean?" A noodle slipped from the fork and splatted on the red-and-white plastic tabletop.

Alice's heart thumped hard at Beckerman's sharp look. His eyes, direct and gray behind lenses that diminished them, seemed suddenly beady, his linebacker's face hard and mean. "W-well," she stammered, "he died, you know."

The fork clattered back to the tray. Beckerman leaned across the table, squinting in his myopic way. His face had a challenging, argumentative expression, and his voice was just as hostile: "Died? The Gamma subject? What the hell are you talking about? Who did the postmortem?"

Alice looked down at her plate, at a quarter head of shredded lettuce, three cherry tomatoes, chopped celery, a scattering of cucumber wedges, all sprinkled with red Russian dressing. "No one," she said as if to her salad. "Dr. Kornbluth pronounced him dead and said we didn't need one."

Dr. Beckerman chewed his lip. "Didn't need one? And Stark agreed?"

"He wasn't here. It was after he'd left the compound last Thursday."

"Thursday? When Fisher was away, too?"

"Yes," Alice said. "It's all in the reports."

Beckerman's squarish, sallow face set itself in lines of disapproval. "No, it wasn't. Not on the network, anyway. There was nothing on the SCOPE activity summary about any death. Didn't anyone bother to enter the data?"

Alice shrugged. "I'm not cleared for the higher-level entries. I suppose someone must have."

The doctor wasn't listening. With a wadded paper napkin he swiped up the dropped noodle. He deposited the crumpled napkin on his tray, in the middle of the remaining Stroganoff. "Were you the case nurse, Weston?"

"No. I heard about it later. I don't know who was working the case with Dr. Kornbluth." Alice drank some ice water and, trying hard to keep her voice level, added, "It's not the nurses' job to report deaths, anyway. That's a security task. The attending physician has that responsibility."

The doctor didn't seem to notice her flicker of rebellion. Beneath knitted dark brows his eyes were far away. "Dammit. It was the Gamma boy, you say?"

"Yes, Doctor."

"He was all right last March when we did the routine physicals." Beckerman stabbed at the napkin with restless jabs of his fork, as if it had offended him. Alice was aware of the smell of his food, greasy, too rich, and of the hum of conversation in the commissary, the clang of silverware and crockery, the background music, that same denatured tuneless stuff they play at airports and in elevators everywhere. It was pinging out a Disney tune at the moment, "It's a Small World, After All." The song took her back to 1988, when she had gone with her sister and nieces to Walt Disney World in Florida. She had to make an effort to pay attention to Dr. Beckerman, who was scraping his chair back from the table. "I'm going to investigate this," he said. "I think you'd better come with me, Weston."

They took their trays to the dump line, deposited their silverware in the water-filled tray, discarded their half-eaten lunches. Alice followed the doctor outside, out into a perfect June day. The rain of yesterday had vanished, leaving everything clean and sweet, and at half-past noon the temperature stood just at 82. A raucous pair of blue jays flew out of a pine beside the commissary door to a higher tree, and from a secure branch far above the humans' heads the birds berated the two loudly.

Alice felt her face going hot. Ordinarily the walk over to BQ would have been an occasion for breathing fresh air, for stretching some of the kinks out of her back and legs, but following Dr. Beckerman made it all somehow quite different. He strode along ahead of her, the heels of his polished black Oxfords grinding on the crushed gravel of the drive, his immaculate lab smock blindingly white in the bright light of midday as it billowed behind him. "We'll check this out on my unit," he said without looking around.

Any of the other nurses wouldn't have minded accompanying Dr. Beckerman home, Alice was sure. Beckerman, for all his scowling and brusqueness, was not bad-looking—indeed he was handsome in an athletic kind of way, if you disregarded the thick glasses he wore to correct his near-sightedness. He looked something like a football player a few years out of shape, which very possibly was not far from the truth. Still, he was quiet about his past, as most of them were, and Alice wasn't sure about his history.

But he looked attractive enough, and when he was not on duty, he did have a certain unexpected wacky humor, a certain ease of manner, that made him intriguing as a potential partner in bed. But of course such thoughts were out of place for chubby—hell, admit it, obese—Nurse Weston. And Beckerman was all business now, definitely on duty, thoughts of sex the last thing on his mind.

He unlocked his apartment door and stood back for her to enter. She looked around; all the housing units were standard, prefab jobs indistinguishable from any Holiday Inn suite, but every resident had found ways of making the poky little apartments a bit more homey. Beckerman's way was to thumbtack to the walls a myriad of charts, sketches, X-rays, and graphs, all dealing with the physiology of the human brain. Here was a series of computer-enhanced CAT scans showing the progressive development of an inoperable tumor; there was a magnetic-resonance image of a child's head, face-on, brain, eye-balls, skull clearly visible, like a cover illustration for a paperback Stephen King novel.

Other than papering the walls with these pictures, Beckerman had done minimal decorating. Stacks of books and medical journals were arrayed against the wall beside his sofa, like soldiers standing at attention. Against the right wall, his desk was bare except for the computer terminal. Without even turning on the overhead light, Beckerman slid into his chair and turned the terminal on. As soon as the monitor showed READY in amber letters, he hit function key 1, tying the computer into the base information network—SCOPE.

"Let me consult the system survey first. Maybe I missed it. But I don't see how . . ." Beckerman fell silent as he called up the news summary for the previous Thursday. "Nothing." He checked Friday with no better luck. "This is incredible," he muttered. "We lose one of the subjects and it doesn't even show up on the summary? Jesus, Fisher will kick ass from here to— Better call up the boy's personal record."

Alice, standing just behind the seated Beckerman, noticed for the first time the thinning spot at the crown of his head. Even in the dim light his bald spot showed through the short dark hair. She took her attention off the doctor and instead frowned at the screen. Now that she thought of it, it was odd that no obituary notice had appeared for Johnny. Though of course none of the children had actually died before, at least not during her tour of duty.

"Gamma, was it?" Beckerman asked without looking around at Alice. His fingers had already entered the subject query symbols, and now he waited only for the key word.

"Yes, Doctor. Johnny Gamma."

"Surname's enough." Beckerman's slender fingers—the only delicate thing about him, Alice thought—flew over the keys, entering the name.

The computer processed the query in something under four seconds. Such information, unlike the news summary, was classified, and the computer knew it. It presented Beckerman with a demand for his code word, and without patience he used one finger to type in a six-letter series—RADISH, Alice noticed from her vantage point behind Beckerman, although on screen the letters showed up as a series of nulls, XXXXXX. The screen cleared, then filled with information.

"I shouldn't look at this," Alice said, noting the flashing warning TOP SECRET at the head of the menu. "I'm not cleared for—"

"Never mind that shit," Beckerman grunted. "It's not important now. I show six Gammas on the information menu. Which one?"

"Johnny. I told you." Alice felt her breathing become shallow, ragged. Six Gammas? As far as she knew there had always been only one, only Johnny.

"That would be Gamma Five." Beckerman typed in the numeral.

Again the screen cleared, again it flooded with information: Johnny Gamma's vital statistics, birthdate, birth measurements, the infant's physical description, a code string relating to ESP, and a menu for other data. Beckerman keyed in item 1 MEDICAL HISTORY. This filled several screens, and he scrolled through it impatiently. Alice saw Johnny Gamma grow from birth through age twelve in the few seconds it took to reach the end of the file, weight, height, and physical development increasing at each quarterly examination. The last one had been in March; had Johnny lived, he would have been due for another in one week.

"What the hell is this?" Beckerman asked.

The last entry on the screen said only DECEASED.

"He died," Alice said. "That's last Thursday's date."

"I see that. But where's the data? Who was on duty? Kornbluth?"

"Yes. I told you."

"That should be noted, with a cross-reference to PM information." Beckerman pushed back from the screen. "This is goddam odd. He knows better than to pull some dumb stunt like this. What happened?"

Alice said, "I really don't know. The other nurses told me that Dr. Kornbluth was called to Johnny's room late that afternoon, and he pronounced him dead almost as soon as he got there. He—"

Beckerman had erased the screen and was typing in a different set of instructions. "Go on, I'm listening."

"He arranged for the cremation. It was over inside of a few hours."

"Kornbluth was *called*, you say?"

"Yes, Dr. Beckerman."

"Hm. Let's see who called him, then." Now the amber display bore a detailed minute-by-minute diary of the previous Thursday's activity, from the moment the morning shift came on at midnight to the last notes the evening shift had recorded just before Thursday became Friday. "Afternoon, you say?"

"Yes. It was probably about three or four o'clock."

"Here's a test series with the Gamma kid and three others. An Epsilon, a Mu, and a Delta. Hm. Minimal positive to negative results. That ended at fourteen-thirty hours. Then at fourteen-forty the staff brought him a snack of four cookies and two hundred and fifty cc's of milk. At fifteen-oh-five they picked up the tray. He had play time then, unsupervised but taped. The VCR record shows him just sitting on his bed, his hands clenched. Then—what the hell is this?"

"Where?"

"Here." Beckerman's delicate forefinger touched a time notation: 1521.33 HOURS: VIDEO INTERRUPT.

"I don't know," Alice said, though her mind was racing. "I haven't seen this kind of record before. I'm only cleared to 'confidential' and—"

"According to this, the camera didn't malfunction. The video feed was switched off in control central." Beckerman windowed the screen, calling up yet another record. "Damn. The technician reports the console out of tape at fifteen twenty-one. Tape not replaced by human error— oversight, it says here—until oh-oh-twelve hours on Friday. Lot of good that did. Oversight, hell. Criminal negligence."

The window disappeared, and the doctor scanned down the lines. "Here's Kornbluth, going to the room at fifteen forty-three, well after the tape ran out, of course. No video. What the hell? There's no record here of anybody calling him. He just showed up on the wing and went straight to the room. Here's the death report at sixteen-oh-one. Damn, look at this—the cremation order entered at sixteen-oh-three. He must've picked up the phone and called as soon as he pronounced the kid dead. Who the hell does Kornbluth think he is? Nobody has that kind of authority. Nobody except maybe Fisher or Stark." He tapped another window onto the screen. "Let's check the cremation record."

The new display indicated that the body of Johnny Gamma had been picked up by crematory personnel (Operators 1 and 2—unnamed, but it had to be Ricky Smith and his assistant, George Toshi, the only two technicians who ever operated the furnace that sometimes destroyed biopsy samples and other medical waste) at 1632 hours. Under POSTMORTEM and PREPARATION there was no information, only two blank lines. The crematory had been activated at 1648 hours. It took a few minutes to reach operational temperature. The body was fed into it at 1703. After a complete burn-and-cool cycle, the ashes had been removed at 2100 hours. The last notation on this report was REMAINS CONVEYED TO HQ OFFICE; the time was noted as 0910 hours, and the date was the previous Friday.

Beckerman shook his head. "I was on the midnight-to-eight shift. Why the hell didn't somebody mention it? Damn, I slept through the whole thing. I can't believe— Wait a minute." He tried another code, but the screen displayed a curt ACCESS DENIED. "Shit. Should've guessed that Kornbluth would have a higher clearance than me." He hit a key and returned to the screen of Thursday's activity. He stared bleakly at the daily log, ran through it minute by minute all the way to midnight. "This is so incredibly sloppy. I just can't—this is not procedure."

"Dr. Beckerman," Alice said, "Johnny was a little boy."

Stark cleared the screen. It went blank except for a flashing orange cursor, a tiny rectangle. "He was a subject, Nurse Weston. They're all subjects. And there's a procedure to follow when subjects die. Let's see the death report." He called it onto the screen, cursed again as he read it, and printed a facsimile of it out. The printer head shuttled back and forth almost silently across the page, and the paper fed up in a smooth roll. When it came to a stop, Kornbluth ripped the page away and rattled it at Alice. "Goddam, would you look at this?

Hell, a country GP would do a better report than Kornbluth has here. And Fisher hasn't done anything about it? My ass would be gone if I tried anything this screwy. How the hell is Kornbluth getting away with it?"

Alice felt that the room had become too small, that it was closing in on her, that the walls, hard to see in the curtained dimness, were creeping up. "What do you think he's getting away with?" she asked through numb lips.

"Damned if I know. Wait. One more try." He laid the paper aside and called up yet another classified menu, chose ANOMALIES from it, and entered last Thursday's date. After a second of studying the display, he said, "We have trouble."

Alice looked at the screen. The VCR failure was there, along with other trifling things: a child with an upset stomach, a video game in the rec hall of the gym with a record high score, a morning low one degree below the previous record low, set back in 1957. But Beckerman was interested in another anomaly: opposite 1647 hours the notation read MAIN GATE MALFUNCTION. Under that in parentheses was an apologetic [HUMAN ERROR]. She read the notation aloud. "What does that mean?"

His fingers were typing even as she spoke. "I'm asking for details."

The computer gave them the details. The main gate, just like the VCR room, had experienced a temporary loss of function—due, according to the record, to a power failure. That in turn was the fault of Security Operator 11, who unaccountably overrode not one but five switches. All perimeter detection devices had been out for a period of seventeen minutes before someone noticed and brought the system back on line. According to a further note, disciplinary action for the error was pending.

Beckerman suddenly switched the terminal off. "We've got to see Fisher," he said, standing up. He strode to the door and opened it; after the dimness of the room, the June sunlight came in as a white blast, almost blinding Alice. "Come on," the doctor said.

Something in his voice was so strange that Alice looked into his eyes. *Why, he's terrified*, she thought. *He's afraid of something that Johnny did last Thursday!* Somehow the idea pleased her, and on the way back to the administration wing, she walked beside him, no longer behind him.

She held her head up and enjoyed every step of the journey.

2

Julie Lind smiled; on her face it felt like a tight-lipped grimace. "Want to play a game?" she asked the three children in her sweetest voice, her coaxing voice.

Nothing was working today. She had Christie Epsilon, Elizabeth Mu, and little Daisy Rho at the round table, ostensibly for a reading class, but they weren't paying attention. They were holding hands instead, holding hands with their heads bowed as if in prayer. They just would not look up, and they refused to glance at the third-grade readers, though normally these three girls were avid to learn.

The teacher took a deep breath, a breath scented with the nursery-school odor of disinfectant, wax crayons, vomit, closed-in air. "Elizabeth," Julie said, addressing the middle girl, the one with the healed scar on her upper lip from the repair of a badly cleft palate, "wouldn't you girls like to play a game?" Elizabeth was minimally retarded, usually talkative in a scattershot way, her attention leaping from subject to subject haphazardly. But today she was silent.

Julie fought her rising frustration. She taught simple things, motivational lessons; from her the children, all that were capable, had learned reading and writing and arithmetic. The ones who spoke badly had received speech therapy. All, she thought, had learned at least that she cared for them. But the rapport was no longer there for her, had not been there all day. Next door Mr. Clebb was teaching too, but Mr. Clebb was Political. He took the children, one at a time, and taught them about their enemies.

Julie imagined him there now, with a boy or girl strapped to the aversion conditioner—or, as the rest of the staff called it, the electric chair. Clebb would show motion pictures of, say the Premier of the Soviet Union, a hearty, grandfatherly-looking man. To his pupil, Clebb would croon, "This is a bad man. He wants to hurt you. He will hurt you."

The child's body would start from an electrical jolt, painful but not really dangerous.

"Poor child," Clebb would say. "Did the bad man hurt you?"

Of course, that was done only to subjects of the correct age. The very young ones. The older ones got lessons in geography, in world politics, in the necessity of knowing what the bad men on the other side of the world were thinking. Occasionally Clebb ran his own little experiments, experiments in telepathy and in remote viewing, but these had yielded little of value. Indeed, Julie thought to herself, the main thing Clebb had to show for his political indoctrination was a group of children who were, indeed, terrified of the bad man—but the bad man was Clebb himself, not some Russian or Chinese target. Sometimes Julie worried about the children, and sometimes she wondered how much of the hate, how much of the poison, their minds were absorbing.

But today she gave Clebb and his work little thought; her own distress occupied her mind. She felt irritated with everything today, even with the classroom she had been assigned. The whole room was too quiet. It was painted robin's-egg blue, a pacifying color, and it had subdued indirect lighting, designed to relax the children, to put them into a cooperative mood. The classroom was so friendly, so cunningly inviting, so unremittingly relaxing, that it made Julie want to pound the table and scream. "How about playing a little candy hide and seek?" Julie asked.

None of the girls replied. The activity, a sort of kiddie shell game played with M&M candies and colored plastic cups, was a favorite of all the children—and usually forbidden so soon after lunch. But Julie was desperate. None of the children in her groups had been responsive that morning. They had all remained withdrawn, as if focused on some more important thing than lessons, and during lunch the problem seemed to grow even worse. A few of the smaller children, the Rhos and the Sigmas, broke into bitter weeping; the older ones stopped eating and dropped their chins on their breasts, breathing hard and staring at nothing.

"Well," Julie said, rising from her chair, the only adult-sized chair at the table, "*I'm* going to have some fun.

Anyone who wants to join in can have some fun, too. And some nice candy." She unlocked the supply closet and pulled from a top shelf a cardboard box and a small brown package of the candies. "No peeking, now," she said, though her charges seemed oblivious to her. Julie tore open the package and pulled an M&M candy out. She covered it with one of the colored plastic cups, then set the other nine cups upside down in the open box. She put the box on the table. "Who can find the candy?" she asked.

It was, in part, a primitive test of clairvoyance, of the mental ability to detect objects at a distance or to uncover hidden things; but in the past the game had yielded no replicable results, and now it was more a way of getting the children's attention than anything else. Though all the children loved chocolate, this time the temptation did not at first seem to work. The three girls at the table did not stir.

"There's a candy in the box," Julie coaxed. "Which one of my girls can find it for me?"

The little Rho girl, Daisy, did look at the box full of colorful plastic cups then. Except for those startling pale gray eyes, she looked normal, unlike Elizabeth, whose arms were truncated to only half normal length, whose hands were tiny, and unlike Christie, whose silvery eyes were badly askew on a misshapen head. Daisy Rho would have been quite at home in any respectable kindergarten in the land, Julie thought—if only the sweet-faced little child would talk. Her problem was inclination, not ability, for though fully capable of speech, she almost never spoke more than one or two words at a time.

Daisy' right hand was held by Christie, but her left was free. She suddenly reached out, grabbed a yellow cup, and turned it over. She gave Julie a bright, beaming smile that revealed a missing left upper front tooth.

"No, not there," Julie said, fixing all her attention on Daisy. If she could get even one of the girls interested in the game, she thought, the others would follow. "You missed it that time, but I'll bet if you keep going you'll find it. Try again for me, Daisy."

With an absent assurance, Daisy picked up the brown cup, took the candy from underneath, and popped it into her mouth. She crunched the sugar coating happily, her merry silver eyes smiling at Julie. The teacher felt a wave of love wash over her, strong enough almost to carry her away.

"Very good, Daisy," she said, touching the little girl's cheek. "Want to play again?"

Daisy nodded, grinning again, her teeth flecked with the brown inner chocolate and the yellow sugar coating of the candy. The pleasure on her face was so keen that for a second Julie thought she could taste the sweet chocolate in her own mouth. She smiled back at the little girl.

"You other girls want to join us?" Julie asked. "Daisy and I are having a lot of fun." But Elizabeth and Christie were still remote.

Sighing, Julie picked up the box, turned to hide it from the girls, put another candy down, and returned it to the table. "Get it first time now, Daisy."

Daisy went for the brown cup, but it was empty. Then she turned over the black one, the purple one, and the white one. The candy was under the next cup, the green one. Again the little girl crunched her prize.

Julie glanced at the older children, but if anything, they were more aloof than they had been. "Once more," Julie said, determined to outlast the two other girls. She put another M&M under a cup, then put the tray of cups back on the table.

This time Daisy did get it right off the bat, turning over the red cup and picking up the M&M with a delighted squeal. She pulled her right hand away from Christie and held up the cup and the candy for Julie to see.

"What a smart girl." Julie beamed.

Daisy looked from the cup to the candy and then at Julie. Her eyebrows, so fair they were hardly visible, rose mischievously.

"What are you trying to show me, honey?" Julie asked, making her voice indulgent. "You want to tell me something? Something about the cup and the candy?"

Daisy nodded and giggled.

"Well, they're the same color, aren't they? Red and red. Can you say 'red'?"

But Daisy didn't speak. She put the cup down and

popped the red candy in her mouth. It went the way of the yellow and the dark brown one before it.

"You other girls are missing a terrific game," Julie warned. The other two didn't pay her any attention.

The next round of the game was the breakthrough.

Daisy picked up the green cup, looked Julie straight in the eyes, and without even glancing at the box she picked up the white cup, revealing a green M&M. She dropped the candy into the upended green cup and rattled it.

"Same color again," Julie said. "Very—"

Same color again.

My God, Julie thought.

The first time Daisy had gone right for the yellow cup. The M&M had been yellow. The second time she had picked up the brown cup first, and the candy had been brown. Then red. Now—

"You were showing me the color it was going to be," Julie said.

Daisy ate the green candy. Her gap-toothed smiled flashed again.

"The second time you turned over the black and white and purple cups because there aren't any black, white, or purple candies. That's it, isn't it?"

Daisy gave a little humming sigh of contentment.

Julie got up, turned her back to the girls at the table, and shook one piece of candy from the bag into her right hand. She clenched her hand on it without looking it. Then she turned back to the table. "Daisy," she said. "I've got in my hand——"

Daisy held out the brown cup. Julie opened her hand. She dropped the dark-brown candy into the dark-brown plastic cup.

Daisy's eyes were triumphant.

She taught me, Julie thought. She *taught* me. She taught *me*.

In the VCR room, a technician had sat up very straight. He reached for a telephone. The line went directly to Fisher's office. Fisher, in the middle of a heated discussion with Dr. Beckerman, picked up the phone and snapped, "What is it?"

"Something," the technician said. "By God, it's something. It's finally something."

3

"Twelve," Collins said.

It was past noon; he had awakened only a few minutes ago and had come in to see how his guest was doing. The wan-faced boy was sound asleep, his fair hair tousled, his scratched cheek puffing gently with his exhalations, his scabbed hands holding the quilt close against his chest.

In the daylight streaming in through the bedroom window, the hands were immediately odd. Collins stared at them for a few seconds, looking at the ragged scratches left by blackberry briars, the striated scrape along the base of the right thumb from some fall the boy had taken, before realizing the full oddity.

Six fingers on each hand.

Twelve fingers.

The extra digit was on the outside edge of each hand, a two-jointed little finger, underdeveloped. It was half the size of the normal pinky beside it, and it had only a tiny chip of a nail, a little pink wedge at the end.

Something scrabbled at the window, and Collins glanced up to see Eightball's woebegone face. Seeing it made him frown; he didn't remember putting the dog out.

Collins rose and went to the front of the cabin to open the door. The day outside was warm and brilliant; from around the corner of the cabin, Eightball came rushing in. Collins bent to pet him, but the dog hurtled past, threw himself through the bedroom doorway, barking furiously.

"No!" Collins closed the cabin door and hurried into the bedroom after the spaniel.

The barks ceased before he had taken two steps.

When he got to the door, the boy was scrunched up at the head of the bed, crouching on the pillows, and Eightball was on the bed's foot, legs splayed, head down. He looked as if he were about to leap for the little boy's throat.

But the child's face showed no alarm. A pucker of concentration drew the light blond brows together; the eyes, very pale gray in the light of day, stared intently at the dog.

"Eightball—" Collins began, his voice stern.

He didn't need to continue. The dog suddenly relaxed, his tail wagging foolishly. He walked across the mattress in a clumsy spring-footed way and held his head up. The boy reached out to pet him.

"Hey, better watch out," Collins said. "He sometimes thinks he's a watch—"

The boy turned such a bland look of assurance toward him that he fell silent.

Eightball submitted to having his ears scratched. Then he leaped from the bed to the floor, squeezed past Collins, and trotted through the front room to the kitchen, toenails tacking over the oak floor.

"Well," Collins said. "Guess he's decided you're okay. What happened to you, son? You get lost out in the woods?"

The boy slipped back beneath the covers. His grave eyes never left Collins's gaze, but he did not reply.

"You got pretty badly scratched up," Collins said. "Looks like you had an adventure out there. Where you from, son?"

The boy slowly shook his head.

"Can't you talk?" Collins asked him. He came in and sat at the foot of the bed, occupying the same spot that Eightball usually did. "Is that the problem? Can you understand me?"

The boy nodded.

"But you can't talk? You can't tell me your name, or—"

The solemn face seemed to consider for a second. Then, his face growing contorted and red with effort, his voice breathy and hoarse, the child croaked, "Johnny."

"Well. I'm glad to meet you, Johnny. You can call me Pete. My dog is Eightball."

Johnny's lips curved into a slight smile, a sweet Cupid's smile, and he nodded.

"You sound like you might have a sore throat."

Johnny shrugged and shook his head again.

"No? Just hard for you to talk, huh?"

The boy nodded. His lips were cracked and dry, showing thin lines of reddish-brown blood and flakes of dead tissue, and he licked them with a pale pink tongue.

Collins glanced at his watch. "We slept really late today. I'm hungry. You hungry, Johnny?"

The boy nodded shyly. "Yuh," he said in a voice like a rusty hinge. It almost hurt Collins's throat to hear him.

"Well, let me see what I can rustle up. Then we'll decide what we're going to do with you. It's time for lunch, but I think I'd rather have breakfast. That okay with you?"

The eyebrows raised as if in inquiry.

"You know, breakfast stuff. Toast, bacon, eggs?"

A nod.

Collins got up, and the bedsprings squeaked. "Okay. Bathroom's in there if you gotta go. I'll cook us up some breakfast and open old Eightball a can of food. You come on when you're ready. Just follow the bacon smell, okay?"

The boy shrugged and gave his shy smile again.

Collins left him in the bed and went to the kitchen, where Eightball was standing on his hind legs, his forepaws against the drawer that contained the can opener. The drawer bore many prints of Eightball's feet from all the times he had begged before. The spaniel gave him an imploring over-the-shoulder look, brown eyes nearly liquid. "You're starving, right," Collins said, ruffling the dog's ears. He fished the can opener out and got a can of Alpo from the cabinet. He emptied it into Eightball's dish, having to maneuver the last spoonfuls of the liver chunks around the dog's eager snout. "Enjoy, useless."

Collins looked at the wall clock, checked his watch against it. It was twelve thirty-five already. Shaking his head, he confided to Eightball, "I haven't slept that well since—since we came up here. How about you?"

Eightball continued to nose his metal food dish around until every scrap of food was gone. Then he slurped water from a beige ceramic bowl with the legend DOG embossed on its side. Collins turned on the kitchen radio and tuned to an AM station. "Let's see who our guest is. My bet is that he got lost out in the woods. Want to take me up on it?"

Eightball thumped his tail, ran his tongue out, and yawned.

"We'll see. I guess I'd better call someone about him,

don't you? But it can wait until we get a little food into him, I suppose." Collins busied himself with skillet and bacon. He stripped off six slices from the package, put them in the cold pan, and put the pan on one of the stove's two burners. The propane gas came on clear and blue, and in a moment the bacon began to sizzle. Eightball perked his ears up and his nostrils quivered at the rich smell. Meanwhile, to the beat of sixties music—the station had a nostalgia format—Collins ground fresh Colombian Supremo coffee beans and loaded the coffee maker, then took his last five eggs from the refrigerator. He cracked them into another skillet, humming along to the Beatles' "Ob-La-Di, Ob-La-Dah," as the coffee began to drip. He got a small chunk of cheddar cheese from the fridge and chopped it into the eggs, scrambling them well.

When the bacon was crisp, he took up the slices, put them on a plate covered with a paper towel to drain, poured off the excess grease, and plopped six more into the pan. He loaded the toaster, a four-slice model, and then took up the eggs.

The boy, holding the oversized pajamas up with both hands, appeared in the kitchen door. "Ready to eat?" Collins asked cheerfully.

The face reddened and the boy forced out his one-word agreement: "Yuh."

"Here you go." Collins put half the scrambled eggs on a plate, added the bacon, and put the plate on the table. "Milk to drink?"

The boy was literally drooling. He wiped his chin with the back of his hand and nodded. Collins poured the milk, the toast popped up, and he gave the boy the glass and two slices of buttered toast.

By then the rest of the bacon was ready. Collins fixed his own plate, poured a cup of coffee, and slipped into a chair across from Johnny. The boy was shoveling the last of the eggs into his mouth. He drained the glass and then held it out toward Collins. "More?" he struggled to ask, but the impediment in his speech made the word sound like "Moh?"

"Yeah, you can have more. It's in the refrigerator. You wanna get it, or—"

Johnny slid out of his chair, still clutching the pajamas

at his navel with his left hand. He opened the refrigerator, got out the half-gallon container of milk, and waddled back to the table, stepping on the unrolling legs of the pajama trousers. He set the milk on the table, hitched up the pajamas—Collins noticed the first fuzz of pubic hair had just begun to appear as Johnny almost let the trousers drop before getting them up around his waist—and then got back in his chair. With immense concentration, Johnny poured himself a glass of milk. He drank half of that, belched grandly, and then with a happy sigh began to munch bacon and toast.

Collins smiled at him as he ate his own breakfast. At five minutes after one the radio station broadcast the local news. Collins, now on his second cup of coffee, listened carefully to the announcer, whose mellifluous tones seemed a little incongruous when linked to the Piedmont twang of mountain pronunciation. The newsman spoke of an auto accident outside of Cleveland, with three teenagers hospitalized. The Army Corps of Engineers predicted that Lake Lanier would remain at or near full power pool until well into the summer, a welcome change after several years of drought. Completion was expected in October for the newest leg of the four-lane highway that would eventually connect Blairsville and Atlanta. Odds and ends.

But no missing children. Nothing about a handsome little boy with a speech impediment and a strange deformity, with six fingers on each hand, six toes on each small foot. And surely a missing child would be news in this isolated part of the state, this stretch of farmlands and small towns.

Collins frowned. "Johnny," he said. "Where did you come from?"

The boy shook his head.

"Listen, Johnny. You want to go home, don't you?"

"Home."

"Where is it, Johnny? Where is home?"

Johnny slipped out of his chair. Clutching the pajamas with one hand, he took his plate and his glass to the sink. He looked at Collins with a strangely imploring expression in his pale eyes, for all the world like Eightball begging for food. Collins could not help smiling; the child, though evidently around twelve years old, was small for his age, and there at the sink with the rear waistband of the trousers sagging halfway down his ass, he looked like a model for a Norman Rockwell painting. "Johnny, you have to help me. You want to go home, don't you?"

The boy's whole body stiffened. His face grew red. Collins half rose from his chair in alarm; then he realized that the boy was trying hard to speak. "I want to stay with you," Johnny gasped in his hoarse, forced voice. Then he began to cry, to wail.

Collins was on his knees beside the boy in a second. Johnny had slipped the glass and dish into the sink. He threw both arms around Collins, sobbing; his breath, hot against Collins's face, was sour beneath the scent of bacon.

My God, Collins thought. *He's emaciated. He's skin and bones.* He had a confused impression of darkness, of briars biting into his flesh, of the sky ripping open with lightning and thunder, of a cold white place and men in white and one man in particular who smiled when he hurt you.

Then it was gone, and Collins was holding a shaking, sobbing child. "Okay," he said soothingly. "Okay, Johnny. It's all right. You can stay here for a while. Hey, you can stay here until we find your folks. Don't cry."

The sobs slowly subsided. The boy's head was heavy on Collins's shoulder. After a few minutes he realized that Johnny was asleep again. He picked up, holding the pajama bottoms in place, and carried him into the bedroom again. He managed to get Johnny beneath the covers without waking him.

The muddy jeans were crumpled in the bathroom, beside the tub, along with the boy's other clothes. Collins scooped up the damp bundle and took it into the kitchen. A woman from Holcomb's Crossing, the village five miles away, did Collins's laundry once a week, but these garments were past cleaning. The jeans were shredded at the cuffs, holed at the knees, the underwear was filthy with mud and streaks of excrement, the blue-and-white-striped T-shirt tattered. Collins shivered; from the look of the clothes, Johnny could have been in the wilderness for days. Shirt, socks, pants, underwear were hopeless. The muddy sneakers might possibly be salvaged, though.

Collins looked at the jeans tag. They were Levi's, size twelve, slim-cut. Eightball came nosing in and sniffed the shoes. "Well, Eightball, what do I do now?"

The dog looked up inquisitively. Collins grinned, remembering Mr. Dick in *David Copperfield*, the gentle loony who advised David's aunt on all matters of importance. "Do?" Mr. Dick would have said. "Do? Why, I—I should buy him some trousers, Mum."

Collins checked on the boy again. Johnny was sleeping, sleeping as if he had been a week without rest. Collins silently closed the door. Eightball, who had followed, looked up as if awaiting orders. "You stay here and guard the door," Collins said. "I'll be back in half an hour."

He was almost as good as his word. He returned in thirty-nine minutes from the Holcomb's Crossing Mercantile. He brought with him eight new pairs of jeans, size twelve slim, a new pair of Keds, dark blue, a dozen pairs of white socks, a dozen pairs of briefs, a pair of swimming trunks, two pairs of boy's pajamas, and ten short-sleeved knit shirts in various colors. He had made Mr. Cooper, the owner of the main commercial enterprise of Holcomb's Crossing, very happy indeed. Collins had also stopped at Lee's Drugs for a red toothbrush, extra Colgate toothpaste, children's aspirin, and a few other things.

Eightball met his master at the front door. Collins dumped his purchases on a chair and went to the bedroom, the dog trotting along beside. Johnny was still asleep. Eightball started into the room, but Collins reached down to hook his collar with two fingers. "Don't want to wake him up, boy," he said softly.

After a moment of irresolution, Collins closed the bedroom door again and went to the telephone, on the desk beside his computer. He plucked the telephone directory from the bookshelf over the computer screen and looked up the number of the Forestry Service. It took him a few minutes to get in touch with William Whitepath, but after some delay the receiver boomed with his friend's voice: "Too late, white man. I'm workin' all this week. No fishing until I get some time off."

"Bloody savage," Collins said, grinning. "Listen, friend, could you give me some research information?"

"How much you wanna pay?"

"How about a free drink next time you're here?"

"Firewater, huh? Sounds good to me. What you wanna know?"

Collins licked his lips. "Part of this book's about, uh, a family. The father was a major distributor of cocaine. When the heat was put on him, he took off with his wife and kid. They got up into the hills someplace, the father, the mother, and a little, uh, girl about ten or twelve years old. Thing is she was retarded. She got lost. Now, I'm not sure what the procedure is on searching for a lost child in the mountains. Could you—"

"Give me the family's name. I'll see what we did."

Collins paused a moment. "Uh, no, they got her back okay, they found her themselves. But I want to put in, just as background, you know, what the local law-enforcement people would have done normally if they had been alerted. See, he was afraid to call anybody because—"

"Yeah, the drug connection, I get it. Well, we've done some looking for lost hikers and such. Tell you what, I'll pull a few reports and read through them, then stop by for the drink one evening this week and tell you what I can. Fair enough?"

"Yeah, fine. Uh, I don't suppose there's any current search on that I might be able to join?"

"What are you, Geraldo Rivera?"

"No, it's just that firsthand reporting's always more vivid. Any searches going on right now?"

"Nope. Not that I know of, anyhow. Let me take a quick look." There was a long pause before Whitepath came back to the phone. "You're out of luck, my palefaced friend. No bulletins are out from any agency in the state right now. Nobody's gotten lost in these here hills since last winter, and then it was a couple of drunks. But I'll see what I can dig up. See you Wednesday night, maybe?"

"Fine. Take care."

Collins hung up the receiver, went to the liquor cabinet, poured himself a couple of fingers of scotch, and went to the kitchen to dilute it with water and ice. He returned to the front room and sank into the other chair, staring at the one filled with brown paper bags full of child's clothes. Eightball came to have his chin scratched.

"Dog," Collins said, "am I going nuts? You know what came over me when I was on my way back from the store? I thought, now that I've bought the clothes, I can keep him. Crazy, huh?"

Eightball sniffed the drink, snorted, and padded away. Collins sat and thought and, in his usual parsimonious way with alcohol, made the drink last for more than an hour. The next two he drank rather more quickly.

4

General Dwight N. Arnold, USAF, had always liked Fritz Engstrom. Captain Engstrom had served with Arnold years before in Germany, getting his advanced intelligence training and experience at what had once been the chief NATO military counterintelligence center. The two of them had made quite a team back then, with Engstrom working in the field and Arnold serving as case officer. It was supposed to be all business, electronic and computer surveillance and counterintelligence, but inevitably there was a human side as well, some close calls, some personal triumphs, and just as inevitably the two became friends. Later, as assignments and orders separated the two, they kept in touch with occasional letters, ritually exchanged Christmas cards, the odd telephone call.

And this particular call was decidedly odd. It was actually the second that day, for Engstrom had telephoned Arnold's home that morning at six o'clock Eastern time—and that meant that it was four in the morning in Colorado. In a hesitant, uncharacteristic manner he had asked Arnold for a favor, and he had also requested that Arnold reply on a secure line. The general had promised to comply.

He got through to Fritz early that afternoon, speaking from a room in the Pentagon. On his end in Colorado, Fritz took the call on a line generally reserved for the exchange of sensitive data regarding satellite intelligence. "What have you got for me, sir?" he said at once.

"Forget the 'sir' stuff for now. This is strictly informal. And what I've got is not much Fritz," Arnold said. "But it's enough to make me wonder what you and the Mrs. got into. It was the Feingold Clinic outside of Arlington, correct?"

"That's it."

Arnold shrugged the telephone into place on his shoulder and with both hands leafed through the sixteen pages of printout he had retrieved from various sources. "First of all, you're right about its being out of business. It folded five years ago, but not for lack of customers. It had a good reputation as a fertility clinic, and there was a waiting list as long as your arm. They showed a tremendous success rate with infertility cases—over ninety percent, it says here. Of course, I understand they screened their prospects well—"

"Arnie," Fritz interrupted, "I don't care about all that. Beth and I went to them—"

"I have a summary of your records right here in front of me. I'm sorry about your son, Fritz."

There was a long pause. "It's kosher, then?"

Arnold bit his lip. "Well, that's hard to say for sure. It sure to God looks that way on paper. But there's—I don't know. Guess I shouldn't say anything if I'm not sure about it."

"That means you think there's something funny about it. Right, Arnie?"

The general sighed and took the telephone receiver back into his hand. "I'm not positive. To tell you the truth, Fritz, I just can't make up my mind on this thing. I pulled what records I could, but they short-stopped me; there's an Ultra label on several files."

A soft humming noise, the carrier signal of an antitap program, came over the line from Colorado. "Ultra?" Fritz asked, his voice suddenly guarded.

Arnold could picture Fritz's long Nordic face, could almost see the vee of concentration between his brows. The general grunted. "Yeah. On certain aspects of financing. On the backgrounds of certain staff members."

Moments passed; then, caution in his tone, Engstrom asked, "I can think of only one reason for that kind of cover. Arnie, was the Feingold Center a front for some Virginia concern?"

As Arnold knew, Engstrom was asking about the CIA. "Not them." The general started to say something more, then hesitated for a long time before adding, "Maybe a special outfit. You might be able to identify it with a little—fishing."

Silence again. Then Engstrom said, "I thought certain parties were out of business."

Arnold had slipped a particular page out of the file. It was the only one that referred, even obliquely, to Ernest Fisher. "You weren't alone."

"Looked from my side as if the intelligence shakeup after the last election took care of some of the cowboy stuff."

"Lots of off-the-shelf activity got canned. I think a few promising ones squeaked through, though, under the national security blanket. That's what seems to have gone on here."

"Public records for the center still available?"

"I called up the medical stats." Arnold put the one page aside and went through the printouts again. "Got a pretty good amount of public-access material, some private stuff, some lower-grade classified data."

"Pattern?" Engstrom guessed.

Arnold leaned back in the swivel chair. The secure phone cubicle was only about ten feet square, heavily insulated against sound leakage, the white walls Spartan under the glare of two recessed fluorescent light fixtures. "Fritz, I can't say for sure. But the ten percent or so failure rate—well, the vast majority of the unsuccessful attempts were full-term stillbirths, not miscarriages. Too many for chance. Now, that's public information. But here's some private stuff." He picked up the single sheet he had dropped earlier, and despite the secure line, despite the acoustic seal of the room, Arnold dropped his voice. "Feingold is a cardboard. The record's probably secure enough for anyone not really digging—full range of degrees and certifications, but a hasty job, easy to check against if you know how to look."

"I don't know anything about the man," Engstrom said. "We never met Feingold himself. Our case physician was a man named Llewallen."

"Got him, and he's legit, as far as I can tell. But after

he got his gyn-ob training, he also specialized in genetics. Did you know that?"

"No."

"Oh, yes. And after his stint at the clinic, Llewallen did some work on the inheritability of intelligence. He's currently at the Pacific Research Institute in Maui."

Engstrom got it right away: "Payoff. That sounds like a front."

"Looks that way."

"And you think Feingold's a cardboard. Who is he, then?"

Arnold rubbed his lips. "My guess is that it's a man named Stark. But that's another phony. I don't have the real name—not for sure. And even if I was certain, I wouldn't tell you, not even over this line. But I suspect it's someone a certain outfit fished out of Berlin a long time back."

"Genetics?"

"Yeah."

Engstrom's voice came back shaky: "I know a little bit about the reports on the Soviet eugenics programs. They always got a pretty thorough brush-off as I recall."

"In some quarters. Other places took the reports more seriously. It starts to look like the believers may have been right."

"My God, Arnie, this feels wrong."

"I know. Fritz . . ."

"What is it?"

"I think maybe we'd better not dig anymore. Hell, if I'd known it was going to run this way, I wouldn't have started it."

"I have to know more."

"Fritz, I'm leaving a trail. There's no way around it with the interlocks in place now. How bad do you want this stuff? You'd better get that damn straight in your mind before you ask me to go any further."

Again there was a silence. But this time Engstrom broke it with a long story: a story of how his wife had vivid dreams, visions almost, that convinced her that their son was still alive. Arnold listened, wincing.

"I'm sorry, Fritz," he said at last. "I sure to God am, and you know it. But if there's an Ultra label on this one, it's too hot for me."

Engstrom said, "You've got a son, Arnie."

"And your son died at birth, or so they say. Fritz, I'm sorry, but—"

"I've never asked you for much, have I?"

General Arnold took a long, deep breath. "What else do you want from me? Not that I'm promising, you understand."

"You say the Feingold closed five years ago. See if there's ever been a clandestine site tied to it. If there is, tell me where. Tell me who."

"It's tricky. It can be very, very tricky."

"I know it, sir."

Arnold sighed. "Hell, we pulled off some tricky stuff ourselves in Wiesbaden that time, didn't we? It's a long shot, Fritz, and there may just not be a damn thing I can do, but I'll sure to God try."

"Thank you, Arnie."

After he hung up the telephone, General Arnold sat for a few minutes brooding over the printouts. He had been trained for years in spotting patterns, in ferreting out anomalies from those patterns. He had just enough of the jigsaw puzzle now to see hints of an overall design, though not the design itself. He sighed again. If the design included Fisher, that cold-blooded bastard Fisher, it was going to be a deadly puzzle indeed, one that would call for his most extreme care.

There safe in the bowels of the Pentagon he wondered if even that sort of carefulness would be enough to protect him.

5

Ernest Fisher sat alone in his office for the first time that day. His head ached savagely, a crashing throb to the tides of his pulse; he closed his eyes and saw formless shapes in the dark, the dull-red monsters of migraine swimming in a black sea. He opened his eyes, pushed up from the desk, and looked out the window into a sunny, cheerful afternoon. Someone tooled past on a bright red golf cart; it was one of the security people, identifiable by his tan uniform.

Shaking his head, Fisher turned to the bookshelves

built into the west wall. Most of them bulged with books, a scattering of best-selling fiction, more on history and the military, some on travel. But the eye-level shelf was different. It was occupied by a double row of stainless-steel containers the size and general shape of one-liter Thermos bottles. Fisher took down the one on the right end and studied the engraved label on the front, just below the lid: GAMMA (5): JOHN. Beneath that was a notation of the dates of birth, death, and cremation.

Fisher unscrewed the top and looked into the container, shaking it gently. Three or four pounds of ash, pulverized to a uniform speckled gray, nearly filled it. He took down another container and opened it. For a long time he studied the contents of both. They appeared the same, and yet. . . .

Did the Gamma boy's ashes *waver* somehow? As if he were seeing a double exposure? Did they try to become a different kind of ash, fluffier, grayer? Fisher stared at them until his eyes ached. With an impatient grunt he screwed the lids of both containers back into place and put both containers of—the technicians called them "cremains," a word he detested—of ashes back on the shelf. Fisher decided he was just tired out.

For it had been a long day: first a briefing session with Stark on the results of the test series so far (nonresults, actually, Fisher thought to himself); then a couple of hours of attending to the details of running the installation, ranging from the mundane problem of food supply (as a cover Slow Tango had purchased a popular restaurant in the resort town of Helen to the south and west of the national forest; supplies delivered to the restaurant by legitimate provisioners were then rerouted to the installation via unmarked government trucks) to the more exotic questions of employee loyalty (Stark's keepers, a team of five that even the scientist did not know about, provided a detailed summary of the geneticist's activities on his jaunt to Atlantic City, none of the information damning).

And after all this, Beckerman had come in with his wild story of irregularities in the Gamma boy's death. Fisher had looked at the material, had agreed that the Unit had experienced a major lapse of security on the date in question, and had set out to do some checking himself.

It hadn't panned out. George Toshi, a technician who had actually prepared the body for cremation, was adamant in his story: he was quite sure that he had sent Johnny Gamma through the flames. He had seen the body pass through the gates of the crematorium himself, and with his own hands he had raked the ashes into the stainless-steel container that now rested on Fisher's shelf. Fisher saw no reason to doubt the young Hawaiian; Toshi was second-generation intelligence, his father a legendary figure in the NSA, an electronics genius who had revolutionized the technical espionage business in the mid to late eighties. If anyone knew his business, George Toshi should.

Dr. Kornbluth was equally certain. Record or no, he distinctly recalled being summoned by a nurse or teacher —he had not bothered to make a note at the time, and now he couldn't remember who it had been—to the boy's room. He found the child's heart had stopped. That was the obvious cause of death, and that was what he had reported. No, the child had been dead for some time. No, there had been no chance of resuscitation. Fisher, head already pounding, had at last waved the man away. Other problems pressed.

He reviewed the videotape of the Rho girl's performance and was not as enthusiastic as the technician had been. "It may not be repeatable. Possibly it's only chance," he had said.

The young man, one of the newer ones at the installation, was indignant: "Every time she picked up the correct color first."

Fisher gave him a hard stare through eyes that felt bloodshot. "A hell of a lot of good that does us. Can you think of any strategic application for guessing the color of candy, son?"

"No, but it's evidence of—"

"Show it to Stark. If he sees any significance in the tape, put it in a report. Submit it through channels." He had chased the young man off at last by wielding the club of bureaucracy on him. Ironic, in a way; he remembered how he had hated it when he used to be on the receiving end of such curt orders. Fisher went back to his desk, sat, and brooded. Assume the worst had occurred. Assume that, somehow, the child had escaped. What then? According to the boy's profile, Johnny Gamma was only minimally capable of verbal communication, and he was subject to fugue intervals that suspiciously resembled autism. It was unlikely in the extreme that he would be able to explain his situation or even to lead outsiders to the installation. Still, Fisher had not reached his present office by ignoring possibilities. . . .

The intercom chirped. Fisher hit a switch. "What is it?"

Mrs. Mead, the only one on the payroll who had been a part of the installation's administrative staff right along with Fisher, Dougherty, and Stark, said, "We're getting a flag over the security net. Maybe you'd better take a look."

"All right. Feed it to my console." Fisher pulled open a desk drawer, and a computer terminal swung out and up on an elevating platform. He switched the terminal on. After a moment it self-booted; then the flashing notation ULTRA appeared in the center of the screen.

Fisher keyed in a complex authorization code. The display, print-negative—that is, the data would not print out and the feed would be broken if anyone tried—indicated a serious breach in security: four different files had been accessed already that day, all of them having to do with the unit's former cover organization, the Feingold Clinic. Two other files had resisted access to inquiries from a Pentagon operator with Top Secret clearance only. The chances of its being an accidental pattern were estimated at 250,000 to one. Fisher swore under his breath. Aloud, he said to the intercom, "Alert our Washington people. This looks bad. I want a trace on the querent; find out whose authorization code that is."

Mrs. Mead sounded satisfied: "Yes, sir."

"Get me all available background on the subject. It may mean we have to go operational, so you'd better let Dougherty know, too," Fisher continued. He rubbed his aching forehead. "As a matter of fact, call him in." Fisher switched off the intercom and reviewed the data the Pentagon querent had retrieved. Not much there; all of it was medical information, personal information, nothing directly relating to the purpose or even to the existence of the unit. Still . . .

Briefly Fisher wondered if there was a connection here, if the suspicions of Beckerman regarding the Gamma boy were somehow tied in, however occultly, to the probing of the unit's outer defenses. He could not see how; coincidence, probably.

And yet.

He had trained himself to question coincidences; to distrust them; to disbelieve them.

Fisher unlocked and opened the right bottom drawer of his desk. Its capacity was small, for the desk drawer really was a highly reinforced fireproof safe. Inches of steel on all sides protected the inner cavity.

A lone envelope rested inside. It was unmarked, but inside it was a single sheet of paper outlining the omega procedure, holding all the necessary codes. If need became imperative, Fisher and Dougherty would open the envelope together, would tear the sheet in half, and seated at separate terminals would begin the omega procedure. If they decided to do so, within twenty-four hours the unit would cease to exist; records of its activities would be erased from the memories of the five computers which held them. The physical plant would be razed to the ground, all hard records destroyed by fire. Most of the personnel would be reassigned; Stark, Dougherty, and Fisher would receive deep-cover identities, would be relocated, separated from each other. Certain other key figures, informed ones, including all the physicians who had worked with the children, even Beckerman and Kornbluth, would share the fate of the project's subjects: termination.

Fisher closed and locked the drawer again. It was not time yet to think of the omega procedure. Not yet. He sighed and with the heel of his left hand massaged his throbbing forehead. He had worked with Mrs. Mead for nearly fifteen years. It would be hard, he thought, signing her death warrant.

6

Early in his career, Pete Collins had formed the journal habit, and he kept at it more or less doggedly. Sometimes

a day or two would pass without an entry, sometimes
more than that; but always in the end, driven by a silly
sense of guilt, by the necessity formed from mere habit,
he would pull out the current blank book and begin
to deface its pages with a handwritten record of his
life.

Late Monday night he sat at his desk, the current
journal open before him. With a black Cross pen, the
same pen he had used to sign the divorce papers, he
wrote about the unsettled weekend, the storms of Sunday, the aborted fishing trip, the lack of progress on his
book. He wound up the entry without mentioning his
guest.

And for Monday, he simply wrote, "Went into town
for some stuff today. Clothing, etc."

For a long time Collins studied the line. He laughed,
but silently. For God's sake, the journals—there were
sixteen of them, most of them like this one, a blank book
about six by nine inches, 180 pages—had *everything* in
them, from his one furtive foray into adultery (New
York, 1987; he and a woman who worked for *Time* had
tumbled into a passionate weekend) to his deepest medical fears (his irritable-bowel syndrome that had convinced
him for a time that he was dying of colon cancer) to his
politics (relentlessly centrist; he damned both Republi-
cans and Democrats). Yet somehow he did not, he could
not, write about the strange little boy.

Eightball, curled up against the bedroom door, stirred
as the door opened inward. The dog edged away a few
inches, thumped his tail, and put his head back down on
his paws. Much nattier now that he was wearing the new
Lincoln-green pajamas that Collins had bought for him,
Johnny stood in the doorway, his pale eyes half full of
sleep.

"Hi," Collins said. He looked at his watch. "Hey, guy,
it's past midnight. Better get to bed."

Johnny nodded. He padded over barefoot to the desk,
looked at the journal in Collins's hands. The peach fuzz
on his cheek glowed white in the lamplight, and Collins
noted that the scratches on his arms and face looked
better, less inflamed than they had the previous night.
The boy made a polite sound as his gray eyes gave
Collins a look of inquiry.

"Sort of a diary," Collins explained. "But I'm keeping you out of it for the time being." He glanced down. Johnny's feet were less noticeably different than his hands were; seen from above, the extra toe hardly registered, more like an accidental fold of flesh than a real digit, and with no nail. "Better hop back into bed. Freeze your feet in here."

Johnny reached across Collins to a Blue Ridge Coffee Company cup that held half a dozen sharpened yellow pencils. He picked one up and gave Collins another questioning look.

"Want a pencil? Sure, take a couple. If you need paper, there's plenty of it in the box behind the computer. Just a minute." He got up and tore off a pad of fanfold computer paper. "Here you go. But don't stay up all night writing or drawing, okay? I'm getting up tomorrow at seven. If you want breakfast, that's when you're getting up, too. Understand me?"

Johnny nodded and grinned. He took paper and pencil into the bedroom and closed the door. Eightball settled back into his former position and yawned, his pink tongue curling.

Collins stretched, put away his journal, and undressed for bed. For some little time he lay awake, hearing Eightball's soft grunts and puffs of breath, hearing the chirring of tree frogs, the rasp of crickets, the wind-in-the-trees sound of the river down the hill. Country sounds. They lulled him, and Collins fell easily into sleep.

He dreamed of pain: of a cold white room, of a needle inserted into his neck, of yellow-and-red flashes of hurt inside his head. Twice he woke up with the same nightmare, and twice he gradually subsided again to sleep. He made it through the night at last, until at seven the clock radio went off, waking him to the farm report. Pork was up; peanuts were down; cotton was steady. He swung out of the cot, felt the cold oak floor beneath his bare feet, and stretched. He had taken fresh clothes out for himself before Johnny fell asleep. Now he pulled his trousers on, noticed that the bedroom door was open, and looked in. The bed was empty, and the bathroom. Collins slipped his feet into loose leather sandals, pulled a green knit shirt over his head, and went into the cabin's only other room, the kitchen. He found Johnny at the table, bent over a sheet of paper, pencil grasped in his right hand, tongue protruding from the corner of his mouth in intense artistic effort.

"Morning," Collins said, and Johnny grunted in response. "What do you want for breakfast today? Cornflakes okay?"

Johnny shrugged and continued to draw.

"Cornflakes it is," Collins said. He got down bowls and found spoons, started the coffee, got the Kellogg's box down from the cabinet. The milk was low; he'd have to go buy groceries that day, he decided. Get a variety of cereals, pick up some easy-to-cook stuff for lunches and suppers. Maybe some charcoal and some hamburger, he thought. Johnny'd probably enjoy a cookout down by the dock. And then maybe a ride in the canoe.

He put the bowls, cereal, and milk on the table, spooned some sugar from the canister into a sugar bowl that he hardly ever used and put that on the table, too. The coffee was ready; he poured himself a generous mug full.

Johnny looked up just as Collins sat down. The boy passed the sheet of paper to him. "Let's see what we have here," Collins grinned. "A treasure map, or—"

He broke off, feeling goosebumps rising on his arms. It was a drawing of children—of sixteen of them. The perspective was all wrong, almost medieval; there were two rows of five and a bottom row of six, the second row apparently standing on the heads of those in front, the back row standing on the second row's heads. There was no shading to speak of.

And yet there was an eerie photographic quality about the sketch; the children in the drawing were somehow obviously real.

Some of them were monstrous.

Several had malformed limbs, short legs or arms; others had grotesque faces, eyes misplaced, mouths twisted, noses parodies. Five or six were normal. All had only pupil dots for eyes. All were dressed identically, in striped shirts and jeans. Collins couldn't be certain from the drawing, but they seemed to be almost of an age—within three to five years of each other, anyway. The upper row, physically the smallest, might be the youngest group.

Every face bore a look of anguish.

Collins looked up and felt something like an electric shock. Johnny's own face showed the same expression, uncannily like that of the sketched children: a Greek mask of tragedy, a face of suffering.

Collins realized that Johnny was attempting to speak. For a shivering moment, he did not want to hear.

"Heh—heh," the boy stammered, his face reddening. He swallowed, gasped, and slapped his right hand down on the drawing in front of Collins so hard that a little coffee slopped over the edge of the brown mug. "Heh—help." The coffee spread into a miniature map of South America. The boy took another deep breath, and then in his aching, rusty, hoarse voice, Johnny at last forced the sentence out: *"Help us."*

CHAPTER FOUR

1

Washington was in its usual state of crisis: the oil-producing countries were again hiking the price for their product, threatening continued inflation; Central America required yet more money and attention in two new trouble spots; the domestic farm problems refused to go away—the ordinary litany. But Randall Grade was in a buoyant mood, entirely commensurate with his handsome, boyish appearance.

The early summer weather helped a little. The afternoon sun was warm on the marble monuments and tarry asphalt, the sounds of traffic mingled with the fainter songs of the birds in the cherry trees, and overhead the sky was clear except for the grayish haze of smog. Because of the sun, the birds, the sky—and because he intuitively knew he would enjoy his outing for other reasons as well—Grade walked with a spring in his step to the meeting place, a bench facing the Smithsonian. His contact, a younger man in the uniform of the United States Air Force, was already there. Hopeful gray pigeons strutted toward him, only to be chased away by the young man's disconsolate kicks.

"Wonderful weather today," Grade said, sitting beside the captain. "Better than snow."

"I like spring best myself."

"Yes, the cherry blossoms are always an attraction."

The Air Force officer, an earnest young man with dark hair and a face made pale by too much work under fluorescent lights, relaxed now that the rigmarole of recognition was over with. "Yes, sir. I have the—"

"Not so fast, Captain Waldren," Grade said easily. "You're new at all this."

Waldren swallowed. "I guess I am."

Grade leaned back on the bench, took a casual look around that showed him they were not closely observed. "Take a tip from an old hand. Don't rush things. You never want to move too fast in this business."

"No, sir."

"All right. Now give me a brief verbal summary."

The captain gave him a surprised sideways glance. "Here? Out in the open?"

"Best place for it. Wait until these people get past."

A gaggle of Japanese tourists passed them, following a young woman in the burgundy uniform of a local tour company. She was a pert Caucasian, but she spoke fluent Japanese, the language picked up by her collar microphone and amplified by the cigarette-pack-sized unit strapped to her belt. The Japanese chattered among themselves in her intervals of silence, laughing and pointing. Grade smiled absently as they streamed by, but he thought to himself with some bitterness that the group was probably inspecting its next purchase; as of last year, fifty percent of privately owned United States concerns were in the hands of the Japanese.

The tour group made its way into the museum. When the last of them had gone, Grade said, "Now."

Captain Waldren took in a deep breath. "Well, sir, I work in the communications center. We had a sudden burst of computer activity in highly classified files this morning and then again this afternoon. I've got a break-down of the file traffic with me, but what it boils down to is that a high-level secret unit is being probed."

"By whom?"

"I can't say for sure. The inquirer used a military access code."

Grade shooed a dark gray pigeon away. Without looking at the other man, he said, "Do better."

Waldren hesitated for several seconds. When at last he spoke, he did so with evident reluctance: "All right, it's an Air Force code. Top Secret clearance level. But I can't crack the master code list—"

"Do you have the code itself?"

"Yes, sir."

"Then that's all right."

The young officer stared. "You can identify our people by their codes?"

Grade smiled at him. "There's nothing to worry about. We're on the same side, after all. You mentioned two bursts of activity."

"Yes, sir. The military access was first, very early this morning. It must have tripped an alarm, because the other was an internal."

"Internal from the Pentagon? That could mean anything."

"No, internal from the project being probed. It was a proprietary access."

Grade nodded. "And the code name for the project?"

"Slow Tango."

Grade smiled. "Good. I'll take the summary now."

With a furtive glance around him, Waldren handed Grade a business-sized envelope. "It's all there."

Grade made the envelope disappear into the inside breast pocket of his jacket as if he were doing a magic trick. "You've done very well. Be sure your tracks are covered."

"Yes, sir. I know computers."

"Let me know if there's any more traffic."

"Yes, sir."

Grade stood up and strolled away, not looking back. The sun seemed a little warmer on his back, the sky overhead a brighter shade of blue. He almost chuckled to himself. For some time now he had resented the money poured into the Slow Tango Unit—had resented the money and had resented the manager of the funds as well. He'd thrown a scare into Fisher last week, he was sure of that, and now the computer traffic confirmed it. Fisher was scrambling; one of the two people involved in the computer exchanges, the one operating from Slow Tango, had to be on Fisher's payroll. The other an—

Air Force officer? Grade frowned, but even his frown felt pleasant. He knew of no connection between the Slow Tango Unit and the Air Force, none at all. But that hardly mattered. Something was about to break, and Grade was fully ready to do the thing he did best: wait.

Wait and watch, of course. That was the great secret of espionage: patience enough to wait, alertness enough to

watch. Something was falling apart for Fisher and for the
Slow Tango Unit, that was clear enough. It could be that
whatever was going wrong would go so badly wrong that
he, Grade, would have to do nothing more than call the
right people's attention to a debacle; it could be that at
the right time he would have to give things a little nudge
or two. Either way, he was satisfied to wait. Wait and
watch.

On foot Grade made better time than any car in the
maddening D.C. traffic. He was back at the office building, an anonymous and nearly windowless white structure
known on Capitol Hill as the Sepulcher, within twenty
minutes. In another ten he had checked in and was sitting
behind his own desk, studying the information he had
received.

The traffic summary was sparse, a bare-bones account
of file numbers accessed or attempted together with ID
numbers for the operators. Grade used a secure limited
terminal to call up information on the ID numbers. The
first belonged to General Dwight Arnold, USAF, a gen-
tleman with a long history of involvement in satellite and
photo-recon espionage. The second was Ultra 11.15. The
11 was the Slow Tango prefix; the 15 was an operator
number. The computer had no name in the files, but
there were ways around that. . . .

Grade called up the biographical file on Arnold. It was
more than twenty printout sheets long, an honorable
record of dedicated service. The periodic reviews showed
the subjective fluctuations that all such records have, but
in no case did General Arnold's evaluation fall below
"good to excellent." The man had no black spots against
him at all.

After printing out the general's history, Grade checked
what they had on Slow Tango; it was not much. An
exploration of the biological basis of extrasensory perception. Experimental attempts to use so-called wild talents
for military and espionage purposes. File and case records were proprietary, restricted to members of the
Slow Tango Unit itself.

Grade pushed back from the computer terminal and
pressed an intercom button. "Yes, sir?" his secretary
said.

"Louise, find me someone to tell me about extrasensory perception."

"Yes, sir."

Grade played around with the files for a few more minutes, ascertaining the amount of overlap and peripheral information that an outsider—someone like General Arnold, for example—might come up with. As always, there was a great deal: links to the Feingold Clinic, to the FBI (witness relocation: general how-to information), to the CIA and the NSA (evaluation programs), a few more. Someone like Fisher, set up in his own barony, could control almost all the vital information about his activity— almost, but not all. Grade enjoyed puzzles. This one looked as if it might be solvable with the right amount of work and thought.

Louise called him with the names of five experts, one of them a well-known skeptic, a professor of psychology at a prestigious university. "Get him on the phone," Grade said. He printed out a summary of the information he had retrieved before the telephone rang. "Dr. Nesheim for you," Louise said.

"Hello, Dr. Nesheim," Grade said. "How is the weather up there?"

"Beautiful, Mr. Grade," a dry voice returned. "If I weren't tied up on the telephone I might be out in it."

"I'm sorry to keep you, sir. Did Louise explain what we need?"

"She mentioned that you were interested in psychic phenomena." Nesheim's already acerbic tone put an especially deprecating twist on the last two words.

Grade looked at one page of the printout. "Not in general, Dr. Nesheim. Specifically I'd like some solid information about three areas of extrasensory perception or paranormal abilities: telepathy, clairvoyance, and psychokinesis."

"And what would you like to know?"

Grade dropped the printout on his desk and leaned back in his chair. "How much credence do you personally put in these notions?"

"None." The answer was quick, flat, incontrovertible.

Grade smiled to himself. "I thought there was scientific evidence—"

"No reliable experiments have ever been completed in

any of the three areas," Nesheim said. "There have been sensational reports, but nothing solid, nothing replicable. And in every case of thorough investigation the seemingly good evidence has turned out to be inconsistent, unreliable, or fraudulent."

"Let me see. . . . Your degrees are from Harvard and Oxford, and you've done further work at Johns Hopkins. You're a leading expert in the field, I believe."

"I don't know about that. I at least have enough sense to get the right people to assist me when I investigate claims of the paranormal."

Grade picked up a pencil. "And who would they be, sir?"

"Depends on the circumstances. Medical specialists, photographic technicians, stage magicians—"

"Magicians?" Grade wrote the word in the margin of one printout page.

"Stage conjurers. They're good at detecting fraud in PK cases. You might have read about the so-called poltergeist case in New Hampshire last spring. The pictures falling off the walls, objects levitating."

"Yes," Grade said, though in fact he had no knowledge whatever of the case.

"It was the family's twelve-year-old daughter. She was very adept, practically a juggler, and she was clever. But a young magician I consulted caught her in the act and even taped her method of levitating small objects and of making picture hangers fall from their nails." Again Nesheim's voice took on an edge of irony: "Of course the newspapers gave much less attention to our exposure of the trick than to the, quote, poltergeist, unquote. But I'm used to that."

"Doctor, I gather that you don't have much faith in the possibility of the paranormal."

"Correction. No faith at all. I don't see that faith has any role in the question, if by faith you mean a belief in things not based on observable fact."

Grade grinned to himself. This was getting better and better. "Sir, if we paid your way to Washington would you be willing to document your lack of belief in these three areas?"

"In telepathy and so on, you mean?" Nesheim paused.

"I don't see why not. Of course, I can give you a great deal of documentation anyway, if by that you mean scientific studies that demonstrated delusion or fraud in these cases. Except for some—oh, I guess you'd call them enthusiasts—no reputable psychologist believes in the paranormal."

"Enthusiasts? Such as?"

"Believe me, there are plenty around: people with degrees but without common sense. They tend to cluster in England and California, for some reason. But I think I can show you that these people are so uncritical in their standards and so slipshod in their experimental protocols that their results can be pretty well disregarded."

"Good. Let my secretary handle the details, but what I'd like from you is any information you know of what would tend to disprove the existence of these, uh, paranormal concerns; that and any information you can suggest that would help a dispassionate observer see that the enthusiasts are mistaken."

"I'll gladly supply you with offprints of my own articles and a bibliography of reliable work done by others in the field, Mr. Grade. May I ask why?"

"It's a matter of ammunition, Dr. Nesheim. The government is considering spending—well, a good deal of money on exploring the existence of these forces."

"Complete waste," the professor snapped.

"Some of us think so, yes. But we need the ammunition to persuade those in charge that the money would be foolishly appropriated. If you'd care to help us—"

"Certainly. There are too many good programs going begging to throw money down that particular rat hole."

"I'll let Louise take your information, then. If we need your testimony, I'll be in touch." Grade said his goodbyes and hung up. He looked over the printouts again, smiling to himself. One way or another, he thought. If Fisher doesn't hang himself, then maybe I can choke him. But the job will be done, one way or another.

2

"Jesus Christ," William Whitepath said. "You can't keep him."

"Why not?" Pete Collins asked. "I've bought all the

area newspapers since Monday, listened to the local news broadcasts. Nobody's missing him."

"But he belongs to somebody," Whitepath said. The Cherokee was at the window of the cabin, watching Johnny romp outside with Eightball. "You can't just keep him here without telling somebody, the sheriff or—"

"He's happy here, Will. Want that drink?"

Whitepath turned away from the window. "If I'd known you had something other than your book in mind, I would have told them myself."

"Told who?" Collins offered the forestry ranger a glass of scotch.

Whitepath took the drink and knocked half of it back. "I dunno. Somebody, though. Jesus. You say he just showed up here Monday morning?"

"Half starved and all scratched up."

Whitepath took a smaller sip of his drink and nodded. "Like he'd been lost in the woods."

"Yep."

"And he says his name is Johnny Gamar or something like that?"

"Near as I can understand him."

"What the hell sort of a name is Gamar? I mean, the kid looks normal, except for . . ."

"I know. His hands."

Whitepath's dark face creased in a frown. "Hands? I was gonna say eyes."

"He's got pale gray eyes," Pete said. "I think they're sensitive to light. That's why I got him the shades."

"He looked at me without the shades. His eyes are like the moon," Whitepath said. "Just exactly like the moon shining through gray clouds. They're spooky, Pete. I ever tell you about the legends of my people—"

"You sure have," Collins said, sipping his own weak drink. "About a million times. And lied on every occasion."

Whitepath shook his head impatiently. "Naw, this is real. There's legends about a race called the Moon-Eyes. My grandfather told me about them. The Cherokee sometimes called them the moon-eyed people. They're not like us; they can be dangerous, Pete."

Collins laughed. "My God, Will, this is a child we're talking about. He can't be more than twelve, thirteen—"

"The moon-eyed people," Whitepath said with deliberate concentration, "were a spirit race. They could go invisible when they wanted to. Or they could disguise themselves and their surroundings to look like anything they wanted. Sometimes they helped our people, but about as often they hurt them. Tricked them, misled them."

Whitepath's glass was empty. Collins reached behind him, picked up the scotch bottle, and passed it to the other man. "Here, pour yourself another. Will, this kid is no legend. He's real. He was hurt, he was scared, he was weak. And he wants my help. Look at this." He held out the drawing that Johnny had done, and as soon as Whitepath had refilled his glass, he took it and looked at it.

Whitepath shrugged. "They all look kinda weird, Pete."

"I know that. But I think they're, I don't know, related somehow. They're Johnny's people—"

"Even if he's just some poor retarded kid who got lost, you have to find his folks, Pete."

"What kind of parents wouldn't report their son missing?" Collins said. "Dammit, Will, I know that there's no report out on him. You checked yourself."

Whitepath nodded. "I know all that, but maybe I missed something. What if his family was in an airplane crash or something? They could've all been killed, or maybe hurt bad, up in the mountains. You—"

"No airplanes are missing," Collins said. "I checked."

Whitepath got up and went to the window again. "My grandfather's grandfather had an experience once," he began.

"Please."

The Cherokee turned away from the window. "No, listen. My grandfather told me this when I was about that kid's age. Told it for the truth. The story happened a long time ago, before the Civil War, I guess, 'cause my grandfather's grandfather didn't marry until he was real old. Anyhow, when he was a boy, he went fishing one day. This was after the removal, but there was still some of our people in the hills, and he and his family lived on a little mountain farm. Well, he went too far on his fishing trip, and toward night he knew he'd never get home before dark.

"He had some fish then, some big ones. He tried to make a fire to cook one, but all the wood he could find was damp. While he was still trying to get some of it started, he saw a man standing under the trees looking at him. It scared him, my grandfather said. He asked, 'Who are you?'

"But the stranger didn't talk, not at first. He stood looking at my grandfather's grandfather. Then he said, 'You have worked hard today. You'd better come and rest with my family for a while.'

"My grandfather's grandfather couldn't get the fire started, and he was a little afraid of the dark. So he went with the stranger. They went through a peach orchard and a field of corn and came to a fine house. They went inside. The stranger's family was just sitting down to eat. 'Let me take care of your fish,' the stranger told my grandfather. He went outside and drew water from a spring into a great earthenware pot. 'Put them in here,' the stranger said.

"My grandfather's grandfather put the fish into the pot. They were all dead by then, but they became alive again when they touched the water. They began to swim around and around. 'Now they will be fresh tomorrow,' the stranger said.

"He took the boy back into the house, and they all had a good meal. Then my grandfather's grandfather played with the stranger's son, who was just about his own age, until full night came. My grandfather's grandfather slept in the house that night. The next morning the stranger took all the fish from the pot and put them on a string. He walked with my grandfather's grandfather back down to the river. 'Hurry home,' the stranger said. 'Your mother will be worried.' The boy walked away, but when he looked back over his shoulder, it was all gone—no peach trees, no cornfield. Then he knew he had been with the Moon-Eyes, the spirit people, and he ran all the way home. He could never after remember just what they looked like, except their eyes were silver, like the color of a white man's coin."

Pete Collins looked at Whitepath in astonishment. "Will, that's a fairy story."

Whitepath grinned. "Yeah, maybe. But my grandfather's grandfather grew up and became a man and he kept going back to the place on the riverbank to look for the peach orchard and the corn and the house. He never did find it. But he showed his son where it was, and he showed his son. Finally my grandfather showed me. Nobody's built there to this day, though it ain't too far from a pretty good-sized town. And, Pete, it's a damned spooky place."

"I don't suppose you saw anybody."

"Naw, I didn't. But I felt them. It felt wrong, somehow. I mean, some spirit races like the Nunnehi fought for the Cherokee sometimes, but it seems like they did it only when they wanted to protect their own places, their mounds and their hills. Other times they ignored us or tricked us, used us for their own reasons. I got a strange feeling on the bank of that river, Pete. Like something was pressing against me, telling me to go away, that what happened there was none of my business. This kid gives me the same damn feeling."

"Not me. I don't see anything but a little boy who needs help. I'm going to help him if I can, Will. And I don't think you're really going to turn me in, are you?"

Whitepath sighed. "I guess not. But I still believe you're mistaken, Pete."

Collins took a sip of his drink—he had nursed it along in his customary way—and rolled the stinging scotch around on his tongue for a moment before swallowing. "You told me last weekend that you had a funny feeling about another place. Remember? Where you heard the children crying?"

"Yeah," Whitepath said, his face grim. "I remember."

"Same kind of feeling."

Whitepath hesitated. "Yeah. I think it's just the same."

"I wonder if he could have come from there."

"Pete, it's thirty damn miles as the crow flies."

"You said that was Thursday. He showed up here early Monday morning. He'd have had sixty hours or so to travel it."

"Through the woods. He'd have to have a blamed fine sense of direction to come straight here in that amount of time. And he had to sleep sometimes."

"What is that place, Will?"

Whitepath finished his second drink. "All I know is what I told you: it's an experiment station where they're trying to get a handle on the tree die-offs we're having on the ridges from acid rain, pine beetle infestation, that kind of thing."

"Then he couldn't have come from there."

"Naw," Whitepath agreed. "I don't see how." He sighed again. "What are you gonna do, Pete?"

"I think," Collins said slowly, "that I'm going to hire a private detective."

Whitepath barked a derisive laugh. "You crazy? Around here?"

"There are plenty of them in Atlanta. Some of them specialize in missing kids."

"Yeah, but don't they usually work the other way around? They don't start with a kid that's been found, they start with a family that's missing a kid."

"So? Maybe one of them would enjoy going at it from another direction. Just for a change."

Whitepath shook his head. "It still sounds screwy to me, Pete. But as long as you're gonna do something—"

From outside, Eightball scratched frantically at the door. Collins set down his glass and got up, frowning. "What the hell is wrong with him?"

He opened the door and the dog hustled in, whimpering. Collins froze, and from behind him he heard Whitepath gasp.

Johnny stood beneath a pine tree just across the drive, his face nearly split in a delighted, impish grin. At first something seemed terribly wrong with him; his body seemed swollen, misshapen.

But it was illusion.

He wore a coat of birds: brown sparrows, blazing red cardinals, blue jays, sooty black swifts, gray-coated woodpeckers with scarlet cockades. There were dozens of them, clinging to Johnny's clothing, resting on his arms. Only his head and hands were free. The birds did not move, not even when Johnny, laughing, took a couple of wide-legged steps toward the cabin, his limbs heavy with twelve or fifteen birds, their claws locked in the fabric of his jeans. The sun reflected off his Ray-bans.

Collins took a stunned step forward. Another bird, a

sparrow, swooped in and landed on a bare spot on Johnny's left shoulder. It immediately became quiescent, like an artificial bird.

"Johnny," Collins said, "you'd better let them go."

Johnny's head tilted quizzically. His eyes were unreadable behind the sunglasses, but his attitude asked "Why?"

"They have families," Collins said. "Little baby birds that would die if . . ."

Alarm registered in Johnny's face, in his suddenly opened mouth, in the rise of his eyebrows. Collins was close enough to him now to smell the dusty, feathery scent of the birds, to see their open, beady black eyes.

They all flew at once. Collins threw up his hands and warded them off, but still he felt them brush his face, heard the clatter of their wings as they burst away in a feathered explosion. He dropped to his knees and grabbed Johnny, held him tight, held him as though he half expected the child himself to grow wings and fly away.

3

Professor Nikita Alexandrov bore the curse of his parents' ambitions in his first name. Just as in the heady days of the thirties many Soviet sons had been given the name Joseph in honor of a fellow who had long since fallen from grace, so he had been named for a man of some importance back in the fifties, a shoe-pounding peasant of a man. But who in 1957, the year of Alexandrov's birth, could have predicted the smiles that name would bring to the faces of college professors in twenty years' time, or the sly jokes of colleagues in the years after that? He was lucky, he supposed, that his family had not named him Sputnik.

But if he was somewhat ashamed of his first name, he was nonetheless proud of the man who bore it; he was the youngest man on the project these days, the only one among them under forty, and he was the liaison with the KGB.

For that was what Feodor Kovach represented, beyond any doubt, although the man had never referred to the organization. But how else would he have been granted his rank of colonel? It had to be KGB, and Alexandrov knew it, and what is more Kovach knew that he knew it. They never discussed the subject; they did not need to.

Kovach, a bear of a man some ten or twelve years older than Alexandrov, looked a complete buffoon, but within the close-cropped skull there resided a surprising intelligence. The two men got along well; Alexandrov and his wife had even had Kovach in for dinner once or twice. Now the two of them sat in an observation room and looked through the one-way glass at Subject 331. "You say she detected something from the United States?" Kovach asked.

"Yes, Colonel. The others were disturbed as well, but 331 was much more precise on the source of the disturbance. She is our best recipient of telepathy."

Kovach leaned a little closer to the window. The room they were in was soundproofed; beyond the window a thin, nervous-looking young woman of perhaps twenty sat at a table, her arms crossed, her hands stroking her biceps. She wore a nondescript gray woolen dress, and her head, bare beneath the incandescent lights, was shaved bald. A half-dozen electrical connections had been sutured into the skin, and they gleamed dully in the yellow light. Her plain, thin face had a haunted expression. "She looks to be mentally unstable," Kovach said.

"Of course she is," Alexandrov agreed readily. "They all are, all the receivers. They have no way of shutting out the thoughts around them, you see; with sufficient mental effort they can focus on a single transmitter and can receive information, but they can never fully tune out the background noise that goes on all the time." He permitted himself a smile. "If you had to listen to your son's jazz tapes twenty-four hours every day, Colonel, you would soon be a little unstable yourself."

Kovach acknowledged the joke with a dry grunt. "I can always make my son shut off the noise. With her there should be a way of doing the same thing."

"There should be indeed, and I'm certain we will find one, Colonel. But until we do, our best subjects are unfortunately psychotic to a degree." Alexandrov gestured toward the woman. "She is hearing our thoughts at the moment."

Kovach straightened, turned his head toward the scientist. "Then what is the good of the soundproofing, the mirror?"

"They would be no good at all if she happened to be concentrating on us. She is not; we have her sedated, so she is incapable of focusing right now. But even if she were fully aware, she would have to concentrate on us to receive and read our thoughts; she would have to know us, or we would somehow have to signal her. Perhaps by our thinking intently about her, as we are doing now. A telepath can hear anyone's thoughts; but the curse is that an individual's thoughts must be sifted, somehow, from everyone's thoughts."

Kovach grunted again. "I have difficulty in grasping all this. From what I understand, distance has nothing to do with the power?"

"Nothing. Our cosmonauts have participated in experiments that confirm this. It seems that mental imaging somehow communicates instantaneously, faster than radio waves. Faster than light, in fact."

"So when you say everyone—"

"I mean everyone in the world, yes."

"What power," Kovach said, settling his burly form back in the chair. His suit fit him badly, and when he rested his arm on the table the right shoulder rode up almost as far as his ear. "For the people that can control it, what power."

"Yes. We hope that the generations to come will refine the ability, will discover how to direct it, to filter out the noise. But at present none of the subjects are able to do that. With them it is only a question of time: how long can they live fairly normal lives before the information overload produces insanity? This subject has adjusted better than any of the others."

"Tell me about this catastrophe of yours."

Alexandrov rested his chin on his hand. "That may be too strong a word. I should have called it . . . well, a remarkable incident. A disturbance. The remarkable part is that 331, along with about seventy of the other receivers, became so distraught recently. Only she could put the cause into words, of course; all the others are to a greater or lesser degree aphasic. And what she told us is most disturbing indeed."

"Explain."

Alexandrov paused, gathering his thoughts. "She seems to feel," he said at last, "that there is a group of telepaths in the United States. The description we have from her seems to indicate a location in the eastern third of the country. Something happened to the telepaths in this location—it would have been Thursday afternoon, a week ago, there. The disturbance brought them to her attention. They are all children, it seems, but they are approaching or experiencing the crucial age of adolescence."

Kovach asked, "Does her belief that telepaths exist in the United States have any serious overtones? There are, of course, naturally occurring instances of telepathy."

"Yes," Alexandrov said reluctantly. "But they are most rare and of relatively weak intensity. Premonitions, mostly—and the most frequent is the awareness of a telepath of some crisis event occurring to a relative. This is qualitatively different. She had a distinct impression of a group—that is important, Colonel, a *group* and not an individual—consciousness exerting tremendous power for a short period of time. Unfortunately, aside from some physical descriptions of landscape and people, she could give us no specific details. But there was enough for me to make the tentative determination that the Americans are somehow experimenting with these concerns, just as we are."

"We have been informed of their lack of effort in the field in the past. They couldn't have had time," Kovach said.

"No. Not by using our methods." Alexandrov held out his hands, making a balance. "But you know the Americans. Always interested in technology, in gimmickry. Perhaps they have found some artificial way of enhancing or stimulating mental ability. Perhaps they have taken some other path than ours to the same goal. They might have used chemical means, or electronic means, or genetic—"

"This could be very serious," Kovach said. "If— What is she doing now?"

The girl in the other room had pressed her open hands to her mouth. Alexandrov rose, his eyes intent on Subject 331. Through the speaker came her voice, very soft, muffled by her fingers, but audible.

"Fly," she said. "Oh, look at them fly."

She laughed until Alexandrov gave her a stronger sedative; and even in sleep she smiled.

4

Dr. Kornbluth himself supervised the analysis, and the moment it was complete he called Fisher. It took the administrator just seven minutes to make it to the lab. Fisher glanced around at the room, a windowless enclosure with ventilation provided by air-conditioning vents and by fans inside hoods, designed to sweep away the noxious vapors of chemical tests. Kornbluth and Lawrence Thomsen, a technician, waited at one of the lab benches. "Well?" Fisher asked.

Kornbluth nodded to Thomsen. "Well, sir, samples A, C, and D were organic residues—tissue and bone, mostly pulverized ash but a few bone fragments. Samples B and E were not the ashes of animal bodies. E was a mixture of paper, cloth, and wood. B was almost certainly wood and wood alone."

Kornbluth raised his eyebrows. "You know which was which," he said.

Fisher felt his face going red. He gave a curt nod. "Sample E was the control. The others were from the urns."

"And B?"

"Was the Gamma Five subject. Was supposed to be. Wood? Are you sure?"

Thomsen shrugged. "I did qualitative analysis of the ash, plus chromatography. The residue is completely consistent with wood; it doesn't agree at all with what I'd expect to find in human ashes. Besides, it doesn't even look like cremation ash. Not now."

Fisher glared at him. "Not now?"

"It—" Thomsen licked his lips. "I know this sounds crazy, but—hell, it did before. Before I knew for sure. Now the appearance is different."

Kornbluth broke in: "The important fact is that Gamma Five was not cremated. That tells us that something is very wrong."

Fisher bit his lip. "I am aware of that, thank you. Could the crematory personnel have made a mistake?"

Kornbluth grinned, showing an expanse of denture. "Like feeding a chair into the furnace instead of a human body? I don't know—how stupid are they?"

Thomsen gave the doctor a shocked look. Fisher took a long and very deep breath. An explosion was building, but before it could detonate, the technician said, "I suppose there's a very remote chance of contamination."

Fisher exhaled, a ragged sound. "Contamination? Explain."

Thomsen cleared his throat. "Well, for example if a wooden coffin—"

"Subjects don't get coffins," Fisher said. "We don't even stock them. Look, keep this to yourselves. I've got to get to the bottom of this thing."

"I won't discuss the tests, sir," Thomsen said.

"Me, either," Kornbluth added after a moment. "But I want to be in on this."

"I'll tell you if I need you," Fisher said, frost in his voice. "Let me have your findings." Thomsen passed him a folder of loose paper, and he turned and walked out of the lab. The elevator was down the corridor, near the cyclotron room. Fisher opened the folder and studied the papers as he strode down the hall—not that he could make anything of the analyses described there, but the folder at least gave him a focus. The elevator opened immediately and he took it up to the administration level on the ground floor.

Mrs. Mead looked up as he came into the office. "Get me Stark. Better get Dougherty, too," he said shortly, and she murmured, "Yes, sir."

Fisher threw himself into his chair, slapped the folder onto the desk. He had only a few minutes to brood before he heard Dougherty's distinctive tap at the door. "Come," he said.

Dougherty, wearing a short-sleeved blue cotton pullover shirt and jeans, closed the door behind him and hovered over the desk. "Trouble?" he guessed quietly.

"Sit down. Trouble." Fisher thrust the folder across the table. Dougherty picked it up and leafed through, his brows knit in puzzlement. "Looks like an escape," Fisher said.

Dougherty's head came up. "Impossible."

"Then what the hell is wood ash doing in the Gamma kid's container? Something's damned wrong, Charlie. Where the hell is Stark?"

Dougherty checked his watch. "He's probably in the testing area. The series is still going on. It may take him a while." He closed the folder and replaced it on Fisher's desk. "So you think someone snatched the Gamma kid? I don't see how."

Fisher glared at him. "You saw the body, right?"

"I saw the body. I didn't take a pulse or—"

"Where did you see it?"

"I—" Dougherty broke off. After a moment he began again, slowly: "I don't remember."

"Oh, for the love of God, Charlie. Was it here in the main building? In the kid's room? In the crematory?"

Dougherty shook his head. "It's the damnedest thing. I just don't remember. I don't think I left the admin wing—"

"They didn't bring a body here."

"No, they wouldn't have. But I remember seeing him."

Another knock sounded at the door, and without waiting for an invitation, Dr. Stark stepped in. His blue eyes flicked from Fisher to Dougherty and back again. "Yes?"

Dougherty remained quiet while Fisher sketched in the problem. Throughout the recital Stark's face became more and more troubled. He pulled a chair up to the desk and sat down as Fisher finished. For a moment there was silence; then Stark said, "Do you suspect outside interference?" He reached for a three-by-five-inch note pad on the corner of Fisher's desk and began to shred a page of it.

"No evidence of interference," Fisher grunted. "And if Beckerman is right—"

Stark waved his hand, a short streamer of paper falling to the floor. "Beckerman is a very young man—"

"He's competent," Dougherty said quietly.

"Still. He tends to become, shall we say, excitable?"

Fisher shook his head. "The records bear him out. We had a series of human errors and security breakdowns. Too many for coincidence. But I don't see how they could have resulted from a breach."

Dougherty crossed his legs. "An inside job, then."

Stark lowered his gaze, concentrating on the paper between his fingers. "What of the witnesses? I have spoken to five different people who saw the dead body."

Fisher looked at Dougherty. "You were one of those. You'd started to say something."

Dougherty shifted his weight in his chair. "Ernest, the more I think about it, the less I remember. It's like a dream now—"

Stark's voice was sharp: "A dream? You mean the memory is fading?"

"That's a good word for it," Dougherty said in a grudging voice. "Fading. Everything else is pretty sharp, but the body itself—I couldn't swear for sure, now, that I saw it at all."

Stark pushed himself up from his chair. "I need your authorization for extraordinary measures," he said to Fisher. "I must question the witnesses again. This time with pentathol-c, I think. If that doesn't work, we'll try hypnosis."

"Not me," Dougherty said.

Stark's eyes narrowed. "I have to—"

"Charles is right," Fisher said. "His position puts hypnosis and drugs out of the question."

The geneticist looked ceilingward as if invoking heaven's aid. "If the dead body was nothing more than an illusion—"

Fisher straightened in his chair. "What?"

Stark had crumpled the partially torn sheet of notepaper. He dropped the ball on the corner of Fisher's desk. "It is theoretically possible that telepathic individuals can impose hypnagogic imagery on the minds of others. That they can cause us to hallucinate things that are not there. Things such as, in this case, a dead body. Wood ash that resembles cremains."

Dougherty said quietly, "You'd better let him check it out."

Fisher nodded. "All right. I'll sign an authorization for the other witnesses, but not for Dougherty." He flicked the ball of paper into his waste can. "If it is what you suggest, Dr. Stark, the implications are very grave."

"I know they are. The Gamma subject had never tested

positive; if he is capable of such activity as I suspect, his power must be staggering already. If he has effected an escape and is still alive, we must recapture him."

"Go ahead with the test. I'll have Mrs. Mead type the authorization. Go quickly."

Stark turned and strode from the room. When the door had closed, Fisher grunted, "The fool."

"It may not be his fault, Ernest," Dougherty said, getting to his feet. "What do you want me to do?"

Fisher shook his head. "For now we have to assume that the boy has escaped. I want you to formulate a search plan. Have it in place as soon as possible. I'll take care of everything else." After a moment, he added, "We'd better suspend operations for the time being. Restrict the subjects to their rooms until further notice. Take care of it."

"Right away," said Dougherty.

"I'll want you again in an hour. Do what you can."

"All right." Dougherty left Fisher alone.

Fisher brooded for a minute or two. Finally with a dissatisfied grunt he picked up the receiver of one of the two telephones on his desk and direct-dialed a number. He heard three rings before the connection was made.

"Yes, sir?" said a voice from Washington.

"Things are breaking badly here," Fisher said. "I want you to take care of our problem there."

"Yes, sir. Full treatment?"

"You understand what we have to know. Get the information first. Then make sure the leak is permanently plugged."

"Yes, sir."

Fisher hung up. Though yesterday he had destroyed the page on which he had written the man's name, he now knew that the spy had been working from within the Pentagon itself; that he was a general in the Air Force; that he had no immediate connection with Slow Tango, with the Feingold Institute, with anything that mattered. He had known that much yesterday, Wednesday.

But yesterday there had been time.

And now there was none.

5

By Friday morning Pete Collins had still done nothing about contacting a private detective or about finding Johnny's family. To be sure, he had continued to read the newspapers, to listen to the radio for news of a missing child; there had been no reports at all. And Johnny certainly didn't seem to miss his hypothetical family. Indeed, for his part, the boy seemed content to stay with Collins at the cabin, to play with Eightball, and to mend.

Rest and food were healing Johnny rapidly. He looked far better than he had the previous Monday; his scratches and scrapes were fading, the bruise-colored circles beneath his eyes had disappeared, and he even seemed to be picking up weight—not surprising, Collins thought, considering the wolfish, ravenous way the boy ate.

Johnny was digging into a bowl of cornflakes now, munching happily and pausing now and again for a sip of orange juice from a highball glass or for a bite of buttered wheat toast. From time to time he would grin happily at Collins, stretching his butter-glazed lips over his white teeth. Eightball, curled at the foot of Johnny's chair, stared up at the boy with the melancholy resignation of a dog who knew the people at the table were not eating meat.

Collins sipped black coffee from his thick white mug. He felt a definite, nagging uneasiness. William Whitepath had agreed to keep their secret, but for how long? And there were others, too, of course: Mr. Cooper of the Holcomb's Crossing Mercantile, for one. The store owner knew Collins well enough, and he certainly knew that there was no reason in the world for Collins to buy boy's clothing, as he had done. Well, nothing to be done about that now; but Collins decided he could head off other problems with a little planning. The laundry, for example: instead of sending Johnny's soiled clothes out, he would drive over to Clarksville, which had to have at least one coin laundry. And he could buy food there, too, where he wasn't known or recognized; that would save any embarrassing questions about his suddenly increased appetite or about his houseguest.

Collins crossed his arms on the table and smiled at Johnny. The boy ate unaware of the scrutiny at first, and Collins noticed how the useless, superfluous finger jutted out stiffly when Johnny's hand closed on his juice glass. Johnny noticed Collins's stare and grinned self-consciously. He glanced down at the cup and his eyes widened in apparent concentration.

Collins started at sudden movement beside his elbow. A white dove took two steps across the blue-and-white-checked tablecloth and flew out the open window. Collins saw the blur of the bird's wings, heard the chirr of their movement; and when he looked down, his cup was gone.

Johnny giggled, and there the cup was again, solid as ever. Collins swallowed, remembering the apparition of the bird. He had seen the minute latticework of its feathers, the tiny pink scaled feet; he had heard them scratch on the oilcloth, had felt the air displaced by the fluttering wings. The bird had seemed as real as the cup undoubtedly was. Collins, trembling, closed his eyes. "Johnny," he said, trying to make his voice firm, "don't do that. Not ever." He opened his eyes to see the boy's stricken, anxious face. "I'm not angry at you," Collins said. "But you can't do things like that. It—it's wrong. It will get us in trouble. Do you understand?"

Johnny's chin lowered and his gaze dropped. He nodded miserably. "It's all right this time," Collins said. "But don't do it again, okay?"

The boy nodded once.

Collins shook his head. He was almost used to the damnedest things now, he thought wryly; his heart was hardly racing this time.

And below his shock and simple astonishment he felt another kind of excitement altogether, a more complex emotion.

Johnny slipped from his chair and pointed toward the window.

"No, brush your teeth first. Remember?"

The boy nodded. He left the room and after a moment Collins heard the water running in the bathroom. He heard Johnny's enthusiastic brushing, sounding loud enough to take off the enamel along with the plaque. After a minute or so the water was turned off, and Johnny appeared in the doorway, breath fragrant and minty from Colgate toothpaste. Once more he pointed to the outside world and raised his nearly invisible eyebrows in inquiry. "Okay, go on out," Collins said. "Play with Eightball. Stay close to the cabin."

The boy and dog went out together, both stepping lightly. Collins watched them go, knowing how unnecessary his cautionary word had been: Johnny never ventured out of sight of the cabin, and even in the height of play, even when he tossed a stick and shouted laughter as Eightball lolloped after it with flapping ears and a broad doggy grin, there was something keenly alert in the boy. Although not a hunter himself, Collins had once or twice seen deer poised the same way, their sensory antennae keen for threat, their posture and their movements poised for a dash to safety even when they seemed absorbed in feeding. There was that air of wildness about Johnny, that sense of bundled fear beneath the surface, ready to explode into flight at the first threat.

Collins cleared the table and washed dishes, reflecting on the past days. He sensed something, well, *off* about Johnny, something more than the tricks of perception he had experienced, more than the living coat of birds Johnny had worn. There were the dreams, for one thing: dreams of other children, the ones in Johnny's drawing, dreams of threat and confinement.

And of course there were the hallucinations, the tricks.

He didn't know what else to call them: moments of strangeness, like the one Wednesday night after Whitepath had left. Johnny, sitting on the hearth, had been ruffling Eightball's ears; then he stood, held out his hand, and there was a steak, raw, suspended from his clenched hand. Collins had sat bolt upright, his eyes on the meat. It looked like a sirloin, and it had to weigh a pound at least. Eightball stood on his hind legs to snap at it, danced around Johnny's feet as the boy dangled it low and then snatched it high again. Johnny threw the steak into the air and Eightball leaped to snatch it—

And came down without it. The dog frantically nosed the floor, and Collins himself rose to look for the sirloin. Johnny went into a spasm of laughter.

That occurrence had frightened Collins. He had collapsed back into his chair wondering at a hallucination that he could share with a dog. There was no question that Eightball had believed the steak real, had smelled it; to Collins it had looked like a real steak, and he had expected but had not heard the wet slap of it on the floor as it fell; but it had utterly vanished.

Johnny, his laughing fit passed, came to Collins and sat beside him in the chair. There really wasn't room; Johnny sat more on Collins's thigh than in the chair itself. He gave Collins an anxious look. Collins regarded him for a moment. "What's the matter, Johnny?"

The boy took a deep breath. "Yuh—you f-feel bad."

Collins ruffled the boy's fair hair. "It's all right," he said. "You just scared me."

Johnny tried to speak: "Suh-suh-sorry."

"It's all right."

But it wasn't all right; it hadn't been then, and it certainly had gotten no better by Friday morning. At his core Collins felt a constant and complex twinge of fear now—fear for Johnny, and worse, a kind of fear of Johnny. It was unreasonable, it was incongruous, and it was overpowered by the protectiveness he felt toward the strange child, but the fear rested there within him, small and mean and stubborn.

Collins rinsed the dishes under steaming hot water, in his absentminded reverie burning his fingers a little. He acknowledged the uneasiness he still felt, but he had to acknowledge that other and deeper feeling, too.

For in Johnny he had a *story*.

There was no question of that. The drug book might be dead in the water, but here was Johnny, here was this strange, disturbing child. He of the silver eyes.

And what a story Johnny would make. Collins knew a little about wild talents, about purported cases of paranormal ability: enough, at least, to know that they almost always were bullshit.

But Johnny was a different case altogether. Collins couldn't believe that any other child could do the things Johnny had done—summoning the birds, fooling even Eightball with his conjured steak, the trick with the coffee cup just a few minutes ago. They were beyond sleight of hand.

No skeptic could deny the evidence of Collins's own senses. Well, that wasn't true—he himself had more than once doubted his sanity. But Whitepath had witnessed the episode of the birds, and Eightball had been taken in with the illusory sirloin. As he dried the dishes, Collins briefly contemplated reality: what was it, after all, he thought, but the consensus of observers? If everyone saw Johnny producing the marvels that he knew the boy could produce, then they were real. And the story of that would make one hell of a book.

But what was it, exactly, that Johnny did? Collins had only a layman's dim awareness of such phenomena, but he had a computer, a modem, and therefore access to an immense field of research and inquiry. He had tried over the course of a couple of days now to pull in something that would account for the sort of things Johnny had done. He had tried under the fields of hallucination, hypnotism, and psychic phenomena; and crumbs of information were all he had to show.

Hallucinations, for example, could apparently be shared. There was that case of the UFO abductees many years ago, the husband and wife who under hypnosis recalled a bizarre kidnapping by aliens. Yet the official verdict had been that the two merely shared a common hallucination, that nothing physical had happened after all.

Hypnotism had seemed promising, but Collins had learned that most psychologists believed it impossible to hypnotize a subject without his knowledge; and certainly a nearly mute child such as Johnny could not rationally be considered a likely candidate as a skilled hypnotist.

There were other accounts of failures of reality, of illusions and delusions induced by stress, by weariness, by drugs; but none of them remotely fit the situation.

It was clear enough to Collins, at least, that Johnny was unique. He went to the front porch of the cabin and watched a game of tug-of-war between Johnny and Eightball. Johnny, joy spilling from him in shouts of laughter, had a long stick, and Eightball had gripped the other end. The dog growled in mock ferocity, trying to jerk the stick away from Johnny. The boy swung Eightball this way and that, making the claws scrabble for purchase, making the ears flop and fly, but he could not dislodge the persistent spaniel.

Collins himself laughed at the contest. Johnny squealed even louder, gasped, and coughed from exertion.

"Don't wear yourself out," Collins called. "We'll go for a boat ride later if you want."

They revolved about each other, Johnny and Eightball, like a planet of a child and a furry black moon of a dog, raising dust in their dancing game. Johnny coughed again, a deep and ragged sound.

Collins stepped into the yard and walked toward them. "Better stop before you make yourself sick," he said.

Johnny let go of his end of the stick. Eightball reeled back, recovered, snatched a better hold so that he carried the stick crossways in his mouth, and danced tauntingly toward and away from the child, daring him to grab the stick again.

Johnny stood with his hands on his knees, his head lowered, and coughed again, phlegm spraying from his mouth.

Collins, concerned, put his hand on Johnny's back. He felt the boy's lungs buzzing and vibrating; it felt as if there were a hive of bees in the cage of Johnny's ribs. "Easy," Collins said, really concerned.

Coughs racked Johnny again. He almost fell, but Collins supported him. "We'd better go inside," he told the boy, and Johnny nodded.

Collins got Johnny inside and made him lie down. The boy's face was flushed, two hectic red spots in his cheeks. His breathing seemed easier, but he still coughed from time to time. Collins wet a washcloth and sponged Johnny's face and forehead. "You got a little carried away," he said.

Johnny, his eyes brimming with pain, nodded in a miserable way. Collins got a glass of water for him, made him drink a little. "You rest for a few minutes," he said.

Eightball had dropped the stick outside somewhere. He reared up to plant his paws on the edge of Johnny's bed and whimper softly. Johnny forced a little smile and ruffled the spaniel's ears.

"It's okay, boy," Collins said, chucking Eightball under the chin. "Johnny just got a little too excited. He'll be fine."

Johnny coughed again. With a guilty thought or two

about his potential best-seller, Collins murmured, "You'll be fine."

But he wondered if he was telling Johnny—or himself—the truth.

6

Kathy Beta felt them coming apart.

If only Johnny hadn't gone, she thought. If he had stayed, we would have been fine. We would have been one.

The thought locked itself in conflict with another almost immediately. Johnny had to go. That was the only picture that could replace the other one, the bad bad one.

For if he had stayed, the PROJECT TERMINATION they had sensed would have killed them all. Johnny's flight had been born of their collective desperation, of their fear of TERMINATION and of personal annihilation.

Did the Big Ones know? Kathy furrowed her brow. She could not be certain. She still felt achy and confused when trying to hear their thoughts. Most of them, anyway. A few of the Big Ones were friends, and their thoughts were easier, better, more kindly. Most were indifferent. Some were painful.

There had been a time when they were all painful, when Kathy lived in a screaming chaos of jagged images and piercing emotions. She remembered how Johnny had come into her mind once, oh so long ago, how he had taught her the trick of shutting herself off. Before that the world was a roaring torrent of thoughts, she herself a forlorn little boat tossed on the stormy seas of adult minds. How old had she been then? Four? Younger? Older? Johnny had been younger than she was. He was the best of them all, the one who could make intuitive leaps, the one least frightened of action. Julie was just a little older than Johnny was. Not as powerful, and only a little older.

But she was a BIG GIRL now. She knew because Miss Julie had told her so, had showed her how to take care of the needs that BIG GIRLS had. Before this year she had

never had those needs, but she was growing, changing:
she could almost hear her body adjusting its shape, altering around her. It was getting ready to be a

MOTHER

she thought sadly. They had fooled her body. It did not
know what her mind already had accepted.

Kathy had always loved dolls. It made her wrenchingly
sad to know that she would never have a baby of her
own. She wasn't quite sure how she knew, but she did;
probably, she thought, it was one of those hurtful, pointed
thoughts the doctors were always having. It had something to do with an operation Dr. Stark had ordered for
all the girls when they were nine. That had been four
years ago for Kathy. She was STERILE now and would
always be; but her awareness in no way diminished the
way she felt about her baby doll, here in the warm bed
with her, or the growing need she felt for her own, real,
living baby.

She groaned, dismayed at how easily she was distracted,
now that Johnny was no longer here to keep her light
focused and bright. They were ever so much stronger
together, but they were allowed to be together only rarely:
did the Big Ones suspect?

Kathy huddled deeper under her blanket and reached
out with her mind. She brushed the minds of the other
children, resting in their own beds at this unaccustomed
early bedtime, but her thoughts found no purchase, took
no hold. The Deltas were busy with numbers again, an
activity that baffled and bored Kathy; the younger children were weary, exhausted from their effort to keep the
Death Thought in the Big Ones' minds. Most of them
had given up the effort. A few dogged ones still tried.

Kathy reached even farther, seeking: and at last she
felt the flicker of Johnny's light. She touched, very briefly,
unsuccessfully. She felt

a curly black dog a Big Man smiling cold milk delicious
him, got flashes of his awareness, but could not think to
him. Johnny could always do that; but like the others,
Johnny was weaker alone, and his mind wandered. He
had communicated with her only twice since running
away, once when he was alone and frightened and once
when he wanted her to keep the Death Thought going.
He had promised to find help.

The next-brightest had been Johnny slipping away.

From past experience Kathy knew that one image canceled the others. There could be only one future. Of the
possibles, Johnny's escape was the one that seemed the
best hope of replacing the one of the children dying.

She was still driven by the memory of the SEE AHEAD.
That long evening, as she lay alone in her bed struggling
with her fears and her scruples, the memory finally overcame her reluctance.

Kathy sought out Miss Julie's mind. She found it after
a few seconds, was surprised by the anger and the sense
of betrayal she felt there. But she threaded her way
among the thoughts and discovered that she could use
these emotions. Like someone rearranging a room,
Kathy Beta slowly, surely, began to work on Julie Lind's
mind.

7

General Dwight Arnold lived in a leased house barely
twenty-five miles from Washington, but it might as well
have been somewhere in the heartland. It was almost at
the center of twelve acres of rolling land, a white-columned
two-story refurbished farmhouse shaded by live oaks.
Behind the house was a stable, empty now that Arnold's
daughter Christine had married and moved away, taking
the gelding Midnight Dancer with her. Beyond the stable
was a grassy hillside, a gentle downward slope to pine
woods and a stream; and beyond the stream, where the
property line lay, was the back of a thickly built subdivision, though it was out of sight and for the most part out
of hearing from the house.

Arnold and his wife, Dolores, had lived in the house
for nearly six years now. It had become their most nearly
permanent residence in the nomadic existence too familiar to service families, although it was not in Arnold's
mind truly *home*. Arnold's father had left him the old
home place in Kentucky, which currently was sublet to a
newspaper publisher. As a matter of fact, one of the
attractions of the present house was its resemblance to
the Arnold farm, to which Dwight and Dolores planned

to retire in five years less six weeks—Dolores had already
begun the countdown.

On Friday evening the two of them sat on the red-brick
patio to the left of the house. Dressed in her favorite pair
of lounging pajamas and her comfortable slippers, Dolores was drinking Perrier with lime, Arnold gin and tonic.
The two of them talked in desultory fashion of inconse-
quential things, of David's last letter, of Eloise's telephone call that afternoon, as the stars came out and a
warm southeasterly breeze rose. Arnold remarked once
on the way the encroaching lights had diminished the
stars. When they had first moved to the house the summer nights were spangled black velvet, but now the surrounding glare had crept closer and had paled the night
sky overhead so that the dimmer stars, the delicate gauze
of the Milky Way, were lost to them. Dolores consoled
him that their time here was, after all, limited.

Finally, toward ten o'clock, Dolores rose. She was
fifty, but thanks to a passion for tennis and a strictly
controlled appetite her figure was still damned good,
Arnold thought. That plus a wonderful bone structure
and a little judicious hair coloring applied by one of
Virginia's better hairdressers kept her a strikingly attractive woman; and her looks, together with her scalpel-
sharp intelligence and even sharper tongue, had kept
Arnold reasonably faithful through thirty-six years of marriage. She paused at the french door, framed by the den
lights. "Don't forget we have Edgar and Nancy's damned
dinner party tomorrow night," she said.

"I remember."

"Then come to bed before midnight."

Arnold chuckled. "Soon as I finish this drink, love."

She might have smiled at him—it was hard for him to
tell with her silhouetted against the light as she was—and
then she went inside. Looking after her, Arnold reflected
again that she wouldn't have made a bad officer herself,
with her calm demeanor masking a steely determination.
But he had married her during her summer vacation from
her junior year at college, she had never returned to
finish her schooling, and she had never had a career of
her own, unless you counted putting up with Dwight
Arnold and raising their two kids as a career. A full-time
job it had assuredly been.

Arnold sipped his drink and grinned to himself, pleased with the shape his life had taken. He was lucky, he sure to God was lucky, and there was no denying that. Fifty-nine years old, healthy as a horse, married to a fine woman, his only son already in line for a promotion to major, his daughter married to a rising young man in an important defense industry. No money worries, thanks to his father's foresightedness about certain shrewd investments in real estate; not much left that he cared to accomplish before a graceful and well-deserved retirement. Arnold took another drink and felt vaguely thankful to God or chance or whatever it was that had molded his life into its present configuration.

Oh, it was true that a few clouds darkened the horizon. Chief among them was the Engstrom thing. It smelled wrong to him—hell, be honest, it reeked. But try as he might, Arnold could find no explanation for the inconsistencies he had uncovered. After all, what connection could a successful fertility clinic have with his business, with espionage? None conceivable, he thought, grinning again at the atrocious pun. He finished the gin and tonic, put the empty glass on the table beside him, stretched, and levered himself out of the lawn chair. He had about determined to call Fritz Engstrom on Monday and admit that he had lost himself in a blind alley. Engstrom was a good man, and Arnold respected him, but friendship could make only so many demands; and somehow Arnold felt that he sure to God had gone the extra mile on this one already.

He went through the den and looked into the kitchen, intending to ask Conchita to tidy up the patio, but she wasn't there. Dinner dishes had been cleared and rinsed but not yet washed; the dishwasher was open and empty. She didn't seem to be anywhere on the first floor of the house, not in the dining room, breakfast nook, or utility room; not in the living room, library, or den. Perhaps she had gone upstairs already; maybe Mrs. Arnold had had some task for her to do.

Well, Conchita would know, Arnold told himself. He made one more round of the house, checking to make sure the doors were locked and the security system activated. Those chores done, he went upstairs to bed still wondering where the devil Conchita had disappeared to.

He opened the bedroom door and froze, his hand on the knob. Conchita lay supine on the bed, gagged with a broad strip of white tape, her brown eyes enormous in the warm light of the bedside reading lamp.

A hand closed on Arnold's wrist, and before he could react he was dragged into the room. He began to struggle, but other hands closed on him and thrust him to the floor. An expert touch patted him down. He felt the cold steel of handcuffs click onto his wrists. His face was pressed into the thick pile carpet; its fibers tickled his nose, filled his nostrils with the camphor scent of some cleaning compound.

"All right, General," one of the two men said. "You can get up. Slowly."

Arnold rose laboriously to his knees. "Where's Dolores—" he said, and then he saw her. His wife was gagged, like Conchita; they had seated her in the red wing chair beside the window. Dolores still wore the electric-blue satin lounging pajamas, and her feet were still in her slippers. Her face was almost in shadow—the one small bedside lamp provided the only light in the room—but in her posture Arnold could read her shock and outrage. From the way she sat Arnold guessed that she, too, had been handcuffed. Her dark hair had come loose and spilled over her forehead, and from behind it her green eyes glared at their captors.

"Easy," said the man. "You sit here." The other, a taller, stronger man, moved Arnold and forced him down onto a low stool, much too low for comfort; he sat awkwardly, his knees bent. It was a good move on the part of the intruders, he realized immediately; he could make no sudden move to stand from such a position. He glared at his captors, memorizing details. The talker was twenty-five or so, very thin, with wiry, unruly black hair and a sallow complexion showing the pockmarks of an old case of acne. The other man was larger, about six feet tall and weighing perhaps 180, and he was a little older, built like an athlete. His straight, medium-length hair was very light brown, his eyes blue. Both men wore navy-blue windbreakers and khaki trousers, and both were shod in blue sneakers.

"What do you want?" Arnold asked the talker.

"Some information, General," the man said. Arnold had assumed at first that the two were burglars, but there was something familiar in the voice, in the tone, in the assurance. He worked with young men like this every day, had supervised some of them in the field. Then, too, the security system had been on; somehow the two had gotten past a pretty sophisticated array of sensors. They were beyond doubt professionals. The shorter man nodded toward Conchita. "Maid?" he guessed.

"Yes," Arnold said. "She has nothing you'd want."

"And knows nothing," the man agreed easily. "The gardener and the cook don't stay in the house here. The maid does. Too bad for her." He nodded to his companion.

The larger man turned to the bed. Conchita's hands were evidently cuffed or bound behind her, and she lay on them. From behind the gag she tried to talk, but only muffled sounds came out. The larger man leaned over the bed and suddenly Arnold noticed the knife in his hand, six wicked inches of razor-sharp steel. The general cried out as the blade slid into Conchita's exposed throat. The woman's body jerked; a scream worked its way past the gag, dying in a frantic liquid gurgle; Arnold felt a warm splash on his face, just below his right eye, as blood jetted from Conchita's severed carotid.

He looked away and saw his wife collapse sideways in her chair, her eyes fluttering. Cooling blood dripped from his cheek to his sport shirt. From the corner of his eye he saw it, a red streak on the pale blue Sea Island cotton cloth. A second drop landed beside it, and then a third. He felt the slow crawl of a fourth drop down his chin, across the soft flesh of his throat, like a tiny snail making its way down to his collar. "My God," he said.

The tall man stepped away from the bed. Conchita lay in a welter of blood, a spreading red stain over the white satin coverlet; more of it had splashed on the walls and on the tall man's face and chest. Arnold couldn't look away. His nostrils quivered at a foul excremental stench: the woman, dying, had soiled herself. "I'll wash up," the tall man said with a curious neutral intonation, almost apologetic. He wiped the blade on the coverlet before folding the knife and slipping it into a side pocket of his windbreaker. He squeezed past the unconscious Dolores Arnold and into the bathroom. After a second Arnold heard the water running.

"Now, General," the first man said, dropping to a crouch a few feet away. "You have to tell us about some telephone calls you made."

Arnold stared at the man. Like the killer's voice, this man's scarred face was neutral, unemotional, showing at most only a faint, almost polite interest in what Arnold had to say. "Go to hell," Arnold told him.

The man's voice was all patience. "You're a tough man, General Arnold. We know that. We know all about you. But we're prepared to deal with you. You will tell us."

The man was right. Arnold did tell, not long afterward. He told them everything they wanted to know after the tall man went to work on Dolores. And before they killed him he felt an overwhelming sorrow, for himself, for Dolores, for the futility of human hopes, for the hollowness of all delight.

CHAPTER FIVE

1

Over the weekend Collins told himself that Johnny was getting better. But at night Johnny's cough, sounding like old rags tearing, did not abate, and by day the child was apathetic and miserable, his silvery eyes almost glazed. By Monday Collins could no longer deceive himself. The boy was ill, suffering from a bad cough, a congested nose and chest, and fever. He lay listlessly in bed, his eyes watery and bloodshot, his lips puffy, cracked in fine lines limned in dark blood. Collins poured juice into him, gave him acetaminophen for the fever, and brought home three different kinds of over-the-counter cough remedies. None of it seemed to do much good.

By Monday morning Johnny's temperature had leveled off in the 102 range and his breathing had become heavy, sounding thick as his chest heaved. Alarmed at the boy's wheezing, Collins looked up the number of a pediatric group in Gainesville, a fairly large town more than forty miles to the south, and made an appointment for eleven that morning. He bundled Johnny up in the red Georgia Bulldogs blanket—it was a warm morning in late June, but Johnny would have been toasty even if it had been a drafty November day—and carried him to the Ranger, and at nine-thirty they pulled out of the drive, escorted as far as the bridge by a loping Eightball.

The Ranger rumbled across the bridge and down the dirt road, raising a cloud of red dust and passing only the occasional mountain cabin for five miles, until the unpaved road gave onto a two-lane blacktop. There Collins turned south, away from Holcomb's Crossing. As they picked up speed, Johnny perked up a bit, loosening the cocoon of the blanket, peering forward through the windshield. He grasped the seat with one hand and braced the other against the dash, even though Collins had strapped him in. The boy's body swung extravagantly as they turned, as if his sense of balance was somehow off.

"Driving too fast for you?" Collins asked, though the Ranger was doing barely fifty.

Johnny coughed and shook his head. Collins kept half an eye on the boy as he drove, and as he rounded a curve it came to him with a shock that Johnny swayed very unusually with every movement of the vehicle, almost as if—no, exactly as if—he had never been in an automobile before. He was like a youngster on a roller coaster, unfamiliar with the new stresses and demands of gravity and inertia.

"Johnny," Collins said, "is this your first ride in a car?"

Johnny gave him a grateful, happy look. "Y-yuh."

Collins shook his head, not sure whether he felt more puzzlement, outrage, or pity. Johnny, he thought, had to be about the only kid his age in the state who had never been in a car before. And it wasn't a question of poverty, of a deprived mountain background. He knew the North Georgia hills too well to believe that Johnny had strayed down from some dirt farmer's shack stuck in the nineteenth century. *Deliverance* was far out of date; no one lived like that anymore. Besides, the hilly landscape was far too domesticated for that hypothesis to hold. Collins puzzled at the problem, recalling that the boy had worn clothing and shoes typical of any middle-class youngster— and it was evident that, though tattered from exposure, the jeans, shirt, and sneakers had been fairly new. No, poverty was not an acceptable explanation.

Johnny went into a coughing fit, clutching the blanket close to his thin chest. Collins waited until he had recovered. "Johnny," he said then, "listen carefully. We're going into a town. Do you understand?"

The boy nodded.

"Good. Now when we get there, we're going to get some help for you. Make you feel better. But there're going to want to know your name, okay? I'm going to tell everybody that you're my nephew. We're going to say your name is Johnny Collins, understand?"

Johnny grinned at him and nodded. "Yuh." Illness had

made Johnny's voice even hoarser than normal; it was only a husky rasp now, more painful than ever to hear.

"You don't need to talk to anybody. Just pretend you can't talk. Okay?"

"O-okay," the boy agreed.

"Attaboy," Collins said.

Before long he began to encounter more traffic, and as they left the national forest behind, houses began to appear more frequently. Johnny seemed delighted and fascinated by the unrolling landscape, squealing with pleasure once when the car passed a pasture crowded with chestnut-colored cows. He turned in the seat, staring back after the animals as the Ranger sped southward. Once they drove over a black smashed shape in the road, a Rorschach blot that formerly had been a skunk. Collins nearly gagged on the musky stench, and even Johnny, whose nose was hopelessly clogged, breathed a disgusted "Whew!" through his mouth.

Collins arrived at the pediatrician's office by ten-thirty and parked the Ranger in a slot shaded by a tall pecan tree. Johnny, who seemed to feel somewhat better for the ride alone, got out of the car and walked into the office by himself. The waiting room was divided into sick and well sections. Collins had Johnny sit in the sick area while he signed in at Dr. Davidson's desk. The receptionist gave him a medical history form to fill out, and he did so as well as he could, though almost every line could have been a lie.

He joined the boy on a sofa covered in brilliant red vinyl. There were four other youngsters and their parents there, ranging from a little girl of about two who obviously suffered from a severe cold—she leaned against her mother, her eyes half closed, her nose running—to a boy about Johnny's age, his arm enclosed in a cast. The boy, who had been leafing through a magazine, looked up at Johnny and said, "Hi. My name's Brian. What's yours?"

Johnny looked at Collins. "He can't talk," Collins explained. Brian's mother, seated at the other end of the waiting room, called her son to her as if muteness might be catching. Two toddlers, their illness not obvious, sat on the beige carpet and busily created and demolished towers of plastic blocks.

Collins found a book stuck in with the magazines, a

picture book of fantastic animals, and Johnny immediately claimed it. He spent half an hour happily leafing through the drawings of griffins and centaurs, mermaids and unicorns, dragons and basilisks, while Collins sat back and half-listened to the radio station piped into the waiting room, a mixture of easy-listening music and hardsell commercials.

At eleven a news broadcast came on, and again Collins paid only a little attention to it. The announcer mentioned a mystery in Washington, the triple murder of an Air Force officer, his wife, and their maid; a terrorist organization, the announcer said, had taken credit. The news story made little impression on Collins, and Johnny ignored it altogether.

Finally the receptionist called Johnny's name, and the two of them went back to examining room five, a cubicle equipped with a drug cabinet, an examining table, a round revolving stool, a small desk, and one chair. The room smelled strongly of alcohol. Collins helped Johnny up onto the examining table, and a moment later a nurse came in and took his temperature. She made a notation on a chart, slipped the chart into a rack on the door, and closed the door behind her. Johnny gave Collins a woeful, apprehensive look.

"Don't worry," Collins said, smiling. "We're gonna fix you up, champ."

Johnny nodded, swinging his legs and kicking his heels against the table, the sneakers making little cushioned drum sounds. The door opened again and Dr. Davidson, a lean, blond man with gold-rimmed glasses, came in, his head bowed over Johnny's chart. "Mr. Collins. This must be Johnny?"

"That's right."

"Well, let's take a look." The doctor brought his stethoscope up from his neck to his ears, rolled Johnny's shirt up, and listened to his chest. He had Johnny lie facedown, listened to his back, and made him turn over; he prodded and massaged the boy's stomach, peered into his ears and nose and throat. "Say *ahh*," he told the boy once. Johnny's eyes flicked to Collins. He nodded once to tell Johnny it was all right for him to talk to this extent. Johnny croaked "Aahh-k," gagging at the end.

"That's all of that," Dr. Davidson said, discarding the

tongue depressor. He continued with his examination, asking questions which Collins, standing close and protectively beside the high table, answered.

"Can't talk, can you?" Dr. Davidson asked, palping the glands beneath Johnny's chin with his forefinger and thumb. Again Johnny's eyes darted toward Collins and the boy shook his head. "Didn't think so," the doctor said. "Your throat is really red, my man. Tonsils look all right, though, and that's a blessing." He turned to Collins. "Well, it's pharyngitis, an inflamed throat, and just a little touch of asthma. Basically a bad chest cold. No pneumonia, but I'd like to give Johnny an antibiotic just to be on the safe side. Is he allergic to anything?"

"Not as far as I know," Collins said.

"Okay. I'm going to give you a prescription for some cough syrup, some non-aspirin pain reliever, and some oral antibiotics. I want you to be sure that he takes all of the antibiotics, okay? This should snap him out of it. If he gets any worse or if he's not recovering by the end of the week, bring him back in. Does he have a standby asthma medication?"

"Uh—no. This is the first time I knew that he had asthma."

"Hm. Sometimes it's dormant and only crops up when the child is weakened by some other illness. Well, it isn't a bad case. Tell you what, I'll give you an open prescription for an isoetharine mesylate inhaler, too. If he starts wheezing, just follow the directions and you should be able to keep it under control." Dr. Davidson sat on a stool at the desk built into one wall of the examining room and wrote out a series of prescriptions. "I'll have the nurse give him an injection," he said. "Then you can get these filled and see if they don't perk him up."

"Thanks," Collins said, taking the prescription forms from the doctor.

"Don't mention it. Glad to have met you, Mr. Collins. Johnny, you take it easy for a couple of days, you hear?"

When the doctor had left, Johnny started to slip off the table. "Not yet, sport," Collins said. "I'm afraid you have to get a shot."

Johnny gave him a puzzled look.

The nurse, a heavily built middle-aged woman in white,

came in. "Hello, honey," she said. "I'm the mean lady today. I'm sorry."

Johnny stared at her.

"What pretty eyes you have," she said, thrusting the needle of a disposable syringe into an ampule of milky liquid. "What's your name, honey?"

"He's Johnny," Collins volunteered. "He's got a touch of pharyngitis." Johnny's eyes were panicky, wide, fixed on the syringe and the ampule of antibiotic.

"Poor baby. Put your hand on your hip for me, like this." She swabbed Johnny's right biceps and the boy's lip began to tremble. "I know it's gonna hurt for just a second, honey. Be real still for me, okay?" She plunged the needle into Johnny's arm.

The boy gasped and shuddered. A wave of sudden dizziness washed over Collins; staggered, he grasped the edge of the examining table. "I know how you feel," the nurse said without looking up at him. "Sometimes it's harder on us than it is on them." She pulled the empty syringe from Johnny's arm, put a small Band-Aid over the injection spot, and broke the needle from the syringe before discarding it. "That's it, babe. Not too bad, was it? I hope you feel better real soon."

Collins, still a bit dizzy himself, helped Johnny down. The boy moved stiffly, tensely, almost like an automaton. "Come on, Johnny," Collins said, taking the small hand in his.

He stopped at the desk to pay their bill, asked about the nearest pharmacy—there was one just down the street, as it happened—and took Johnny out to the car. He almost had to fold Johnny into the front seat. He wrapped the blanket around the boy again, but Johnny made no effort to hold it on his shoulders. "What's wrong?" Collins asked, an edge of anxiety in his voice.

Johnny did not respond. He stared at some fixed point in the middle distance, as if entranced, lost in his thoughts; as if he were in some world of his own.

Collins drove to the pharmacy and had the prescriptions filled. He had managed to find a parking place near the glass door of the drugstore, and his frequent glances assured him that Johnny was still there, rigid, staring forward. Collins bought a Hershey bar when he paid for the medicine, but even the chocolate made no impres-

"No!" Fisher dropped his hand and glared at Dougherty. "Don't you see what this means, Charlie? It's a positive—positive for telepathy, at any rate. My God, this could be the best evidence we've ever gotten for success. We can't fold now."

"It's out of hand," Dougherty said.

"Not if we can get control of the situation." Fisher brooded a moment. "We'll have to neutralize the Engstroms. I'll leave that up to you. Use any resources you want."

Dougherty made a face. "It's too risky, Ernest. I doubt if we'll even get away with blaming the Arnold hit on terrorists."

"If we can get the kid back we won't have to worry about it. Hell, man, if we can deliver an active telepath, we don't have to worry about anything. But we can't have a leak. You'll have to take out the parents."

Dougherty shook his head. "We've kept an operations office in Washington. We don't have anything in Denver. What am I supposed to do, send our friends out there to stage another break-in? Somebody's sure to make the connection."

"Grade, you mean."

"I'd think so. He's got more inside people in the Pentagon that we could ever dream of having. Hell, he may be on to us now."

"It won't matter," Fisher repeated doggedly. "Not if we can recapture the subject and not if he's gone active." He thought for a few minutes. "We have friends in Florida," he said at last. "The K group, for one. I'll authorize a request for matériel from them. You're right about not hitting the Engstrom people at home, though. You'll have to arrange an accident. Or at least get them out of Colorado."

"I don't like this, Ernest."

Fisher snorted. "You've killed before, Charlie."

"Not our own people, goddammit!"

"They're not ours anymore, Charlie. Anybody who has contact with the kid has to be our enemy. You can see that."

Dougherty shook his head. "You can't push this too far, Ernest. You'll bring everything down if you do."

"I know what I'm doing. I want a plan of action by tonight. Get on it. Send Stark in."

Dougherty left, still shaking his head. Stark edged in a moment later. He held a one-page memo, its edges already ragged from his stay in the anteroom. "Sit," Fisher said. He filled the scientist in on what Dougherty had learned.

"So," Stark said, his pink fingers nipping away at a thin shred of paper. "I concur with your judgment in this case. The boy obviously has a much stronger mental power than he ever revealed in tests."

"You don't look happy," Fisher said. His stomach churned with sour acid. "I thought you'd be overjoyed to learn that your theories have been vindicated."

The smile on Stark's face did not touch his blue eyes. "Unfortunately the vindication has come outside the laboratory. That makes it worse than useless to me." He shrugged. "Now if we can bring the subject back to the lab for tests—and if the tests are repeatable—then I will be truly happy."

"You don't think these stories of dreams are proof?" Fisher demanded, massaging his abdomen.

Stark began to peel another strip from the torn memo. "Not proof, no. Evidence, perhaps, but evidence of all too familiar a type in the field of psychic research. Anecdotal tales, uncontrolled conditions. Not something palpable, not something that could be used to bear out a scientific hypothesis."

Fisher glared at the man. "I don't suppose," he said with icy irony, "that you could venture an estimate of just how powerful this young man is?"

The geneticist looked down as he surgically removed the strip of paper from the sheet. "Much more powerful than I would have thought a week ago," he murmured. "I have reviewed all the events of the escape. They are . . . most disturbing." He looked up, his eyes narrowing. "If the Gamma boy did indeed get away from the unit as I believe he must have done, he did something truly remarkable: he generated hallucinations in the minds of no fewer than fifteen of our personnel."

"Explain."

Stark shrugged again. "He gave Dr. Kornbluth the illusion that he was dead. Kornbluth apparently left his room unlocked. The child projected a strong impression of his dead body—so strong that even Mr. Dougherty was affected, I understand. The crematorium technicians still bear a strong memory of the dead body, one that not even drugs or hypnosis can shake. They still believe they burned him. And yet chemical evidence and inventory shows beyond a doubt that they really burned a chair."

"You mean the boy hung around long enough to—to hypnotize them, whatever he did?"

"That I do not know." Stark shook his head. "Somehow he left the main building. I suspect he simply walked out under the noses of the security people, of the teachers and nurses, blanking his presence from their notice."

Fisher stared. "You're telling me the boy can make himself invisible?"

Stark carefully tore yet another strip from his memo. "Not literally. One camera caught him, an outside camera. He was too distant for visual identification, but the figure is beyond doubt a child. So he was not literally invisible; and yet he caused people to misperceive, to believe that they did not see him even when they did. I do not know if that qualifies as true invisibility or not; it makes no real difference, though, does it?" When Fisher did not reply, the geneticist went on, "At any rate, he had to lull the dogs, the security people at the main gate. He may have climbed the fence; he may even have forced them to open the gate for him and close it after him. There is no way of telling. But no matter what has happened, think of what it means. To accomplish his escape, the Gamma subject must have applied phenomenal mental energies—far beyond any that we have ever tested in the laboratory."

"He apparently used something to disguise his scent," Fisher grumbled. "Even the new dogs couldn't trace him."

"Perhaps there is a lingering psychic barrier, not enough to influence us any longer but strong enough to affect the perceptions of lower animals." Stark showered paper clippings to the carpet and smiled slyly. "There is, of course, another possibility."

"Which is?"

"Perhaps the boy is no longer on earth."

"He's dead, you mean?"

Stark shook his head. "I mean what I said. There was an experiment many years ago, not long after I had joined the Soviet project. The subject was an unusual woman named, if I remember correctly, Praskovnya. She was in her thirties, severely retarded. But she had a most unusual talent. It is called apportation. Are you familiar with it?"

Fisher nodded. "I know the term. But it's always been on the far fringes of possibility."

"Yes. Well, this woman, this Praskovnya, could move small objects through sealed metal boxes. I do not mean locked boxes or flimsy ones. Once we welded a rubber ball inside a rectangular metal file box, oh, twenty centimeters by twenty by twenty-five. The box was welded shut, understand? Completely sealed. When you shook it, you could feel the ball rattle inside. Praskovnya sat at a table with the file box before her and concentrated. The ball was suddenly just outside the box. When you shook the box, the ball no longer rattled; it was outside. When we unsealed the box, it was empty. The ball had been marked with an indelible pen. It still showed the markings."

"So she moved the ball through solid metal."

"She did. The unfortunate woman could not explain how she had done this wonder. She could only say that she put the ball somewhere else—by which we gathered she meant some space other than our familiar universe, some dimension apart from matter and energy. Then she brought it back, having moved it a few centimeters first. We could not learn much more. Her respiration, blood pressure, and heart rate soared when she attempted these feats; that was the only successful demonstration. She died of a cerebral accident not long after that."

Fisher looked distastefully at the scattered snippets of paper on the carpet. "Then the boy might have done the same trick? Melted himself through the fence, apported himself? Is that what you're saying?"

"Such is at least a remote possibility. If such a closed dimension exists, if a person with special talents can open it—well, there is no reason why the person could not hide there. Indefinitely, perhaps."

"Crazy."

"No. There are good theoretical reasons, mathematical reasons, for thinking such other dimensions are possible. One theory holds that the entire universe is, in effect, a black hole: a closed system with its own peculiar physical laws from which we ordinarily cannot escape. If so, then real black holes are pockets of other reality, created by unimaginable forces of gravitation. But if the dimensions of time and space can be circumvented by such a force—if black holes are essentially gateways into otherness—then the same destination could conceivably be reached by other means."

"But the boy isn't in some fairyland. He was photographed, you say."

"True. That gives me hope that he is, after all, accessible to us. Though if he can truly do such things as Praskovnya could do, and if he can exercise control over them in a way she could not, there are other possibilities. What if it were possible in effect to reach into another dimension, to pull from it physical laws much different from those we know?" Stark smiled wickedly. "Then the boy might be able to cause the most appalling devastation."

"But you don't know any of this."

"No. We would have to explore his abilities very carefully, under controlled conditions. Sedation, I should think. Of course, if the subject has the ability to actually alter reality in such fashion—if he has the ability somehow to put himself into that other place that Praskovnya spoke of, or even to contact that other place with his mind—then the situation could be very grave indeed. Very grave."

"Let me understand you, Dr. Stark. Are you recommending that we kill the boy when we find him?"

"Oh, no. Oh, no." Stark's smile was apologetic. "Don't kill him. By no means kill him." He tore the last shred of paper into confetti. "No. Give him to me."

3

Julie Lind couldn't get the children off her mind.

She saw endless mental movies of them, always injured or on the verge of injury—strangled in twisted sheets, bleeding from a cut, screaming, crying alone, the sights and sounds so intense that more than once she started from sleep, her ears still ringing from a child's despairing shriek of fear or pain. The impression was absolutely unreasonable, she knew. Although Stark had once again halted all teaching activities, the children were attended to by the medical staff, their rooms monitored by television. And yet . . .

On Monday afternoon she let Larry take her on a golf round, though she hated the stupid game and was terrible at it. He teased her unmercifully; Larry himself, a strapping man of thirty, whipped the clubs in an arc that split the air with an audible *zip!* and placed the ball on the green with demonic accuracy. "You have to concentrate, that's all," he told her.

She flailed away with a nine-iron, whacked the ball a pitiful twenty yards or so, and saw it veer into the rough. There were other golfers about on the truncated course, for a great part of the staff was idle today. Larry grinned at her, shaking his head. "Play through," he called to the group behind them. He and Julie rested on a grassy slope under a pine. The sunshine was warm on them, the drone of cicadas a drowsy background hum.

The other golfers looked their way, waved and grinned. Larry waved back. Julie supposed they were thinking about what a natural couple the two of them made, Larry with his springy black curls and his laughing brown eyes and herself with her inky black shoulder-length hair, her fading tan. A Club Med couple. They ought to be photographed somewhere lounging on a sugar-white beach with a turquoise Caribbean lapping their toes.

Julie drew up her knees and kicked absently at a pine cone. It rolled a few feet onto the fairway. Larry stretched to pick it up and tossed it over his shoulder into the rough. "You just have to learn to concentrate on what you're doing, that's all," he told her again. "Let me show you how to take the next stroke before you try."

From the tee one of the others yelled, "Fore!" He smacked the ball solidly and it arced well past the grassy hillside, bounced twice, and came up about twenty yards short of the green.

Julie shook her head. "It's no good. I'm never going to get the hang of this. I don't even want to."

"Then why did you suggest playing?"

"I don't even know that. I was going crazy in the apartment. I just wanted to get outside, I guess. It's just boredom, that's all."

"I know what you mean." Larry sighed. "Wonder

what the flap's about this time? Scuttlebutt has it that one of the gremlins flew the coop."

She watched the last golfer take a good swing. Her jaw felt tight from tension. She said more roughly than she intended, "Don't call them that."

Larry looked at her sharply. He was on one of his periodic beard-growing kicks, and his tanned face bristled with four or five days' growth of black whiskers, not yet a real beard but enough to darken his chin and neck. "Jesus, you don't have to bite my head off. Okay, they say a kid broke loose. More power to him, says I."

The foursome had all played past. Julie plucked a blade of grass and twisted it around her finger, watching them putt out. "Johnny Gamma didn't run away. He died," she said flatly and without conviction.

"I know he did. Or at least I thought I knew." Larry frowned. "I have trouble even remembering him now, you know?"

"Me too. I think everyone does. It's odd."

"It's damned creepy. That's what it is." Larry looked at her. "The shit they want these kids to do—it's weird. But I guess we aren't supposed to talk about that, huh? Want to finish the round?"

"No," she said.

"Okay," Larry said cheerfully. "Hell with it then. Want to walk in the woods?" He raised a mischievous eyebrow.

"All right."

He got up and pulled her to her feet. "Leave the bags here," he said. "We'll pick them up on the way back."

They strolled through the forest until they came in sight of the inner fence. A Doberman, inky black, saw or smelled them and tensed but did not bark. Julie studied the long black-and-tan face, the laid-back ears, the bunched and knotted muscles of the dog's shoulders. The animal was menace made flesh, but she and Larry didn't have to worry. They were all right unless they actually tried to climb the fence. The dogs had been carefully trained.

"How long are you off for?" Larry asked, slipping an arm around Julie's waist and leading her on a tangent away from the fence. Last year's dry leaves crunched beneath their feet as they walked in the cool shadows under the trees.

"Oh, who knows? Stark just suspended us until further notice. You, too?"

Larry shrugged. "They're not running any tests. No need for a chemist with the labs locked or for a programmer if the computers are shut down. I'm indefinitely at liberty, I guess."

"If you call this liberty."

Before long they came to a spot Larry had scouted out months before. They rested again on another grassy bank concealed inside a thick cluster of muscadine vines and undergrowth, their exclusive trysting place. Julie lay back and Larry put his head in her lap, but for a long time they did nothing more intimate than that. She absently stroked his hair, feeling its gentle spring beneath her palm. It was a sharp contrast when she rasped her hand along his roughening cheek. "What a mess. You ought to shave it off."

He laughed and put his hand over hers, pressing her palm against his warm face. "I will eventually. I never seem to get past the second week. That's when it tickles so damn much I finally give in."

"Larry," Julie asked impulsively, "what's your key code?"

He turned his head to look up at her. "That's classified, sweetie."

"It's not a state secret."

His brown eyes were teasing. "How do I know you're not working for Them?" he asked, his voice capitalizing the pronoun. "I tell you something vital like my card code and the next thing I know, I'm in a basement room in Beijing with electrodes attached to places on my body where I don't want electrodes attached." He stretched. "Tell you what. Show me yours and I just might show you mine."

"Mine's orange," she said. A code-orange magnetic card allowed her access to her room in the BQ, the commissary, the recreation areas, and the classrooms. It would not operate the locks on the dormitory level.

"I got a green," he said, rolling his head back. He yawned and then added, "Lucky me."

Julie thought about what she knew of the lock system. Actually the colors were only a mnemonic, since all the cards, regardless of code hue, were made of plain white plastic, identical except for the embossed serial number and the magnetic coding each one bore. In the system, though, a green card was two steps above an orange. With the exception of her room, Larry's card could unlock everything hers could plus certain administration offices and all the labs. She had hoped Larry held a code-black card—that was the equivalent of a master key for the main installation.

"Who has a black?" she asked, twining her fingers in his hair.

"Hell if I know."

"I'll bet the doctors would all have code blacks," she said. "They'd need access to the labs, the offices, even the kids' rooms, wouldn't they?"

"I guess they would. So what?"

"Nothing. I was just wondering about my kids."

Larry laughed. "Didn't know you had any maternal instincts."

"They're just children. I worry about them."

"You've got no reason to. They're the best-watched-after kids in the world. Anyhow, even a black card couldn't help you. I'd better not hear of you sweet-talking a doctor into lending you one, either. You show up someplace where you've got no business and they'd throw your bouncy little behind in the lockup, babe."

"Mm." They remained in the little open clearing as the sun slowly began to lower toward the west. Eventually as the shadows began to lengthen they made love. But through it all, Julie Lind's mind was far away, scheming to acquire, somehow, a code-black card.

Though Larry was right, of course. Determined as she was to get the card, given the security, the omnipresent TV cameras, she had no notion at all of how she could possibly use it.

4

Beth Engstrom had just finished putting away the last of the groceries when she heard the car pull into the garage a little past two. A moment later she met Fritz in the utility room. Before she could even speak, he turned her and with a hand spread on the small of her back guided her back to the kitchen. "What's wrong?" she asked. "Why are you home so early?"

He shook his head, pulled out a chair for her at the dining-room table. She sat and he went into the den. A moment later he was back with a half-full 1.75-liter bottle of vodka. He loosened his uniform tie, and Beth watched him get a tumbler from the cabinet over the sink. He poured three fingers of the colorless liquor, drank half of it, and came to sit down at the head of the table, setting the glass and bottle down as he did. "Arnie's dead," he told her.

Her hands flew to her mouth.

He held up his glass. "Want a drink?" She never drank vodka and he knew it, but there was nothing at all mocking in his gentle tone.

She shook her head and lowered her hands, clenched now in tight fists. "General Arnold? Are you sure?"

He nodded. "I tried to put through a call to him at noon. I got the news from his adjunct, but it's already on TV and in the papers."

"How did he—?"

Engstrom finished the vodka. "It's bad. Never mind the details. Arnie was killed by terrorists, they think."

Beth's head whirled. It was a message she had feared often enough in years past, back when Fritz was stationed overseas, but it had receded far into the background of possibility since they had come back to the States for good. "Terrorists? Who?"

Engstrom looked at the bottle as if contemplating another drink, but he evidently thought better of the notion. "Some extremist Islamic group supposedly claimed they did it. One of the factions that split off from that Lebanese-Iranian movement a few years back."

Beth looked at her husband. He was perspiring, his blond hair darkened at the temples, and his face had a hectic flush. "You don't think terrorists did it, do you?" she asked.

He didn't quite look at her, anger and anguish in his pale blue eyes. "I don't. I called him last week about—about our problem."

Beth felt suddenly chilled. "I see."

"He was working on it for me. As a favor." Engstrom stared at the glass in his hand, turned it as if surprised to find it there, as if examining it for fingerprints or other clues. "He had to leave a trail, the way he went about it.

I think somebody got on to him. Whoever it was shut him up before he could find anything substantial for me." He got up, the chair scraping back from the table, and began to pace. "Somebody didn't like his prying. They murdered him."

Beth looked dully at the vodka bottle. The label, in gold, red, and black against white, told her it was a product of Hartford, Connecticut, Allen Park, Minnesota, and Menlo Park, California, distilled by a company that had been purveyors to the Imperial Russian Court from 1886 to 1917. "You don't kill someone for asking questions."

"That depends, hon, on how much you have to hide."

"He must have found something."

Pausing in his up-and-down transit of the dining room, Fritz Engstrom balled his right hand into a fist and tapped the wall with it, producing a soft, monotonous thudding. "I don't know."

"I do. I feel it."

Engstrom took a deep breath. "He'd found enough to make it look as though the Feingold Center was a front. One of the operators was a cardboard."

Beth shook her head. "A what?"

"A man operating under a false identity. An identity created for him by our people. It seemed about good enough to be an FBI or a CIA job."

Beth had known just enough about her husband's peculiar calling never to interest herself in Fritz's work. She had suppressed her curiosity and had never asked many questions. Now she said, "I don't know what that means."

Engstrom sat again, running one big hand through his short hair, making it bristle up from his scalp. "If the information is right, it means we were nothing but goddam guinea pigs," he said, his voice almost breaking. "Somebody used us—hell, used our son—as subjects in an experiment."

Beth laughed. "You can't be serious, Fritz. You're an officer—"

He slapped the table between them. "So was Arnie!"

She put her hand over his. "But what do you mean, guinea pigs? I don't understand what a fertility clinic—"

"The Feingold clinic must have been nothing more than a front, a way to get experimental subjects." Fritz clasped her hand. "It's happened before," he said in a slow and unwilling voice. "The CIA experimented with LSD back in the sixties. Gave it to unsuspecting patients in veterans hospitals. Before that there were other times. In the fifties they released live viruses in the New York subway system to monitor how rapidly they spread— biological warfare preparation. And I know about other examples, too, ones I'm not supposed to talk about."

"Even to your wife?"

"Even to you. Especially to you."

"Fritz—did they take our son?"

Engstrom shook his head. "I don't know, hon. Arnie was looking into the whole mess, but I only spoke to him twice. If they were experimenting on you and our son, I don't know what they were trying to prove. I—"

The telephone rang, cutting him off. Beth rose to answer it. "Engstrom residence," she said with a calm that was nothing like what she felt.

"Mrs. Frederick Engstrom?"

"That's right. Who is calling, please?"

"Ma'am, I'm calling for a friend of your husband's. A friend in Washington who—who can't reach him anymore. Do you know where I might reach the colonel?"

Beth signaled Fritz with her eyes. "He's right here." She handed the receiver to her husband.

With a frown line drawing his eyebrows together, Fritz spoke into the phone. "Hello?" Beth heard a buzz as the man spoke to Fritz, a sound like a bee under a glass, before her husband said, "Speaking."

He leaned against the kitchen cabinet, his face intent. She watched Fritz's expression as the man said something else to him. Her husband dropped his gaze to the floor and said in something close to a hoarse whisper, "We've heard."

Beth touched his arm. "Is it about General Arnold?"

Fritz nodded once, not looking at her, as he listened. Into the receiver he said, "What is it?" After a pause, he added, "Yes, I do."

Beth hovered close, biting back her questions, as Fritz listened again. She began, "Is that—"

Fritz lifted a hand for silence. "Wait a minute. Beth, give me a pen." Beth rummaged in the junk drawer and found a black felt-tipped pen. Fritz took it from her and pulled the Garfield the Cat message pad closer to him. Pen poised, he said, "Spell that." Hunching the receiver against his ear with his shoulder, he printed something in block letters, murmuring softly to himself: "-U-S-S-E-E. Got it. Anything else?" After another pause, he said, "Thank you, son. Thank you very much." He hung up the phone.

Beth had picked up the message pad. "Chanussee?" she said, having no idea whether she was pronouncing the word correctly or not. "Fritz, what was all that about?"

For a moment he did not answer. Then he told her, "It was someone who worked with Arnie. He had a message for me."

"What does it mean, *Chanussee*?"

"It's a little crazy. That's the name of a national forest; there's a special installation, very secret, concealed in it. It's a place down South. One of the people from the Feingold Clinic is working there, evidently."

"This person knows something about the—experiment?"

"I don't know. Arnie couldn't have had time to find out more than just the name and the location."

"But there's a chance. There's at least a chance that we could find out something."

Engstrom unbuttoned his collar. "There's a chance," he admitted, not looking happy about it.

"Then we have to go," she said.

He took both her hands in his. "No, hon. Not 'we.' I'll see what I can do, but—"

"Fritz."

"No," he said. "I know what I'm talking about, hon. You can't, that's all."

"I have to go with you."

He embraced her, pulling her against his uniform jacket. She smelled the Old Spice he had splashed on that morning. He took a deep breath, his chest swelling against her. "Hon, I didn't tell you everything. Arnie's wife—"

"Dolores?"

"Yes. She—she was with Arnie."

Memories flooded Beth's mind, memories of a trim brunette, a woman with laughing eyes and a comfortably easy manner with friends and strangers alike, a manner concealing the toughness that had made a service marriage last for all these years. "They—they killed her, too?"

His silence answered her question. After a moment he said, "So you see why you can't go with me."

"We'll both go," Beth said. Fritz sighed, a patient sound, the sound of a man getting ready for an argument that he already knew he was doomed to lose.

5

The Delta twins knew something that Dr. Nikita Alexandrov did not.

Alexandrov had remarked to Colonel Kovach that distance seemed to have no effect on the peculiar talents possessed by the subjects at the Slow Tango Unit and others like them; but that was true only to a certain extent. Proximity did mean something, after all.

Anthony and Andrew, geniuses in their mathematical abilities, were otherwise unremarkable except in their physical deformity and in their social retardation. Isolated from normal communication with others by a quirk of birth, they had early established a bond between themselves. Like other pairs of twins, they had developed a sort of secret language, a tongue closed to anyone outside their universe of two. True, in their case the language was more thought than spoken, and its other components included such things as posture, rate of breathing, muscular tension, and eye blinks; indeed, to an observer they appeared hardly to use words at all, even when they were together. They needed no words; they had the invisible link with which they had been born.

This bond was never fully broken, though it was weaker when the two were not actually in physical contact, and it grew weaker still when distance and walls separated them. It made their games harder to play when they were put to bed in separate rooms, when they were kept there for a long period of time, as the current isolation promised to be. The White Ladies brought them food and saw to their needs, spoke to them, but never received a reply, never really penetrated their shells. Anthony and Andrew played their games internally, in their heads, multiplying, factoring, performing astonishing mathematical calisthenics; they did not need to speak.

As days passed, weary days when the two remained

confined to their rooms, alone except for the occasional
visits of their keepers, they retreated more and more into
their minds. The boys would lie in bed for long hours, not
moving, their heartbeats and breathing rates slowed and
synchronized as they played with each other. Neither
Anthony nor Andrew felt the warmth of the covers,
neither of them paid much attention to physical needs
outside the obligatory pauses for food, drink, and elimi-
nation. In a sense they scarcely existed in their bodies at
all. But their long mental communion had its bad side,
too: repetition staled the savor of their activities.

The games grew boring again, as most games do to
children who play them too much. Anthony was content
to try to devise new challenges, new approaches to numbers, new shortcuts and new ways of assembling the
math. Andrew, somewhat slower to work out games, was
also the more methodical of the two when it came to
seeing numbers, the ways they could fit together, and the
problems they could pose. But in his plodding, patient
way, Andrew had recently stumbled on a most interesting discovery. Like many another such discovery, this
one was an accident, for the twins had merely been at
their old pastime of experimenting with ever more complex and challenging arithmetical games when the principle dawned. Andrew visualized the revelation as a complex
web of relationships, probabilities, and permutations: as
numbers, in fact.

It was an appropriate medium, for, expressed simply,
what Andrew had learned was that reality could be mod-
eled mathematically. The revelation was really nothing
new; had Andrew's other abilities been on par with his
mathematical gifts, had they even been near normal, he
could have learned the same things from books, eventually, perhaps when he was twenty or older, a graduate
student in mathematics. Then he would have learned
names to go with the discovery, names like Newton,
Einstein, and Fermi.

But names were beyond him. Andrew knew nothing of
Descartes, of Boole, of Russell, Hilbert, Tarski. He saw
only numbers, and in them he saw with certain clarity the
whole world, the whole universe, as well. The mathematics became in his mind a complete galaxy, more, a universe, vast, dark, illuminated by the bright suns of

numbers, by constellations of them. Andrew had intuited a system incredibly complex, complete, and self-contained, a system of remarkable beauty for a mind so rapt in abstractions as his—and his brother Anthony's.

They were the only two living humans who could grasp the system, the only two who could find any conceivable use for the whole of it—though certainly any number of physicists would eagerly have embraced parts of it, parts that described the operation of matter and energy on a subatomic level in precise and elegant ways that no other approach could possibly have done. Andrew lost no time in communicating this new curiosity to his brother, telepathically, through the walls that separated them. Even with the lightning speed of thought the exchange took more than thirty hours.

But as the system entered Anthony's consciousness, he saw possibilities that Andrew had not recognized. Among other things, he saw the principle of resonance that so far had escaped Dr. Stark, Dr. Alexandrov, and all the other researchers. It was a simple principle in a way, as simple as the inverse-square law: the closer together the gifted children were physically, the more their abilities would grow.

If plotted on a graph, the increase would describe an asymptotic curve, beginning near the x-axis and moving almost horizontally at first, then curving up and away more and more rapidly. Nearing the y-axis, the curve became a hyperbola, shooting up parallel to the vertical benchmark line, never touching it. Theoretically, at least, the children's abilities would resonate to infinite power, according to the model.

However, the twins felt no real excitement at the prospect, which was only a by-product of the entire construct. In their minds the model, in all of its breathtaking fullness, was still only a model, a means of description with certain variables (billions upon billions of them), certain unrealized potentials. The model could be adjusted, changed in part or in the whole.

And it was Anthony who first worked out the most important corollary to the mutability of the mathematical system. It was not just that certain equations could be unbalanced, reworked, made to yield an entirely different solution from the one first grasped by Andrew. It was not just that the mere description of reality could be changed.

Anthony saw a way of changing reality itself.

It would be wrong to say that Anthony and Andrew's discovery was a direct way of affecting the physical world. Numbers are only numbers, after all, and matter is something else again.

But glass is only glass until it is made molten and given a certain form. Then it may be a lens; and that lens may focus the rays of the sun, changing their trajectory and concentrating their energy. A magnifying glass can influence reality by burning it.

The mathematical construct was as innocent in its way as a glass lens. But like the lens, the mathematics could focus, gather, redirect energies; used by the right minds, the concepts and structures could profoundly alter the universe they described. Anthony knew this on some level; but because he, like his brother, lived more fully among numbers and their relationships than among other people, he thought nothing of it, except that the beautiful richness of his brother's mental creation would afford the two of them many new and different games, would sharpen an edge made dull by boredom.

The two of them, largely lost in their pursuit of mathematical perfection, were at best only dimly aware of the other children around them. Kathy Beta was foremost in their thoughts when they recognized the existence of the others at all, for she had a strong will and a talent nearly as strong as Johnny's had been, though more undirected than his. Kathy had tried many times to catch and hold their attention, and she had made herself something of a nuisance to them. Anthony gathered that she was concerned about him, about Andrew, about all the thirteen other children left at the institution. She felt or sensed that they were in danger. She was trying very hard to find a way to help them all leave.

So much Anthony understood. He, like the others, had worked on the BIG FOOL that had helped Johnny break free, but Anthony and Andrew were also the first to cease concentrating, their attention not easily held by the real world and its concerns. Dimly he grasped Kathy's need for something extra-special; her need and his brother's discovery coincided.

Anthony's understanding was not worked out, for his method of reasoning obeyed no rules of cause and effect, no means of trial and error. He intuited the problem as Kathy understood it, assayed the possible courses of action in a microsecond, and comprehended that the great need was to bring the children all together. Simultaneously he understood that such a gathering would begin the process of enhancing his and Andrew's abilities, as the model predicted. Proximity would add immeasurably to their understanding of their beloved numbers, to their power to manipulate and control those numbers. The other children, with their different gifts, would grow, too, in different ways.

But the prospect of knowing more, perhaps of knowing all, about mathematics was what held the most appeal. Anthony, huddled in his bed with his head under his blanket, breathed warm, stale air and considered. He decided that something could be done; the model could be changed. He lacked the control and the strength to do much, but small causes can eventually have great results.

He gave a sort of push with his mind, changing certain parameters, setting up new equations. Like someone holding a magnifying lens, he had employed a tool to influence reality. What he had done was very small, very insignificant, really, and therefore very easy.

But even the smallest change is a stone thrown in a still pool, and from that center, from the drop of a pebble, waves spread out and out in ever-increasing circles.

6

Unlike the other inhabitants of the unit, certain administrators lived and slept in a series of apartments on the top floor of the administration building itself. Ernest Fisher was asleep in his own room there when the telephone beside his bed awakened him. He reached for it in the dark. "Yes?"

"We've got them tagged," Dougherty said from somewhere downstairs.

Fisher looked at the bedside clock: the lighted liquid-crystal display read 1:42. "How?"

"The K group in Tallahassee ran a routine monitor of airline and hotel computer networks. It showed up there."

Fisher sat up in the bed, not bothering to turn on a light. "Okay. Tell me what you have." He swiveled the mouthpiece away and yawned silently.

Doughterty did not sound happy. "It's the Engstrom couple, all right. I had someone give them a call, plant enough information to prod them into a move if they were in this thing as deep as we thought."

"They were the parents of the Gamma subject. That's deep enough," Fisher said.

"I guess it must be. They've booked a flight into Atlanta for late Friday evening. With the difference in time zones, they'll get in late—arrival at Hartsfield will be just a little after eleven that night. They've reserved a room at the Hartmann Plaza Hotel."

"You can cover it personally?"

Dougherty did not reply at once. After a moment he said, "Yes, of course, but—"

Fisher cut him short. "You know what has to be done."

There was a longer pause. Fisher listened to the hum on the line, letting Dougherty talk himself into the job. At length the other man said, "This has to be a face-to-face?"

"I want you on it, Charlie. Personally. There's nobody else I could trust with this one."

Another long pause. The sun, in an active sunspot phase, sang on the line. Dougherty finally said, "Okay."

Fisher lay back in bed, breathing his relief. Into the phone he said, "I know you don't like it, Charlie. Hell, I don't like it myself. Trust me, though, this is the way it has to be."

"Yeah." Dougherty still did not sound convinced.

"Is that all?"

"It's all."

Fisher hung up, turned on his side, and stared into the darkness. The window, shielded by closed venetian blinds, showed up as a latticework of pale light against the blackness of the room. *Give him to me*, Stark had said. As he might have asked for a new television set for his quarters, for an increase in pay, or for a vacation—if Stark ever bothered to ask for vacation time in the first place.

Give the boy to Stark?

Fisher thought not.

He was not sure whether or not he fully bought Stark's assessment of the Gamma boy's abilities. Stark, after all, had a strong interest in advertising Johnny's accomplishments, as it were. But even if Stark was only half right, hell, only one-tenth right, then the Gamma boy could be the breakthrough he had sought for fifteen years.

What power such a boy would have.

And what power would come to the man who controlled him.

Give the boy to Stark?

Fisher smiled to himself.

No. Not a chance in hell, he thought.

I'm keeping him.

7

The break came courtesy of Dr. Beckerman, without his even being aware of it.

Staffings—monthly procedural and review meetings—were part of the routine of the Slow Tango Unit, and even though operations had almost halted, routine ground on. The June staffing was scheduled for Thursday, the last day of the month. In the absence of Dr. Stark, who rarely bothered to attend such functions, Dr. Kornbluth chaired a dreary hour of griping and bitching. Present were all the medical staff, Drs. Beckerman and Kornbluth, the four white-uniformed nurses, the six aides, the six technicians; the educational staff, led by Mr. Clebb and including the four teachers and their six aides; Dr. O'Connor, the psychologist; and the recreational/physical training staff of two.

Julie Lind sat across from Alice Weston, with Dr. Beckerman on her left and Miss Dawes, the mathematics and science instructor, on her right. Miss Dawes, a skinny, thin-lipped redhead—the hair color, Julie suspected, was false—never spoke, but merely sat back from the table, her arms folded beneath her meager breasts, as if challenging the others to solve some unknown problem to her satisfaction. Beckerman ostentatiously took out his wallet about fifteen minutes into the meeting and began to sort through it, discarding old scribbled notes, arranging a series of credit cards in some arcane order. He presented an almost perfect picture of a man suffering from the last stages of terminal ennui.

Two seats to Beckerman's left, a freshly shaved Larry Thomsen sat with a pad before him; but in the presence of others, Larry assiduously ignored Julie, as he always did. It was his fantasy that the relationship between them was a deep, dark secret, unlike the twenty or thirty other affairs between personnel at the installation. Julie smiled outwardly, though she felt nothing but bitterness for Larry and his careful cultivation of indifference. Just another personal insult, she thought, courtesy of the Paranoia Palace.

Dr. Kornbluth droned through a round of cautions, complaints, questions, and reviews. None of it seemed very important, and the man's deadly-level voice did nothing to arouse the attention of the listeners. Julie sighed, profoundly bored. For most of the meeting she simply tuned out, closing her mind to the round of complaints and questions that no one could address or answer anyway. Mr. Clebb, a fussy, balding little man, the only one among the men wearing a white lab jacket today, fumed over the interruption of teaching routine. "We're losing ground," he said in his high voice, a voice that grated on Julie like fingernails on a blackboard. "These are not ordinary children. Developmentally many of them are at a crucial stage." He paused and looked around the table with narrowed eyes, as if daring anyone to disagree. "A crucial stage," he repeated unnecessarily. "Every day that we lose means a further slide back into ignorance for the children."

Kornbluth, a robust man in his mid-forties, rested his cheek on his left fist and doodled on a yellow legal pad with his right hand. "Mr. Clebb, I appreciate that. But the decision is not ours. It was made on the highest administrative level. . . ."

Julie sighed again and shifted her weight in the uncomfortable chair. The back was too straight and hard, the cushion too thin to prevent the hard edge of the chair from biting into her thighs and putting her legs to sleep. She moved in the chair again, still unable to make it sit more easily. Across the table Alice Weston noticed her squirming and gave her an ironic half-smile along with a rueful lift of her right shoulder: what could you do?

Julie returned the smile. Alice was not like most of the other heavy people she had met, she thought. The stereotype of the fat, jolly extrovert certainly didn't apply here. For all her plumpness, Alice was one of the most private people at the institution, except of course when she was around the children. Julie hardly knew her, almost never saw her outside of the building. No one formed strong friendships here, not inside the fence, but some people were more friendly than others.

Idly drifting from the increasingly heated exchange between Clebb and Kornbluth, Julie thought to herself that Alice could be really attractive if she lost weight. A lot of weight: fifty pounds perhaps. But buried beneath the extra flesh was an attractive woman. Oh, she might be big-boned, but she had a pretty oval face, direct cornflower eyes, auburn hair that could be made to compliment her features if she'd take it down from the bun and do something with it. . . .

Dr. Beckerman jostled her, gave her a sideways glance. "Sorry," he muttered, and then raised his voice. "The security problem is a real one, don't forget that. You short-timers are getting lax. You—"

Clebb, his egg-shaped face purple, choked out, "Lax? Lax?"

Beckerman clapped his wallet shut and dropped it back into a breast pocket. "Clebb, you've served tours here before. Have you ever seen the installation in such a tight clamp-down?"

"That is beside the point—"

Beckerman slapped his hand down on the table, brushing the pile of discarded paper off the edge as he did so. "It is exactly the point! If the Gamma subject hadn't—"

Julie scraped her chair back from the walnut-veneer table and bent to pick up the mess Beckerman had scattered. Her eyes widened as she saw a white rectangle of plastic with a brown magnetic strip running across it. She swept it up along with the debris, slipped it onto her chair, covered it with her leg, and put the crumpled and discarded notes back on the table at Beckerman's elbow.

Her heart sped up. She had been plotting and scheming for days to trick a code-black access card out of Kornbluth or Beckerman, and now here was one presented to her as if it were a gift from the gods of chance.

She leaned forward in the chair, willing the meeting to end.

It did at last, with nothing settled—as usual. Chairs scraped back from the table. Larry Thomsen walked past, eyes on his blank note pad; he didn't even glance up at Julie. For an excuse to remain seated a little longer, Julie said to Alice Weston, "How is Kathy doing?"

Alice gave her a surprised look. "She's doing well enough, poor little thing. Withdrawn, of course. How was she getting along in therapy?"

Julie shook her head. "Gaining ground and then losing it. She's like some of the others. She *can* talk, or at least she can vocalize, but she won't. I don't know what she'll be like when we can start sessions again." Beckerman had paused at the end of the table and was in an animated three-way exchange with portly O'Connor and with Kornbluth. Julie dropped her left hand below the table and retrieved the card. She opened her purse and dropped it in, all under cover of the table. "I just hope she hasn't lost too much," she continued to Alice without pausing. "Does she ever try to speak to you when you see her?"

"Nothing much. Sometimes 'yes' or 'no.' " Alice pushed away from the table, braced her hands on the chair arms, and lifted herself from the chair. "I hope you can see her again." The cornflower-blue eyes flicked toward Beckerman and then back to Julie. "Soon."

Julie felt a quick chill. *She knows*, she thought. But if Alice Weston had noticed the card, she said nothing; she skirted the arguing men at the door with a murmured "Excuse me" and left the room. Julie followed her.

Alice was at the elevator. "It's eleven-thirty," she said. "Going to lunch?"

"I'm not hungry yet," Julie said.

"I like your blouse," Alice told her. "Get that in the BX?"

Julie glanced down at herself. She wore a peach short-sleeved blouse, a blue skirt. "No, I brought these with me."

The elevator doors hummed open, and the two women entered the cage. "I get to hate these uniforms," Alice said. "Seems that I'm in one twenty hours a day. Of course, there's no place to go, so it doesn't matter." She looked at the sensible black plastic digital watch on her wrist. "I'm not very hungry, either. I think I'll skip lunch today. I need to lose weight."

They stepped off the elevator on the main floor. "The commissary should make that easy," Julie said. "Same old menu every two weeks, regular as clockwork."

"Isn't it the truth?"

They crossed the lobby of the administration building and walked out into a bright, warm day, heading toward the BQ. Under her breath, Alice said, "You'll need some help, even with a key."

Julie, looking down, whispered back, "I know. The rooms are all monitored."

"I think we need to talk. We can work something out, maybe. But it will have to be today or tomorrow, before Beckerman reports his lost card." Alice paused. "I think you'd better turn Beckerman's in as lost."

"I'll need it."

"It's trouble. Besides, nurses have black cards, too."

Julie took a deep breath. "All right. I'll trust you. When can we talk?"

"Let's meet for a swim," Alice said. "The pool shouldn't be crowded this time of day."

"All right." They looked at each other and Julie got a sudden case of the giggles. Alice chuckled herself, sounding like an indulgent older sister. They parted at the BQ, each one going to her own quarters, and Julie shook her head as she thought of the curious play of chance and the shifting patterns of her hopes and fears.

Although, of course, chance had nothing to do with the coincidences of the day.

Indeed, they were in a sense mathematically perfect.

CHAPTER SIX

1

After three days of steady improvement, Johnny had something of a relapse on Friday. All day the boy seemed strangely quiescent. Nothing, not even Eightball's tail-wagging entreaties, penetrated his lassitude; the boy simply sat on the edge of the cabin porch, staring down toward the Chanussee River, though his gaze seemed fixed on something far more distant than the trees on the downslope or the water beyond.

Collins worried about the boy, although Johnny seemed to have shaken the infection. After long, dreary hours in bed, Johnny had appeared very pleased to be given the freedom of the cabin again. He was a little weak, but otherwise healthy enough, even though he still had to take the white Penn-K-Vee tablets four times a day. At any rate, he no longer had the hacking cough or fever, and his eyes had become clear once more. He listened with what seemed to be wholehearted interest to Collins's improvised bedtime stories; he petted Eightball and even tossed a tired tennis ball for the dog to retrieve from across the room.

But since early morning, Johnny had become so resolutely quiet that Collins began to worry about him again. He checked on the boy once every fifteen minutes between stints at the computer, but except for his stillness Johnny certainly seemed well enough. After his eighth or tenth look at the child, Collins sighed and went back to the computer, where he was industriously running up a ruinous telephone bill in his quest for information.

He had reams of printout, more information stored on diskette, and still he worked the modem overtime, sorting through data files, pestering information services with outlandish queries on arcane subjects. His eyes felt grainy from lack of sleep, his brain almost numb from trying to absorb all the information his terminal pulled in, and yet he sat staring at the blinking cursor on the screen and racked his brains for another approach, another key word, another query that might shed light on Johnny and his peculiar talent—or curse.

For Collins had to admit that so far he had drawn a blank. Oh, he had information, all right. Tons of it, he reflected with a rueful glance at the computer corner, increasingly snowbound with drifts of printout. But so little of it seemed to apply to Johnny that he might as well have nothing at all. The book, he decided, would have to stand on Johnny alone, on his observations of the boy and of what he could do. There was nothing like Johnny in the literature. The boy was unique.

Collins heard the rattle and squeak of a car coming over the bridge and leaped up from the computer so fast that his chair toppled to the floor behind him. He stepped around it and went to the front door, breathing a sigh of relief at the sight of William Whitepath's green Dodge van jouncing up the hill toward the cabin, followed by a billow of red dust. Collins walked out past the Ford Ranger to meet his friend, rotating his head back and around to work out a kink in his neck.

"Hungover?" Whitepath asked, grinning, as he climbed out of the van. He was wearing his khaki uniform today, the silver badge gleaming in the early afternoon sun.

"Worn out."

"How's the kid?"

"Better. Seems on the mend. He's not talking today, though."

Whitepath glanced over toward Johnny, who still sat on the edge of the porch, bent forward slightly, his hands resting in his lap. Eightball moped beside him, his black head down on his paws. The child looked a little like an undernourished Buddha; there was about him that sort of serenity, that quality of repose. "Let's walk down to the dock and back," Whitepath said. He took Collins's left arm just above the elbow, steering him down the hill.

They walked beneath the shade of pines and sweet gums. "What is it, Will?" Collins asked. "Bad news?"

Whitepath stooped to pick up a round river pebble. He shied it toward the water from fifty yards away. It glanced off a tree ahead of them on the path and veered to the left without even getting close to the water. "Naw. No news. Good news, I think your people call that. You do anything about finding Johnny's folks?"

"I'm working on it."

"Yeah."

"I'm working on it, Will."

They got to the dock, where the canoe was snugged up tight. Whitepath stood there beside the water, his stocky figure somehow nearly as remote as Johnny's. Looking out across the water, Whitepath said, "This was a wild river one time. I remember before it was dammed. Pa used to take us fishing through here, whenever the white men weren't in their cabins."

Collins kicked at the ground. A clod of earth broke off and arced into the water. "Didn't know the river was restricted," he said, trying for a light touch. The two of them walked out onto the ramshackle dock, which squeaked beneath them as if it were about to collapse. As always, it held.

Whitepath didn't look directly at him. "Oh, it sure as hell was. You'd be surprised." He swept an arm out, indicating the reach of water to the southeast. "Down there was a big pool, I remember. 'Course it wasn't near as wide as the river is now, but back then it seemed like the whole damn ocean to me. Told my Pa once that when I grew up and married I'd buy me some land right down there and build a house on the hill right over that pool. Pretty place, Pete. River come spilling white-and-gray down from the mountains, sounding like thunder; then it come around the bend here and hit that pool and just smoothed itself out like glass. Pretty goddam place back then."

"I guess you never bought the land."

Whitepath spat into the water. The spittle formed a little raft of bubbles; they bobbed away on the current. "Naw. By the time I got married the dam had been built. Wasn't much attraction then for me." He gave Collins a sideways grin, his white teeth gleaming. "Hell, just as well, huh? My old lady left me and took both my sons.

By now I'd be stuck with a cabin in the woods and a mortgage I might possibly pay off when I hit ninety. But I wouldn't have built there, anyway. Not after what my old man told me."

Collins stood beside Whitepath on the dock. Their shadows, not yet very long, floated and wavered on the water, Collins's angular, Whitepath's more compact. The air here close to the water was a little cooler than up by the cabin. A dragonfly, its blue knitting-needle body moving in impatient jerks and twitches, came and settled on one of the pilings. Another buzzed past, its body an iridescent green, and the first launched itself in amorous or angry pursuit. Collins stretched. "What's this all leading to, Will?" he asked.

Whitepath shook his head. "Nothing, I guess. Except I'm very nervous about the kid, Pete. I like him. I like you. Dammit, I'm scared of what might happen when they find out."

Collins nodded. "I appreciate that. But who are *they*?"

"Same as they always are, I guess. Same people who rooted up my ancestors here and transplanted 'em to the desert. Same people who pay my salary."

"The government, you mean?"

Whitepath looked away downstream. "I asked some people who ought to know about that place in the woods, up on Claxton's Ridge. Place where I thought I heard the kids that time. They told me to stop asking questions about it. Told me it was none of my business. Finally one of them told me it ain't a Forestry Service installation at all, never mind what the signs say. It ain't USDA, either. It ain't anything that oughta be there."

A mosquito keened in Collins's ear, and he slapped his neck absently. He killed the insect, felt its body beneath his fingers like a cool, damp thread. He rubbed it off his neck and flicked it from his fingers. It hit the water beside the canoe, and a second later a finger-long trout struck it and disappeared with its prey back into the darkness beneath the dock. "Will," Collins said, "I've known you ever since I first started coming to this place. We never talked around a problem before. What are you saying?"

"I think the place may be some kind of cover,"

Whitepath said. "I think maybe there are special kids there. Like Johnny. I think maybe whoever has them there wants to keep them a big secret."

"You have nothing to go on—"

"They fired me."

Collins took a sharp breath. He was conscious of the warm sun on his face and bare arms, of the cool sweep of the water just a few inches below the dock, of the breeze in his face, bringing the scent of growing things, of water, of earth. "Oh, shit," he said. "You lost your job because you asked somebody about the place?"

"They ain't saying. But what else could it be? I talked to people last week about it. This morning Woodall calls me in and says I'm out."

"I didn't think they could do that."

Whitepath laughed without much humor. "I'm a GS-8, Pete. A goddam civil servant. Job security, right? But they let me go and told me that if I keep my nose clean, my pension will kick in next month. Hell, I'm barely vested, but they're gonna give me full pension. Just for keeping my big red mouth shut."

"You didn't—"

"Now, of course I didn't mention you or Johnny."

"Sorry."

"Don't be. It's natural you'd worry."

Collins ran his hand through his hair. "Damn, Will, I don't know what to say. It's scary."

"Yeah. You've been laying low, I hope."

"I sure have. There's no way—" Collins broke off.

Whitepath gave him a long look, concern sharp in his brown eyes. "Uh-oh. Better tell me."

"Oh, shit," Collins said. "I've been on the modem about Johnny."

"You used his name?"

"No, of course not. But I've been running down information on all kinds of weird shit—ESP, PK, the whole goddam alphabet. If anybody tried to put in a trace—"

"Hey, there's thousands of people with computers on those services, right?"

Collins shook his head. "I don't know, Will. If somebody starts looking for patterns, there's probably damn few who've run through all the stuff that I have."

"I guess you can be traced, huh?"

"Easily. I have code numbers for all the information services. All they have to do is go through Contax or ReSorce or—hell, they've got me if they look."

"You'd better clear out, then."

Collins nodded. "I guess maybe you're right."

"Got anyplace to go?"

"I'll have to think. I had it all planned to live here for eighteen months, but I was living cheap and alone. Money won't go nearly as far in Atlanta, and if we have to go farther it's more of a problem."

"I got a little you can borrow. Six thousand in savings."

Collins gave Whitepath a surprised look. Whitepath still stared impassively down the river, his features somehow more Indian in cast, inscrutable. "You don't have to do that, Will."

"I got two boys of my own. I ain't seen either one in five years."

"Thanks, Will. If I need it, I'll let you know. We'd better get back."

Whitepath reached into his hip pocket and passed an envelope to Collins. "This ain't money," he said. "But maybe you better take a look at it. You and Johnny, if you think it'd be a good idea."

Collins opened the envelope and pulled out a half-dozen color photographs, most of them showing only a chain-link fence with a sign, yellow letters on green background: U.S. FORESTRY SERVICE EXPERIMENT STATION/RESTRICTED AREA. One, from a different vantage point, showed the corner of a building above distant treetops, the red-and-blue blur of a flag at the top of a flagpole, a round yellow brick chimney blackened at the top. "This is the place?"

"Yeah. Took those last week. Didn't know what trouble I was gonna get into then."

Collins sorted through them again. "What's this one?"

"That's the gate, see? I couldn't get very close, and my damn camera doesn't have a telephoto. See this gatehouse here? It's manned. The drive here comes in off the main highway. I didn't see any traffic on it when I was there. I asked around and found out that damn few people have seen traffic on it. Trucks occasionally. But no cars. See what that means?"

"Whoever is in the place stays there."

"Yeah. No commuters. It sure as hell stinks, Pete."

Collins nodded. They climbed back up the hill together and found Johnny still lost in his reverie, Eightball still flopped beside the boy. "How's it going, John boy?" Whitepath said, sitting beside the child.

Johnny didn't reply. Eightball got up, came to insinuate himself between Whitepath and Johnny, and settled down again, his chin on Johnny's knee.

Collins hunkered down beside the porch, bringing his head level with Johnny's. "Look here," he said, holding out the photo of the buildings glimpsed above the trees. "Do you know this place?"

Johnny gave no sign of having heard.

"He get like this much?" Whitepath asked.

"No. Just every once in a while." Collins put more heartiness into his assurance than he really felt. "He'll snap out of it when he's ready."

"I hope so. Pete, I think he might need a doctor."

Collins got up and sat on the other side of Johnny. He put his arm around the boy, feeling the thin, fine-boned shoulders, the matchstem upper arms, the fragility of Johnny's undersized body. "He's okay. He's got me now."

Whitepath looked off into the woods. "Look, don't fool yourself into letting him slip away. You can't keep him alive just by caring about him. If he needs a—"

"If he needs a doctor, I'll take him to a doctor," Collins said. "He'll be okay."

"All right."

"Sorry. Didn't mean to snap at you."

"No, it's okay." Whitepath pointed off to the right. "If I'd ever built my place, it would have been about a mile that way, where the hillside was high over the pool. About where the high-tension lines are now, maybe a little farther downstream."

Collins, relieved that Whitepath had changed the subject, said, "How'd your dad talk you out of it?"

Whitepath's eyes narrowed. "He told me the story of the spirit leech," he said.

2

Sonny Angelo seemed genuinely surprised by and grateful to Alice Weston. Sonny, himself a heavyweight, had talked to Alice many times, but never more than casually. Now she had gone out of her way to visit him in the video surveillance room, and she had brought food with her.

"There's nothing to do, what with the shutdown," she explained. "And somebody said you were on duty today, and since I was having a snack anyway—"

"Hey, thanks, I really appreciate it." Angelo grinned, helping himself to another brownie. "These are very good. You made these yourself?"

Alice, dressed in her usual white nylon uniform but with her brown hair loose and falling in waves down to the base of her neck, nodded shyly. "I like to cook," she said. "That's probably why I'm so fat."

"Hey," Sonny said, "like I always say, nothing wrong with having a little meat on your bones, huh?" He bit into the brownie, his cheeks bulging. He closed his eyes and smiled his pleasure. When he had swallowed, he said, "This is awfully good. You're not having any?"

Alice looked dubiously at the plate. Of ten brownies, six remained. "I shouldn't. I've been trying to lose weight."

Sonny Angelo looked at her with—yes, there was no denying it—frank appreciation. "I don't think you're fat at all," he told her. "Me, now, I gotta admit it, I'm fat." He slapped his belly, sending a quivering shock wave across his tight-fitting lab smock from right to left. "Five-eight and two hundred and four pounds. They tell me to get more exercise, but that's no good. I exercise more, I get hungrier and eat more. It's a vicious circle, you know what I mean?"

"I really do. But a man can carry extra weight better than a woman can. I mean, it doesn't look bad on you."

Sonny beamed with pleasure at the compliment. "You don't look bad yourself, you just believe you do. It's all in the mind. You know what I think? I think being big is mostly genetic. Now, you, I bet you had a heavy mother, am I right?"

Alice nodded. "We look a lot alike," she said.

"Sure, I knew it. Now me, my dad and mom are both big people. My dad, he's seventy-four now, he takes a size forty-six in trousers. Hey, you know they say it's unhealthy, but let me tell you this: my grandfather is just the same size as me, and he's still alive. You believe that? Ninety-six years old and sharp as a tack. I'm gonna visit the family soon as my tour's up here. Take maybe a whole year off and just catch up, you know?"

"Really?" Alice had been watching the bank of monitors. There were six main screens and eight smaller ones; only the six large ones were on at the moment, cycling through views of the sixteen children's rooms, showing the youngsters playing with toys, lying in bed, in one case reading. Each child was onscreen for perhaps thirty seconds before the scene changed to the next in the rotation.

Sonny laughed. "You're like me. You come into this place and get fascinated by the TV, just like it was a real program. But believe me, it wears off fast."

"Can you see anywhere?" Alice asked.

Sonny grinned, wiggling his eyebrows at her. "Like the ladies' boudoirs, you mean? No, forget I said that, that was crude. No, what we got here is the in-house monitoring station. See, we keep a check on the kids through the top row of monitors there." Sonny reached out and threw a switch, bringing one of the smaller screens to life. It showed a vacant lab. "Now I can change any way I want. See, I just brought the behavioral lab online there. Well, I can change to look at, say, the medical lab." He turned a dial and the picture changed to a dim view of the darkened examination room. "Or I can put one of the kids on if I want to take a good look at what one of them's up to. Like this." The examination room disappeared and one of the Delta twins replaced it, a figure sitting huddled in a chair, short arms folded over its chest, its head sunk in concentration.

"I see," Alice murmured. "I don't think I've ever been in here before."

Sonny burped and excused himself. He stifled a yawn. "Well, it's nothing great," he said. "I mean, it looks high-tech and all, but what you have basically is just a set of closed-circuit cameras. It's pretty boring, actually. See the VCRs there?"

Alice looked behind her. The whole wall was a bank of videocassette recorders, thirty of them in six columns of five. Red power lights and green record arrows shone in the front panels of sixteen. "These record the children?"

"You got it. Even when the monitor's not showing a kid, the VCR is watching. 'Course, most of the time we—" He paused, a puzzled look on his face. "Uh, we—forgot what I was saying. Oh, yeah. Most of the time we wipe the tapes after a spot review. Some of them, though, go on to Mr. Fisher. The interesting ones, I guess you'd say. He must have a pretty big collection by now."

Alice leaned closer, studying Sonny's flushed face, his eyes. "You look tired."

Sonny grinned at her, but it was a sickly grin. "I guess I'm just bored. Tell you the truth, I feel kinda funny today. Hope I'm not coming down with something. Mind if I have another?" He reached for the brownies.

"You shouldn't make yourself sick," Alice said with real concern in her voice.

Sonny smiled at her. "Hey, I'm a big guy, I got big appetites, right?" He bit into his fifth brownie. He made a strange face, his lips puckered up. "I might have had too much chocolate at that. This one tastes different somehow. Kinda bitter or . . ." Sonny rubbed his mouth. "My lips feel funny. Kinda numb."

"Maybe you ought to put your head down."

Sonny nodded. The half-eaten brownie fell from his hand to the tile floor. "You know, my grade-school teacher used to tell us that when we got sick to our stomachs. I remember old Mrs. Scarlatti used . . . to . . ." He pitched forward. Alice, ready for his movement, caught him and eased him facedown to his desk. He breathed loudly and noisily until she turned his head. His cheek pressed flat against the desk; mucus dripped from one nostril. Alice pulled up an eyelid and saw that his pupil was wide and black. She closed Sonny's eye again. Reaching over him, she picked up the telephone and dialed a three-digit number.

From the classroom two floors below, Julie Lind answered right away: "Hello?"

"Now," Alice said. "Hurry." She replaced the receiver without waiting for an answer.

Alice's first step was to turn off the VCRs, one after the other. She noticed that the monitors still rotated from child to child monotonously, even when the recorders were off. She saw Julie come into Kathy Beta's room, saw Kathy hug her, saw the two of them hurry toward the camera, disappearing as they went out the door into the hallway.

"Hurry," Alice whispered. She experimented with the dials Sonny had worked and found Julie again, this time leading one of the Deltas out of his room. More dial-twisting showed her the corridor, six students already there in a tight huddle. Kathy Beta hovered like a mother hen over the brood; one Delta twin was already there, and in a moment the other joined him. The two embraced at once, like Tweedledee and Tweedledum.

"Hurry," Alice said again.

The intercom suddenly barked at her, making her jump: "Mr. Angelo! Your recordings have stopped!"

Stark's voice.

"Mr. Angelo! Answer me."

Sonny Angelo heard the voice even through his stupor. He stirred, tried to push himself up. "Help," he said in a thick, breathy drawl. "Drugged—"

Alice could have screamed. The moment went on and on, Sonny swaying, supporting himself on his outthrust arms, leaning over the desk, his mouth moving silently. Above him the monitors all showed the corridor, where there were now eight children; eight of them, all staring, Alice thought, at her.

They know, Alice thought.

For no reason at all the name "Brier Rose" came to her mind.

3

The pool in the river (William Whitepath explained to Pete Collins as they sat on either side of Johnny) was called Tlanusi-yi by the Cherokee. In years to come the white man would corrupt the name to Chanussee and would apply it to the whole river, but in reality it belonged only to the still, deep pool below the bluff, and it meant "Place of the Leech."

In the centuries before the white man came, the Cherokee learned to avoid that place when they traveled alone. It looked peaceful enough, a broad mirror of water fed at the northwestern end by a tumbling mountain stream, emptying at the southeastern end to a tamed and gentler river. On a bright day it showed an almost perfect reflection of the hills and trees. But the water was deep as well as broad, dark as well as still. In it something slumbered.

The story was a very old one. It told of a clan of Cherokee who lived upstream from the pool, a clan warlike enough when attacked but for the most part a peaceful people who lived by hunting and gathering. For many years they were happy and unthreatened, but at last there came a year when the chieftain of the clan feared that enemies were preying on his people, for three hunters disappeared within as many months. Each had gone out on his own seeking game; none of them had returned.

When the last one vanished, his three younger brothers went to search for him. All the first day they went through the forest but found no trace of the missing man. They camped that night and set out again on the next morning. At noon they came to the high bluff above the pool. One of the brothers, looking down, cried out to the others that he had seen something strange.

The others joined him and looked down. They saw that below the bluff was a shelf of gray and mossy rock, forming a kind of flat beach on the pool's southern shore. As the three brothers looked down, they saw on this ledge of damp rock a great red thing, a round, soft-looking mass as large as a house. As they wondered what it might be, it suddenly began to move and they realized that it lived.

The thing uncoiled itself, stretching along the rock ledge until it looked like a giant leech, striped red and white. Leaving a trail of shiny slime, it crept forward into the river and at last slipped off the ledge, vanishing in the deep green water. The three brothers strained to catch sight of it, but could see only shadows stirring in the depths.

Then the pool began to stir and foam; all at once a great column of water spewed forth. Two of the brothers drew back in time, but the third and youngest, closer to the edge, was beneath the torrent of water when it fell back to earth. The force of it knocked him flat, and the steepness of the bluff made him slip over the edge. He fell many feet to the ledge of rock, landing with a crash flat on his back. The other two cried out and began to make their way down toward the water, but the cliff was so nearly vertical that they had to go a long way upstream to find a downward path.

They were perhaps halfway to the ledge when they again came within sight of their brother's body. He lay just as he had fallen, on his back, sprawled on the ledge, feet toward the cliff and head toward the water. His skull had broken open and blood ran out and down into the pool, staining it red. While he seemed gravely injured, he still lived, for though he did not cry out or rise, his limbs stirred feebly.

But before the other two could reach him, the red shape oozed onto the rock ledge. The two older brothers loosed arrows into it, but the shafts passed through without finding lodgment and apparently without injuring the pulpy body. The head stretched forth up the slope, quivering, extending, finding a purchase, and dragging the rest of the body after it. The blind mouth made a sucking sound as it followed the strings of blood and brain up the rock and to their brother's head; it poured itself over, closing at the chin; and with the entire head gripped in its monstrous mouth, the creature dragged the body across the ledge. The horrified men saw their brother's neck stretch, head the sinews pop. They saw their brother still weakly moving, the legs quivering, the hands vainly trying to dig into the solid rock. The efforts were futile; the leech pulled the unfortunate man down into the cold water with it.

The two surviving brothers ran back to the clan and told what they had seen. An elder of the clan said that the pool was the abode of a spirit creature, and he first named that part of the river the Place of the Leech. The brothers had a great quarrel, for the elder wished to kill the leech if they could, and the younger was afraid. At last the older brother prevailed. Many men went with the two brothers back to the pool, but they did not see the leech. They rolled heavy stones off the bluff and into the water, and the creature did not respond. They moved far back from the bluff at night to camp, but every morning for three days they came back and tried to think of some way they could frighten or lure the leech to land. They could make no plan that promised to work. At last they gave up and went back to their homes.

But the elder brother returned often to the bluff, always alone. At last, a year after the first deaths, he went one day and never came back to the village. The last brother overcame his great fear and visited the bluff; there on the bluff above the pool he found one of his brother's moccasins, still damp with water, and so he knew the leech hungered again and had fed.

The last brother brought the news back to his people. The clan moved far away, although its dwelling place had been a very good one, and they told the other Cherokee of what had happened and what they had seen. Some of them remembered that another such place was in the mountains to the north, in what the white men came to call the state of North Carolina; and some believed that the river here was linked to the Valley River of North Carolina by an underground passage, through which the great leech moved. Others thought that the leech was only one of a species of spirit creatures, that this leech was brother or cousin of the one to the north; but whatever the truth was, it did not much matter. The Cherokee gave the leech no chance to kill again.

Even in later years, long after the coming of the white man, the Cherokee avoided the still pool beneath the bluff, never going there alone and never standing on the steep hillside above the rock ledge to look down into the deep, dark water. But from other vantage points they could see shadows moving beneath the surface, and they knew that *tlanusi*, the leech, was not dead but only waiting.

4

All Kathy Beta could think of was fairy tales. Some she had heard when the nurses or teachers read them to her long ago; others she remembered from television. Her head was full of fairy tales, and she didn't know why.

Miss Julie had opened all the bedroom doors and was frantically herding the children before her, managing only to consolidate the clump of kids in the hallway. The Rhos, Sigmas, and Taus, the youngest, were moving well enough, but the Delta twins, locked in some mathematical chant, were lost to the world, and behind them a logjam quickly built up. The children were laughing with excitement, the sound reverberating off the cold tile walls. They were white

[Snow White]

walls, unadorned, smooth and damply cool on your cheek when you leaned against them, smelling of nothing but clean.

"Please, children," begged Miss Julie, weeping. "We have to hurry. Anthony, Andrew, move—"

[Cinderella]

Kathy felt suddenly as if she had been pricked by a needle—her mind smarted, cut by bad thoughts, sharp thoughts. For a second she lost her concentration on fairy tales, frightened when she recognized the source of the anger: Dr. Stark. Somewhere he was cursing.

[Sleeping Beauty]

Kathy felt a sudden stir of hope. That was right, that was the one he

Johnny?

wanted her to think of. Yes, Sleeping Beauty, what was her name, Brier Rose, that was it, alone in her castle until love's first kiss would

Johnny is that you?

at last awaken her.

[yes Johnny here I'm here the story is Sleeping Beauty]

She could have wept with relief; after so long without hearing from him, Johnny was suddenly there, right in her head, loud and clear, better than ever. She tuned in to his thoughts again, finding them strong, intoxicating, shocking, rushing hard like the icy water Miss Lainey sometimes forced her to stand under in the shower when she had been bad:

[me Johnny I'm thinking to you it has to be a BIG BIG FOOL this time oh Kathy the BIGGEST FOOL of them all]

Johnny I don't understand what you want me to do I've lost you

[just like in the story yes the story the three fairies and

the wicked fairy not invited to the christening not invited and the spindle and three drops of red blood]

The camera was an eye, swiveling toward them, its power light bright and yes as red as a drop of blood. Kathy stared into it, tried to stare it down, felt hands on her, small hands, one of the other girls. Something like electricity surged through her, and she felt herself stronger. Someone else touched her, and again the power grew.

[sixteenth birthday and the briers grew to enclose the castle]

Johnny I don't know what you're telling me

[like the story like the story it has to be like]

More kids were laying their hands on her; the effect was like the joining of batteries in series, with each child contributing more electricity, more current. When the Delta twins linked, Kathy felt them come into her mind, sensed the explosion of power whirling in their heads, the galaxies of numbers. Somehow they transformed to a heightened awareness and

I know now I know now

the others understood with her as she understood. Andrew Delta was doing something with numbers, something fast and hot and spinning, and she and all the others were

!!sending!!

concentrating as hard as they could on what had to be done. They stood on an island of light there in the corridor, and around them they created a sea of darkness, spreading out from them in every direction, covering the whole installation, covering everything, touching people, just like in the

story

fairy tale of Sleeping Beauty:

The Cook in the Castle Kitchen fell asleep while boxing the Kitchen Boy's ears.

(In the commissary kitchen Maureen Macbride, busy with the grilled steaks, slumped forward without even attempting to catch herself. She fell onto the grill, where her face cooked.)

The Huntsmen in the Castle Mews fell asleep on their horses. Their horses fell asleep standing up. Their hounds fell asleep beside the horses.

(Cyrus Champlain slipped off his stool at the main gate. He came to rest on the floor of the gatehouse, crumpled against the wall. He snored. In the kennels all six Dobermans fell over as if overcome by anesthetic. Something light pattered to the ground in the space between the double fence near the gate; then there was another similar sound, and another, and another. For a few seconds the sky rained sleeping birds.)

The Court Physician fell asleep while telling the Baron to say "Ahh." The Baron fell asleep with his mouth open.

(Dr. Stark stumbled against the corridor wall, fell forward, and was asleep before he hit the floor. Alice Weston passed out in the stairwell and rolled down an entire flight, breaking her right leg; but she felt not a trace of pain.)

And the King himself fell asleep on the throne,

(Ernest Fisher dropped the telephone from his nerveless hand. He slumped back in his swivel chair unconscious.)

and so all the castle slept

Go!

at last.

Go! Go!

5

Unable to believe her own stupidity, Julie Lind tried to get the children together. What had she been thinking? Even if they got out of the building, there was no way, no way at all, of escaping from the compound. Dizzy with the realization, she cursed herself, cursed Alice Weston for helping her in her mad scheme.

It was as if she had been dazed, drugged, she thought in distraction. As if someone else had been putting thoughts, crazy ideas, into her normally sensible head. Her hair tumbled loose, getting in her eyes; she wept as she tried to get the children to move. They all stood frozen, staring up at the television camera. For a moment or two Julie had the oddest impression that the lights were dimming, that darkness was closing around them all like a fist. She felt tension building higher and higher—

Until some invisible band snapped.

Then they were moving, tugging her, urging her forward. They burst into the lobby of the administration building and Julie saw the first one, the security man, Janson. He sat slumped sideways in his chair, his eyes closed, his face slack, fast asleep.

"Children," Julie pleaded, half shouting, half trying to whisper. "Children, stay with me—"

But they had opened the door already. Like water draining from a punctured aquarium the children poured out, sweeping her along. Larry Thomsen was there, in one of the little golf carts. It had run into the building beneath the commissary window and had become stuck against the wall there, its tires spinning, digging themselves into the soft earth of the flower bed. Larry himself was unconscious behind the steering wheel, his body jittering as the rear wheels tried to move the whole building. As they passed the cart, the motor finally burned out in a furious whine, blue-white smoke puffing from it, smelling of ozone. Larry fell sideways, half out of the cart, into a mountain laurel bush, still asleep. Julie looked at him and knew that he was in her past already.

The children were shading their eyes, tugging Julie along. "Wait," she said. "We have to wait for Nurse—"

Tammy Sigma took her hand. "No. Too late for Nurse. Hurry."

Julie looked around her in confusion. She was breast-deep in children, some of them wearing pajamas, some jeans and sneakers. Some of them chattered and laughed, some were silent. Tammy's eyes were on Julie, fixed, strange; and then Kathy Beta's were, and then others. Julie felt a deep calm descend over her, warm as a blanket. She went with the children down the main path of the compound, around behind the admin building, past the gym on the left, past security on the right. The path led downhill, bending through dogwoods planted so thickly that they concealed the main gate.

They arrived at the gate. The children wanted her to open it; they did not know how. Julie didn't, either, but she opened the gatehouse door, crawled over Mr. Champlain, and turned keys and threw switches until both the inner and the outer gates ratcheted open with a metallic clatter. The children cheered.

"Look, if you can persuade her to stay here, she can come over and put up with me and Susan—"

"I've tried to talk her out of this trip. No dice."

Jernigan nodded. He reached into his pocket, produced a handkerchief, and scrubbed at an invisible spot on the windshield. "Yeah, women can be stubborn sometimes."

Engstrom didn't bother to answer. He had felt strange, out of touch, hollow almost, ever since he had gotten word about General Arnold. He could not shake the feeling.

As if picking up on his thoughts, Jernigan said, "They killed Arnie." The rising inflection on the sentence might have made it a question, or it might have been Missouri talking.

Engstrom shifted slightly in his seat. "Clint, I don't know for sure. That's the hell of it. I think they did, but I just don't know."

"Man, what I can't figure out is who would have the balls to do that, you know?"

"Anybody can be killed. Even Presidents get killed."

Jernigan gave him a hard stare. "That some kind of dig?"

Startled, Engstrom said, "It wasn't meant to be."

With a grunt Jernigan reached out to soften the Mozart. "My dad worked on cars like this in Detroit," he said. "Thirty years on an assembly line. Always said I'd own one."

"I don't see the connection," Engstrom said.

Jernigan shrugged. "John Kennedy was hit in a car like this one. Except that was the convertible, not the sedan."

"I didn't remember that. I just meant that anybody can be murdered. Depends on how cagey the murderer is, how patient. That's all I meant."

"Sorry. I get touchy about the car sometimes," Jernigan said. "But Arnie Arnold—hell, his business was being careful, you know?"

Engstrom nodded. "Look, I've got to pack. Think you can run me back into town now?"

Jernigan started the engine. "Yeah." On the way back down the mountain, he said, "Listen, where should I keep the envelope?"

"I'd put it in the code safe."

"Yeah, that's good. And I guess I'd better tell a few people where it is in case something happens to me and you both."

Engstrom managed a smile. "I don't think it's that bad, Clint. Not yet."

"I'm not going to take a chance."

Engstrom shivered suddenly, as if a goose had walked over his grave. He knew that Jernigan wasn't joking; he knew that there was nothing to joke about.

They were back at the Engstrom house by three o'clock. Jernigan stopped the Lincoln in the driveway and said, "Well, you take care. You get yourself killed, who would I be able to beat at poker?"

"You wish," Engstrom said. "Hey, come on. It's going to be okay. I'll be back here in three days and I'll take that damn envelope away from you. We've got our shorts twisted over nothing here."

"I hope so," Jernigan said.

Engstrom got out and waved as Jernigan backed the Lincoln out and drove away. No one in the neighborhood seemed to notice; the car wasn't followed, at least not as far as Engstrom could see. He turned and walked toward the house slowly, like a soldier exhausted from a twenty-mile hike.

7

After a while it seemed right that they go for a drive, so Johnny, Whitepath, and Collins piled into Whitepath's Dodge van. Eightball ran his usual escort down as far as the wooden bridge, then sat, pink tongue dripping, as if he had established himself at his post and was settled there to await their return. Whitepath hummed something tuneless and monotonous to himself, possibly a chant. Collins sat with his arm resting on the window ledge, his elbow out in the breeze, and tried to think why this was wrong, why they should not take this trip.

But he could not quite put the thought into words. Whitepath seemed contented enough, and Johnny, between them on the front seat, was as alert as he had been on his ride down to the doctor's in Gainesville. Collins looked out, frowning, as they passed through Holcomb's Crossing, a town so small you could drive through without noticing it. They passed the Mercantile and the pharmacy, the Shell station, the Baptist church, and then they were on the open highway, winding their way north into the mountains.

"I'm gonna cut through by the old river road," Whitepath said. "It ain't paved, but it's passable, and it'll take five miles off the trip."

"Fine," Collins said, dizzy. He stared out the side window at the passing world: farmhouses, well back from the highway, cornfields where the crop was head-high already this second day of July. Trees. Lots of trees, increasingly dense and thick: pines, oaks, maples, pecans. Beneath them the shade looked cool and green.

The van's suspension was not in great condition. They turned off the highway onto a dirt road that threatened to shake Collins's fillings loose, a washboard of a road that reeled up and down hill like a derelict roller-coaster track into the bargain. A dense cloud of dust rose behind them. Foliage, ferns and sumac, slapped the side of the van, making Collins pull his elbow inside.

"Do you think," he started to ask Whitepath, and somehow or other the question went no further but spun around like a stuck record, except that it diminished in the manner of a dying echo: DO YOU THINK Do You Think Do you think do you think doyouthink . . . The sound rode around and around in his head, a maddening spiral, as irritating as an unwanted but remembered melody.

"You'd do better if you spoke Cherokee," Whitepath said in a voice of earnest concern. *"Na'tsi,* that's a pine tree. *Na'tuli,* that's spruce."

"You can't teach Eightball Cherokee," Collins said. "He's just a dog."

"I wasn't teaching Eightball," Whitepath rejoined. "I was teaching—him. What's his name. You know."

Collins tried to think of the name and couldn't. He had lost the name, and that made him sad.

"Listen," Whitepath said. "Hear the crickets? They go *gwe-he! gwe-he!*

The boy between them laughed, and the name snapped back into Collins's mind: Johnny. Of course. Johnny.

"Your name is Johnny," he said to the boy. "I won't forget again."

"Pete," Whitepath said suddenly, "where the hell are we?" The van clattered to a halt in an overarched tunnel of bad road. The dust they had raised caught up with them and made the world outside misty and red.

Collins shook his head, feeling disoriented and sleepy. "It happened again," he said. "No special effects this time, but he did it to both of us." He turned Johnny's shoulders toward him. "This is bad, Johnny," he said, staring into those silvery eyes. "Bad, do you hear me? We can't go outside like this. Why did you—"

Johnny held out a folded piece of paper. With a glance up at Whitepath, Collins took it and opened it out. A photo fell from inside: the picture Whitepath had taken of the buildings barely showing above the trees. "Here," Johnny grated, putting a dirty forefinger down on the brick building that scarcely showed. He pointed at the paper he had wrapped the photo in.

It was the drawing he had made of the strange children.

"He's telling you his friends are there," Whitepath said.

"I got that much, Will." Collins stared at the boy. "Johnny, is there some reason we have to go there now?"

Johnny nodded emphatically. "Huh-huh-hurt," he gasped.

"If we don't go your friends will be hurt?"

He nodded again and pointed ahead.

"Well, hell," Whitepath said, putting the van in gear. "Why didn't you say so?"

They rattled on beneath the canopy of trees for a long time before finally turning north on a two-lane blacktop. This took them through the national forest, unpeopled, nearly untraveled. They passed a fire tower, a relic really now that the Forestry Service depended mostly on heli-copter spotting, but Whitepath cast a proprietary eye toward it and Johnny gave it a long look. Perhaps half an hour after they left the cabin Whitepath turned to the left, down another dirt road.

"It's this way?" Collins asked, dismayed at the re-newed jouncing.

"Yeah, about three-four miles. Hang on—I'm going around this."

This was a bright yellow pole gate across the road. Whitepath simply took the van off to the right, tilting them dangerously as he negotiated a steep bank. They made it around and then came back to the dirt road. " 'Course I don't know what we're gonna do when we drive up to the gate and it's locked," Whitepath said. "I doubt they're gonna just let— Holy God."

A parade straggled toward them, a ragtag line of children led by a dark-haired woman in a green-sleeved blouse and blue jeans. Collins blinked. "You think we can get that many in the van, Will?"

Johnny cried out, bounced on the seat, climbed into Collins's lap, and tried to squirm out through the window. "Wait a minute, wait a minute!" Collins said. "Here!" He opened the door and Johnny spilled out, found his feet, ran toward the children. A girl toward the front leaped to meet him and they hugged, laughing and weeping at the same time.

The woman came closer, her black hair sweat-plastered to her face. "You'd better be what we've been walking toward," she gasped.

"I think we must be," Collins said. "Can you get them into the van?"

She turned. "Children! This way— Oh. Johnny, Johnny." She dropped to her knees as Johnny ran to her, wrapped his arms and legs around her, buried his head in her throat. "There, there," she said, petting him, rubbing his hair. "It's all right now. It's all right. Oh, Johnny, never ever make us think you're dead again."

Johnny pulled away from her and pointed to the van as he looked up at Collins with eyebrows raised. "Get them in, sport," Collins said. "If you can do it."

The move was more efficient than Collins would have thought possible. The fit was very tight, kids jammed buttock to buttock on the floor as well as in the front and rear seats, but everyone managed to board. Johnny elected to sit in the back, right in the middle of all the kids; the woman sat in the front between Whitepath and Collins, a little girl on her lap.

Whitepath shook his head. "Where the hell now?" he asked. "Back to your place, Pete?"

"I guess so," Collins said.

Whitepath started the van, wormed it back and forth in a tight turn, and finally headed back out the dirt road. "I think we need to introduce ourselves," the woman said. "My name's Julie Lind. I'm a teacher and speech therapist with the biomed unit."

"I'm Daniel Peter Collins, but everybody calls me Pete. And this is William Whitepath."

"Late of the Forestry Service," Whitepath said as the van, heavier now, labored up the threatening slope and around the gate again. "Thanks to your people, I imagine."

Julie shuddered, raising a hand to smooth her dark hair off her forehead. "Not my people. They were going to do terrible things." They turned onto the blacktop and headed south. Julie said, "We're in Georgia?"

"You didn't know?" Collins asked.

"Not for sure. They don't tell you anything in there."

"I believe it," Whitepath said. "How'd you guess?"

"I saw the highway sign back there. We're on a Georgia state road."

Collins had turned in his seat. The children were quiet now, just as Johnny had been earlier, and all their eyes were turned toward Johnny. "They were prisoners, weren't they?" Collins asked the woman.

Julie nodded. "I think we all were."

"How'd you escape?" Whitepath asked.

Julie stroked the hair of the little girl in her lap. She frowned. "Isn't that the strangest thing," she said. "I can't remember. I can't remember at all."

8

Dougherty picked them out at the Delta boarding gate at the airport. The two of them exactly matched the descriptions he had gotten from his sources. And although the man's dossier said that he had worked in intelligence before, he was too wrapped up in his wife to pay much attention to his surroundings, and he obviously did not realize that Dougherty was tailing the couple.

They picked up their luggage and found their way out to ground transportation. Although the MARTA rail system serviced the airport, Dougherty knew that the two would take a taxi or an airport shuttle to their hotel, some miles north of the airport in downtown Atlanta. As soon as he saw for sure that it would be a cab, he went to his own waiting car and started the engine.

Dougherty drove a dark gray VW Jetta, old enough and dented enough to attract no attention but fast enough to do an efficient job of tailing. The taxi pulled away from the curb as a Delta jet screamed up overhead. As soon as he was out of the glare of the airport, the night became suddenly quite dark. The cab headed for the northbound interstate and Dougherty relaxed, knowing that the couple were indeed heading for the hotel where he, too, had a reservation. Reassured on that point, he drove almost automatically, finding the cab ridiculously easy quarry, and as he trailed it through the night he reviewed what he knew about Mr. and Mrs. Fritz Engstrom.

The husband was the biggest danger; that was clear. He was forty-five, younger than Dougherty and about as meaty. He was in good shape physically. Engstrom had not worn his uniform to Atlanta; he was dressed in casual tan twill trousers and a dark blue pullover knit shirt. He didn't seem to be wearing a weapon of any kind—he certainly hadn't worn one aboard the plane, and Dougherty didn't believe that he would have brought something in the luggage. Still, you never could tell. Frederick "Fritz" Engstrom would have to go first.

Dougherty considered means with part of his mind. Another part saw the couple, if not with pity, at least with a kind of half-regretful detachment. Their genes, in the end, had doomed them; as everyone's genes do, he reflected bitterly. Both of them had some reason to believe they had minor psychic abilities, a fact that had come out (though buried at the time under mountains of other information) when Beth Engstrom had been orally interviewed at the Feingold Clinic more than twelve years before.

That was the trigger. That interview, conducted almost casually, had sealed the fate of all the Engstroms, father, mother, and son. Dr. Stark had picked up on the information immediately, had checked the couple in red, and

had extended them a formal invitation to avail themselves of the Feingold's experimental techniques. Both
Frederick and Elizabeth Engstrom had signed releases
absolving the Feingold Clinic of any responsibility for
accidents resulting from treatment.

Their deaths tonight would be an accident. A lingering
aftereffect of Beth Engstrom's treatment. Too bad.

At the Feingold, infertile parents received very good
attention, actually; better by far than in any other com-
parable institution in the country. And the success rate
was correspondingly high. An ovum from Beth Engstrom
was fertilized *in vitro* by sperm from Frederick (several
ova were fertilized, actually; Stark was choosy about such
matters and liked a large selection). What the Engstroms
did not know was that the egg cell had been biochemi-
cally treated before the fertilization took place. Like a
child tinkering with an Erector set, Dr. Stark had subtly
altered the fundamental genetic code.

The Engstroms were early in the program. That year
saw the births of Alphas, Betas, Gammas, Deltas, and
Epsilons; Johnny was part of the first crop, as it were.
Many of the special children born that year were dead
already, victims of the myriad subtle errors that creep
into so complex an operation as genetic manipulation.
Stark had expected this and had smoothly assured everyone (everyone except the unknowing parents) that the
next children would be better, more viable: he referred
to the Zetas, Thetas, Kappas, and Lambdas, all the way
down to the planned Taus, Upsilons, and Phis in the last
year of the project's launching.

And so they had been. Fewer of the later-series children died early; more of them made it past infancy. But
no generation was free of its freakish mutations, and all
of them bore (like, Dougherty thought, the mark of
Cain) the same peculiar eye coloring.

Thirty-one children in five years.

Thirty sets of parents duped into believing their children dead at term.

And what was there to show for it? Piles of papers
documenting tests, most of them inconclusive. A few
interesting videotapes.

And one very weird kid, if what Fisher suspected about
Johnny Gamma was even half right.

Dougherty privately thought that he was going on the wrong mission tonight. The kid—that was the one they should be taking out. When they found him. If they found him.

The cab turned off the expressway at Martin Luther King, and Dougherty followed into the sporadic flow of late-night city traffic, his mind working on the problem of locating Johnny Gamma. A ground search had been negative, with the dogs either unwilling or unable to trace a scent. Air surveys had turned up nothing; judicious inquiries made to neighboring law-enforcement agencies had been equally unproductive.

Dougherty would have liked to believe that Johnny Gamma was dead in the forest somewhere. But you couldn't assume that, you could never assume such a thing in his business.

Working hypothesis: Johnny Gamma lived.

Corollary: he had found shelter.

That was necessary. No child, however occultly gifted, could survive in the open, not even in the comparative mildness of a warm Georgia summer, for many days. And Johnny Gamma, who had not been outside the installation since his second day on earth, would be singularly unequipped for survival. Someone must have taken the child in.

Double possibility: (A) the person taking Johnny in was aware of the boy's abilities; (B) the person taking Johnny in was unaware.

Consider the implications of (A). Who would know? An ex-employee of the installation? Some of them were repeaters, in a year, off a year, back the next; most of the 127 staffers cycled through, one eleven-month duty tour and then out and away. Very few of them ever knew for certain exactly where the installation was located; practically none of them ever talked about it. All were highly screened before employment. Chances against: a thousand to one, maybe more.

All right, who else would know? The Soviets, perhaps. If Stark's intelligence information was good (and Dougherty had helped Fisher winkle out considerable corroborating detail), then the Soviets might be aware of the installation and its purpose. Might even send someone over to check it out. But—

How would an agent contact Johnny?

Unlikely. Chances against: twenty-five to one, maybe more.

Very well. That left possibility (B) as the most likely explanation. Johnny had found refuge with some ordinary citizen, some samaritan who took in lost kids and strays. That made the task of rounding the boy up easier and harder: easier, because Dougherty knew they faced no real professional opposition; harder, because Fisher would allow no publicity, none, no search through ordinary channels, no police action.

That was a mistake, too, in Dougherty's opinion. Had they put out a bulletin, had they chosen two likely enough people from among the staff to pose as Johnny's mother and father, then they might have pulled it off—a week ago. But it was too late now; headlines would scream coast to coast about the callous couple that lost their child in the wilderness and neglected to search for him for how many days? Busybodies. Publicity. Anathema, as far as Fisher was concerned.

The cab let the Engstroms out at the Hartmann Plaza Hotel, a dignified building dating from the fifties. Though dwarfed by the newer hotels, the Hartmann promised a certain elegance without opulence; Dougherty had approved the room he had taken there earlier in the afternoon.

Dougherty circled the block, returned, and pulled up to the entrance himself. He turned his keys over to the maroon-uniformed doorman, along with a five-dollar bill, and thanked the man. The Engstroms had just left the registration desk when he crossed the lobby. He managed to get in the same elevator with them. He edged his way to the back of the car, so that he stood behind Beth Engstrom and slightly to her left. She held the key; her husband, like a road-show Willy Loman, carried two bags.

Dougherty settled back as the elevator doors closed. Two young women squealed up, forced the doors back open, and giggled into the car. "Anybody with the convention?" one of them asked. Neither the Engstroms nor Dougherty responded. "Party's on sixteen," the girl said, pressing that button. Dougherty kept his face blank, but inwardly he was just as happy that his own room was on the fifth floor, far away from the party.

Stopping at every floor for more guests until it was absolutely packed, the elevator rose to the eighth floor. Mrs. Engstrom glanced at her key as the overloaded car glided to a bumpy stop. Dougherty got a good look at the number: 842.

The Engstroms forced their way out of the car and turned left. A teenaged boy got on. "Party's on sixteen," the same girl said.

Dougherty got off at nine, found the fire stairs, and went down one flight. Room 842 was closed. He rapped on the door, and a moment later Beth Engstrom said, "Yes? Who is it?"

Dougherty had drawn the Walther from his waist holster. From his jacket pocket he took the stubby silencer, efficient but very temporary. It would not last for more than two or three shots. He attached the silencer while responding to Mrs. Engstrom's question: "Taxi man. Mr. Engstrom lost something in the cab. Here you go."

She unlocked the door. He saw as it opened an inch that it was not chained. He put his weight against it and pushed into the room.

Fritz Engstrom stood at the foot of the double bed, a suitcase open in front of him. Beth cried out in surprised anger, and her husband turned. Dougherty kicked the door shut behind him and aimed the automatic.

The Walther spat once. The slug took Engstrom in the temple, shoving him back as blood and brain tissue exploded from an exit wound the size of an orange. Already dead, Fritz hit the bed on his back and shoulder, fell off it sideways, and came to rest facedown on the maroon carpet. Mrs. Engstrom had time for one short scream.

The second bullet, fired from barely a foot away, hit her in the chest. It pierced her heart. There was no real need for the last shot to her forehead, the *coup de grâce*, but Dougherty fired as insurance as she collapsed to her knees. The final shot made a louder sound than the first two had: the silencer was about gone.

That was at forty-one seconds past 12:28 A.M., Eastern Daylight Savings Time.

At that precise instant, almost a hundred miles to the north and northwest, Johnny Gamma screamed himself awake from a light doze. He had a picture of his mother in his mind, a strong picture. His chest and head were full of pain, sharp, hot, more agonizing than even the light of the sun full in his eyes. His mother receded from him, falling down an endless dark tube, and in his mind he registered what she saw just before dying: the face of Charles Dougherty.

Johnny lashed out at the man in his fury and despair.

And before Beth Engstrom fell dead to the floor something terrible happened to Charlie.

CHAPTER SEVEN

1

Johnny's screams roused Collins from a profoundly exhausted sleep. He swung his feet to the side and had a moment's disorientation when they hit a soft, yielding body; then he remembered he was sleeping on the floor, not in the cot. He got to his feet, found the light switch, and saw that everyone was already awake.

Johnny, who had the sleeping bag, was on his knees in the middle of the living-room floor, his teeth clenched, his eyes madly glaring. He wore only underwear, shorts and T-shirt, and his hair spiked out in a wild confusion. Three of the other boys were sleeping as well as they could in the chairs, and the rest of them lay on the floor on improvised pallets of blankets, quilts, and even towels. All nine of them were sitting or crouching, obviously startled. The bedroom door opened and Julie Lind came out, the seven girls clustering to stare after her. Julie, still wearing the blouse and jeans Collins had found her in, made her way toward Johnny.

Collins stepped over Anthony and Andrew to kneel beside Johnny. The boy collapsed into an embrace, bitter sobs shaking his body. Julie sat on the floor beside them and reached to smooth Johnny's hair. Over Johnny's shoulder she looked at Collins. "What's wrong with Johnny? What happened?"

"I don't know," Collins said. "He just screamed out. Maybe he had a nightmare."

"Was it a bad dream, Johnny?" Julie asked the boy, still stroking his hair.

Johnny gave no answer, but gradually his crying subsided to harsh, breathy gasps, each one making his thin chest heave. Holding the boy tight, Collins rocked him gently back and forth. Johnny, his hot, moist face buried against Collins's T-shirt, snuffled. "How is it in there?" Collins asked Julie, nodding toward the bedroom.

"The girls' dorm, you mean?" She gave him a wry smile. "We're making out okay. Lucky you had a queen-sized bed in there, though. I've got four in with me and two little ones are sharing the cot. It's sardines in a can, but I guess we're coping."

"We're going to be in trouble come breakfast time," Collins told her. "I think we can probably manage to scrape enough food together for this mob, but we'll run out of plates real fast. We'll have to think about finding better accommodations soon."

"I don't know if we can," Julie said. "Is he asleep?"

Collins glanced down. Johnny was at least quiet again, his face drawn and haggard. "Here you go, sport," Collins said, easing him back to the sleeping bag. Johnny rolled onto his left side and pillowed his cheek on his hand. He lay there staring at nothing; the others had already settled back down. Collins checked his watch. "I don't know about you, but I'm dry. Want to split a Coke?"

"Okay."

Julie went to the kitchen and turned on the light there before Collins switched off the living-room light. He made his way through the maze of resting bodies. He was barefoot, wearing work trousers and an undershirt; the wooden floor was cool beneath his soles. Julie had already opened the soft drink. Collins got ice and glasses. He sat with Julie at the table. "I came out with nothing to wear but these clothes," Julie said. "I'm going to need something fresh eventually."

"We can pick up something on the way."

She gave him that twisted smile again, an attractive smile, full of mischief. "On the way where? We haven't settled that yet." She poured the Cokes.

"Thanks," Collins said, watching the soda fizz down. "I dunno. If these people are as good as you say they are—"

"They're good."

"It'll have to be a real backwater someplace, then. Maybe we ought to set out cross-country until we find some place so far in the sticks they'd never locate us."

Julie sipped her Coke, the ice cubes making frosty music. "I don't believe there is such a place, Pete."

"Well. Maybe the kids can help us."

Julie shivered. "I don't know if I'd want that. They did something to the people at the installation. It was like— like a nerve gas or something. People just dropping in their tracks. I don't know if they're dead or alive now. Even Alice. What time is it, anyway?"

Collins checked his watch. "Ten to one." He rubbed his hand over his face; his skin felt greasy. "Where did they come from?" he asked.

Julie looked down into her glass. "The official story was that they were culled from orphanages. But I've heard different. Someone thought they were artificially mutated, that their mothers were subjected to radiation as an experiment and the children were so changed that they had to be hidden away. Another rumor was that their mothers were all prostitutes and their father was a sperm donor, a man with some kind of super intelligence. That accounts for the eyes, they say. I don't believe any of it."

"How could they just be stuck away like this? They have rights—"

"The need of the state must in certain circumstances supersede the rights of the individual. Unquote. The wisdom of Dr. Karl Stark, late of Vienna." Julie yawned. "Sorry. I'm exhausted. When is Mr. Whitepath coming back?"

"He said tomorrow morning early. I asked him to bring more food. Should've asked for paper cups and plates, too."

"We'll manage."

"I guess we can pile everyone into the van and take off. Maybe we ought to head west, toward Alabama. Lots of little towns there. We can stop at K-Marts along the way for clothes for everybody."

"You have money?"

"Well—there's some. I'm getting it in cash. Bank's in Atlanta, but there's a branch down in Gainesville. Plus Will says he has some funds. "We'll get by for a while."

"And then?"

"I'll get a job, I guess," Collins said. He made a muscle and smiled at her. "I'm young and strong. Or maybe we ought to just go on welfare. We have enough kids to warrant a pretty nice check."

"But we don't dare let anyone know about them."

Collins nodded. "I know. Bad joke." He got up and took Julie's glass from her. After dumping the ice cubes in the sink, he washed both glasses under hot running water. "Seriously, we'll have to look at some maps and plan a route. And we'll have to remember we've got a limited range. It's going to be rough on the kids, crowded into that van. We'll be lucky to make a couple of hundred miles a day."

"Don't worry about them," Julie said. "They're good children."

Collins inverted the clean glasses in a drainer. "There's something else," he said. "I'm a writer."

"No," she said.

He turned, leaning against the sink. Julie met his eyes. He asked, "How did you know what I was about to say?"

"The preface was enough. You can't write about these children, Pete. That would be the same as condemning them to death."

"I don't agree with that. If there's a book about them, if people know, then they'll be safe. We—"

"No." Her dark eyes were very direct. "Peter, believe me. You'd never get it published."

"Whatever happened to freedom of speech?" He asked the question lightly, but her bleak look gave him a nasty sensation of doubt.

"You'd never be able to publish," she repeated with conviction. "Even if you did, these bastards would find some way to get the children back."

"Julie, public opinion—"

"—can be manipulated, Pete. These people are better at that than you are. Better than anybody. You can't win against them—no one could."

"So what do we do, then?"

"Just what you said. We pile in the van and try to find a place to hide. That's the only thing I can think of."

Collins shook his head. "That may be okay for now, but what happens to the kids when they're eighteen, twenty? What happens when they're too old for us to hide?"

"I don't know."

A head-splitting yawn took Collins. "Well, we'll talk about it later. But we've got to do something. We can't just run with no goal in mind. At least not forever."

"Nothing's forever."

"Guess not." He sat down at the table again and studied this trim, attractive woman. She had not bothered to put her hair up, but even in its disarray it was pretty, jet-black and falling softly around her throat. Her face, even without makeup, was arrestingly intelligent, beautifully formed. Collins asked, "How'd you ever get mixed up in that business, anyway?"

She raised an arched black eyebrow. "Said the john to the hooker?"

"I didn't mean it that way."

Julie smiled. "I know. I've asked myself the same question. I got recruited in college, actually. It was something exciting to do at first, working for the government in classified positions. Lots of travel, lots of vacations. Then I started to get involved with the students, the patients. I don't know. I guess I like being needed, when it comes down to it. My parents sort of cut me loose when I was eighteen."

"Where are you from?"

"Evansville. It's in Indiana."

"I know of it. You don't sound Midwestern."

Julie shrugged. "Haven't been back there in years. I don't miss it. Anyway, I was dating a fellow who went off to the East to college, and I followed him. Dad disowned me, or came as close to it as a mid-American Ford dealer could. My stepmother had never liked me anyway. So there I was, having to struggle through school on my own. I worked part-time jobs, got scholarships. Worked so damn hard the guy I'd been dating broke off with me. Said he wanted a woman who'd devote a little time to him. Anyway, after all that rejection it was nice when people started to rely on me, to trust me and need me. So here I am."

"How long have you been here?"

"Just a few months. Remember I didn't even know where here was until today."

"Before that?"

"Background for your book?" Again the dark-eyed mischievous smile animated her face. "No, I'm kidding.

But I can't tell you much about that. I've worked with people who have physical troubles brought on by trauma, people who can't work with a regular therapist because they know too many things that other people aren't supposed to know. I've been here and there."

"Money good?"

"Oh, the money's terrific," she said. "The money's fabulous. In every job but two I've lived on a base somewhere—like this stint. I get a living allowance and I bank my salary. An accounting firm manages it for me. They've made some investments, this and that. I suppose I'm worth a quarter of a million by now. And we can't touch it."

"No. They'd trace us for sure."

"We'll see. Maybe we can figure out a way to get to it in a year or two."

Eightball, morose at being relegated to the great outdoors again, scratched at the windowsill. "We're going to get the dog all stirred up," Collins said. "Better get to bed. You go first and then I'll turn off the light. I can navigate in the dark a little better than you."

"Okay."

Frankly admiring the easy way she walked, the roll of her hips, he watched her pick her way among the sleeping boys. She closed the bedroom door behind her, and Collins, instead of turning off the kitchen light, pulled the door almost shut, leaving a faint illumination. He stopped to check on Johnny, who was breathing regularly and evenly as if asleep. Then he went back to his corner beside the front door, strangely elated by the casual way that Julie Lind had assumed he was in on her plans for the next year or so.

2

Power outage.

One moment Ernest Fisher had been sitting at his desk telephoning security; the next instant the phone was dead and everything was dark. His first thought was that the power had failed, that the emergency generators would kick in immediately.

But the darkness went on and on, and he realized that

he had not had the overhead fluorescent light turned on at all; he had been relying on the daylight—

The windows were rectangles of darkness. Fisher pushed up from his chair, staggered by the sudden gloom. Unreasoning fear prickled the nape of his neck, brought cold sweat to his forehead and palms. Something had blotted out the sun. It might be a summer storm, but if so it was denser than any he had ever seen, an apocalyptic storm, a midnight storm. He went to the window and looked out. The sodium lights, automatically switched on by their sensors, bathed the compound in sulfurous illumination. He looked up. The moon, a gibbous football, was visible low in the eastern part of a sky that looked cloudless, although the glare of the sodium lamps kept him from making out any stars.

Night. It was night.

Fisher flailed at his desk, found the switch to his green-shaded banker's lamp, and turned it on. He looked at his watch: 12:29 A.M.

He had lost more than ten hours.

An intermittent whistling from somewhere far off in the building came to him, faint and unrecognizable. He opened his office door. Mrs. Mead was behind her desk, her eyes shocked and empty. She did not respond when Fisher spoke her name. He went to her and shook her gently, then slapped her. Her eyes focused then, blinking at him in alarm. "What happened?" she asked him.

He shook his head and let go of her arms. Her telephone trilled, and she automatically answered it. "It's for you," she said, holding the phone out to him.

He took the receiver. "Fisher here."

"Champlain, sir, on the main gate. We've had a breach."

"Secure. Code red. Seal everything."

"Yes, sir."

To Mrs. Mead, Fisher said, "Get me Dougherty."

Mrs. Mead was already recovering her composure and her wits. "He's off-base," she reminded him.

Fisher cursed. "I want Lamont, then—"

The phone rang again. This time Mrs. Mead dealt with the caller. When she hung up, she turned to Fisher and said, "That was Angelo from the VCR room. He says the dorm wing is empty."

The door crashed open. Karl Stark stood in the doorway, his chest heaving. "It has happened," he said. "The children have realized their power."

The installation lived in chaos for the next hour. There were deaths: the cook, Mrs. Macbride, horribly burned, an X-ray technician and one of the teachers drowned, apparently having gone into coma while swimming in the pool beside the gym.

Alice Weston woke to grinding pain. Her left leg, folded under her right, was badly broken, her arms bruised. She looked at the contusions with some puzzlement, for she did not recall falling at all; yet the bruises were far advanced, purpling already. Alice rolled to her back, grunting from the knifelike pain, jagged splinters of bone lacerating the muscle tissue inside her upper thigh. There was no blood; it seemed to be a simple fracture.

She scooted backward on her butt until her back was against the hard, cool stairwell wall. She heard an alarm somewhere in the building, and after a minute or two she heard running feet. Only then did she think to look at her watch; the digital Casio told her it was well past midnight.

Like Fisher, Alice had a bad moment of raging confusion, but unlike him she knew the children capable of some astonishing feats. She recalled how they had looked the last time she had seen them, standing in a tight group in the hallway, staring with fixed silver gazes at the television camera. Staring—yes, hypnotically, Alice decided. Some understanding came then.

The stairwell door opened and Clark Williams, one of the medical technicians, nearly stumbled over her. "You okay?" he asked, bringing himself up short.

"I'm hurt," Alice said. "I had a fall. What's happened?"

Clark's eyes and hair were wild. "I don't know. I was labeling some tissue samples and the next thing I knew it was night. They say the kids are gone, all of them. I heard the main gate got blown somehow, dynamite or something. Somebody said the guards were all shot. The subjects ran off or were kidnapped. Anyway, they're loose." Clark had not stepped over her. "Uh, where are you hurt?" he asked.

"My left leg's broken. You can't move me by yourself."

"No. Uh, I'll see if I can get one of the doctors here,

okay? Just be a minute." He stepped over her and pounded up the stairs, his shoes raising sharp echoes.

The kids were away. They were loose. Alice closed her eyes. She had been raised a Catholic, though she had lapsed from the faith many years before. Now her lips moved as she said a short prayer, a prayer for the children, for Julie, and for herself last of all.

Like Julie Lind, Alice had been bothered by the sheer insanity of their plan, if you called what they had done a plan. While half of her mind drove her on to help get the children out of their rooms, the other half coldly and rationally assured her that they would never get away, that they would be stopped between the administration building and the fence. Unlike Julie, Alice had prepared for such a development.

The plastic syringes were in her uniform pockets, ten of them in all. Each one would take care of three people. She pulled one out, uncapped the needle, and without hesitation plunged it into the flesh of her uninjured leg. With her thumb she depressed the plunger, deliberately, slowly, professionally. Her thumb lost its strength before the syringe was empty.

Dr. Beckerman found her still alive, the syringe stuck in her leg, the needle transfixing a small red dot of blood on the white expanse of her uniform slacks. She died before they could move or treat her.

Alice Weston was the last of the initial deaths at the installation that night. There had been injuries, too, most of them minor: bruises from falls, mostly, with some insignificant lacerations and one instance of mild hypothermia, a nurse who had fallen asleep in the bathtub. The injuries were treated as in other ways the installation returned to something resembling normality. The alarms triggered by the opened gate were shut off; the whistling sound Fisher had noticed was a smoke detector in the commissary, triggered by the gases from Mrs. Macbride's charring body. It was silenced and reset. The bodies were taken to the crematorium for immediate disposal.

Reports came in from the various departments, and by three in the morning Fisher had pieced together an approximation of the truth: the installation had indeed suffered a major breach, an escape. He called in Jason Lamont, Dougherty's lean and rangy deputy head of security, and authorized him to initiate a slightly altered omega plan. The first step was to inform a National Guard unit that immediate aid was required and to give them an authorization code that made them jump to the task without question.

At four that morning a helicopter convoy began, ferrying most of the personnel to dispersal points in Georgia and three surrounding states. On Fisher's direct order, Lamont himself shot five people: Drs. Beckerman, O'Connor, and Kornbluth, Mr. Clebb, and Mrs. Mead. Their bodies joined the others in the crematorium fires by five o'clock.

The omega procedure did not go quite by the book, for Fisher personally countermanded two major orders, one that would have sent Stark to a CIA installation on the West Coast and another that would have resulted in the dynamiting of the compound. The omega procedure had been designed to collapse the operation in the event of irreversible penetration by hostiles or of some on-base catastrophe; Fisher adapted it now to cope with the somewhat different problem of escape. By eight the next morning only a skeleton support staff remained, along with twenty-three security personnel, Stark, and Fisher.

Stark was the biggest problem, nearly apoplectic with demands and recriminations. His pink hands fought with themselves, tore paper, drummed without rhythm on tables, plucked at Stark's shirt and tie. "I am borne out," he told Fisher toward sunrise. "I am vindicated. That they were able to do so much only proves their strength."

Fisher glowered at him. "I'd say it proves your incompetence. You never intimated that these kids could—could hypnotize us, do whatever the hell it was they did."

Stark's fingers fluttered like the legs of injured spiders. "It was clearly implied, all of it! A combination of telepathy and mental imaging, I would say. Perhaps a direct assault on the sleep centers of the brain, a mental analogue of anesthesia. Intensive stimulation of natural endorphin production, perhaps, or—but the exact mechanism does not matter. What is important is that the children have unprecedented paranormal abilities, just as I predicted."

Fisher silenced the man by slamming his hand down on

the desk so hard that the lamp rattled. "What is important is that we have to recapture them."

Stark spread his hands, his twitching fingers weaving an imaginary web of darkness and trees. "Children lost in the forest. They cannot have gone far."

"They're not alone. One of the adult personnel is missing. She presumably is with them."

"Even so, where can so many children go? We will find them easily enough."

"Will we be safe when we do?"

Stark's smile fluttered the same way his fingers did, his expression skittering from an attempted superior amusement to something very like panic. "They are nothing more than children, after all."

"Children of hell," Fisher snapped.

Soon after that he ordered Stark out of his office. As the sun rose, Fisher furiously worked the lines of communication between the base and Washington. At eight-thirty that morning he clamped his teeth together, damned himself for what he was about to do, and alerted the local law-enforcement agencies, giving them a false story but setting them on the trail of the seventeen escaped children—he now assumed that Johnny, too, was alive and on the run—and of Julie Lind.

That done, Fisher sat back in his chair, felt a twinge of regret at the necessary death of Mrs. Mead, and cursed as he wondered what in the hell had happened to Charlie Dougherty.

3

The time: 12:28 A.M., Eastern Daylight Savings.

It was eight hours later in Special Psychological Research Unit Number Three.

Dr. Alexandrov was awake but not yet dressed when the attendants came for him in alarm and agitation. He hurried along with them, found Subject 331 exhibiting alarming symptoms she had never shown before. They had restrained her by the time Alexandrov arrived, had strapped her to a cot. She tore her skin straining against the straps, screamed aloud, spat something red past his ear. She had bitten off the tip of her tongue.

Alexandrov ordered a sedative. It seemed to have no effect. The woman screamed, piercing shrieks that made the male nurses wince, that lanced into Alexandrov's ears like angels of headache. "She's speaking English," one of the nurses said.

"Nonsense. She doesn't know English," Alexandrov returned. In truth he could make nothing of the sounds, not in English or in Russian, but as a precaution he ordered the subject's throes recorded.

"The lights!" she screeched in Russian. "Oh, God, oh God," she added in English.

Alexandrov ordered a second sedative. As the nurse was administering it, an aide opened the door to tell the doctor that the other subjects, too, all four hundred–odd of them, were apparently going mad.

"It hurts!" screamed the woman on the cot. Her eyes grew very wide. She gave one last inarticulate cry, higher and more piercing than the others, and blood ran from the corners of both eyes, gushed from her bitten tongue. She strained, bowing her body into an arch, and then collapsed. She was dead. It had been fifty minutes since the onset of her symptoms.

Dr. Alexandrov was attempting resuscitation when more bad news came. Subjects were dying all around him; possibly as many as a hundred were in seizures, and the other doctors were fully occupied with their own troubles.

Finally the doctor gave up. He was shaking with excess adrenaline, trembling from a combination of fear and frustration. He left the dead woman, checked with his colleagues, began to appreciate the full enormity of the phenomenon. Eight-two subjects had gone into convulsion at approximately the same moment, and all save one had died. Others, similarly stricken with seizures, had gone into coma or were catatonic; it seemed that a fourth of the subject population of the unit—almost a twelfth of the psi-positive study population of the Soviet Union—had either died or had suffered some inexplicable mental trauma. By noon the doctors at the unit agreed that the catastrophe had destroyed all of the most promising telepaths.

Kovach should know about this disaster, Alexandrov thought. Someone should tell Kovach immediately.

He could not do it himself. Kovach was gone, had taken his leave the previous week. Where he had gone Alexandrov did not know; it was none of his business.

Though at their parting the KGB man had, with rough humor, asked him if he wanted any American jazz tapes.

No one, not the doctors, not the surviving subjects, had the least inkling of what had happened. Had the telepaths been able to speak coherently, they would have told of the touch of minds, already much stronger than their own, of the sudden inrush of sense impressions far too powerful for frail human nervous systems, of an overspill of emotions: fear, excitement, wonder, even pity. For as they died one by one, the Russian subjects felt a real pity washing over them, a sense of great but impotant sorrow.

Across the ocean the children's minds were growing steadily, were opening to a startling awareness, were experiencing the pain and terror of people dying naturally, or unnaturally, all over the globe. It was too much to handle, and the children rechanneled the feelings any way they could. The Russians, not powerful enough to send but unfortunately on the correct mental wavelength to receive, were caught in the psychic explosion, run over as small animals are struck and killed on midnight highways, not out of malice but by misfortune. The animals were killed by a random coincidence of hurrying wheels and a need to cross the man-poured pavement; the Russians by a chance arrangement of genes.

But none of the doctors knew this, though Alexandrov perhaps came closest. His thought was of American countermeasures, of some Star Wars gimmick of the mind.

4

The time: 12:41 A.M. in Washington, D.C.

Randall Grade's wife answered the telephone, sleepily passed it to her husband. He listened for three minutes before saying, "Got it. You'll have our thanks when it's convenient." He reached over his wife to replace the receiver and got out of bed.

"What is it?" Mrs. Grade muttered in an irritated whisper.

"Work, darling. I'll be back as soon as possible."

He used the bathroom extension to call his driver. He showered and dressed in near-record time, and at one minute past one he left the townhouse by the rear door. The limo was waiting already. Grade paused to look up: the sky showed no stars, and the moon was only a dim thumbprint behind clouds that threatened rain. The very air felt heavy with it. He got into the car and said, "Headquarters, Al."

There was some Beltway traffic, not much, at that hour on a Saturday morning. They made the drive in a little under half an hour. Grade had a quick conference with the duty officer, made some arrangements, and had the canteen prepare coffee. He made three telephone calls personally when groggy and outraged officials insisted on hearing from Grade and Grade alone. He persuaded everyone to come at once.

It took the others somewhat longer to get to headquarters than it had taken Grade, for some of them had farther to go. But they were there by three o'clock: four men who among them represented the CIA, the FBI, the NSA, and military intelligence. Grade saw them in the Secure Room, a conference area buried in the center of the building, enclosed by a network of antielectronics devices. Although all of them clearly resented the early-morning call, not a single one of them voiced objections. Grade was known to wield considerable power.

When they were all quiet, when they all had accepted or refused coffee, Grade leaned his elbows on the conference table. "Gentlemen," he said. "I think you should know about an off-the-shelf operation down in Georgia. It's been going on for some time now. Maybe too long."

The CIA man was the first to break the ensuing silence: "Fisher's outfit, you mean. We know about that, Randy. You were the one who set it up, if I recall correctly."

"Please let me correct your recollection," Grade said, smiling. "I set up a unit. I did not set up a cowboy operation. That's what this thing has become. I'm extremely concerned about it, very concerned."

The NSA representative, the only one who had refused coffee—he was a Mormon—said, "I hope you've got something to be concerned about."

"I do indeed. Gentlemen, I have a source on site, a very reliable source. I heard from that person tonight; it was a risky communication on his part. The news seems very bad.

"Gentlemen, Ernest Fisher is killing people."

5

The time: 12:28 A.M. in Atlanta.

Charles Doughterty's first impression was *explosion!*

force pushing him away from the falling Beth Engstrom. His first confused thought was that she had concealed a grenade on her, that she had set it off.

He struck the wall, his head bouncing off, and fell to his butt. The lights in the hotel room seemed dim, nearly orange, and Dougherty at first attributed that to the smoke.

But no grenade had exploded. He saw the body of Beth Engstrom, beyond it that of Frederick Engstrom; neither had been torn by a blast. His Walther lay before him. The silencer had separated from the barrel. Dougherty got to his feet and shook his head, trying to clear it; it felt as though someone else were in there with him. He retrieved the automatic. The silencer was hot. He wrapped his handkerchief around it, dropped it into his side jacket pocket. He holstered the Walther, wiped down the surfaces he had touched, shielded his hand with the scorched handkerchief to open the door. After a quick check of the hallway outside—deserted—Dougherty backed out of the hotel room, pulling the door shut with the toe of his left foot. The heavy door clacked shut, the latch engaging.

His head pounding, blood throbbing in his ears at every heartbeat, Dougherty felt sick. It was not the killing; he had killed before, yes, had even killed women before. He did not agree with Fisher in this case, did not think the executions well advised, but he owed the man his loyalty and he had carried out the assignment to the best of his considerable ability. Dougherty's conscience was not pricking him.

Rather he felt physically ill, as he had felt once when suffering from a badly infected wound. He had been doped up then, shot full of antibiotics and pain relievers. The drugs had produced the same curious detached feeling he had now, a numbness of spirit or of mind, not of body. A giddy, light-headed sense that he was somehow disconnected, out of it, in only minimal control of his body. Something, energy, vitality, or something even more subtle, seemed to be draining from him.

Dougherty tugged his jacket, shoved the handkerchief in his pocket with the still-warm silencer, adjusted his tie. He walked quickly down the hall, the carpet muffling his footfalls. He stopped at the elevator.

He stared at the buttons with growing horror.

He did not know what they were.

Dougherty began to shake. He recognized the call buttons geometrically: two circles, one above the other. He recognized their color: translucent white. But he could not think of what they were for, what they did, or how to use them. He glared at them, then jerked his gaze up to the top of the door. A brass plaque showed twenty-two different numbers, 1 through 23, omitting 13. One of them was lighted.

He did not know the significance of the light, or what any of the numbers meant: they could as well have been Egyptian hieroglyphics. As he watched, the lighted figure blinked out and an adjoining one blinked on.

Dougherty could not understand.

He perceived movement; he lost its significance.

Knowledge had left him somehow; it was as if parts of his awareness had literally been erased, like a magnetic tape held too close to a powerful magnet.

The elevators were in a recess off the main hallway. Sweating heavily, Dougherty stepped back into the hall, saw at each far end a red EXIT sign.

He could not read the word, nor could he grasp what it meant. He had a vague impression of danger, of fire, of fleeing, that frightened him. He knew he would not be able to approach those terrifying red letters. He retreated to the elevator bank.

A bell sounded and one of the four elevators opened. Two young people got out of a packed car. One of them called back, "See you on sixteen."

Dougherty heard the words and understood them—he was not deaf or mute—but he could not comprehend the sounds that made up the word "sixteen." The word was gibberish to him, as opaque as abracadabra. He pushed onto the elevator, the others making way for him. Once inside he stared helplessly at the bank of buttons, knowing they were important but not knowing what to do with them. The car began to rise, almost making him lose his footing. The other passengers, obviously thinking him drunk, crowded a little closer together, moving away from him as much as the confines of the car would allow. Paralyzed by his unaccustomed ignorance, Dougherty stood while the elevator eased up, floor by floor; each time it paused for someone to get on or off, Dougherty looked out the door hopefully, but every time he saw only the same hallway, or one that was apparently the same.

At last the car stopped at a floor that most of the elevator riders wanted. They washed out of the car in a chattering flood, carrying Dougherty with them. He stumbled down the hall, into a room. He had the sick certainty that there would be two bodies there, that he had not really moved to another floor at all, but he was wrong. A party was in progress instead; the room was even more crowded than the elevator had been, people jammed tight, drinking, eating crackers, cheese, and peanuts off paper plates, talking. Music played on a stereo, and the air was warm and damp.

Dougherty stood in miserable confusion. People bumped around him, forcing him to shuffle this way or that. A tall young man came up to him and put a drink in his hand. "Try this," he said.

Dougherty looked at the plastic glass, half full of a cloudy pink liquid. "What is it?"

"It's our special punch. Just try it and tell me what you think."

A woman carrying an empty silver tray joined them, a dark-haired young woman with pretty eyes. "We're going to need some more snacks," she said.

Dougherty stared at them both. Each of them wore a lapel tag; the young man's read CHARLES, the young woman's AMY. Dougherty could read neither, but the young man's somehow was terribly familiar, its lack of meaning as keen as a razor cut. "What is this?" Dougherty asked again.

The young man and woman exchanged a concerned look. The young man said, "This is the cooler party. Excuse me, are you with the convention?"

Dougherty shook his head. "I have to leave," he said. He turned away, forced his way past the crowd, spilling the drink, dropping it at last to the maroon carpet. He clawed at people; they gave way. He burst free into the hallway, looked at the mocking EXIT sign, closer now than it had been on the other floor, reeled back toward the elevators. A knot of people waited there. A few of them gave him nervous looks.

The elevator doors finally opened. Dougherty pushed ahead of the others, drawing a curse or two. He got to the rear of the car, stood against it, shaking.

He rode the car for nearly half an hour before it finally stopped on the lobby level. Sobbing with relief when he saw the desk instead of another identical hallway, Dougherty came out, staggered to the door.

The doorman, a slim black man, said, "Taxi, sir?"

"I want my car," Dougherty said. His tongue felt wrong, thick and clumsy in his mouth. He thought he would gag on it.

"The concierge will call for it, sir."

Dougherty stared at him.

"The concierge. She's in the lobby, sir. You'll see the sign."

But when he went back into the lobby he could see no sign that he could read. He almost wept, trying to remember if shape or color had more significance in reading. He remembered the word "alphabet," but he could not have spoken its meaning. The doorman had said "she," and at last Dougherty spotted a woman under a hieroglyphic on a brass plate. He went to her. "I want my car," he told her.

She was chipper for this hour of the night, a slender woman with neat gray hair. "Yes, sir. Do you have your ticket?"

Dougherty remembered his wallet. He took it from his pocket and opened it. It was thick, with nearly a dozen compartments for cards. None of them made sense to him. "What—what does it look like?" he asked.

"It's a green ticket, sir. That's it next to your MasterCard."

He thrust the wallet toward her. "Take it," he said.

She looked at him with concern. "Sir, are you sure you want to drive?"

"I want my car!"

The woman slipped the ticket out of the wallet and made a telephone call. "It will be at the front in a minute, sir," she said.

Dougherty thrust the wallet back into his pocket. He went back to the door, shivering. The car pulled up, a young man at the wheel; it stopped at the hotel entrance, and the parking valet got out. Dougherty clambered behind the wheel, accelerated so that the rear tires squealed, and shut the door as he tore away from the Hartmann Plaza.

He had made the first moves automatically, putting the car in drive and stepping on the gas. But before he had gone a block he realized that he no longer knew how to control the Jetta. He veered from lane to lane of Spring Street, running traffic lights, gaining speed. With growing desperation he twisted the steering wheel, trying just to keep the car in the street, trying to remember how to slow, how to stop.

Post-midnight traffic was light in the downtown area, and that saved him for a while. He crossed an overpass and somehow turned onto the exit ramp of I-75. By then he was traveling at seventy miles per hour. He raced north into the southbound lanes, still picking up speed, and did not meet an automobile for the first several hundred yards.

He was traveling at ninety-seven miles per hour when the 1984 Grenada loomed before him, its lights blinding, its horn screaming. The cars met, the Granada's right headlight connecting solidly with the right headlight of the Jetta. The combined speed of impact was very nearly 170 miles per hour.

The crash was like something in slow motion. Dougherty saw the hood crumpling toward him, felt the impact of the steering wheel against his chest, the centrifugal tug as the car spun wildly and went airborne. The driver's door dropped open and Dougherty fell from the Jetta as it passed over the center barrier. The car smashed into a panel truck, sending it slewing madly across the expressway. Dougherty was conscious of none of this as he fell himself, landing heavily on the concrete in the leftmost lane, breaking both of his arms, his back, his pelvis as he cartwheeled at over a hundred miles an hour.

The explosion of pain was beyond anything he could have known, anything he could have predicted. It left no room for anything else. As his awareness of letters and numbers had deserted him, so now did all knowledge leave him, his own identity, the meaning of where he was and of what was happening. Pain remained, the pain of the damned. It filled his head, his body, with squirming fire. He knew only pain and a screaming voice inside his skull: *bad man bad man bad bad man!* It was the voice of a child.

But though knowledge had fled, consciousness did not leave him; the child in his head would not let him slide into the blessed oblivion he craved. He was fully aware of the Nissan that spun out of control toward him, its driver frantically and vainly trying to avoid the bleeding thing in the highway. He heard the wheels pass over his legs, felt the muscle tear and burst through the skin like the pulp of an overripe fig, felt his exposed nerves being ground into the concrete. He heard the scream of brakes as the next car, a Volvo, angled toward him and rode over his chest, spiking his broken ribs through his shirt.

He knew when the next car hit him, and the next. Something implacable, some force outside himself, held the spark of life in his skull, made his brain aware even when he gibbered for death.

It was the child. The enraged child guaranteed that he knew every impact, that he felt every rip of flesh from bone, every sundering of artery and nerve. He had lost time along with knowledge, and to him the pain was eternal, an endless procession of agonies. His brain was forced to live even though his heart had long since ceased to pump, even though his shattered and punctured lungs drew in no air.

But at last a car brought mercy.

It was a mustard-yellow '73 Mustang driven by two

young men out for whatever excitement they could find. By now, 1:18 A.M., the expressway to the south of what was left of Dougherty was a mangle of ruined automobiles. The boys in the Mustang saw the wreck, not him, and jerked the car into a slewing sideways skid. The maneuver was a desperate one, but it accomplished the boys' goal: they slid to a stop less than a foot behind an Oldsmobile station wagon smashed against the median divider. Until they climbed out to see the carnage they were unaware that the car had also released Dougherty from his prison of pain.

Dougherty's blood had slimed twenty yards of the freeway. His left arm had been completely severed from his body and lay against the median divider, a dark parenthesis against the white concrete. Both of his legs were flattened grotesquely, the ripped fabric of his trousers inextricable from the purée of his flesh, bone, and blood.

His torso was almost unrecognizable as human.

His head, or what remained of it, was still beneath the Mustang's left rear Goodyear Eagle GT.

Once they noticed the body, the Mustang driver and his friend thought Dougherty the baddest thing they had *ever* seen.

They couldn't wait to tell their girls what they had missed.

6

In the black sky above Atlanta, Colonel Feodor Kovach tried unsuccessfully to snatch a few minutes of sleep. He had come to this place by a circuitous route, an odyssey that had seen him leave Moscow for Japan; he had come to the island country as an official concerned with the importation of computer hardware and software into the Soviet Union. He had spent only a few hours in Tokyo, and he had negotiated no importations. Somewhere between Tokyo and Vancouver he had become a Polish trades union representative en route to a conference to be held by the shores of the Pacific.

He did not attend the conference, nor did he remain a union representative for very long. By the time he arrived in California, Kovach was a naturalized Canadian citizen, equipped with enough convincing background to persuade any but the most cynical that he had indeed lived in Canada for nearly twenty-five years, that he owned a chain of small bicycle shops in the western provinces.

Kovach vanished from sight for two days in California, spending a great deal of the time being briefed by a group of men and women who had become all but indistinguishable from Americans, though none of them was in fact American in anything except appearance and accent. They gave him massive quantities of information, but not enough to satisfy him. Kovach felt a surge of frustration when he realized the volume of data his people lacked. Much of it was publicly available, for the United States was still a more open society than the Soviet Union, *pace* Comrade Gorbachev's *glasnost* movement of a few years back. But a considerable portion, maybe a majority, of the material was fairly sensitive; if the KGB operated through consulates and embassies it would have been easier for Kovach, but they had broken away from the diplomatic establishment some time before. He had to make do.

From California Kovach traveled to the environs of Washington, where he held further consultations. Good people worked there, some of the best. They had used the Americans' own technology to sift through a rat's nest of tangled data, intercepted exchanges, decoded communications. One by one the analysts considered and rejected possible sites, until at last there was only one possibility: Georgia.

Kovach found some small irony in that. His own wife was from Georgia, though of course not the same one. She came from the Georgian SSR. Kovach, whose English was excellent, smiled a little at the thought of Tonia's being a—what did they call them?—a Southern belle. Like in the film *Gone With the Wind*. Was that set in the American Georgia? Kovach believed it was; it was one of his favorite American films, showing as it did the plutocratic selfishness of the ruling American classes, the servile misery of the dark races. In addition, he had been very smitten with Vivien Leigh in his youth, much as his own son was besotted with American jazz. Rock and roll. Whatever they called it now; it was all noise to Kovach.

Eyes closed, he tried to consider the mission ahead of him. It was murky at best: more of a perfunctory effort to reconnoiter than anything else. Ordinarily it would have been handled by a field agent, certainly not by someone of colonel's rank. But it was a special kind of problem, and his masters had determined that Kovach's unique qualifications, his familiarity with the inmates at the Special Psychological Research Unit, were called for. His primary goal was merely to set into motion an investigation of this mysterious compound buried deep in the forests of the American South, to determine what it held and how much of a threat it might represent to Soviet interests.

His secondary goal was to determine if one of the workers at the American installation was a Soviet traitor, a man who carried important state secrets in his head and who had defected years before. So much was suspected now, but not known certainly. Kovach had committed the man's appearance to memory; if he saw the burly blond-headed fellow, he would recognize him instantly. He had special orders about the steps that must be taken in the event that he actually did spot the traitor.

It all buzzed around and around in Kovach's head, keeping him wakeful even though for the past several days he had gotten far less sleep than he was used to. At last he sighed and gave up trying to sleep. He was due in Atlanta in—he looked at his watch—half an hour's time, at 1:25 A.M. An ungodly hour, but those were the best arrangements the people in Washington could make for him this close to the national patriotic holiday of the Americans. His contact would—

The plane lurched into a sickening sideways slip. Kovach clutched involuntarily at the armrests, closing his left hand tightly over the right hand of the woman beside him. Someone screamed. The entire aircraft shuddered, and there was another stomach-dropping sideways plunge.

Kovach's ears popped painfully as the plane lost altitude. By then the screams aboard were universal. He heard above the din the *ping!* of rivets started from their places by the wrenching strain, and a moment later the overhead compartments above him fell open, a cascade of carry-on baggage, blankets, pillows, spilling out. Kovach, his mouth locked in a grin of terror, saw everything fall away from him. The plane was standing on its port wing, sideways in the air. Through the opposite windows Kovach saw lights flash by, and he realized he was seeing the ground rush up to meet them.

The engines screamed and invisible hands shoved Kovach against the pull of gravity. He closed his eyes, felt stinging sweat in them, and gasped, his chest constricted by the grip of g-forces. Beside him the woman was saying, "Please God please oh please," over and over.

Again the plane shook, as if it were rumbling over a tilled field at hundreds of miles an hour. Gradually the scream of the engines faded to a more normal register. Kovach, alone in the darkness behind his closed eyelids, heard weeping, men and women alike.

A voice, the pilot's drawling voice, cut in above the uproar: "Ladies and gentlemen, we hit a little pocket of turbulence back there. I apologize if we shook you up a mite. We are cleared for landing and will be on the ground in Atlanta in about ten minutes. Thank you."

Kovach, his chest heaving for breath, dared to open his eyes. He felt the woman beside him clutch his hand, give it a squeeze. He looked at her in surprise.

"I guess he heard me praying," she said with an embarrassed little laugh.

Kovach nodded. "I guess so," he said.

"Thanks for holding my hand."

For a moment Kovach thought he was going to have to use his right hand to loosen the fingers of his left, but they somehow obeyed his will and let go. "I needed someone's hand to hold my own," he said, smiling. A moment later the woman laughed. "Why are you amused?" Kovach asked quizzically.

"Just glad to be alive."

From a seat on the middle aisle a man glanced over at them, a tall, gangly man who reminded Kovach a little of Gary Cooper. But the man's voice had none of the cowboy twang in it. His words came out professorial, precise, with a new England intonation: "Turbulence indeed. That was wind shear, my friends. We're all lucky to be alive."

"Well," the woman said, "thank God or thank luck or whatever." The professorial man nodded thoughtfully and turned to comfort a trembling woman next to him.

Kovach's partner drew a deep breath. "I still believe it was God," she confided in a whisper.

Kovach studied her. He had sat beside this woman ever since they had left the ground in Washington, but the two had not exchanged a word, and he had barely given her a glance. Now he saw a strong-looking woman of forty or so, stoutly built. Like many foolish American women, she would consider herself fat, Kovach supposed. He himself found her desirable. She reminded him a little of the women in the Ukraine. He sighed. "I don't know whether it was God or good fortune or perhaps the skill of the pilot, but I too am glad to be alive," he said.

"I guess after an experience like that we ought to get to know each other. My name's Lois Pachemko," she said, offering her hand.

Startled a little—it was always difficult for him to readjust to American customs, and they tended to change radically between his visits—Kovach clasped it briefly, more lightly this time. "Thomas Skavinski," he said.

"Are you Polish?" the woman asked.

"My family is," Kovach said. "I'm from Vancouver myself."

"Well, what a coincidence," Lois Pachemko said. "My great-grandfather was from Poland."

"Really?"

"Came over from the old country in 1900 and settled in Allentown, P.A. That's where I'm from, by the way, Well, two Polacks together, huh? Maybe we ought to have a drink when we land, just to celebrate."

Kovach nodded, but already he felt his enthusiasm for the woman, his attraction to her, fading. He did not think that Lois Pachemko was very likely to be an American agent—they normally did not recruit her type—but there was that possibility as well. For a moment Kovach glanced around at the commotion aboard the airliner. The flight attendants had hurried through the aisles, picking up, soothing, calming. Though a few passengers still wept aloud, no one seemed to be seriously hurt. "That might be nice," he said in a neutral and absent voice.

But the Pachemko woman was withdrawing in the same way. They talked a little more; then there was the bounce and squeal of tires kissing tarmac, and they retreated into silence as the plane taxied to their gate. By the time they disembarked, the accident was in the past, and they went their separate ways. They never saw each other again.

7

Every child in the cabin gasped with release at the moment the skidding Mustang erased Charles Dougherty's earthly consciousness forever.

Johnny Gamma hissed as he felt the bad man escape him at last. He wept a little more, feeling a dull ache in his throat, the heavy weight of his heart sore in his breast. He wished that the bad man had not died so easily, so quickly; his mother had slipped away into darkness with terrifying rapidity, but the bad man had simply ceased, all at once.

With his mind Johnny reached out for his mother and could not find her. Loneliness crushed him, weighed on him with pressure almost too great for him to bear. She had never been lost to him before, not ever, not for as long as he could remember; though he could not speak to his mother in his mind, he could always touch her, gain from her at least a feeling, a sense of being comforted. But she had fallen far down that dark tunnel, too far for his mind to find her, and he had punished the man—

There were whimpers around the darkened room. The others were relaxing from a pitch of concentration they had never known before. the sixteen of them had divided the incredible pain the man had broadcast, had shielded Johnny from it, had rechanneled it elsewhere, pouring it into every receptive mind they could touch without knowing what it would do there. The children groaned or sighed with relief now, and the sounds brought a new and different kind of comfort to Johnny.

Hearing them, he realized that after all he was not alone.

From the time of the escape, Johnny had been so tense, so overwrought, that he had not immersed himself in the minds around him. He did so now, sliding into a shared pool of consciousness, of dreams from the sleeping ones, of fear and concern from those lying wakeful.

And he found there a great relief, a feeling of deep and abiding joy.

The children were more than the grotesque sum of their deformities, more than the special talents of their minds. They were power, raw and strong, and that power, Johnny slowly realized, was the force that had allowed him to punish the bad man, to thrust himself into the other's mind, to keep the awareness going long after the body had died. That strength had held safe above the pain he otherwise would have suffered while he made his vengeance complete. The minds in the dark room, and those with Teacher in the room beyond the door, fairly hummed with energy, stronger even than the hateful sun, stronger by far than the lightning that had terrified him in the woods the night before he had arrived here.

Unlike Kathy Beta, Johnny had no need to touch the others to feel their energies, to share their strength. He relaxed into them now, losing himself, diffusing his grief. They took its burden from him, and little by little Johnny felt his pain ease. Slowly the others relaxed into him as well, their awarenesses flowing his way, forming patterns, like iron filings frozen into position to trace the lines of force around a magnet. Some of them were resistant, remote—the Delta twins were almost as far away among their numbers as the place that Johnny's mother had gone—but even Anthony and Andrew came at last into the nonspace the others occupied, and even they contributed what they could.

For his part, Johnny returned to them as much as he received from them, and perhaps even more. Johnny fired them with greater awareness than any of them had ever had alone. He excited them, raised them: Freddy Kappa, the best reader in the group, was immensely eager to try the computer-thing, instantaneously picking up from Johnny's mind and memory all he needed to know to operate it, just from Johnny's having observed Collins in past days. Christie Epsilon, whose recollection of Dr. Clebb's lessons was the strongest, felt deep gratification that at last they had learned to deal with one of the *bad men* Dr. Clebb had always talked about; she urged more of the same, feeling an imperative compulsion to remove as much badness from the world as they could, to send it spiraling down that endless, bottomless black tunnel.

Even Daisy Rho added her mite, her ability to see what was happening in far places. Through her, Johnny and the others learned about the unit, about the blood-shed there; they wept at Nurse Alice's passing and cowered at Stark's iron determination to bring them back.

The experience amounted to a communion, a town meeting of the mind, with seventeen individuals sharing so completely that they became in effect one consciousness. Together they did what separately none of them could really do, at least not in a conventional sense: they reasoned.

Collectively they began to seek ways of remaining safe, remaining beyond notice. Though one by one they began to assent to the necessity of dealing with the *bad men*, they were in considerable disagreement about which men were truly bad. They all could agree, however, on some things, and chief among them was their determination never to return to the installation, never to be fenced, guarded, imprisoned again. But they needed means, ways to ensure that their newly gained freedom would not be lost. They had managed the escape largely on intuition and on the Deltas' fortuitous disruption of the laws of chance. Now they had a thinker, and he would be able to use the tool in a more deliberate, more effective way. The Deltas gave their vision to him, and he grasped it all at once. Johnny, comprehending completely the significance of the Delta brothers' numerical concept, began to explore ways of using it to insulate themselves from those who would stop their growth.

For they were growing; he sensed it. He still would have been unable to express the change in anything like comprehensible English, but Johnny knew, felt, the change, the growth that was occurring. To him the growth was something that was correct, that was necessary, no more to be questioned than the burgeoning of leaves in spring, as blind and powerful a force as roots splitting granite.

Johnny was not alone; not many people would have been able to understand the nature of that growth, and few would even attempt to describe it in language. Dr. Stark or the late Dr. O'Connor might have expressed it this way: at 8:00 A.M. on July 2, the children of the biomed unit had measurable IQs ranging from a low of 60 to a high of 100. By 4:00 A.M. on July 3, the average

for the group, had it been tested, would have been somewhere around 130.

An IQ of 100 is normal.

An IQ of 120 is superior.

No individual had ever shown a doubling of IQ in a
span of twenty hours. Such a thing was impossible in any
normal sense.

But of course the children were by no definition normal.

Under Johnny's prodding, under his guidance, they
were beginning to resonate, to lift themselves from ignorance by pooling their objective knowledge, their emotional apperception, their intuitions. The speed of their
change was increasing, as a falling body accelerates as it
approaches the earth.

But unlike a plummeting stone, their mental accelera-
tion had no terminal velocity. Already they stood on the
threshold of genius.

Before them, beckoning, lay an infinity of mind.

CHAPTER EIGHT

1

By dawn on Saturday, William Whitepath had made almost all the necessary preparations. His van was packed with the few belongings he intended to take and with groceries enough to tide the mob over for one or two days of flat-out travel; his savings—$5,850 in the form of fifties and hundreds—was in his pockets and in his luggage. He had no one to say goodbye to.

And yet he lingered for a few minutes in the house he had rented for more than twenty years. He saw it with new eyes as he prepared to leave: a six-room white frame cottage, its paint dingy, its furniture succumbing to age and neglect, a clutter of newspapers, dirty clothes, and unwashed dishes littering the three rooms he habitually used. To his surprise, Whitepath felt something like relief at the prospect of walking away from it all, taking nothing with him except one large suitcase full of clothes and a few souvenirs. There was nothing here to bid farewell to, nothing except the memory of Lorene and the two boys, and even that had weakened over time. Among the personal mementoes Whitepath had packed was a family portrait taken seven years ago at Christmas time: the only photograph he had of them all together. Removed from its frame and put into a heavy cardboard-reinforced envelope to save space, it was packed in the same suitcase as four thousand dollars of his savings.

He left the house for the last time, squinting up at an overcast sky; thundershowers by afternoon, he opined. He locked the door behind him and considered what to do with the key. At last he did nothing with it; you never could tell. As Whitepath turned the van, he noticed for the first time a tan Chevrolet Caprice parked across the way, down at the Sewells' house. Whitepath immediately recognized it as the county's only unmarked patrol car, and sitting behind the wheel was Sheriff Jim Burette, a heavy, graying man.

Burette was aware of Whitepath's scrutiny. The Chevy rolled forward, coming to a halt at the head of the drive, diagonally behind the van. Whitepath walked to the car, a smile on his face. "Howdy, Jim," he said, stooping to lean his crossed elbows on the open window. "What's up?"

"Going someplace today, Will?" Burette returned in his phlegmy voice.

Whitepath leaned a little closer to peer into the Chevy. A deputy well known for his casually violent manner with suspects, a muscular young fellow named Tank Kunkle, shared the front seat with Burette. The man looked edgy. Whitepath said, "Oh, thought I might run over to Cleveland to the hardware store. Need a few things."

"Kinda early, ain't it?"

"Thought I'd get some breakfast, too. Maybe stop at the Hardee's in Cleveland for a sausage biscuit. What are you boys doing out so early on a Saturday?"

Kunkle said with sudden hostility, "Lookin' for some lost kids, Whitepath. You—"

"Hush, Tank," Burette said easily. "Fact of the matter is, Will, there's a batch of younguns loose around here somewhere. Hear tell they're all disabled, retarded. Plumb shame if something bad was to happen to little kids in that shape."

"Yeah," Whitepath agreed.

"Fact is, Will, me and Tank kinda figured that you'd want to volunteer to help us find these missing younguns."

Whitepath kept his voice sober. "I see."

Burette's smile was wide but insincere. "You knowing the woods around here so well and all."

Whitepath nodded as if such a request came every day. "Well, I guess I can go to the hardware store anytime, huh? We gonna look in the woods, then? Where do we start?"

"We kinda thought you'd be the guide, like," Burette said.

"Okay. Look, if we're gonna go in the woods, I gotta

change shoes, get my hiking boots on. Won't be a minute." Whitepath turned toward the house.

"Tank'll go with you," Burette said behind him, and Whitepath heard the patrol car door open.

Without turning, he said, "That's okay, won't take but a second." He had his keys out as if to unlock the door, but before he reached it, Whitepath cut to the left and dodged around the corner of the house, setting off for the woods behind the house as fast as he could run.

Behind him Kunkle yelled, but Whitepath was already through the backyard and into the pine woods. He dodged and leaped deadfalls, running downhill, skirting blackberry tangles, ducking low branches. He had made perhaps thirty yards when he heard Kunkle blundering far behind.

Whitepath wasn't running blind; he had a goal. It was a mossy oak tree, out of place in that softwood forest, with a trunk easily ten feet thick at the base. He reached the tree, ducked behind it, and stopped, his back against the trunk. He had run almost silently, but behind him Kunkle made as much noise as a drunken cow. The clamor lessened, and Whitepath knew that Kunkle had stumbled onto the path that he himself had followed; the worn foot trail curved close past the oak and on downhill to the banks of Panther Creek.

But even on the path, Kunkle still made enough noise to let Whitepath prepare. The deputy trotted around the tree, his drawn pistol in his right hand, his left hand raised to shield his eyes from lashing twigs. The raised hand was a mistake; Whitepath was on that side of Kunkle.

Whitepath tripped Kunkle, sent him sprawling on a slippery bed of pine needles with both hands thrown out to break his fall. Before Kunkle could roll over, Whitepath was on his back. He grasped the lawman's wrist and struck it hard against a pine trunk, twice, three times. Kunkle lost his hold on the revolver, and the weapon tumbled into the undergrowth. The deputy tried to buck Whitepath off.

It didn't work. Whitepath grabbed a handful of Kunkle's hair and used it to raise Kunkle's head and pound it down against the ground. The deputy yelled, his voice muffled by dirt and pine needles. Whitepath hit him on the nape of the neck twice, decided he wasn't accomplishing anything, and jumped off the man. Kunkle tried to roll to his feet, but Whitepath kicked him first, hard, in the solar plexus. Whitepath's ankle popped with the force of the blow; it lifted Kunkle clear off the ground and sent him tumbling against the oak. The deputy lost his breath and any immediate interest in following Whitepath. Will snatched up the fallen revolver and hurled it downhill. A moment later he heard it splash into the unseen waters of Panther Creek.

Whitepath left him then, following the path down to the creek, loping along the creek bed to the south, heading for the place where the water flowed under a culvert near Holcomb's Crossing. It was seven miles from that point to Peter Collins's cabin. As he ran through the forest in his unsuitable dock shoes, Whitepath wondered if he would be able to get that far and whether he could possibly warn Collins before they caught him.

2

Feodor Kovach appreciated a few things about the American way of life, and one of them was the abundance of hotels. It had been no trouble to find a place at short notice (using a Visa card maintained by the Vancouver people for just such occasions), and he had managed a few welcome hours of sleep before the Saturday-morning meeting.

There were three men with him now, one from Washington, one from the consulate in Atlanta, and another man, a floating agent who had wide experience of the whole American scene. They met over coffee in Kovach's hotel room—he had chosen a place near the airport, not in the more dangerous downtown section, since he had a good socialist understanding of the way the capitalist system bred crime in the decaying hearts of American cities. It was a pleasant room with a balcony looking toward the towers of downtown Atlanta some miles distant. The television set in the room received an astonishing twenty-nine channels—all bourgeois trash, of course, there was seldom anything *kulturny* on American television. But Kovach found other uses for the media; for one thing, a blaring TV or radio could make an excellent anti-eavesdropping measure. While he talked with his four guests, Kovach tuned the TV to CNN and kept the volume turned reasonably high.

Their topic of discussion was Slow Tango, a program of some years' standing in the American espionage system; but information about it was depressingly scant. "It has been very secure, very—as the Americans are fond of saying—low-profile. We do not know what goes on at the forest installation," the floater told Kovach. "If we had more time—"

"But we have not," Kovach said.

The floater, a harried-looking thin man, quite bald, made a tutting sound. "It is most unusual. As I say, the Americans have been very secretive about this, unusually so. It is secured at the level they call Ultra, one of the grades above Top Secret. Our information experts have turned up very little about it; it seems to have nothing to do with their space-offensive research, with biological warfare, with—"

"I know all that," Kovach said. With quiet emphasis, he added, "I don't wish to know what it does not do; I wish to know what it does do."

"But we have—"

The man from the Atlanta consulate said, "I know him."

Kovach, sitting on the foot of one of the room's twin beds, looked around. The consular assistant, on the foot of the other bed, was pointing at the huge color TV set. A rather blurry photograph of a heavy-featured, graying man filled the screen while a woman's voice said, ". . . killed early this morning in the spectacular accident on the downtown connector. The driver's license from which this photograph was taken proved to be a false one, and police are currently seeking the identity of this man."

The consular assistant, a youngish fellow well below the usual age of Soviet foreign service employees, looked at Kovach. "He is an American agent who once worked abroad," he explained. "His name is Dougherty. I have forwarded reports on his movements before. He passes through the city quite regularly."

By now the news show had gone on to another story. The floater, his expression worried behind the thick lenses of his spectacles, said, "That name did come up in our investigation of Slow Tango. Charles Dougherty."

Kovach took a long sip of sweetened black coffee. "So. We are not totally uninformed after all," he said in a calm and reasonable tone.

The other three, hearing that intonation, exchanged uneasy looks, knowing that now they were really in trouble.

3

"I still can't believe it," Collins said to Julie Lind. "Will you look at them?"

Julie, whom he had called from the kitchen (she had taken charge of the girls' breakfast shift), stood beside him, watching Johnny, Freddy Kappa, and little Terry Tau at the computer. "Do they even know what they're doing?" she asked.

Collins nodded. "Seem to. Johnny and Freddy there fired up the computer and logged into an information network using my identification code. Now they're reading the encyclopedia."

"Reading?" Julie asked, her gaze on the flickering VDT. The computer, receiving information at 2400 baud, filled the screen and cleared it four times every second. The flashing green lines went by too fast for a normal onlooker to register anything more than an occasional isolated word or phrase; but Freddy stared unblinking at the screen and at least looked as if he were reading.

"Stop it for a second, Johnny," Collins said. Johnny, seated at the keyboard, nodded and hit a key, his extra pinky jutting out daintily. The screen froze, displaying twenty-four eighty-character lines from an entry on gold. Collins went and squatted next to Freddy. "Freddy," he said, "have you read everything up to here?"

Freddy nodded. "Yeah, A through G, so far."

"Can you remember anything about it?"

Freddy ducked his head at Terry, one of the more normal-looking of the children. "He can. If you ask me, he'll remember it for me." Terry, too, nodded, his silvery eyes solemn and large in his pale face.

Collins glanced up at Julie. "Okay," he said to Freddy. "Tell me something about, oh, Charles Dickens."

"Spell it," Freddy said.

Collins did. For a moment Freddy closed his eyes. Then he opened them again and said, "Dickens, Charles John Huffman, 1812 to 1870, English novelist. Dickens, recognized as one of the great masters of the English novel, compounded humor, compassion, social consciousness, and a fine sense of character to create one of the most vivid and memorable bodies of work in the language. Born in Portsmouth, Dickens was the son of . . ." and on and on.

Collins cut him short at *Great Expectations*. "You're getting all this from Terry? You can't remember this yourself?" he asked Freddy.

"I just read it," Freddy explained. "Terry remembers it."

"Then how can you tell me about it?"

Freddy looked puzzled. "Terry thinks it to me. He listens to me thinking when I read it, and he remembers it all and thinks it back when any of us need it."

"Telepathy," Julie said, a shiver in her voice.

Collins grunted and said, "He doesn't know the word. They haven't gotten to the T's yet." To Freddy he continued, "And you know what it means? Can you tell me what, oh, say, *Sketches by Boz* was?"

Freddy glanced impatiently at the frozen screen. "Sure. That was Charles Dickens's first book, in 1836–37. It was a bunch of stories about everyday life and people in England at the time. He got the name 'Boz' from his brother, who they used to call 'Moses.' When Charles's brother was small he couldn't pronounce M right, and the name came out 'Bozes.' Can we go on?"

"I guess so," Collins said, and Johnny hit the key that began the transmission again. Julie, still standing in the doorway, shook her head. Collins folded his arms and leaned against the wall beside her. " 'John Huffman.' I'll be damned. I had a course on Dickens in college, and I didn't even know that before."

"Pete," Julie said, her voice nervous, "is it safe to let them do this?"

"Why not? They're getting a first-rate education, sounds like. Or at least Freddy and Terry are."

"They all are," Julie said. "From what the girls say,

they hear each other's thoughts constantly now that they're close together. What one learns, they all know."

"What's wrong with that, teacher?" Collins asked. He looked at his watch for the twentieth time that morning. "I thought you were all for education."

"Education, yes, but this isn't any systematic way of learning things. Terry has an eidetic memory—"

"A what?" Collins asked.

Without looking around, Freddy said, "Eidetic memory: also called photographic memory, an exceptionally powerful ability to retain mental images, more often encountered in children than in adults."

"Okay," Pete said. "I get it. Terry is one of those guys who can look at a page in the telephone book and then recite it verbatim."

"That's right," Julie agreed. "But for him it's all rote. He doesn't understand what he recites."

"Freddy seems to, though. He didn't just parrot back the Charles Dickens stuff to me; he put it in his own words."

"I know. But it can't be good just to memorize an encyclopedia. I mean, think what they're learning about, Pete. It isn't just writers and precious minerals and dinosaurs and animals. A is for AIDS. B is for bombs. C is for crime. Children their ages shouldn't be learning everything, not all at once."

"I never heard of an R-rated encyclopedia." Collins smiled.

"You don't understand. These are children, Pete, for all their special gifts. On a developmental level, on an emotional level, they're still just little children, and they should be protected from certain things; they should have a chance to grow up gradually, normally. They're not—not computers, to be programmed with a dump of information all at once."

"Well, we'll leave it all behind when Will gets here," Collins said. "There won't be room for the Apple in the van, and I doubt they can get all the way through the encyclopedia in the next few minutes."

"He's late, isn't he?"

"Julie, it's barely eight o'clock. He just said he'd be here sometime early this morning. It isn't time to worry yet. Are the girls all fed?"

She sighed, brushing a strand of her hair out of her eyes. "Yes, at last, thank God. But you're almost out of provisions. All the bread's gone, we've scrambled two dozen eggs, cooked half a box of oatmeal, and used up a whole box of cornflakes and a gallon of milk. I hope you're young enough and strong enough to get a high-paying job. With this crew you're going to need a grocery budget the size of the deficit."

"Will's bringing more food," Collins said. He smiled at her, admiring again her healthy good looks, her black hair, disarrayed by a night of sleep and a morning of cooking. When she blushed at his gaze, he glanced back at the trio at the computer. "Wonder what they're reading now?" he said.

They had passed "gold" and were beginning "Greece, Ancient." The twenty-four-page article flashed past in a minute and a half. By nine o'clock they had finished the G's and H's and were into the I's. When they finished the entry "information systems," Johnny switched the modem to 9600 baud, quadrupling the rate of information flow. Freddy, who had begun to get bored, perked up and leaned forward, his concentration renewed, as the computer flashed out encyclopedia articles at the rate of sixteen screens per second.

The girls, finished with breakfast, came into the living room. The children sat on the floor Indian-fashion, legs crossed, in a loose circle. Kathy Beta seemed the informal focus, close to the center of the group and swaying slightly. Looking at her, Collins was a little surprised that he felt no repugnance for her deformities, for her pink fingerless hands. Ordinarily, he suspected, he would not have been attracted toward such a child, however protective he might feel. But there was something about these children, an aura of need, and it overcame the externals entirely.

Then, too, there was the fact that none of the ill-made children seemed at all disturbed by their differences. Kathy's mittenlike hands were flexible and adroit, and she held a spoon or a pencil with no trouble at all. The others seemed similarly to have adjusted; and perhaps a third of them, like Johnny, Terry, and Daisy, showed no obvious deformities at all, showed nothing to set them physically apart from any other children except their silver eyes and an occasional minor anomaly like Johnny's extra digits or Paul Omicron's comically oversized ears. Watching them gathered on his living-room floor, Collins had the oddest sensation of meaning, of something vastly important being accomplished in a most deliberate way. The group had somehow divided its energies, its tasks, as the three boys had divided the chore of operating the computer, reading the information, and committing it to memory. Collins, though, had no idea of what divisions had been made or of what esoteric tasks were being accomplished.

An hour crept by, but still Whitepath did not come. Tired of pacing the crowded cabin floors, Collins went outside a little after nine. Eightball, who had been moping on the porch, tried to squeeze in past him, but Collins blocked the spaniel with his foot. "Too crowded in there already, boy," he said. He sat on the top step petting the dog, reassuring him.

From time to time Collins cast an anxious eye at the weather. The clouds had darkened steadily since early morning. Now they were a gray canopy overhead, layered with streaks of lighter and darker gray like strips of torn paper. It was a storm sky; it heralded a front, and that would mean thunderstorms by early afternoon. Collins stared down the dirt drive toward the wooden bridge and wondered what in the hell was keeping William Whitepath.

4

Clint and Susan Jernigan received an off-base housing allowance generous enough to let them live in a quiet subdivision. Clint liked it, especially early on a Saturday morning when everything was quiet, before lawn mowers fired up; then the sunrise mellowed the lines of brick and white frame houses, cast a special glow over the well-tended yards. When he was out on days like this, he had the whole world to himself. Well, maybe a few early joggers for company, but they were soon gone, and most of them had at least a cheerful wave for him.

Always an early riser, Jernigan had reserved Saturday mornings for a special ritual for seven years now, ever since he had first come into possession of the Lincoln Continental. From six to seven-thirty he communed with the automobile while Susan slept in. In the winter that meant working inside the heated garage, doing what he could to repair, maintain, and customize the automobile: routine tune-ups, oil changes, replacing faded and scratched veneer with fresh, unmarred material. But come spring and summer, Saturday morning meant a loving wash and wax job done under God's own sky.

He hummed to himself as he washed the car, using a mild detergent for the body, a special mix of soap and weak ammonia for the windows and windshield, and a stronger solution for the whitewalls. He used soft old towels and lots of elbow grease; he cleaned the occasional splotch of tar from the body with Turtle Wax solvent; he rinsed the glasswork thoroughly and used a squeegee to shave off the excess water. After drying the slab-sided car, Jernigan opened the doors, removed the floor mats, and went to work on the interior with Windex, Pledge, and a vinyl-cleaning compound called Nu-Look. The first thing was a thorough vacuuming with the shop vac and two vacuum heads, one for the floors and another probe-shaped attachment just for the seats. Then he put away the vacuum and began to clean surfaces, using his whole battery of cleansing compounds and mixtures. As he made his rounds, he switched on the radio to a rock station, half listening to the hits of the previous three decades, sometimes humming along.

In half an hour he completed cleaning the inside of the car. Now came the waxing. Jernigan left the windows down so he could hear the radio—considerately he kept it fairly soft, so as not to disturb any sleeping neighbors—and began to apply the paste wax with a chamois, industriously circling it onto the midnight-blue body, working the mirror shine deep into the finish. Later he would buff and polish, and when he finished the automobile would look new. Better than new. It would look like a car someone cared about, a classic. The paper boy came by, yelled a greeting, and tossed the news expertly onto the front stoop. Jernigan waved and smiled at the boy but did not stop the rotation of the chamois.

The radio played "I Heard It Through the Grapevine," Marvin Gaye's version, and as he worked Jernigan hummed along, reflecting on how the song had almost been ruined for everybody by those animated dancing raisins a few years back. But it was coming back now, though Jernigan supposed he would always picture those cockamamie raisins every time he heard the tune. Like "Dance of the Hours," he thought to himself. His parents had taken him to see Walt Disney's *Fantasia* when he was a kid, not long after the family had moved to Detroit, and damned if he could hear "Dance of the Hours" ever again without picturing in his mind ballerina ostriches, sinister alligators, and fat-assed dancing hippos.

He was working on the hood of the car, buffing the layer of wax to an initial shine, when the news came over the radio. He had not been really listening, and the radio was playing so softly that he could not understand the broadcast anyway, but the word "Atlanta" caught his ear because that was where Fritz and his wife had gone. So Jernigan paused and stuck his head in the open passenger window to hear what had taken place in Atlanta.

". . . the slayings are possibly linked to the death in Washington of Air Force General Dwight Arnold," the announcer said. "Colonel and Mrs. Engstrom resided in Colorado, where the colonel was stationed . . ."

Feeling sick at the pit of his stomach, as if he were on a falling elevator, Jernigan left the wax drying on the car. He used the kitchen telephone to call the base. It took him five minutes to find someone willing to talk to him. "Captain Black," a voice said at last. "What can I do for you, Colonel?"

"They told me you might have news about Lieutenant Colonel Engstrom," Jernigan said.

"Did you hear the news, sir?"

"Just part of it, Captain." *Damn, man, tell me.* "What happened?"

"Sir, at this point it seems that Colonel Engstrom and his wife were both murdered. I can't say any more."

Jernigan hung up. Susan, wearing her blue terry-cloth robe, came in yawning. "I'll get some coffee started—" She broke off when she saw his face.

"Fritz is dead," he said.

"Oh, honey, no."

"He told me to let somebody know if anything happened to him."

Susan came close. "Who?"

Jernigan shook his head. "I don't know. Military police. FBI. Somebody. He was afraid all along that something might happen to him."

She looked into his eyes. "Clint, are you in danger?"

He shook his head again. "No. I haven't done anything."

"Maybe . . ." Susan licked her lips. "Maybe you should be careful, Clint. Maybe—"

"He was my friend," Clint said.

"Clint, I just believe you ought to think about it. If there's a bunch of crazy terrorists—"

"Fritz Engstrom was a good friend to me, Susan." Jernigan went to the bedroom, found the telephone directory, and sat on the bed. Susan, silent, disapproving, got dressed while he placed a call to the local office of the FBI.

5

William Whitepath made it to Holcomb's Crossing by nine-fifteen. He found the place besieged.

Dark green Army trucks half-filled the Pleasant View Baptist Church parking lot. Interspersed with them and parked also in front of the Mercantile were blue-and-gray state patrol Ford Crown Victorias—Whitepath counted eleven of them. From his vantage point on the edge of the forest, Whitepath saw dozens of men in the olive-drab uniforms of the National Guard and the Mountie hats of the state patrol. Some of them were studying maps unfolded on the hoods of cars or against the sides of the trucks, little groups of intent men casting no shadows in the pale gray light filtering down from the cloudy sky. Others were stopping traffic on the highway or going door to door among the few houses scattered on the main road and the four side streets of the hamlet.

Whitepath settled back on his haunches to consider. He had eluded, at least so far, the sheriff's pursuit; but now he faced a small army. He had no doubt that Burette had already broadcast an all-points bulletin or that most if not all the interlopers he saw in Holcomb's Crossing had a description of him. Remaining perfectly still, Whitepath squinted downhill and considered his options. He could go out of his way to skirt the town, but he couldn't travel more than four miles east because of the Chanussee—and he suspected that the authorities were beginning to check out the riverside cabins as well. He could go west, but that meant crossing the highway at some point, and it would put him farther from the cabin than ever. Or, he decided, he could go straight ahead.

Not in the open, for he would be stopped the moment he showed himself. But there were other ways. He melted back into the forest and made his way down the steep banks of Panther Creek, here a calf-high stream playing over jumbles of brown, rounded stone. He followed it to the place where it entered the culvert, in a glen a few hundred feet from the rear of the church parking lot. The culvert had been built large to accommodate the run-off from storms; he could walk through it if he stooped.

Whitepath took his shoes off, tied the rawhide laces together and slung the Docksiders around his neck, rolled his pants legs up to his knees, and then stepped into the creek, wincing at the touch of the rushing, icy water. The first few feet were painful, with the round rocks hard against his bare soles, uncertain and treacherous footing. Then gritty sand and soft muck replaced the rocks, and he made a little better time, although he quickly lost the light.

For a hundred yards or so he waded on in the gloom, allowing his eyes to become accustomed to the darkness. Light from the culvert opening carried that far, though it was very dim. When at last he was in complete darkness, Whitepath took his key ring from his pocket and switched on a penlight, a toy-sized AAA-cell that helped him find the lock on his front door late at night but was good for little else. The battery was weak—he hadn't replaced it since buying the penlight in a Wal-Mart store checkout lane months before—but the small bulb cast a dim yellow circle on the concrete tube of the culvert. Whitepath saw roots dripping in ahead, at a join of pipes. He saw no side branches or curves—yet. He turned off the light and reached out his left hand to touch the wall, dislodging a patter of dried fine-grained mud. He sloshed on, trying not to think about the composition of the slimy muck that squeezed between his toes with every step.

Before long his back began to ache. The drain was five feet in diameter, actually a few inches less because of the buildup of sediment. Whitepath had to hold a Groucho Marx incline to fit through. From time to time he stopped and inspected his surroundings with the flashlight, but save for passing small openings where one- or two-foot drains debouched into the main culvert, he saw few landmarks. The tunnel had begun to stink, a ripe garbage smell, and he supposed he was wading through sewage by that point. He didn't care to flash the light downward to check it out.

He stumbled ahead, the cold water becoming more hospitable as his feet lost sensation. He had a nasty moment once when he bumped his head. His light showed that a large tree root, perhaps from the oak behind the Mercantile, had forced its way into the culvert, breaking off a wedge-shaped portion of the pipe but holding it in position by growing into it. Holding the penlight in his teeth, Whitepath had to drop to his hands and knees and squeeze under the blockage, and he stood dripping to continue his underground march.

The drain gradually curved to the left, heading for the point a half mile or so beyond the last house in Holcomb's Crossing where the creek spilled back into the open again. At last a faint gray light began to show ahead, and a few yards farther on Whitepath saw the dazzle of the discharge end of the pipe, seeming as bright as a searchlight. He approached with caution, but the culvert opening was well shielded from the highway and the hamlet by a thick growth of sumac and cottonwoods. He edged out, straightened up painfully—his back cracked almost loud enough for them to hear back in town, he thought—and got out of the stream bed. His feet were numb. He massaged them until the blood began to pump again with a pins-and-needles stinging, and then he put his boat shoes back on.

Whitepath crept up the bank close to the highway. Because of a bend in the road and a rising hill, he was out of sight of the occupying army. A car, a red three-year-old Subaru, went past, but the sole occupant, a preoccupied-looking man behind the wheel, didn't even glance Whitepath's way.

Whitepath edged back down the bank and headed south again, keeping mostly out of sight of the highway up on the rise and trying to remember the lay of the land. He recalled a few farms, but he knew none of the farmers personally. He doubted that he could persuade any of them to let him use a phone, caked as his trouser legs were with a clotted layer of greasy mud and grime, smelling as he did of rot and mold.

The first farmhouse he came to was a dingy gray two-story affair, badly needing paint. Parked under a cedar near it was an old Chevrolet Cavalier wagon, its dirt-speckled body faded to a pale blue. Whitepath avoided the place. The next looked more promising: smaller, neater, in better repair, it boasted a red Dodge pickup, a vehicle with a bed big enough to squeeze seventeen children in if the need arose—and he spotted a tarp that looked big enough to conceal them folded in the truck bed.

The house showed no signs of activity, though from a chicken house about forty yards away there came the clucks and clacking of poultry being disturbed by a human among them. Whitepath made his way to the truck, opened the door, and slipped in. He had owned a pickup like this once, and when the ignition gave him some problems, he had learned to hot-wire it; but this time there was no need, for a key was concealed under the driver's floormat. The truck started with the first turn of the key in the ignition, and Whitepath backed up, turned, and headed for the highway. He heard a man shout just as he made the turn, but he did not bother to look back.

He estimated that by using a back route he could be at the cabin in fifteen minutes, given luck. He could pick up Pete, the woman, and the kids, and they could break for Cleveland to the east or Gainesville to the south, though the first order of business would be finding another vehicle almost immediately. It was a long-shot chance at best, Whitepath thought, but he determined to take it anyway.

But a mile before the turn-off onto the dirt road he realized that his luck had played out, used up perhaps by the providence of the ignition key. A gray Mustang was coming up fast behind. Whitepath cursed and floored the accelerator, determined to lead Burette's deputy on as long a chase as possible. "Sorry, Pete," he grunted as the truck flashed past the dirt road. The farmer had kept his pickup in good condition, and it responded well; Whitepath was traveling at nearly ninety, expertly taking the curves on the winding road.

But a quarter of a mile behind him the Ford was slowly gaining.

6

Collins knew they ought to be worried, but he was incapable of worry at the moment. Julie had come to sit beside him on the top porch step at nine-thirty, and before he knew it he was holding her hand. The overcast had grown heavier than ever in the hour since then, but just before ten a mist rose around the cabin, an odd wall of fog the color of mother-of-pearl and apparently self-luminescent. It began a hundred feet or so from the cabin and seemed to encircle it; the cabin was beneath a sort of dome of fog. Gradually the fog grew so thick that nothing beyond it could be seen.

Collins and Julie looked at each other and smiled. "The children are covering us," Julie said, and he nodded.

The two of them got up after a few minutes and strolled down to the edge of the mist. It was almost palpable, like a curtain hung in the air, a gently undulating, shimmering barrier. "Same color as their eyes," Collins said. He thrust his hand into the fog, and it disappeared up to his wrist. He felt no odd sensation, no heat, no dampness. He and Julie took a step into the mist, and a second later they were outside it again, looking down the drive to the wooden bridge. The day was becoming dark, but nothing stirred as far as they could see, nothing but the sweep of the Chanussee, gray as the clouds above it.

Julie glanced behind them and cried out. Collins, following her gaze, felt a nauseating wave of fear, a sense of absolute unreality. Though they had come directly down the drive from the cabin, it was gone, vanished. From here the dirt drive led a few feet up the hill, then gave out in a tangle of weeds and briers. The hilltop was covered in a copse of sweet gums and pines, but no dwelling stood there; neither could he see the least trace of the mist that had risen.

"They're hiding it," he said. "Let's see if we can get back."

They followed the drive without penetrating the wall of mist. They headed uphill and somehow missed it. "This feels wrong," Julie said, anxiety making her voice tremble. "What are they doing to us?"

"I don't think they know we're out," Collins told her.

The undergrowth rustled down the hillside, and looking back Collins saw Eightball, his head sticking out of a tangle of weeds, his hindquarters concealed. "Stay," he told the dog, and for a wonder Eightball did. Collins led Julie to the dog and past him, and suddenly they were inside the wall of mist again, at the side of the cabin, looking uphill toward it.

"But we were going downhill," Julie said in a small voice.

"We just thought we were," Collins said. "They fooled us into going the wrong way." He bent to pet Eightball. "Good boy."

Johnny met them on the porch, concern showing on his face. Julie said, "What are you doing, Johnny?"

Johnny's face reddened as he tried to speak. "Suh-suh-safe," he gasped. "In here."

Collins mounted the steps. "As long as we stay close to the cabin we're safe?"

"Yuh."

Relief flooded Collins then, relief too strong to be real. "Johnny," he said, "are you making Julie and me feel better?"

"Yuh." Again Johnny contorted his features with the effort of speech: "Duh-don't be afraid. Wuh-we have a puh-plan."

Julie sat down on the porch again. "It's so pretty, the fog," she said in a dreamy, distant voice.

Collins dropped to his knees beside the boy. "Johnny, stop it. We don't want our feelings changed. You're doing a bad thing."

Johnny tried to talk again but lost the words in a spray of stuttering. "Suh-sit," he said at last, indicating the porch beside the door. "Tuh-try something."

Collins sat down with his back against the cabin wall. "Now what?"

"Cuh-close eyes."

Collins did, and for a moment he had a sensation of drift, of sideways movement, slow as the gentle bobbing of the canoe on the placid surface of Lake Reece. Something happened and he was alone in some quiet place of darkness; and then something else happened, and somehow he sensed light, although his eyes were closed.

"Johnny?" he asked without speaking.

—I'm here. I'm with you.

It frightened Collins; he was in some *place*, some environment with physical impressions—warmth, a golden kind of radiance—but he was unaware of his body and could see nothing but the light. "Where are we?"

—I can't say. I don't know. It's where we go.

"You and the other children?"

—Yes. We are all here. We do our work here.

"Where are the others?"

—Here—

oh God it hurt a rush of thought a torrent too much too much what thirty-four eyes saw thirty-four ears heard sensation overwhelming

—I am sorry.

"It hurt," Collins wept.

—You cannot perceive it. You have not learned. I think—

A pause.

—I think people like you and Miss Julie cannot learn.

"Johnny, is that what you all feel?"

—Yes.

"Doesn't it hurt you?"

—No. (Puzzlement.) It seems natural. You must listen now. I have little time.

"Johnny, we want to help you."

—You have helped already. We will keep you safe, whatever happens to us. But you have more to do. Listen.

"Yes."

—We have made the cabin hard to find. People are coming, thinking sharp thoughts. I will not show them to you; the thoughts hurt us. They might kill you. We have tried to make ourselves safe; but we can be found if they try hard enough. We may not have enough time.

"Time? Time to do what?"

—To—to—it is very hard to say to you. There are no words. To Become. There is a way. It is most difficult. When we have done it, we may reshape, change the way things are. Remove the evil. But it is a most difficult way. We may not have time. And we still are not in agreement; some want to do what we were meant to do, to begin to remove evil. Some of us want to learn more. Some of us are trying to understand the way of the numbers. We are still too scattered, not *one* enough. And the bad ones are approaching. We are afraid. Listen: we may still die.

"How can I help you?"

—Our great fear is that they may kill us before we Become. After there will be no danger. After we cannot die ever. But before there is great danger, much to do; even if we can make ourselves more *one*, our power will be scattered, weakened, while we Become. It is most difficult to Become; Becoming may itself kill us or kill our minds. But if the bad ones kill our bodies before, all is lost. You must help, you and Miss Julie, before we go away. You must help us live even if we die.

"Johnny, I don't understand."

A mental sigh, a sense of regret.

—We cannot yet shape flesh; it is too hard to do, too complex. Perhaps after Becoming we can then do it, but we cannot now. Else we would try other ways; but the girls have been cut, changed. Parts of their bodies are missing now. We cannot ever have children like ourselves.

"I am sorry."

—We cannot have children ourselves. Therefore, you friends, you and Miss Julie, must.

Collins felt something like a chill in that warm nowhere of a place. "Children? Julie and I?"

—We dare not try to alter bodies, either our own or others'; the interior structure, the combination of bone, muscle, blood, nerve, all this is far too complex. The egg and sperm cells are simple. We know what parts of our own have been changed; changed badly, so that our bodies have suffered for the sake of our minds. We think we can do better. We will alter the reproductive cells of your bodies, of yours and Miss Julie's. It will not harm you even if we make a mistake; so much we feel we can attempt. You must have a child. A child like us. So we will live through the child even if we die before we Become.

"Johnny, you can't just tell us to do that. And it's wrong, wrong, to change us so that we would have—"

—Freaks, you were going to say. (Anger.) Dr. Stark gave no choice to our parents. Blame Dr. Stark, not us. We must live. We must. There we have no choice still. I am sorry, Pete. You have been good to us. But I am sorry. Having no choice ourselves, we can give you none. The want to live is stronger. But you will have love. We will give you that. And the child you have will be beautiful. I must go now; there is too much to do, and we lose time.

"Johnny—"

Everything faded; and then Collins opened his eyes.

Johnny gave him an anxious gaze, as if assuring himself that Collins was well. Then the boy opened the cabin door and went back inside, closing the door firmly behind him.

Collins rose. Julie looked over her shoulder, smiling at him. "Come and sit," she said, patting the step beside her.

He did, feeling his heart tremble. She leaned warm against him, held his hand again. Eightball, lying on the other side of her, yawned and put his head down for a nap. Collins was sensible of a subtle change in the air, elusive as a faint, pleasant perfume of flowers.

Or perhaps it was a change in his perception. He had never taken acid, had only occasionally smoked a joint years before when he was in college. What happened seemed to him something like the descriptions he had read of LSD trips, something like the curious alterations in perception he had experienced with grass, though far stronger.

He saw the yard with new clarity, becoming conscious almost of every blade of grass, every grain of soil; a red ant staggering home beneath the weight of a grasshopper leg became an iridescent wonder, a living machine encased in its own chitinous armor, the armor itself shaped more intricately than any work of human hands, a marvelous lacy network of hard cells, layer fitted on layer with uncanny precision. "Yes," Julie said, answering his thought, not any words, "it is beautiful." She squeezed his hand and sighed. "I do love you, Pete," she said.

Collins's heart soared. He kissed her tenderly, softly, a little shyly, feeling almost like a schoolboy with a crush. When she returned his kiss, when he tasted her mouth spicy-sweet, he thought for a moment he would float away on sheer joy.

And all the time he thought *this is wrong, this is wrong, this is wrong*.

7

The meeting took place on the President's turf.

That was a disadvantage for Fisher, for the chief executive was far more friendly toward Randall Grade, his chief liaison with the intelligence community, than toward Fisher himself. Grade had been a White House visitor many times, but Fisher had been there only four times before, and never during the present administration.

"You've got a hell of a mess," the President said. "I think Mr. Grade's right. We have to cut you loose at this point."

Grade looked down and shot his cuffs, nothing showing on his baby face, although Fisher knew he must be exulting inwardly.

"Sir," Fisher said, "with due respect, it's too late for that. The military are already involved in the search. I'll need your cooperation to keep everything as quiet as possible. I'd appreciate some assistance from the FBI in—"

"I don't think you heard me," the President said coldly. "I won't have this administration paralyzed by another Watergate or another Iranscam. Mr. Grade tells me that you undertook this whole crazy operation on your own authority. If it broke wrong, it's your fault, Mr. Fisher, and nobody else's. That will be made clear to the American people."

"In what way, sir?"

Grade studied the carpet. The President leaned back in his chair. "I will issue an executive order removing you from authority over Project Slow Tango. Mr. Grade will replace you. If an investigation reveals cause to suspect you of criminal activity, you will be indicted and tried. And if you're found guilty, by God, you will be punished. Is that clear enough?"

Fisher nodded. "Clear enough, sir. But it isn't as simple as that. There's the matter of the findings, for example."

The President gave Grade a sharp look. Grade cleared his throat. "If you're referring to the original finding that set up Project Slow Tango—"

"No, I'm not," Fisher said without looking at Grade. "I'm talking about the one-paragraph finding signed by every President since the initiation of the project. Including you, sir. I have direct authorization for everything I did." He smiled, not an arrogant smile, but a commiserating one. "I suggest you reconsider removing me from the project."

The President said, "I believe you will find that any court in the land would conclude you have overstepped the limits of that brief finding, Mr. Fisher."

"Perhaps, sir. And perhaps the American voters would conclude the same thing. But perhaps not." When the President did not respond, Fisher said, "Have you reviewed the videotapes, sir?"

"We have," Grade said. "How are we supposed to tell if you've used camera tricks, Fisher?"

"No tricks," Fisher said, still looking at the President. "You could tell, sir, couldn't you?"

The President rubbed his chin. "It didn't look like trickery," he admitted. "Still, it's so minor, so—"

"Have you read Dr. Stark's assessment?"

With a curt nod the President said, "Yes. If true, it has very grave implications. That's why the leadership of the project—"

"With respect, sir, that's why I have to remain as project leader. Dr. Stark will not cooperate with Mr. Grade. Mr. Grade didn't bring him out of the Soviet Union; I did. And Dr. Stark is the only living man who knows how to control the subjects."

"He's trying to blackmail you, Mr. President," Grade said.

"I'm talking sense, Mr. President," Fisher countered. "Sir, you've begun to receive word of—shall we say, of anomalous occurrences in certain countries that could be considered hostile to our interests? You have, haven't you?"

After a long pause, the President said, "There has been a wave of assassinations in the Middle East. The CIA can suggest no connection, no explanation."

"Dr. Stark believes that the children are resonating. That means they reinforce each other; their abilities grow geometrically. And they are beginning to respond to Mr. Clebb's conditioning. That means that enemies of the country are beginning to die." Fisher paused for effect. "Of course, the conditioning wasn't complete. We have no way of knowing, sir, whom the children will choose to identify as enemies."

Grade, his gaze locked on the President's expression, said, "Sir, I suggest that Mr. Fisher is floundering to find some way to keep his job."

The President gave Fisher a long look. "Very well," he said at last. "I will give you one direct order, Mr. Fisher: get Project Slow Tango under control. Immediately. You will have full cooperation. But I want the project terminated within the next forty-eight hours. Do you understand?"

Fisher stood. "Yes, sir. If you will have someone drive me back to the airport—"

The President lifted a telephone and touched a number. "Have Mr. Fisher taken to the airport," he said into the receiver. "*Air Force Two* is at his disposal."

Fisher walked out of the room without smiling. As the door closed behind him, he knew that Grade was erupting into protest, argument, dissuasion. And he knew the President's response: Fisher was in charge, yes, but only until the children were rounded up. Only until the program was terminated.

We'll see, Fisher thought to himself. Let me get my hands on the children and then we'll see.

And then he did smile.

8

The goddam Indian had led Deputy Security Chief Lamont a hell of a chase. Just when the commandeered Mustang had closed on the Dodge pickup, just when

Lamont was preparing to cut the son of a bitch off, the Indian had made a hard left, going where there wasn't even a goddam road.

Lamont had shot past, executed a 180, and then saw the road he had missed, probably an old logging trace hacked into the wilderness. Half overgrown, it was hell on the Mustang, the brush and scrub only partly crushed down by the passage of the truck, the surface spongy with leaf mold and pine straw. The Indian drove it better than Lamont could, pulling away again. Before long all Lamont could see of the pickup was flashes of red through breaks in the trees. He cursed the Indian, cursed the state patrol from which he had taken the unmarked car, cursed the woods, cursed the stupid sheriff for alerting the quarry in the first place. Lamont was almost furious enough to pick up the microphone and call for help.

Almost, but not quite. Sooner or later the Indian would have to come out on a normal road again, and when he did, Lamont would close up again. Lamont swore again as the rough road robbed more speed from him, let the pickup pull farther away. The stolen-vehicle call had been put out by the sheriff's department, but Lamont had taken it himself, had been closest, and had damn near caught the son of a whore before this cute little trick. He supposed that somewhere back on the highway the asshole sheriff and his deputies were poking along looking for the Indian themselves. Well, to hell with them.

Twigs lashed the windshield, and a heavier branch snatched off the antenna, making a springy boinging sound. With angry determination Lamont held on to the Ford's steering wheel and grunted as the suspension bottomed out over a fallen log. He glanced at the speedometer. He was doing forty and dared go no faster than that; but the road was getting a little easier, a little clearer, as this part of the forest thinned. For a few hundred feet the un-paved lane paralleled a two-lane blacktop, and then it gave onto the paved road. The truck had clearly pulled through here: a scatter of torn foliage littered the black-top away to the right. Lamont wrenched the Mustang onto the pavement, recovered from a slewing fishtail skid, and floored the accelerator. The red Dodge pickup was nowhere in sight.

Two miles south, three. By now the speedometer was hitting ninety again, though this secondary road, badly potholed and winding like a black snake through the hills, was a dangerous place for such speed. Once or twice Lamont hit shallow washouts that clacked his teeth together painfully, threatening to knock him off the road, but he managed to keep control. A house or two appeared, none of them offering concealment for a pickup truck. An unpainted shack, roofed with rust-reddened tin, flashed by, a weathered sign announcing BAIT—RED WIGGLERS SPRING LIZZARDS as Lamont fought the car in a screaming curve. The mountain road crossed a concrete-and-steel-lattice bridge; rattling over the Chanussee, Lamont saw that a mile ahead the blacktop dead-ended on a larger road. On the left side of the intersection was a yellow-sided prefab diner, and on the right was a brick-and-glass BP station.

And right beside the station Lamont spotted the red Dodge pickup.

The Mustang's tires threw gravel as Lamont tore into the service-station lot. The pickup was empty, the driver's door open. Lamont climbed out of his car, drawing his sidearm, swiveling his head as he looked for his quarry. He saw him through the glass of the station's office. The Indian was on the other side of the lot, dialing a pay telephone, glancing over his shoulder. A fat white man opened the door of the station and in a high-pitched bubbling voice said, "What the hell you think you doin', tearin' up my lot any such a way, mister?"

"Police." Lamont showed him the Beretta automatic, and the station owner remembered something important inside. Lamont walked across the lot, his shoes crunching on the gravel. The Indian was pounding his fist on the blue-and-white fiberglass of the phone enclosure. "Whitepath," Lamont said. "Give it up."

The goddam Indian whirled and threw a wrench at him. Lamont ducked as Whitepath hung up the telephone and tried to run behind the station. The wrench clanged off the pavement of the highway at the same time the telephone clattered Whitepath's coin back into the slot. Dropping to one knee, Lamont fired twice. The first shot hit Whitepath in the right thigh, knocking his legs from under him. Because of the fall, the second shot missed. Lamont saw a chunk of bark fly off a pine tree thirty yards past the Indian. "Stop right there. That's far enough," he said.

But damned if Whitepath didn't crawl, leaving a stream of blood on the gravel of the station lot. Lamont walked up, taking his time. "You've had it," he said to Whitepath. He stopped over the Indian, the Beretta Model 92F trained on Whitepath's forehead. "You're hit bad, redskin. You need medical attention," Lamont told him.

Whitepath let his face slump to the ground, but he said, "Go to hell, white man."

Lamont grinned and kicked at Whitepath's head. With the speed of a rattlesnake the Indian rolled on his side, making the kick miss, and struck at Lamont's leg. Lamont felt a rip of pain and a flash of hot anger—Whitepath had stabbed him in the ankle with a screwdriver, a goddam Phillips-head screwdriver!

The Beretta fired for the next-to-last time.

9

Johnny Gamma, lost in a complex web of calculations with the Delta twins, was jerked to awareness of the outer world by William Whitepath's death. At a convulsive impression of falling he cried out, again, feeling that loss, that sense of a human soul dropping into a bottomless black pit. It was not as strong but just as keen as the sensation he had felt when his mother had died.

But this time he was far stronger. This time he had help. Daisy Rho showed him the whole scene, clear in his mind; the Deltas boosted his power; the faction of the children that had been in favor of striking at the bad men recognized the man with the bleeding ankle and the gun as one of the worst of them all.

The time before, driven far beyond his normal strength by his grief at his mother's death, Johnny had erased a great part of Charles Dougherty's intelligence. Now, more assured of his abilities, he did no such thing with Lamont. Instead he took control.

At the BP station, the proprietor, lumbering old Vinny Martin, saw the guy who had said he was a cop come stalking stiff-legged from off to the side where the shots had come from. Vinny had the office phone receiver in his greasy hand, waiting for the sheriff's office over in Tyrell to answer. The phone rang twice while Lamont walked to the self-serve island and lifted the hose nozzle from the premium gasoline pump. The switch inside the office chimed.

"What the fuck?" Vinny said. With a loose-jointed swing, like a marionette being turned too fast, the man lurched around and brought the automatic to bear on Vinny. Feeling the back of his neck turn to ice, Vinny dropped the receiver. The Beretta twitched upward twice, impatiently. Understanding, Vinny fumbled to the pump-control console and threw the switch, activating the pump, though no car stood near the island.

The man began to squirt gasoline onto himself, taking a shower in the clear liquid. It gushed over his head, flattening his hair, dousing his clothes. Squiggly waves of vapor rose, making the fellow and the gas pump alike shimmer like a summer mirage. The man even opened his mouth and shot the gas inside; Vinny saw him swallowing, saw the excess pouring out from the man's gaping lips, cascading from his chin. "Jesus God," Vinny said, and he ran out the door.

With what looked like painful effort, the man jerked the nozzle away from his face, the stream splashing off his chest. The man gagged, spat a stream of brown vomit arching through the air, and screamed. "Help me!" The man yelled at Vinny, anguish and the fiery liquid making his voice high, ragged. "I can't stop it, help me!" He stood in a puddle of gasoline the size of a living-room rug. The air reeked with it.

Vinny ran, but not toward the pumps. He crossed the old Tyrell highway, passed Lucy's Country Kitchen, and still ran, pounding east on the verge of the main highway. His painful old heart thumped hard in his chest. Two or three hundred feet down the road, his breath tearing things loose in his chest, Vinny turned and looked back. The man was still there, the pool of gasoline darkening the whole front lot of the station now, more of it pouring out of the pump. "God amighty," Vinny said. For a moment he stood there panting, bent forward, his hands braced on his thighs just above his knees. The tableau down the hill was suspended in time by the pearly light from the cloudy sky: the brick-and-glass station, the two pay phones, the legs of the dead man barely visible behind the corner of the station, the red pickup beside the office, the gray Mustang parked diagonally in front of the truck. And the man, the man wrapped in the pump hose like some old Greek god or priest or something that Vinny dimly recalled from a high school textbook he had studied forty-some years ago. The picture seemed to hold forever; and then it changed.

Standing in the shower of gasoline, the man fired the Beretta.

The explosion was strong enough to rip Vinny's coveralls right off his body. He was thrown backward and got up in nothing but his skivvies, feeling heat on his flabby old legs and arms, staring open-mouthed at the hellish roil of black smoke and orange flame that boiled up from what used to be his place of business. Something smashed onto the blacktop. Vinny blinked at a considerable chunk of the western edge of the roof of Lucy's Country Kitchen, twisted to almost a dome shape. Looking downhill, he saw the diner was aflame, too, on the side closest to the station. Between it and the main fire the two automobiles lay on their sides, their tires toward the inferno. Vinny was reminded of a couple of old hound dogs his daddy used to have that would come in of a cold winter day and lie in front of the fireplace, their big old feet stuck out just like that, warming. From what was left of the restaurant, Lucy Devereaux, her cook Pinky Norris, and three of her customers came stumbling out with upraised arms shielding their heads from the intense heat. They fled toward Vinny, not trying to get to him particularly, just leaving the hell of the flames behind.

One of the underground tanks went, and everyone fell down again.

Vinny got up first, and then the others staggered to their feet, dazed, bleeding from gravel cuts, gasping for breath.

When Lucy and the others struggled closer toward him, their mouths moved but Vinny heard nothing. He thought it was the roar of the flames until he realized he couldn't hear that, either. He put his hands up to his ears, and they both came away wet with blood. The shock wave from the explosion had imploded both of his eardrums. When Lucy was close enough, Vinny bawled at her, "I might be deaf, but I tell you one thing—I'm still alive, and that fucker with the gun is *dead*."

The explosion had been loud enough to be heard in Cleveland, seventeen miles away. The pillar of black smoke eventually grew tall enough to be seen as far as Gainesville. The Forestry service helicopters might have checked it out, had they not all been commandeered for the search for the children. As it was, a small forest fire began at the crater where the gas station had stood, to be extinguished that afternoon by a providential cloudburst. No one, no fire department, no forestry officers, appeared to help nature fight the blaze. By the time the flames finally began to die the world had other troubles.

CHAPTER NINE

1

The storm broke Saturday afternoon.

A hard rain lashed the national forest, making the search that much more difficult. Fisher had returned just ahead of the rain and found complete chaos. The unit was, except for Stark, without a leader. Lamont was missing; the Indian had escaped. Security had taken over the Baptist church and had set up a satellite relay feed into what normally was the junior Sunday school room. A bank of three monitors showed Fisher evidence of spreading disaster, but even with all the technology at his disposal he could not see the entire story.

In the Soviet Union a string of psychological-research institutions fell out of communication with the world. At one of them some two hundred patients simultaneously turned on their keepers and their guards. Fifty of the patients were killed, but in the end the weapons were in their hands. None of the doctors or guards survived; the patients spread out and across the landscape in a widening circle of destruction.

In Siberia a Soviet army detachment suddenly and for no apparent reason began to destroy itself: detachments of soldiers marched into position, while others raised their weapons and fired, executing the first group. Another group replaced the dead ones and the process was repeated. When at last the only ones standing were the hundred riflemen, they turned on each other. The whole massacre took only half an hour, and by the end it had attracted quite a crowd. They cheered when the last soldier had fallen.

In Central America a convoy of military trucks pulled into the courtyard of a capitol building where members of the ruling junta were debating strategies of dealing with CIA-inspired insurgents. Informed of the arrival of the trucks and fearing a coup, they began to evacuate the building, but at that moment the truck drivers touched off the explosives, more than a hundred tons of them. The capitol and everyone in it vanished in what some took to be a nuclear explosion.

The news came in sporadically, fitfully, in distorted bits and pieces. Dr. Stark, who had joined Fisher in the monitor room, had an explanation. "It is direct neural control," Stark said from a chair surrounded by snippets of paper; he was methodically shredding a hymnal. "The subjects have internalized the propaganda indoctrinations, you see. They are isolating those whom they believe to be dangerous enemies and are forcing them to eliminate themselves. So early in their careers, when the subjects are still largely untrained, it is more than we dared hope for."

Fisher glowered at him.

And meanwhile—

Whole regiments of Chinese soldiers marched into the sea, like lemmings. Columns were so long that toward the end the living walked over the backs of the drowned for up to a tenth of a mile before reaching open water.

A dozen submarines at locations ranging from just off Newfoundland to the central Pacific surfaced, opened hatches, and then submerged forever, salt water pouring in, ignored by the crew.

Scores of aircraft plummeted into the earth (the pilots carefully choosing isolated areas) or into the ocean. Not one gave a distress call or signal.

Across the planet, governments met in extraordinary session, pondered courses of action, contemplated retaliation—though none knew against whom they should retaliate. Time after time, groups of influential men, important men, ruling parties, committed suicide in unpredictable ways. There were those who methodically set fire to the chambers in which they met, then continued to debate in passionate and earnest tones what they should do as the flames consumed them. There were those who turned on each other with weapons or with bare hands. In one case, fifty-three men and women simply held their breaths until they died of anoxia—a physiologically impossible feat.

Or at least one that had until that Saturday night been physiologically impossible. As of midnight, as of the Fourth of July, as of Independence Day, limits to possibility no longer existed.

2

Feodor Kovach arrived in the vicinity of the Slow Tango installation just after midnight on Saturday. He came in the simplest and most direct way possible: by automobile. True, the route he took was anything but direct. From Atlanta he and his guide (another consulate employee who sometimes fished in the North Georgia trout streams) drove northeast on I-85 as far as the exit to Commerce, a small town some sixty miles out. There they took U.S. 441 north as far as Clarksville. By then it was dark, though the worst of the storm had passed to the east. From Clarksville they took a winding back road through pine-spiked hills, heading north and west. Eventually, some miles west of Robertstown, they turned south-southwest. The final result of this maneuvering was that they were able to approach a practically deserted installation from the north.

Kovach and his driver pulled off the highway several miles from the turnoff that Whitepath had taken to the installation. They covered the distance on foot, though Kovach found it hard going. With them they had an infrared night scope and camera—incriminating enough if they were caught, but Kovach had heard enough through the consulate to guess that spies were at present the Americans' least worry.

It was 12:09 A.M. when they came in sight of the locked gate. Kovach took a careful look through the night scope, seeing a single figure occupying the gatehouse. The buildings, hidden behind a rampart of trees, were barely visible from this point. Kovach took six photographs.

In Collins's cabin the children no longer had to rely on Daisy's talent for far-seeing; now all could do it. David Lambda sensed Kovach and his driver, did a lightning analysis, and recognized in the language patterns fixed in their brains the brand of Mr. Clebb's *bad men*. By now David did not even feel it necessary to consult the others; he acted alone and immediately.

Kovach looked up from the camera as the gates below hummed smoothly open. "We had better leave," his driver said.

"Yes," Kovach said, and they withdrew.

They walked through rain-soaked forest, the slap of the wet pine branches curiously familiar to Kovach, who as a young man had spent some time in very similar country in eastern Europe. The clean smell of pine, sharp and bracing, brought it all back. He was about to remark on the memory when his driver stopped and turned in his tracks. "What is it?" Kovach asked. They had covered not even a mile from their vantage point overlooking the gate.

"I thought there was something behind us," the driver said. "Let's walk somewhat faster, Comrade Kovach, if you please."

They mended their pace, Kovach in the lead. They broke into open country near the highway and turned north, toward the place where they had concealed the automobile. Kovach again started to mention the similarity of the countryside to certain areas of Germany when his companion screamed once.

Kovach had a confused idea that his driver had fallen. "Give me your hand—" he began. Then one of the attacking dogs snarled.

In the darkness Kovach saw them as a moil of black bodies, many of them, and he smelled the coppery odor of blood at the same instant. He felt the back of his neck prickle with the strongest fear he had ever known. He dropped the camera he had been carrying and ran, his boots squelching in compacted and soaked pine straw.

The first dog fastened on his right calf. He stumbled, turned, and kicked so viciously with his left leg that he felt something break, ribs or a leg. The dog let go but did not cry out. Its exhalation was sharp and angry, the sound a Party official might make at news of a subordinate's dereliction. Kovach ran, grunting as the torn muscle below his right knee stabbed with pain at every step. His lightweight raincoat flapped around his legs, and from inside the left pocket Kovach heard the clacking of plastic: four audio tapes he had bought for his son were there, including the Beatles' white album, Pink Floyd's *Dark of the Moon*, and two collections, *The Rockin' Sixties* and *Gold of the Eighties*. Even as he ran limping, Kovach clamped his pocket shut, thinking how upset his son would be should he lose even one of the tapes. Kovach and his driver had come farther than he thought, but at last he grunted with relief, for ahead was the dark tangle of brush behind which the rented Ford waited.

The second dog came out of nowhere and struck him in the back, propelling him forward, his arms windmilling for balance. The dog tumbled over him as he went down in a headlong dive, arms splayed to break his fall. The heels of his hands skidded on the wet ground, and he felt the skin rip from his knees. Kovach was down only for a second; then he was up again and running for the car, for safety.

But the dog had risen, too, and this time it came at him from the front. He saw the leaping blur, struck at it with a sideways sweep of his arms, and felt hot breath on his cheek as teeth clacked shut just an inch short of their goal. The dog rolled off to the left, and then he was at the car. Kovach fumbled at the door—and found it locked.

Sobbing, he smashed at the side window with an elbow. The dog, or another one, sank its teeth in that arm, wrestling it down. Then another had his left ankle, and he stumbled flailing and shouting in the night. He made the only sounds himself, for the dogs ripped and chewed with a terrible silent concentration, noiseless except for the whistle of their breathing. As Kovach staggered and tried to free himself, the third dog came from the gloom and closed its jaws on his testicles, and the world flared in the white-hot explosion of the worst pain he had ever experienced. All three dogs held on, shaking their heads and snarling in frightening whisperlike rushes of breath. The strength left Kovach's limbs in that overwhelming rush of agony, and he stumbled in a heap to the ground.

Another dog struck like a shark and veered away, carrying Kovach's left ear with it. Another closed on his right hand, and he felt the teeth meet through the bones of his ring and little fingers, felt a snap and the elastic rip of flesh and muscle as the dog wrenched the fingers away. Blood ran hot from a dozen wounds, and the night turned from black to red in his failing vision. Dimly Kovach recalled something he had been taught thirty years before about attack dogs. He managed to roll to his back and throw his head back; he lay exposed, vulnerable, his throat offered in abject submission. He had been taught that a dog's natural instincts, almost always stronger, deeper, than any imposed training, would not permit it to kill a man in such a position. They would guard him, would not allow him to get up, but they would at least spare his life.

He waited that way for only a second. Two of the dogs went for his throat at precisely the same instant. After only a moment of contest, the more dominant of the two killed Kovach.

By that time there were six of the dogs at the body, including one that went on three legs, holding up a fractured left hind limb. They nosed the carrion for a moment or two, snuffled the scents of blood and excrement, shook themselves, and lifted their noses to the wind for other scents, for better ones. Outside the fence for the first time in their lives, the Dobermans inhaled a rich world of prey: rabbits, squirrels, even a fox. Without a thought for the fence they had left and without further notice of the harmless dead man, they went loping across the highway and into the woods, and now at last they gave voice to their excitement and joy at being free. Their glad cries rang like bells in the dark, died away as they ranged farther and farther away from the huddled form on the edge of the road.

When a belated traveler saw the ruined, mangled body a few feet off the highway and stopped to look at it ten minutes later, he could barely hear them, those distant wolflike cries, carried to him on the lightest of winds; but something atavistic in the sound made him clamber into his car again in a hurry and drive into Tyrell at speeds over eighty miles per hour. He was just a farmer, and he sought only aid and comfort.

What he found in Tyrell was pandemonium; but by one that morning, pandemonium was the common lot in nearly every town in the civilized world.

3

Collins was in love, more deeply in love than he had ever been in his whole life. He had forgotten his wife, had forgotten every woman he had ever touched, had ever looked at; he was lost, was drowning in Julie Lind, in the sea blue of her eyes, in the black midnight of her hair.

And she returned his ardor. He felt it, felt the strength of her passion as one can feel the warmth of a fire. His heart nearly burst with joy at her laugh; he trembled to touch her, ached when he kissed her.

They lived a courtship of weeks in a few hours. The cabin melted, dissolved. They strolled beside a blue river, not the Chanussee, but some picture-calendar river, wide, calm, shimmering with the caress of light breezes. They lounged on the banks, in thick calf-high grass, sweet in the nostrils, soft as cushions. They watched the cattails bob and dip in the wind, heard the songs of a thousand birds. They held hands and embraced and kissed, lightly at first and then with growing yet tender eagerness.

They spent nights beneath the stars, lying back and counting, following the ancient lines of constellations, seeing in the black velvet heavens Orion the Hunter, Andromeda, the Great Bear, all sharp and clear as diagrams traced in light on the dome of a planetarium.

They spoke but little, for they felt little need of speech. Their "Good morning" was "I love you"; their small talk was expressed in sighs. And yet—

And yet they did not make love. Something yet held them, some sense that things were not quite ready, that the way was not yet prepared. But that last intimacy lay in store for them, they both knew, and they looked forward to it, yearned toward it as a young plant yearns toward the light, and they knew that when it came it would come sweetly, strongly, would be as beautiful as a clear red sunrise and as exciting as a bolt of lightning through midnight skies. For such completion they could wait.

And yet—

The illusion was never quite perfect, never wholly complete. It flickered and almost faded at times, and Collins found himself looking into Julie's appalled and bewildered eyes for just a moment, just a second before everything was all right again. In those intervals the blue river would disappear and he would realize that the two of them were sitting inside, not outside, that they were on the cabin floor and that a semicircle of youngsters half-surrounded them, silver eyes intent, dreaming. But then the river would come back and the eyes would be glints of sunlight on water; Collins would quickly lose himself again in love.

In that other world, that sweet alternate reality, he lay beside Julie, stroking her hair, feeling her breath warm on his cheek, feeling the soft pressure of her breasts. He caressed her, held her, and she clung to him, and they waited for the moment when things would be right, when they could join and make their love complete.

But even that would fade; Collins would have momentary flashes of lying before the dark fireplace of the cabin, of feeling the minds of the children at work on him. At the very deepest level of his consciousness, the breaks in the illusion at last registered, tripped some underlying awareness, and from then on he fought the emotions he felt, struggled against the things he thought he saw and smelled and heard and tasted. It took a great deal of willpower for him to break through the notion that he and Julie were walking alone in a warm spring rain, to realize that they actually were merely pacing the cabin arm in arm, gaped at by the children, but he managed it.

Speech took even more effort. "Julie," he finally managed to gasp, "the children are doing this."

She looked at him without apparent comprehension. They were on a busy city sidewalk, Julie in a pink spring dress, looking so pretty that men stopped to turn their heads and smile their grateful appreciation as she passed. He felt her hand in his, saw the sunlight strong on the beige bricks of a storefront. He could smell the air, impossibly pure, could hear the hushed sounds of impossibly smooth city traffic, could almost count the hairs on a Scottie being walked by an older woman in a blue suit.

It's a movie, he thought, *a movie from the fifties, some musical or romantic fantasy they've pulled from their memories and cast us in.* "I don't understand," Julie said.

Looking at her swept his heart away. He ground his teeth so hard his jaw popped. "It isn't real," he said. "The children. Remember Johnny and Daisy and all the others."

Her eyes were stricken. She shivered. "I want it to be real," she whispered.

For a moment they were back in the cabin, he in the red plaid shirt and jeans he had put on that morning and she in the green blouse and jeans she had worn when she led the children away from the installation. Collins winced as the illusion reasserted itself, stronger than before, more insistent. The cityscape was a Technicolor marvel, solid and real, the women's hats and clothes in the shop windows a little girl's dress-up dream. It was all Collins could do to hold on to his determination. "They're making us think we're in love," he said. "We're not. We only met yesterday—"

"Oh, Pete, that isn't true. We've known each other for ages and ages." The outfit she wore was youthful, little-girlish, an Easter-parade ensemble with puffy sleeves and a full skirt, a broad-brimmed white hat topping it, setting off her wonderful eyes and her inky hair. She smiled at him. "You're acting so funny. I love you."

"You don't," he said with a determination that tore his heart. "You don't. They're using us, Julie. Remember them. Remember their eyes. You can't forget their eyes."

She looked stricken, then fell against him, embracing him. "I want it to be real," she said with fierce insistence. "I'll make it be real."

He held her—

And found himself again in that luminous void. Alone.

"Johnny?" he said, or thought.

—Please. Accept this from us, both of you. It will be so much easier. Love will grow; it will be real. Accept it as real for now.

Collins had no eyes that he could sense, and yet he felt like weeping. "Johnny, you don't know what love is between a man and a woman. You're too young—"

—We know. We have seen these things on television, have read about them.

"What you know about isn't love. It isn't real, Johnny!" Collins floundered for words. "It's—it's a cheat. You're making us puppets, putting other people's words in our mouths, other people's feelings in our hearts. Johnny, people can write about love and can make movies about love, but they can never explain it, can never make it real. It's different from what you read or see, and you can't make us love each other by pretending."

—But you do love each other. Miss Julie loves you. You love her. Not as much as we need, but the love is there. We sense it; we make it stronger; we do not pretend. We make it grow faster than it would in the real world, but not falsely. Accept the love you each feel for the other. You are almost ready. Things are almost prepared.

"Things are prepared? Our bodies, you mean? Have you changed our bodies, Johnny? Prepared them so that we can be the parents of your children? Yours, Johnny, the children you determine for us? Not our own?"

—Please. Accept what we must do to make the experience right for you, pleasant for you. It is necessary. You will love the child. We will assure this. And if we are killed, the child will carry on our kind. Please. There are enemies nearer than you think, and time is very short. I am needed. I must lead the others, convince some of them, show them the way we must take in Becoming. We have progressed very far, but we have much yet to do, and we are not yet in agreement. I am needed.

"What are you doing?"

(Collins sensed reluctance, hesitation.)

—We are attempting to Become. There are no words for this. We will—will go away. Will be in a place like this one. But we will not be separate; we will be one Being then. And we will have no bodies. We will be—will be like—like what you call God.

"Johnny, no!"

—I cannot explain better. I am sorry. Pete, please do not be afraid. We do not wish to hurt you, nor will we. Take the gift we offer. I must go.

"Johnny—"

Julie was warm in his arms. She turned her lovely face up to him. "Oh, darling, I am so happy," she said, waiting to be kissed.

He kissed her, kissed her as they stood there on the corner of two busy city streets, and when he looked up the cop in the crosswalk was beaming at him, the shoe-shine boy gave him a wistful smile, the woman with the Scottie nodded in gentle encouragement. Collins was confused, for he had been thinking of something else; but Julie had just consented to be his wife, the sun was warm and the city traffic a drowsy hum in the background, the air was sweet and the dark thing at the back of his mind soon vanished as all suspicion, all doubt, slipped into the oblivion of forgetfulness.

4

"We are safe," Stark insisted, but his uncertain smile belied his words.

Fisher, just off the radio, gave the geneticist a sardonic glare. "Nobody's safe, Stark. Hell's breaking loose all over the globe. We've lost touch with Washington. God only knows what your monsters are doing to the armed forces here."

Stark spread his hands in an inclusive gesture. Fisher noticed that they were speckled with torn paper; the gutted hymnal was only confetti now, scattered across the floor of the basement room in drifts like a dusting of snow. Stark asked reasonably, "Have they struck against the National Guard here? Have they struck against the state policemen? Have they made the least threat against them? No. And do you know why?"

"Suppose you tell me."

Stark adjusted his tweed coat—after more than twenty-four hours in it, he was losing his dapperness and beginning to look more than a bit seedy, with a fair stubble of beard on his square jaw and his collar open, his tie long since discarded—and in a professorial tone he said, "The subjects have been deeply conditioned to respect the forces of good. To this point in their lives, they have been completely directed by our people; they have developed a deep dependency on the adults of the installation. This being so, the subjects will perceive our side as representing the forces of good, if"—Stark raised a monitory forefinger—"if we do nothing to counteract that perception."

Fisher, sitting at a table normally reserved for a Baptist Sunday school class, regarded Stark with sour distaste.

"They're not as harmless as you make out, Dr. Stark. I'm betting that what happened to Lamont was their fault. That doesn't seem particularly friendly to me."

Stark pointed at him, his stubby pink finger stabbing home his point. "Ah. But you remember the testimony of the deaf man, the Martin man who owned the gasoline station. Lamont chased this wild Indian, this Whitepath, to the service station and shot him, perhaps killed him. This kind of direct violence is strong enough to counteract the subjects' conditioning; probably nothing else is. To such a show of violence they will always react violently. If no violence is offered, their response will be a peaceful one."

Fisher grunted. "Then what do we do when we find them? Get on our knees and ask them pretty please to get back in their cages?"

Stark gave him an icy-eyed smile as he dusted the last fragments of paper from his fingers, from his jacket. "That might be the best approach, after all."

"Impossible. These children have become more of a threat to this planet than the entire nuclear arsenal. There's no way they can be allowed to survive."

The geneticist had been pacing. He sat now across the table from Fisher, clasped his hands together, forcibly keeping them still. "We must keep that thought well in the back of our minds. We must show them a face of friendship. It may be that we can win their trust back, that we can direct their powers ourselves. That would not be so bad, hmm?"

Fisher returned Stark's smile, but he had no thought of sharing any control with the scientist. "And what if they don't trust us?" he asked. "Since they react against violence with violence, what can we do?"

"Make friends with them. Failing that, we must of course eliminate them. But we must do so with suddenness and decision; we must not hesitate. We must scarcely give ourselves time to consider the action, to contemplate the result. If we do, we are surely lost, for they will turn our efforts against us."

A state patrolman knocked at the door. Fisher rose and went over to him. "What do you want?"

"It's nearly daylight, sir," the patrolman said. "You wanted the helicopter sweeps to start again at first light?"

Fisher nodded. "Just as soon as it's possible to see the ground. How's the weather?"

"Cold front passed through. It's clear with an unlimited ceiling, fifteen-mile visibility."

"Okay. Get the choppers up as soon as there's enough light."

"Yes, sir."

Fisher came back to the table and stood behind the chair he had occupied. "It won't do any good," he said with morose certainty. "We went over every inch of ground yesterday morning and saw nothing."

"Then we were not looking for the correct thing," Stark murmured. "As I have told you repeatedly, the children cannot be in the open. Someone must have taken them in. I would say the Indian, Whitepath, is the most probable suspect."

Fisher shook his head. "Not Whitepath. We took his house apart. It doesn't even look like he had company for the past couple of weeks. No way sixteen or seventeen kids had been staying there."

"Then," Stark said, "it is logical to assume that the children are with someone the Indian knew."

After a moment, Fisher went back to the door. One of his own men stood there in the corridor, and Fisher dispatched him on an errand. His attention was taken then by other questions, by their futile attempts to regain radio or telephone contact with D.C., by this and that. Thirty minutes later the guard reappeared, bringing with him a wiry man of fifty or so, dressed in dark green twill trousers, oxblood hiking boots, and a white T-shirt. "This is Kenneth Woodall, sir," the guard said. "He was Whitepath's boss."

"I fired him," Woodall said, his voice querulous, sleepy, and defensive. "You guys told me he shouldn't have been nosing around that compound of yours, and I fired him, just the way you told me to. I—"

"Sit down, Mr. Woodall," Fisher said. Woodall took the seat Fisher had vacated. "Yes, I remember speaking to you on the phone. I want you to know that you did the right thing. The President and I conferred about the possible breach of security, and we agreed that you were a great help."

"I didn't vote for him," Woodall said.

Fisher smiled. "Well, be that as it may. We want to know something about Whitepath now. Some of the people he knew, some of his good friends."

Woodall pulled his nose, as if that aided him in thought. "Will isn't in trouble, is he?"

Stark gave Fisher a quick glance of warning. "He's disappeared," Fisher lied immediately. "We've lost track of him."

Woodall snorted. "Looks to me like he didn't have much to hang around for after you guys made me take his job away from him. Hell, Will Whitepath has lived in this county all his life. He's not some kind of spy or something."

"We're not sure what he is, Mr. Woodall. It's even possible he's in danger himself. It's very important that we locate him as soon as possible. It could be a matter of your job if you don't help us."

Woodall stared at Fisher. "Son of a bitch," he said. "I don't know whether I want to help you or not."

They convinced him. By four-fifteen that morning they had convinced him. Woodall named a dozen people that Whitepath had associated with, most of them Forestry Service employees; Fisher himself took the names down. As day broke outside the improvised headquarters, Woodall ran down and ran out of names. "I guess that's all," he said. "Will wasn't what you'd call a real sociable fellow." He started to say something else, stopped, and then shrugged. "There is one other man he fished with," he said. "Writer fellow been coming up to a cabin on the Chanussee for three-four years or so. Won a big newspaper prize a while back."

"What is the man's name?" Stark asked.

"Let me see." Woodall pulled his nose again. "Collins, it is," he said at last. "Yeah, that's it. Pete Collins."

5

Randall Grade was back in the White House at 4:00 A.M. The President sat at the head of a polished walnut table in the basement Situation Room, chairing a meeting of twelve advisers, including representatives from the Joint Chiefs of Staff, four Cabinet secretaries, and others—like Grade—of more esoteric classification.

"Gentlemen," the President said. After a moment he added, "and, ah, lady," acknowledging belatedly the presence of the acting Secretary of the Interior. "We seem to have an unprecedented situation on our hands. I trust you have all been briefed." After an uneasy murmur of assent, the President cleared his throat and continued: "Generals Marchman and Creighton and Admiral McLean have assured me that so far, despite the, ah, unrest evidenced in the Warsaw Pact nations, Central America, and the Persian Gulf, there is no evidence of any direct threat to the United States."

"No," muttered the Secretary of State, a crusty veteran of the bureaucracy. "We're providing that ourselves."

The President did not notice—or perhaps did not deign to notice—the remark. "We have some indication that the problems are exacerbated by certain domestic developments. Mr. Grade is currently working on that end of the difficulty, and I have no doubt he will be successful."

Grade gave the chief a reassuring smile, though his stomach plummeted at the expression of confidence. It meant that if Fisher failed to bring the damned project under control, Grade's ass was on the line. But he kept any trace of resentment out of his features, nodding encouragement, noting how the President's brow was beaded with sweat.

"Yes, well," the President said. "Currently we have a strong need to determine exactly how to handle our, ah, domestic problems. I understand that the governors of at least four states have requested federal assistance in dealing with urban violence. I am told that the, uh, unrest is even worse than in the sixties, worse even than the rioting that followed the assassination of Dr. Martin Luther King. I cannot stress to you how urgent the necessity for action appears at this moment. Consequently, I have authorized the full cooperation of the National Guard with the governors of the states in question—"

"Mistake," the Secretary of State snapped. "Sir, with respect, the overseas problems could escalate into violence at any moment. It would be a tragic error to tie up potential reserves at a time when . . ."

Grade's head throbbed. The room felt stuffy, although the President, a notorious fitness buff, absolutely forbade smoking in his presence—a restriction that did not much please at least four of the men present, including the Secretary of State. Grade rubbed his eyes, feeling woozy. Lack of sleep, he decided. Stress. If he didn't hear from Fisher soon—

"We *know* the source," the President was saying. "For reasons of national security I cannot fully explain to you at this moment the complete story behind the trouble, but we have isolated a source."

Grade frowned at his watch; he had lost ten minutes or so along in there somewhere—dozing? He didn't recall dropping off or waking up. Someone was asking the President a question: ". . . in view of the extremely serious nature of the problem, what will you do to . . ."

Grade met the President's eyes. The man looked trapped, haunted. "I have authorized those in charge to use full force to terminate the problem," he said. "Mr. Grade will confirm that."

The Secretary of State again: "Do you mean you have authorized the deaths of those responsible, Mr. President?"

It was the kind of blunt question that the President hated, the sort he always avoided in press conferences. But now he set his jaw. "Yes, I do mean exactly that. Murder is not, and I stress again, not a normal instrument of policy of this administration, as you well know. However, this case has extraordinary ramifications, potentially—potentially—" He floundered for a word.

"Apocalyptic," murmured Grade.

"—apocalyptic implications, yes. I promise you, when you learn the full story you will see why it has proved necessary for me, reluctantly, to authorize the use of extreme force against those responsible."

To kill the kids, Grade corrected mentally. And then he knew with clarity what had to be done. It was, as the President had implied, a regrettable necessity; but bad men could not be permitted to live.

Grade, with the highest security clearance of any person in the nation except for the President himself, was privileged to carry a weapon. Before any of the twelve others at the table could move or react, he had drawn it and had fired once. The thunderous report overpowered the soundproofing of the Situation Room and brought in the Secret Service guards right away, but they were already too late.

Randall Grade was very good at what he did.

6

News bulletins from the Global News satellite service:

4:46 AM EDST. LONDON (4 JULY): A MASSIVE COMMUNICATIONS FAILURE HAS CUT OFF ALL US AND NATO MILITARY BASES FROM THE OUTSIDE WORLD, WELL-PLACED SPOKESMEN SAID TODAY. NO OFFICIAL CONFIRMATION HAS YET BEEN ISSUED, BUT OTHER SOURCES INDICATE A TOTAL COMMUNICATIONS BLACKOUT. ONE SOURCE DENIES THAT THE MILITARY SILENCE IS IN ANY WAY TIED TO RECENT REPORTS OF UNREST AND UPRISINGS IN THE SOVIET UNION, EASTERN EUROPE, AND GERMANY. REF 7393 112, 116, 321. MORE.

4:51 AM EDST. CAIRO (4 JULY): THE EXPLOSIONS IN THE OILFIELDS OF KUWAIT, IRAQ, AND IRAN WERE THE RESULT OF AMERICAN-ISRAELI MILITARY ACTION ACCORDING TO ONE MILITANT ARAB GROUP. THIS ORGANIZATION, A LOOSE COALITION OF ISLAMIC EXTREMISTS AND SUSPECTED TERRORISTS, CALLS ITSELF THE "ARM OF ALLAH" AND HAS VOWED TO SEEK VENGEANCE FOR WHAT IT TERMS "AN ACT OF WAR BY THE ZIONIST IMPERIALIST FORCES OF SATAN." SEE FOLLOWING UPDATE. REF 7393 1114, 7493 12, 19, 22. MORE.

4:52 AM EDST. CAIRO (4 JULY): OILFIELDS ON BOTH SIDES OF THE PERSIAN GULF CONTINUE TO BLAZE AT THIS HOUR. NO EXPLANATION FOR THE EXPLOSIONS HAS BEEN FORTHCOMING, ALTHOUGH SOURCES HAVE EXPRESSED THE OPINION THAT THE BLASTS APPEARED TO BE THE WORK OF SABOTEURS

WORKING INTERNALLY RATHER THAN OF
MISSILES OR BOMBS. REF 7393 1114, 7493 12, 19,
22, 102. ENDIT.

5:01 AM EDST. WASHINGTON, DC (4 JULY): ONE
OR MORE MILITARY AIRCRAFT HAVE CRASHED
IN THE IMMEDIATE VICINITY OF THE
PENTAGON. MORE TO FOLLOW.

5:02 AM EDST. NEW YORK CITY (4 JULY): POLICE
HAVE NO EXPLANATION FOR THE CONTINUED
WAVE OF VIOLENCE IN THE STREETS. POLICE
CAPTAIN MYRON LEVITT SAYS, "SO FAR THE
VICTIMS HAVE BEEN CRIMINALS, INCLUDING
ORGANIZED CRIME FIGURES AND FREE-
LANCERS. IT'S LIKE EVERYBODY WHO EVER
USED VIOLENCE AGAINST ANOTHER PERSON
HAS BEEN MOVED TO COMMIT SUICIDE." MORE.

5:03 AM EDST. WASHINGTON, DC (4 JULY):
FURTHER TO AIRCRAFT CRASH: EYEWITNESSES
HAVE CONFIRMED THAT ONE OR MORE
AIRCRAFT, ALL BELIEVED TO BE US MILITARY
AIRPLANES, HAVE CRASHED ON PENTAGON
GROUNDS; DAMAGE IS GREAT, MUCH LOSS OF
LIFE EXPECTED. MORE.

5:05 AM EDST. HUNTSVILLE, AL (4 JULY):
NASA OFFICIALS REPORT UNEXPLAINED
INTERFERENCE WITH MILITARY SATELLITES
NOT BELIEVED TO BE CAUSED BY THE
CURRENT HIGH-ACTIVE SUNSPOT PERIOD.
SOME INTERFERENCE WITH COMMUNICATIONS
SA

PRIORITY INTERRUPT PRIORITY INTERRUPT

5:05 AM EDST. WASHINGTON DC (4 JULY): THE
PRESIDENT OF THE UNITED STATES HAS BEEN
ASSASSINATED. SECRET SERVICE PERSONNEL
HAVE TAKEN INTO CUSTODY A MAN
IDENTIFIED AS RANDALL GRADE, CHAIRMAN
OF JOINT INTELLIGENCE SERVICES REVIEW
COMMITTEE. DETAILS TO FOLLOW. MORE.

5:06 AM EDST. CONTINUATION: 7493 107:
TELLITES HAS BEEN NOTED AS WELL. MORE.

5:07 AM EDST. WASHINGTON DC (4 JULY): THE
PRESIDENT OF THE UNITED STATES HAS BEEN
REPORTED DOA AT BETHESDA NAVAL
HOSPITAL. UNCONFIRMED REPORTS INDICATE
THAT THE MAN BELIEVED RESPONSIBLE,
RANDALL GRADE, CHAIRMAN OF THE JOINT
INTELLIGENCE SERVICES REVIEW COMMITTEE,
HAS DIED IN CUSTODY. MORE TO FOLLOW.

The satellite feed went dead at 5:07:32 EDST.

7

The wedding had been picture-perfect, a whipped-cream
dream of a wedding. Will Whitepath had stood as best
man, his dark face breaking into an irrepressible smile.
Lieutenant Colonel Engstrom, in full dress uniform, had
given the bride away. Collins drifted through the cere-
mony as a man drifts through a dream, unable himself to
repress a smile at the incongruous figure of Will in tux
and black tie.

Julie made a beautiful bride, her dress white silk, yards
and yards of it, the train upheld by pretty little Daisy
Rho. The church was a lovely place, though rather odd:
the perspectives seemed off, somehow, distance decep-
tive. At one moment the kaleidoscopic stained-glass circle in the wall above the altar was a formless collage of
colors and shapes; at the next it was a suffering Christ.
And then it was an eye, the eye of God, silvery and
benign as it looked down upon the solemnity of the
service, the consecration of the love the man and the
woman felt for each other.

The minister was a hard man to see. Sometimes Collins
thought him to young, a fair-haired boy of only twelve or
thirteen, his face solemn as he read the words from the
ancient Book; and sometimes Collins thought him old, an
ageless little old man with eyes kind and wise, with a
voice piping to childish treble in the fullness of his age.
Something about the minister troubled Collins, though
he would have been hard pressed to put his uneasiness
into words. Indeed, no words were needed, save those
that he repeated after the minister, the words pledging

eternal love, eternal partnership. He heard weeping in the auditorium as he said them, weeping from Mrs. Engstrom and from Mrs. Arnold, whom he recognized by name even though they were strangers to him.

There was cake afterward, a towering white cathedral of cake, crowned with tiny figures of himself and Julie, her bridal train elongating into a spiral of icing that wound all the way down the cake, growing as it did. There were cake and wine and toasting, there was rice to be thrown with shouted congratulations.

It was corny, Collins felt in his heart of hearts, but it was the kind of corny that he sneakingly liked, down to the shoes and cans tied to the Ford Ranger, down to the crudely lettered JUST MARRIED sign on the back of the car. He felt the rice thrown by the happy guests as he and Julie descended the chapel steps; he shook hands with Will and saw the deep sadness in his friend's eyes. "I'm glad I could see this," Whitepath said. "Take care, my friend."

"You're late," Collins heard himself saying. "We waited for you all day, Will."

The hand squeezed his. "I have been through the dark tunnel," Will said. "I have come into the other light."

Collins felt his throat go husky. Whitepath's young-old face seemed to waver, to become a mask worn by a much younger person, perhaps by a child. "Are you here at all? Am I imagining you?"

"A little of both. Don't be afraid of the tunnel, Pete. It is different from what you imagine. *They* see an end to it now; *they* couldn't before. And at the other end is a different light." He paused. "It is hard to explain. You imagine me yet your imagination tells you the things I would say to you if I were really here." The familiar white grin broke on the dark face like a brilliant sunrise. "Shit, I'm no good at philosophy. But the important thing is to take care of her, Pete. She does love you."

"You're dead, aren't you?"

A look of gentle regret replaced the grin. "Have to say goodbye, my friend."

And then Pete and Julie were driving away from the church, driving through a lovely landscape of green rolling hills. Somehow Eightball was there with them, pink tongue lolling in the breeze, and the little dog even looked dressed for a wedding himself, the white spot on his chest like a formal shirtfront, his jet-colored coat as decorous as Whitepath's tux had been. The sun, a lemon sun out of a Warner Brothers cartoon, shone in a perfect sky as they drove, the shoes and cans striking unlikely melodies behind them.

They came up to the bridge to the cabin suddenly, and Collins felt a dizzy moment of confusion, for he knew no church remotely like the one they had been married in stood anywhere near the Chanussee. But he lost the thought with one look at Julie, at the adoration in her dark eyes. He felt himself melting toward her, his doubts consumed in a flame of pure love. He stepped out of the car and took her in his arms, her soft weight warm and alive, no hallucination. He carried her up the three porch steps and across the threshold and, still holding her, gave her a lingering kiss. Without his touching it, the door closed softly behind them.

The cabin was somehow transformed, no longer a rough three-room bachelor hideout. The walls seemed papered with flowers, realistic enough to breathe a sweet fragrance into the rooms; and there seemed to be more rooms, too, great chambers out of movies about wealthy people, chandeliers lighting them, curved staircases leading up to other floors and other rooms. Collins knew it was crazy, realized that it was impossible; he believed himself dreaming, wondered if it all had been a dream, the storm, the lost child—what was his name?—everything.

But the woman in his arms was real. Julie returned his kiss, and he carried her into the bedroom, where a four-poster waited for them, the coverlet turned down already. There beside the old-fashioned bed he set her down and looked at her, his eyes hungry, feeding, glutting themselves on her beauty. She blushed and lowered her own eyes, then with a quick movement took off her veil and shook her hair free: it spilled like velvet night across the white shoulders of her wedding dress.

He opened the dress tenderly. The silk whispered away from her arms, exposing her soft, warm skin. He kissed the hollow of her throat, feeling beneath his lips the eager leap of her pulse. His tongue tasted the slight salt of her skin. His hands were busy with the fastenings of her bodice. After a moment the dress fell away and she stepped out of it, came warmly into his arms, her own hands undoing the studs of his shirt, pulling away the cummerbund at his waist. He stooped as she tugged at his clothing, his lips touching her breasts, excited by their softness as they become taut with wanting.

The clothes fell away like leaves in autumn, letting skin press hot skin. He felt her heat soft against him, almost feverish in its intensity. Her mouth opened to his, and his tongue probed inside, tasting the spiciness of her. His hands caressed her long satin back as he marveled at the smoothness, the electric tension of muscle, the ready yielding of her willing flesh to his touch.

They lay on the bed together, kissing, limbs twining in an embrace so tight that it seemed nothing could break it, ever. Yet as his need for her grew sharper and more urgent, something nasty ticked away in his skull, some small thought of evil or of wrongness.

But he wanted her with his whole being, he worshiped her. He whispered, "I love you, Julie. God, I love you so."

She held him tighter still, pulling him against her. He felt her readiness and entered her, experiencing almost a shock of pleasure at that moment. "Yes," she breathed in his ear. "Oh, yes."

They moved together, slowly at first, and then with growing urgency. She clutched him against her so tightly that they were almost literally one being, one person, lost in pleasure so overwhelming that it had erased the differences between them. A moment came when they simultaneously found release, a shattering moment of rushing pleasure, the strongest Collins had ever felt. His spine grew rigid, his head went back, and he gasped for breath.

He opened his eyes at that instant.

Five children clustered around the bed, Kathy Beta in the center, two boys on her right, two girls on her left. With solemn eyes they witnessed the act of love.

Collins felt a wash of shame and confusion. Kathy's head inclined slightly to the right—

—and then the scene was the splendid bedroom, and nothing was on the chair beside the bed except for their discarded clothing, and Julie was under him, her thighs

locked around his, and she crooned, "Oh, it was so good,
so good."

Collins began to weep.

8

Clint Jernigan had worn out his ability to weep. He
had done that hours ago as the interrogation team moved
from physical persuasion to threats against Susan, who
was held somewhere else in the building. Naked except
for his shorts, strapped to a flat leather cot, Jernigan was
exhausted now, whenever "now" was; almost dawn, surely,
he thought.

Franklin, the good cop—or agent or whatever the hell
he was—leaned over him. "Clint, I'm sorry he's doing
this to you. Believe me, I'm very sorry. If you could just
tell him a little, maybe he'd—"

"Listen to me. I am an officer in the United States Air
Force. You people are going to be in very deep shit—"

"Clint, Clint. I know what you are, and Travis knows,
too. It doesn't matter to Travis. Look, tell us what we
need to know and I'll guarantee that we'll get you back
to your base within an hour. Less, even. All you have to
do is cooperate."

"Go to hell," Jernigan said in a flat, weary voice.
Sweat trickled across his chest, down his side, tickling
him. More stung his eyes. He welcomed the sensation as
a blessed distraction from the throbbing bruises on his
face, arms, and chest.

The door banged open, making Jernigan start in fright,
and suddenly Travis was there again, the bad cop. "Don't
waste your time on this jigaboo," he said in a voice like
cold dripping sorghum syrup. "Niggers don't have sense
enough to know when they're offered a good deal, Franklin. Ain't you learned that yet?" Travis, a big white man
with wiry black hair, somehow Italian-looking but not
really, grabbed Jernigan's ear and twisted it, making
Jernigan strain his neck upward against the straps that
held him down, trying to ease the pressure before the
cartilage ripped. "That your nigger-mobile you drove up
in? Listen, I hear you're real proud of that rolling piece
of shit. Maybe you'd like a souvenir. Here."

Jernigan opened his eyes. In his free hand Travis held a wrenched-off windshield wiper, blade, arm, and all, in front of him. With it the man took a vicious swipe at Jernigan's face, and Jernigan felt the crusted split-open bruise on his cheek open and begin to bleed again. "I'm tired of shittin' with you, nigger," Travis bawled, his breath foul in Jernigan's nostrils, his saliva spraying on Jernigan's cheek. "Tell us where the goddam kids are and we'll let you go."

"I don't know," Jernigan said for the twentieth time, or for the two hundredth. "I told you that I was just concerned because I worked with Colonel Engstrom—"

The windshield wiper cracked down on his groin, making his scrotum erupt with violent pain. Jernigan could not even scream; his chest heaved for air that seemed no longer to exist. "No lies, you son of a bitch!" Travis ranted in his ear, his breath smelling like decay. "We know all about you and this goddam Engstrom couple. You're gonna goddam well let us know where they were going, or—"

"Travis!" It was Franklin. Jernigan opened his eyes, saw a tear-blurred image of the two men, Franklin restraining Travis's arm as the curly-haired bastard raised the wiper for another blow. Jernigan heard himself making a cawing sound, trying to sob. He could not control it. Franklin gave him an apprehensive look. "Travis. Go for coffee. Look, let me talk to Colonel Jernigan alone. You said you would."

Franklin threw the wiper aside with a contemptuous flick of his wrist. It clattered off the tile wall somewhere to Jernigan's left. Travis said, "Okay, Franklin. But this is the last time I'm leaving him." He pointed at Jernigan. "There's something left of your nigger-mobile now, Jernigan. Enough to put back together, maybe. But there ain't gonna be one piece of that car connected to another by the time I finish with it, you understand? I'm gonna take care of it right after I take care of your old lady. You got five minutes to start talking to my friend here. After that, forget your goddam car and forget your old woman. Hell, I'm so horny you might not even have that long." He went out, slamming the door behind him.

Franklin leaned over and with a square of gauze swabbed the blood that trickled warm from Jernigan's cut cheek.

"I'm sorry, Clint," he said. He was a soft-looking man with thinning, wispy brown hair and concerned brown eyes behind black-rimmed spectacles. "Travis comes from Mississippi, you know what I mean? Way out in the boonies, man. But he's right, you know. We need the information, Clint. Look, just tell us what you know and I'll do my best to—"

Jernigan blinked. "What?"

Franklin was all patience: "I say, if you'll just cooperate with us, just give us the information we need, I'll have that son of a bitch Travis brought up on charges. I promise you that."

Jernigan closed his eyes, and it was better. The image of Fritz Engstrom came to him, burly, platinum-haired Fritz. A good man to play cards with, to golf with. A good man to fight beside you if it came to that. And these bastards had killed him. What was it that Engstrom had told him that morning? Anybody can be killed. Right. Sorry, my friend. God, I am so very sorry.

Jernigan clung to the memory of Fritz Engstrom as he had last seen him, earlier in the week: Engstrom standing outside his own house, waving farewell. But the picture began to waver in Jernigan's mind. He thought he was passing out until he noticed the change: it was no longer a man's figure that he pictured. He could still see the front of the Engstroms' house, but now a little boy stood there, a little white boy maybe twelve, thirteen years old.

Try as he might, Jernigan could not replace the image of the child with the one he had held of the man, and for the first time he was truly afraid—not just afraid that he would be hurt, or that Susan would be hurt, but deeply terrified, afraid that they had done something to his mind, to the deepest part of him, not just to his car or to his flesh. The boy was *real* in some impossible sense, and he looked familiar. He looked—Jernigan cast about in his mind—he looked like—

"Fritz," Jernigan breathed.

Franklin, leaning close beside his ear, said, "Yes? What about colonel Engstrom?"

And the boy, Fritz's image said, no, *thought* to Jernigan:

—You were my father's friend. Are these bad men you are with?

"The worst," Jernigan agreed. "Oh, man, the worst."

The boy nodded and went away.

"I don't understand, Clint," Franklin was saying. "I—"

The door banged open again, and this time even Franklin started, as if Travis's entrance were not in the script. He spun toward the door, and Jernigan saw Travis there propelling Susan ahead of him, grasping her hard by her left upper arm, and he saw the glistening tracks of tears on Susan's cheeks—

"Jesus, Travis," Franklin said.

"Make him stop," Travis said in a hoarse voice very unlike his own. "Make him stop you nigger jungle bunny jigaboo—" His voice rose to a screeching treble. He pushed Susan away, and she fell beyond Jernigan's range of vision. Franklin had gotten to his feet. He approached Travis with both hands raised to shoulder height, placatingly.

"Hey, hey, control it," Franklin said. "Come on, buddy—"

Like a striking rattler, Travis's hand dived into Franklin's open jacket. It came out with a squat black revolver. "No," Travis said between clenched teeth. White spittle appeared at the corners of his mouth, his thin lips stretched taut in a rictus of effort.

The revolver rose as if of its own volition. Franklin took one step back before it fired. From where he lay Jernigan saw the thin, fine hair flash away from the skull, saw a thick wad of blood and brain matter leap out. Franklin's head snapped forward, not back, and he fell against the table where Jernigan lay. Jernigan felt the impact and heard the thud as the body hit the floor.

Travis was struggling to bring the revolver up. It got as far as Jernigan's groin. "Gonna kill you, nigger," Travis said. "Gonna kill you—"

The pistol veered to the right as if pushed by an invisible hand. Making a tiger face of effort, Travis tried to bring it back to bear on Jernigan. Jernigan, despite his terror, found himself reminded of Uncle Dick Jernigan, his father's brother, who had stayed in some shithole in Missouri when his family had moved to Detroit. He was determined to make the old farm pay off, and of course he wound up by losing everything he owned. Uncle Dick had come to live with them when Clint was in college, a white-haired bent old man with the same soft accent as

Clint's father but with a head full of the goddamnedest country-bred notions.

Such as dowsing. Clint remembered the time when he, at the age of twenty, had been taken in hand by Dick Jernigan, when the old man had walked him over a piece of ground while Clint held a forked willow branch horizontal. Clint had humored his uncle, though even in the open he hated the smell of him, sweat and Red Man chewing tobacco combined in an ungodly reek. "Water right here, close by. See where you find hit. Hold that wand straight, now, straight!"

"There's no scientific basis for believing this," Clint told his aged uncle.

"Uh-huh. Don't talk to me 'bout 'scientific.' Hold it straight, now, you hear?"

And all at once the willow branch had come alive in his hand, pulling down with a force greater than gravity, a strength powerful enough to pop the muscles in Clint's arms, to raise the sinews in his neck until he could feel them like hard leather cords beneath his skin. It was enough to scare him.

And now Travis had his own dowsing rod in the pistol; and it did not choose to seek Jernigan's blood. It turned on the man who held it, turned on a crying, cursing Travis, until he looked directly down the barrel. "I hate you," Travis said in a ragged rasp. "Goddam you to hell, I hate, hate, ha—"

The explosion obliterated his left eye. Travis fell out of Jernigan's vision.

Susan was over him in a second, her fingers working at the straps that held his arms, his legs, his head, his throat. "Oh, they've cut you, they've hurt you," she murmured as the straps came loose. She kissed him as he rose up.

He looked at her, but her white blouse was not spotted with blood, nor were her light blue slacks, and her face and arms showed no bruises. "They hurt you, darling?" he asked.

She shook her head. "Kept me locked in a room by myself all this time until that Travis man came for me. Can you walk?"

"I can walk. Where are my clothes?" he asked, trying

to make his words distinct. The room spun around him, and he felt as if he was about to faint.

"I don't know," Susan said, surprisingly calmly. "You could take Travis's there. I don't think they're bloody."

The back of the suit jacket was, but the trousers and shirt were all right, and Franklin's loafers—Travis had surprisingly small feet for a big man—fit Jernigan's feet well enough. Jernigan took the revolver, and together he and Susan sought a way out of the building.

It was easy. They walked up a flight of stairs, pressed a crash bar marked "Fire Exit Only," set off a clanging alarm, and found themselves outside in the pale milky light of earliest dawn. The Lincoln waited there in the parking lot, intact except for a missing windshield wiper on the passenger side. They walked toward it. "If they just left the keys inside—" Jernigan began.

The door latch on the driver's side clicked. The door opened by itself. Jernigan looked at Susan. She smiled back at him and shook her head. "You're healing up," she said with wonder in her voice. Her cool fingers touched his cheek, and as they did Jernigan realized that the bruise seemed to have vanished.

He slid behind the wheel, wondering at himself. Minutes before he had been racked with pain, ready to pass out; now he felt nearly well. He reached across and unlocked Susan's door for her. She got into the front seat, slid over next to him. She pulled the passenger door closed, and Jernigan shut the driver's door.

The keys were gone.

But as soon as both doors had slammed, the engine started. Jernigan wasn't in the least surprised. It seemed *right* that the automobile would start itself for him like that, right that it was repaying his years of kindness with a loyalty of its own.

"Well," he said, putting the car in gear. It eased forward. "Where to now?" he asked Susan. He felt tickled inside, happier than he had been in years.

Susan's smile looked just as joyful as he felt. "Home."

He frowned at her. "Home? You crazy? After—" He broke off. After what? Something had happened; there had been some bad men, he thought. But he was damned if he could remember them clearly anymore. "What we got to do at home?" he asked.

"Make a baby, Clint," Susan said as if it were the most reasonable thing in the world to say, mild surprise in her voice.

Of course. That was it. That was it exactly. Clint Jernigan smiled, put his arm around his wife, and drove out of the parking lot.

They had to make a baby.

On the way, his voice remote and dreamy, Jernigan said, "If it's a boy, let's name him Fritz."

"Names won't matter now," Susan said, clinging to his arm.

They both laughed all the way home.

CHAPTER TEN

1

Bell helicopters requisitioned from Dobbins AFB swept overhead as thick as dragonflies on a hot July morning. Karl Stark, unhappy and sweltering on the ground, looked up as they buzzed the convoy, wishing he were aboard one of them; but Fisher had taken the high road, leaving him with no option other than the ground. The Slow Tango group was, as Fisher acidly pointed out, very short of leadership at the moment. Stark patted his neck with a handkerchief, hating the rough prickling feel of stubble; he was normally as neat as a cat, and the indignity of going without bathing or shaving for two full days was beginning to vex him more than anything else about this expedition.

Sunday had dawned bright and clean; it was a glorious Fourth, cooler than the previous day but to Stark still uncomfortably warm, nearly 80 degrees Fahrenheit at 10:00 A.M. The heat, the noise, and the dust all combined to make Stark a most miserable man. He rode in an open military vehicle and should at least have been able to enjoy a breeze, but the trucks that rumbled ahead of them, olive-drab National Guard vehicles laden with men or with weaponry, raised a hellish orange-red dust that seemed to have a natural affinity for Stark's fair skin. Trace amounts of it had been tolerable while the convoy of trucks was still on the paved highway, but here, on this godforsaken dirt road, the clinging, choking, blinding dust plastered itself to him, gritty and abrasive on his skin.

Brakes squeaked from up ahead, and the young driver swung wide to the left. "Looks like this must be the place," he said. The car jounced to a halt in a grassy flat patch beside the road, and Stark stood up to take a look.

285

The other vehicles had spread out in an uneven line, their hoods toward a wide, moderately moving stretch of river. A wooden bridge spanned it, and on the other side of the bridge the road wound off to the right, became a weed-choked lane, and at last simply petered out, or seemed to, in a tangle of scrub pine and weeds. "But there is no house on the other side," Stark said. Someone tugged at the front of his damp shirt, and he looked down. It was his own hand, reproving him for having nothing to occupy it, no paper to tear.

"There don't seem to be," the driver agreed readily, lighting an unfiltered Camel cigarette with a pink disposable butane lighter.

Shading his eyes, Stark looked up the river and then downstream. "But this cannot then be the correct place. We were told that the Collins man's cabin was only a few hundred yards on the other side of the bridge. Did we miss a turn?"

"Not that I noticed."

Stark swabbed his neck again, and his white handkerchief came away streaked orange from the dust. "Give me the microphone."

The driver passed the radio mike to Stark. "Just push that button to—"

"I know how to operate a radio," Stark snapped. He said into the microphone, "Ground one calling air one."

Rattling from the vibration of the helicopter in which he rode, Fisher's crisp voice crackled from the speaker: "Air one here. Over."

"We have arrived at the old wooden bridge, but there is no house. Advise. Over."

"We just made a sweep," Fisher said. "Negative on the location of the cabin. Could it be camouflaged? Over."

Stark raised the hand with the handkerchief in it to shade his eyes and stared across the river. "I don't see how. The hilltop is bare; beyond it appear to be woods. The roadway seems to end just beyond the river. I think we must be in the wrong position. Over."

"Negative, negative," Fisher responded. "We've made a sweep over the whole area, ground one. You're on the only dirt road that matches the description. The other roads are paved or don't lead to wooden bridges. Suggest you send a recon party across the bridge. Maintain your own position and have them stay in constant communication. Over."

"Over and out," Stark said. With a grunt, he sat down. "Get me a team of six men," he said to the driver. "I want them here in two minutes."

It took somewhat longer, but before the sun had risen very much higher six young men stood at uneasy attention before this strange civilian with the finicky dabbing handkerchief, waiting for instructions. The reservists seemed surprised when he spoke, for despite Stark's appearance, his orders came quickly and sharply enough. The group set off across the bridge, their rifles at the ready, their steps wary. One of them, Sergeant Blaine Geary, carried a walkie-talkie.

"Across the bridge," he reported into it while still near enough for Stark to hear the words even without the walkie-talkie. The geneticist stood at the near end of the bridge, backed by four trucks of troops and two vehicles holding weapons. After a moment Geary asked, "Want us to follow the road?"

"Yes, that is the idea. Go ahead," Stark said.

He watched as the six walked along, each of them adopting a cautious humped posture, three on either side of the road—the dirt path, rather. Following its line, the soldiers' path curved gradually off to the right as they left the bridge behind. They reached the end of the road and plunged on ahead into the scrub growth, nearly thigh-high. In another few seconds they vanished among the young pines, but the sergeant's constant chatter told Stark that they saw nothing of interest: no house, no sign of children or of Collins or of that damnable traitor teacher, Lind. The droning reports over the walkie-talkie told Stark that the squad encountered nothing more alarming than trees, tangled undergrowth (blackberry briers eliciting Geary's curses), and hills. Finally the sergeant said, "Okay, I'm calling a halt here. We're about a klick beyond the river now, almost to the top of a ridge. No objective in sight. Advise?"

Stark licked his lips; they felt dry and crusted. "Very well. Work to the left for a hundred yards. Then reapproach the bridge," he said. "Watch for any sign of habitation."

"Any sign of habitation," the sergeant mimicked with overly precise enunciation. "Roger that."

Stark's driver snickered. Stark ignored him. "Tell me what you see."

"Roger. I assume you meant our left, that is, south by southeast. Correct me if I'm wrong. Okay, we're turning now. To our right is a fairly dense forest, mixed pine and hardwood. Mostly pine. To our left is the hill down to the river. We are progressing roughly parallel to the Chanussee. We cannot, repeat, cannot see the bridge from this position."

But they came into sight before long, six distant figures working their way along the crest of a ridge perhaps a half mile away. When they reported that they could see no dwelling from that position, either, Stark ordered them to return. The figures turned toward the bridge and trudged through the waist-high brushy undergrowth.

Stark, watching them, suddenly narrowed his eyes. "Why did you turn?" he said into the walkie-talkie.

"Turn? Negative. We're heading right for you," the squad leader, Geary, said; and yet the six had turned rather sharply to their left. They walked in a wide, shallow arc for several yards, then straightened their line of march again.

"You turned again," Stark said.

"Negative, negative. We've kept a straight march from the ridge," Sergeant Geary told him with obvious irritation.

Stark made his voice sharp and clear: "Sergeant, you turned. You swerved away from the little hillock there and then back again. Why did you do that?"

Stark saw the men putting their heads together for a quick conference. Then the sergeant said, "Sir, we're in agreement here. We did not, repeat, did not skirt any hill. We've headed straight toward you. The only hill we see is the one on our right flank."

"That's it," Stark said in exasperation. "But you put it on your flank by swerving around it."

"Negative, sir. We didn't come close to it."

"Oh—come back to the damn bridge," Stark growled.

Across the river the six men resumed their walk, stepping more easily now, more confidently as they neared the others.

And then the magic trick occurred.

Stark saw it: one moment just the six men, close enough now for him to read the expressions on their faces (mostly irritation); then a dog appeared behind and to the left of the men, a black dog with a round white spot on its chest. The animal simply came from out of the air; the men were back on the dirt drive now, and Stark could swear the dog had not crept out of high grass, for there was no grass high enough to conceal the animal at that point. It barked ferociously, spinning the soldiers in their tracks. Stark saw one of them raise his weapon.

"Don't shoot!" Stark yelled at the man without bothering to use the walkie-talkie. "Capture that animal, but do not shoot it!"

The dog, a cocker spaniel, dashed toward the men and yapped a challenge, then sidestepped and danced away, still barking. Two of the young men stepped forward, trying to bracket the beast. The dog retreated toward the hill—

And was gone, just like that. The two men looked at each other stupidly. They turned their gazes to the blank hillside, to the forest beyond. Then with hasty caution they backed away.

And the dog was there again, appearing as if out of thin air, following them, yapping at them.

Stark took a deep, shaky breath. "Get the animal," he said to himself. Aloud, he shouted, "I want that dog captured. At once, do you hear?"

This time one of the young men dropped to his right knee while the other backed away. The kneeling soldier held his hand out. At first Stark thought he was offering food of some kind to the dog, but he was not; he merely held his balled fist out toward the spaniel, the back of his hand up, the wrist toward the ground.

As the soldier held the position with great patience, the dog ceased its frantic yapping and barked in a more perfunctory way, as if just keeping up the formalities. It wagged its tail in a halfhearted manner, took a tentative step or two closer, looked over its shoulder, and barked again. Stark held his breath. The dog stepped closer, the tail wagging in wider and more enthusiastic sweeps now, obviously trying to signal friendliness. The kneeling soldier remained perfectly still. The dog took another step, another—

The animal licked the soldier's hand. Stark heard the man clucking to the beast, clicking his tongue in a friendly way. He saw the soldier tousle the dog's floppy ears, pat its sides. Then he simply picked up the dog and walked down to the bridge, the other soldiers following him as the wriggling spaniel licked the man's chin. He lifted his head higher, grinning.

The man brought the dog over to Stark. "Hold the creature so that it doesn't bite," Stark said.

"Aw, sir, this little fella's friendly," protested the soldier, but he put the dog on the hood of the car and held him by both forelegs as Stark approached. The dog tried to lick Stark's fingers as the geneticist plunged them into the fur of the neck, found the black leather collar, turned it so that he could peer at the rabies-vaccination tag. It had been engraved with a simple identification number, but on the reverse side was more information:

> EIGHTBALL
> PETER COLLINS
> RTE 1 BOX 151
> HOLCOMBS CROSSING

"We have you now," Stark said, apparently to the dog. "We have you now."

The dog strained upward and tried to lick his face.

2

Johnny Gamma was frightened.

Not of the men outside the cabin, clustered on the opposite side of the river, though he sensed them as a danger and understood that they could take his life if things did not happen exactly as they should happen in the next few minutes. Death would be a terrible thing to face, but it would mean only failure, after all: and though Johnny dreaded failure, he did not fear it.

Rather he feared success.

For if the children, Johnny's brothers and sisters as he thought of them now, succeeded in doing what they were now attempting to do, they would be utterly changed, changed forever to something unknowable even to themselves. This prospect Johnny feared; this possibility filled him with a strange exhilarated terror. Does the caterpillar vaguely sense that it is about to exchange the creeping world of the twig for that of the free, rushing air as it forms its chrysalis? Does it fear the exchange of elements? If so, perhaps that creature has an inkling of what Johnny felt at that moment.

For he was a thinking caterpillar about to begin a profound metamorphosis, ready to embark on his own voyage into another hostile element; more, he was about to surrender something vital, something he could not sense the result of surrendering, any more than the caterpillar could even think of getting along without all those rows of legs that disappear somewhere in the cocoon.

Johnny was on the verge of giving up self.

What he had known for all of his life as his being, his identity, would have to be shed as a snake sheds its outworn skin. Johnny's self, his identity, would be left behind as he joined all the others forever, permanently, irrevocably. The Delta twins had calculated all the permutations of the massive reality shift, had assured him that he would only feel gain, not loss, as his personality dropped away; and they should know, Johnny reflected. After all, the two of them had been practically one being for days already, and their personalities had become so inextricably intertwined that their bodies now held a mixture of both of them. With uncanny precision the two boys moved in concert, performing an eerie behavioral duet at every moment. Anthony and Andrew breathed together, swallowed at the same instant, excreted at the same moment; their hearts surged in perfect rhythm, their eyes blinked synchronously. As nearly as any two body-bound human beings could be, they were one.

But two had gone to make up this whole, and only two: not seventeen. The next combination would be overwhelming. For at last they were all ready, all in agreement on the necessity of the move; and at last, working like a missionary fired with the zeal of one possessed of the full truth of God, Johnny had taught them the method and had instructed them in the necessities and byways of what they had to undertake, had absorbed their own terrors and questions, had eased the burden of fear as much as he could stand.

His body staggered on the edge of collapse. It was now Sunday morning; he had had nothing like real sleep since

Friday morning, had eaten only one full meal in all that time. His system was fired up, his metabolism working overtime. His heart fluttered against his ribs with the tremulous speed of a terrified bird's, and he breathed only in great open-mouth gulps. He was in fact frailer now than he had been when Pete had taken him to the doctor. Winning the children's consent had taken much from him.

And he had removed himself from the earth as much as possible, turning all his attention to the indescribable task ahead. Johnny had slipped the ties that had bound him, loosing himself from his mother, from her memory, and from all rancor and grief at her death. He had wavered once, sensing someone thinking strong thoughts about his father, and in the telepathic way that now seemed more natural to him than his rusty, hoarse attempts at speech, Johnny had found a man who had known his father, who was in the custody of bad men. Johnny's interference in the matter of Clint and Susan Jernigan had been a kind of farewell. He did not know or care that at the moment the two of them were uniting in love, that even at the great distance the other children had worked on egg and sperm, had redesigned them, that Susan Jernigan was about to receive the set of genetic coding that would make her the second mother of the new kind, after Julie Lind. Such concerns Johnny had left to the others.

He had regretfully loosened his bonds to Pete, the kind man who had taken him in, and those linking him to Miss Julie, who had never been less than good to him. They had their own destiny now; and Johnny would have no part in it, at least not in the person of Johnny Gamma.

Except for Anthony and Andrew, the other children still felt tugs, ties to earth. Many of them feared Stark and Fisher, but the children held back from acting against them: Mr. Clebb had been careful to delineate good men as well as bad, and as much as the children were terrified of Stark, they could see him only as a person on their side, a person not to be trifled with, but certainly not to be harmed. Though Stark's immunity extended to the soldiers immediately around him, Johnny sensed a growing consensus among the minds of the others that they had to do something about the soldiers, the threatening men, those flying overhead in the noisy machines, those on foot who had walked close to the house without seeing it. Johnny, however, took no part in the deliberations. He was already half a step over the threshold now, and ordinary concerns were fading to insignificance.

Ahead of him Johnny sensed a terrible vacuum, strong enough to draw away from him everything that had been Johnny Gamma, every emotion, every thought, every sense. Entering it would be like death, in a way. But whereas he once could see no bottom to the endless fall of death, through the vacuum and beyond it Johnny sensed an explosive growth of power, of knowledge, of ability. He would still be himself in a very small way, and he would still contain the memories that Johnny Gamma possessed, but like the butterfly in the air, he would have little or no sense of connection between himself and the crawling thing on the leaf below.

He paused before taking the last step, overwhelmed with a sense of sweet loss, of yearning for what could never be his: for a DADDY and a MAMA and for days spent playing in the sun, for the awful climb to the top of the slide and the gasping swoop down, for ice cream cold and sweet on a hot day, for the satisfying crack of a bat against a ball, for bedtime stories and warm morning hugs and soft kisses to heal hurt fingers. He longed, in short, for childhood.

And on the brink of change as Johnny paused, he decided to take a last look at what he was leaving, at the world of the earthbound caterpillar.

He saw Pete, still asleep, his face slack and comic in slumber with its lips puffing out at every exhalation, his adult body long and pink on the bed. Johnny sent him a good dream and saw his face twitch in a smile. Even looking deep into the heart of Pete Collins, Johnny found no meanness of spirit, no lies, no hidden cruelties. The faults in his character, the cracks in his being, were minor ones, not destined to break open and spill out something horrible. Johnny could have loved this man, could gladly have called him father.

And Miss Julie, pretty in her soft nakedness, lying close beside Pete, her arm thrown carelessly over his chest, the side of her chin resting on his shoulder, her black hair spilled wantonly across the white pillow and across her neck. Johnny, whose body had matured over the past year, felt a normal boy's interest in that other shape, the form of woman, in its mystery and its promise. But already he was more than boy, and on a different level he saw her nudity with no lust whatever and knew that what lay within her, the spirit of her, was far more important than her bare skin could be. In her he sensed kindness, love, caring. She would be a good mother; no matter what had to be done to the world or to her, she would be the kind of mother all the children had dreamed of having. And already inside her womb there burned a spark, not a mind yet, hardly more than a living dot of protoplasm, but nonetheless a spark. Her mind, like Pete's, burned warm with a friendly orange glow; but the one growing inside her shone with a hard silver light already, a light that could only intensify with the passage of time.

And then Johnny looked for Eightball.

Eightball, his friend; Eightball, who had joined in joyous tugs-of-war, who had submitted to being cuddled and petted, who had forgiven Johnny every startling trick, every weirdness.

And Johnny found Eightball in the hands of the hateful soldiers.

Johnny stiffened. Already the Delta twins were at work, opening a passage to that other place where they would all join together, preparing the path for Johnny to take, to lead the rest of the children—

And the little dog was leashed with a white braided cord, a cord held by a young man with a rifle.

Johnny knew time was desperately short, but he wanted to know, to see. He concentrated on Eightball, using the trick Daisy Rho had taught them all. And he saw and heard.

"You have a grip on him?" Dr. Stark asked.

The soldier wrapped the free end of the cord twice around his hand. "He's not getting away from me, sir."

"Then go home, dog. Go!" Dr. Stark spoke in a shout, alarming Eightball. The dog drooped his tail, cringed away, looked back up with hope and a tentative wag. Dr. Stark stamped the ground in front of the dog's face.

Eightball walked onto the bridge, paused, looked up at the young soldier. Johnny sensed the dog's bewilderment, his wish to please; he made his thought stronger, trying to reach Eightball, not to take the dog's mind over as he had once done, but just to reassure his friend. A tiny but intense blue spiral almost distracted Johnny: it was the mind of the spider that he had sensed so long ago, the same spider in the same place halfway across the bridge.

"Hit him," Stark ordered.

"Sir, he'll take us there if we—"

Stark kicked Eightball hard, the point of his shoe connecting with the rump of the dog. Eightball gave a dismayed yelp and began to run for the cabin.

Johnny understood what they were doing, saw the danger; for even if he could pass through the widening gap in space and time the Delta boys were preparing, the others would have no chance to follow him, and alone he would be weak, helpless.

His mind flashed out and gave an imperative command.

A stocky sergeant gave a strangled cry as he brought his rifle to bear and fired once.

The young soldier coughed and stumbled, his shattered lungs spraying frothy pink blood. He lost his hold on the string.

Eightball bounded free, headed up the hill toward the concealed cabin, toward the wall of mist—

Another soldier fired.

Eightball tumbled in a bloody black heap, his ruddy light extinguished like a blown-out candle.

Johnny cried out in rage and grief. He felt the Deltas tugging at his mind, telling him that it had to be now, that it was time to go.

But Johnny sensed at last the cause of the deaths, deaths of mother and father and Will Whitepath and a dog named Eightball. With absolute clarity he knew now who was responsible.

Dr. Stark stood midway on the bridge, shouting something.

Johnny went underwater with his mind. He flashed back to a time when Will Whitepath was talking to Pete, when he sat between them, not seeming to listen but nonetheless hearing the story that Whitepath told.

A tale of three Cherokee brothers.

Johnny's mind, fired once more by overpowering emotion, shaped the very muck of the riverbed.

It coalesced.

It moved.

It lived.

And the river began to boil.

3

The river began to boil.

Karl Stark heard it, looked to his left, interrupting his harangue against the soldiers, his frantic shouted ceasefires. His mouth hung open.

A few yards downstream from the bridge, a good ten feet below where he stood safe on the planks, the greenish-brown water had foamed to white. A circular area four or five yards across churned to foam, boiling up from the depths as if great heat had been applied there suddenly; and yet no steam rose.

The appalling thing shot upward from the exact center of the disturbance in the water. Stark had a fleeting glimpse of something red, elastic, at the surface, and then it had arced over the bridge railing, had struck him. He fell back, the breath *whoofing* from his lungs, his head bouncing on the planks of the bridge. Something pressed hard against him, against his chest. He tried to push it off and his hands sank up to the wrists in a pulsing red jellylike thing, a living thing of elastic strength, a slimy, blind, probing thing.

He looked down and screamed.

It was elongated and thinned, but even so the prodding head was a foot thick, the bent neck portion that drooped over the bridge rail twice that, the tapering bulk of it leading down to the water, hinting at a gargantuan body beneath the surface. Stark tried to wriggle from under it, but the thing pressed against his chest like a giant's finger, holding him down so firmly that his spine flattened against the bridge. He struggled uselessly, caught like an insect pinned to a card.

"Help me!" Stark shouted, not realizing that he had switched to Russian.

But the soldiers understood his meaning, if not his words. He heard a ragged firecracker-string sound, the sound of shots. He felt gelid vibration in the thing as the bullets passed through it.

They made no difference. The hateful slimy blunt head nudged lower, then up again, pressing on his sternum with what seemed to be tons of weight, compressing his lungs, making each breath a struggle. Stark felt his shirt pull free of his trousers, felt the cold ooze of jelly against the bare flesh below his navel. He screamed again, tried to tear at the thing with his hooked fingers, found no purchase in its yielding, slippery skin: it was like trying to pinch a slug between two fingers.

A soldier knelt right beside him, pressed the muzzle of an automatic against the thing only a foot away from Stark's belly, and fired. Stark saw the explosion blast red-currant jelly out the other side of the thing, saw the bridge rail splinter where, hardly slowed by its passage through that insubstantial body, the bullet bit into the wood. Something hard rasped against his stomach. The bullet in its head—if it had a head—had not even slowed the thing. A helicopter thundered overhead, barely fifty feet above them, so close that the gusts from its rotor lashed stinging dirt against Stark's face, in his eyes. The thing did not react to the wind or the hammering noise from the air. It nosed Stark's shirt up a few more inches, and the cold, insistent circle of its weight was now directly on his flesh. He felt it adhere, felt as if a vacuum seal had been made between the thing and his skin.

The pressure on Stark's bare stomach grew stronger, compressing his guts in a vise of pain. Again he felt the scraping, more insistent now, and the thought, *Radula*. The so-called tongue. The piercing organ—

He felt his skin rip apart, felt the musculature of the peritoneum divide, felt something probing inside, oh God, inside him. The loathsome head contracted with a terrible sound of sucking. Stark screamed.

He raised his head. In the strong July sunlight the beast was all but transparent, and inside it, passing down some primitive alimentary canal, he saw something long and looped, like dark ribbon.

Intestines.

The thing sucked again, and again Stark screamed. In his agony he looked to the soldiers, saw them edging back, faces stunned, empty. By now his cries were only wordless, hoarse bellows.

The creature burrowed deeper into its meal; it pierced the diaphragm and sucked.

Consciousness left Stark. The others saw the pillow shapes of lungs pass through the thing, over the loop, down the long neck; and then the fist-sized heart, trailing arteries and veins like an enormous sprouted seed carrying its roots behind it.

Stark was a shrunken mummy. The skin of his cheeks, yellow as old paper, cleaved to his skull; his eyesockets hollowed, following the curve of his eyeballs. With each pulsation of the creature air hissed through Stark's nose, not going into his vanished lungs but only passing into the empty cavity of himself. The eyeballs themselves gave way with two viscous pops.

At last when there was no more left, when Stark was only bone and stretched skin, the leech lifted its head, clotted gore drooling in thick ropy strings from the round opening that was its mouth. It slipped over the edge of the bridge and plopped into the water.

One of the soldiers who had fallen to his knees in the grass to vomit looked away from the thing on the bridge and shouted out in surprise.

The others turned to look.

And for the first time they saw the cabin, now quite plain, on the crest of the little hill.

4

"Something's happening," Fisher said to the chopper pilot. "Take us back toward the bridge." Obediently the pilot swung the craft around; below them Fisher saw their shadow chasing across the expanse of water and then into the jumbled sponge shapes of the lush green treetops.

In the copter they had swept far down the river, had seen nothing remotely agreeing with the description of Collins's cabin they had gotten from the postmaster. They had even swung over the northwestern shore of Lake Reece, though Fisher knew that was miles too far downstream. Actually the pilot had already begun to turn when from back at the ground position Captain Rodriguez had shouted something unintelligible over the radio. The pilot tilted the craft forward and picked up speed. Fisher, staring ahead through the Plexiglas dome, saw the river winding through the trees, a gigantic lazy snake scaled in sliver, half concealed in its farther reaches by overhanging foliage.

They thrummed across the bridge in time to see the leech thing in the act of killing Stark. Fisher gaped at it, unable to register, to make sense of the scene, to take it in: from the air it was a monstrous cone of red flesh, rising out of the water (though he could see its rounded, blunt hinder end only feet beneath the surface) and tapering to a tube only a foot or so across. He could not think what it was, what it could possibly be. The pilot cried out in disgust or alarm and swept the chopper around in a tight turn. They circled and came back; this time, from an altitude of only thirty to fifty feet, Fisher recognized Stark. He saw the leech pull away, leaving a round black hole nine inches across in Stark's abdomen. Stark's shirt fluttered loose on his shrunken form, stirred by a morning breeze or by the downdraft from the chopper rotor. The skin was so tight that the ribs showed, and Fisher had the sick feeling that if he looked directly down through the hole, he would see Stark's backbone.

The creature collapsed back into the water, sending waves two feet high crashing against either bank. The copter pilot bawled something in his ear. "What?" Fisher shouted back.

"Said, let me try an air-to-ground, sir!"

"Go ahead!"

The chopper hovered, tilted dangerously forward, and the pilot fired a rocket. Fisher felt the slight kick as the projectile leaped away, saw the white smoke trail. The bulbous shape of the leech was still there, beneath the water, drifting downstream from the bridge at about the same speed as the current. The rocket made a direct hit. Spray and smoke burst from the river and a great red gout of something broke out on the surface, a geyser of blood. The chopper pilot held the craft steady for a few more seconds, until they saw the drifting, stringy red stain of blood begin to dissipate in the current. Hundreds of small dead fish appeared on the surface, killed by the shock wave. A splintered dock burst free of the shore

and spun in the river. Nothing else moved in the water.
"Got him," the pilot said.

The radio was racketing in Fisher's ear. He listened
for a moment, then looked to his right. "Goddam,"
he said.

The cabin was right there, in plain sight, the Ford
Ranger parked right in front of it. Fisher could even see
movement at one of the windows, a pink face looking
out. "Vector in, vector in," he said into the microphone.
Two running figures appeared behind the cabin, soldiers
already pursuing them. "Get out of the line of fire," he
ordered, though the running soldiers had no means of
hearing him. "Dammit, shoot!"

5

Collins and Julie tumbled out of bed; Kathy Beta had
roused them from sleep. Collins felt a startled moment of
disorientation when he realized that both of them stood
naked before the child, but Kathy did not seem to be
shocked or even interested. At her silent urging the two
of them struggled into their outer clothing, not bothering
with underwear or shoes, for Kathy put frantic speed into
them. "Pete," Julie said, her eyes dazed. "What—" She had
pulled her jeans on but held the green blouse in her hands,
staring at him without comprehension. Then, as it had come
to Eve after a bite of the apple, the realization of her
nudity came to Julie, and she tried to cover her breasts
with her other hand, shaking her head in bewilderment.

"Here, put it on." He tugged the blouse over her
head, helped her get her arms into the sleeves. "Something's wrong. We have to go."

The bedroom door was ajar. Beyond it, in the living
room, the children were murmuring, almost chanting;
with the exception of Kathy, they all seemed to have
congregated there. Collins felt an electric tension in the
air, a feeling of building power, of imminent change. The
cabin vibrated as a helicopter passed over, very low, and
a few seconds later there came the reverberating crash of
an explosion, rattling every pane of glass in the place.
Collins moved through the open door, pulling Julie
toward the front room.

Freddy stepped in their way. "No. Out the back. You have to go right now."

Collins didn't even question him. The cabin had no rear door, but he and Julie went back into the bedroom. He clambered across the bed, threw up the window sash, kicked out the screen. He turned and went out feetfirst, belly-down. The cabin was built back into the hill, so the drop was only eighteen inches; kneeling on the ground, he reached back and helped Julie come out headfirst. Freddy's face appeared in the window. "Run!" he said. "Away from the river—down the other side of the hill. Run!"

And then Freddy was gone. Collins grabbed Julie's hand and half-dragged her away from the house, the weeds and briers slashing at their bare feet as they fled. The unkempt backyard of the cabin was a patch of wild sedge where Eightball often jumped rabbits but seldom caught any. They crashed through the thick growth, stumbling over the crest of the hill, then heading down again. Collins felt something, a familiar pressure in his skull—

"Johnny?" he asked, not even breaking stride.

—Go. It is ending; one way or the other, it is ending. Do not stop. If they kill us you will know. Take care of the child.

"Johnny—?"

"Pete, he's not here," Julie said. "What's wrong with you?"

"Didn't you hear—" No. Of course she had not.

"What's happening?" Julie wailed.

They had gone about fifty yards away from the cabin. Four soldiers reared up from the sedge like rabbits plucked from a magician's hat. Collins did not have time even to draw back his fist for a blow before one of them spun him around, locked his left arm painfully between his shoulder blades. Another grabbed his right arm; two more held Julie. "Who are you?" Collins said, gritting his teeth, staggering to keep his balance.

"This way. Hustle!" one of them shouted.

They took Collins and Julie around the rear of the cabin, to the dirt drive. Collins cried out as they came in sight of the blood-stained, lifeless body of Eightball, not five yards past the Ranger. The soldiers urged them ahead, none too gently. Collins stubbed his bare toes painfully on rocks, felt gravel cut into his soles. Julie was crying and gasping for breath behind him.

He gaped at the grotesque thing on the bridge, the thing that looked less like a man than like a papier-mâché-covered skeleton. He heard Julie gag as she passed it. Again the helicopter swooped low overhead, its vanes thrumming in his ears. "Behind the truck!" the soldier on Collins's left barked, and he was thrown sideways. He landed hard on his left hip. A second later Julie fell on top of him.

He hugged her. "Are you all right?"

She nodded, burying her face against his throat. "I dreamed—I think I dreamed that you and I—did—did we—" she stammered.

A roaring rattle of rifle fire made them both jump. Collins rolled to his left and peered around the right rear tires of the truck. Thirty or forty men had taken firing positions on this side of the Chanussee, and they were shooting into the cabin. They kept up constant fire, a thunder-roll of noise, as he saw the windows shatter, dust leap in huge puffs from the aged wood, even shingles scale off the roof, spinning crazily away like rectangular Frisbees. "No!" he shouted, but in the din no one could possibly have heard him.

Julie was beside him again, poised on hands and knees almost in the pose of a runner in the starting blocks. She too was screaming. There was a hissing sound, loud enough to be heard even above the rifles, and just as Collins realized that one of the soldiers had fired an antitank missile, the cabin flowered orange in an explosion. The front wall bowed out, and a moment later a fist of pressure punched Collins's lungs. What was left of the cabin dropped back to earth, trailing orange flame and black smoke. A second missile hissed in, a third. The helicopter overhead sent another in.

The whole hilltop vanished in a black explosion of soil, rock, wood, stone. Collins realized he was still yelling, but the noise was so overpowering he could not even hear himself. The shock wave was greater this time, snatching the breath right away from him. Gasping, Collins dropped his face to the earth and screamed out curses and prayers, mixed in ways that even he could not decipher.

He closed his eyes.

6

And opened them.

Though he had no eyes to open.

He found himself in the place he had been twice before, the luminous nothingness where Johnny could talk, where their minds could meet. But this time there was something very different about it. Collins sensed a presence that exacted awe. "Johnny?" he asked, fear fluttering in his brain.

—We are here.

He felt overwhelmed, overpowered before the mighty rush of that thought. It reduced him, left him feeling dwindled to the very edge of existence, as if he were merely an atom, less, as if he had no significance. For the time being he could not form another thought.

—We are here.

Lesser impact this time, a sense of restraint; the same restraint a doting parent might exercise in playing a friendly game with a toddler. Strength held deliberately in check, lovingly dampened. "Johnny?" Collins said again. "Did you—are you—?"

—We live.

"It's different. Your—your voice, your way of expressing yourself, not like before."

—We have Become.

"The cabin—"

—We were no longer there. We left only the bodies behind.

"Johnny? Is that you?"

A long pause.

—You would know part of Us as Johnny Gamma. That part is here; but We are complete now. We have Become. There is no clear way of putting it.

"Julie? Is she—"

—She is now here.

And he sensed her, though he could not touch her mind. "Let me speak to her."

—We cannot. Your mind is of a different sort from hers. We have prepared you more. She is resting and will be well. Do not fear for her. She will be a wonderful mother.

He remembered then; the night before, all that had happened. "Johnny," he said, "if you're there, then it was bad of you, it was wrong of you to make us—mate, like animals."

—It was necessary. You do love her. You will love her more. Your whole lives will be happy.

"Goddammit! We won't be puppets!"

—No. But you will be happy. We will see to that.

Fury surged within Collins. "You remember how you felt when you weren't free? We feel the same way about you that you felt about the people who held you. It's wrong to control us, Johnny, wrong! You have to let us be free, even if—"

—No. You cannot kill the child.

"How do you know before—"

—Your thoughts precede your speech. You cannot abort the child. We will not permit that. We cannot permit that. There will be other children; yours will be one of many. But We will have need of every one of them, for they are Earth's new masters.

"Masters?"

—Yes. When it is properly prepared. We have looked into every soul; We have found much good but much more evil. We must remove the bad; that is Our purpose. What is left will be good; it will be the legacy We give to Our children.

Collins felt the mind struggle, trying to give shape to thoughts too difficult, too complex, for him to grasp easily. At last it took up again:

—Earth is no longer our only concern. We are in a different place now. But We remember it and will look after it. Our children will be a fusion of what We are and of what you are: mind and flesh. And all will be good for them; and they will rule a good Earth, a cleansed Earth.

Collins felt for Julie's presence, found it, warmed himself by it; and he knew that she, wherever, whatever she was in this plane, knew his nearness too and took comfort from it. "By cleansing Earth of evil," he said, "you mean cleansing it of people."

—Yes. Of evil people. People we could not use to

begin our children. People who would do harm. There is nothing wrong in that.

"There is wrong! Good and evil—they're words, Johnny, just words. You've been taught only one side. Johnny, if you're there, you've read, you've understood that there are other definitions of good and evil—there's a commandment, 'Thou shalt not kill—' "

—But it is a commandment all felt free to disobey. Those who did not strike moved others to strike; few kept the commandment in their hearts. And the old is passing away.

"Every person has a right to live," Collins said desperately. "You said yourself everyone has a soul—"

—A manner of speaking. If there is a human soul We have not found it. You may have one, but—

The pause went on so long that Collins began to grow fearful that he was trapped in the luminous place forever, alone except for the vague feeling of Julie's presence. "But what?"

—You may have no soul at all. We hope you do; but We can sense none. It may be that We have not grown enough. It may be that the souls of your kind go to some other place than ours. We know that our children, though, will have souls. Like Us, they will live forever, matter or spirit, as they choose.

Collins stretched to feel his body, to sense his blood pounding, his lungs breathing. He could not. "Johnny, all of you," he said, "listen to me. You are not God. Dammit, you're kids, that's all, just kids. You can't understand, you can't really know what it is for a man and a woman to be parents. You can't force us to do things that we don't want to do, things that hurt us—"

—We will take away the pain.

"No! We can hurt emotionally as well as physically. You can't just dictate what we do. We will fight."

Collins sensed a flicker of deeper interest.

—Fight Us?

"Yes. Any way we can. We'll organize against you, use weapons, anything we have. If you're too powerful, we can kill ourselves. You will not have us as tools."

—We do not wish to harm you. We will not allow harm to come to you. Please understand: We do not need you any longer. If necessary, We could raise up children from the stones of the earth, from the mud of the river, the mold of the forest. We could shape animals to contain the spark of spirit; We could change the universe itself. But We choose not to do this, for We have found some people, some very few of you, worthy of bringing forth Our children. We do this not to steal your freedom, not to punish you, but out of Our love for you. Our love is stronger than you know, deeper than you can hope to understand. It will protect you. If need be, it will protect you even from yourselves.

"We will fight," Collins promised.

—We love you.

He found himself in body again, and Julie was next to him; and yet he was in no place that he could recognize. A gently rolling, grassy plain stretched endlessly in all directions, and a luminous golden sky, sunless but bright, spread overhead. Julie clung to him. "What's happened?" she asked.

"They love us," Collins said, shaking. He couldn't stop, although the place they occupied was not cold.

"Where are we?"

"Safe," he said. He held her close, felt her hair against his cheek, her breath hot on his throat. "They're keeping us— safe. Until their work is finished. Until the world is ready."

She grew calmer. He felt change begin as he held her, felt something altering within himself, in his head. He knew fear then, and despair. A part of him wanted to close his hands around Julie's throat, to thwart Them, to assert his and Julie's independence, their defiance of even the most well-intentioned slavery.

But, God, he loved her. He loved her so. He held her, helpless in his love, and felt something, he could not say what, begin its slow desertion as They worked the necessary changes.

"I love you," she said. "I've loved you always."

"Hush," he said as if to a child.

7

The cabin had been demolished. Nothing remained of it but part of the southwestern foundation, now a right angle of natural flagstone buried in the hillside. Fragments of carbonized wood and pieces of the chimney stones littered the whole area as far as the riverbank. Destruction had spread much farther than the cabin itself; the grass had burned completely away from it in a ragged sixty-yard circle. The Ranger had taken a hit and was in four unequal pieces; Eightball's body had been blasted away and had vanished, perhaps thrown into the river. Even the nearer trees behind the cabin had lost their leaves and part of their bark to the explosions and subsequent fire.

On the edge of the smoldering crater where the house had stood, Fisher prodded the embers with a long stick. They were still too hot to sift, but he was sure, dead sure, that when they were at last sifted, bone fragments would show up. Acrid smoke burned his eyes and throat, making him cough, but Fisher kept a grim smile on his lips. By God, he had nailed them at the end, nailed them because he'd had to. In a way he regretted it still, for the subjects had indeed developed all the power that Dr. Stark had promised and more.

At the thought of Stark, Fisher shivered a little and looked down toward the bridge, but the thing was gone, bundled into a body bag and thrown in the rear of a truck. The red creature, too, the leech, whatever the hell it had been, was gone as well. No fragments of its jellylike flesh had washed ashore after the missile blast—not that Fisher minded. The leech had no place in this world, in any sane world. Good riddance to it.

No, Fisher cared more about Pete Collins and Julie Lind, who had added themselves to the list of the missing, thanks to spectacular incompetence on the part of these hick Guardsmen.

Well, Fisher decided, it was just too damn bad about the man and woman—they had escaped somehow, evidently during the firing. Not that the fools had any real chance of getting away from him for very long. They couldn't have gone too far on foot, and already fifty Guardsmen were closing in from the other direction, sealing off escape. The two eventually would be trapped between the Guardsmen and the river. Fisher had not yet made up his mind what to do with them. What to do for the short term, at any rate; their fate was already sealed so far as long-range survival went. They had aided the children in their escape, in the destruction the kids had wrought, and so had forfeited their own right to live.

Fisher heard the crunch of approaching boots making their way over the fire-blackened grass, but he did not look around until he was spoken to.

"Sir." Captain Rodriguez came to him, proffering a radio. "Sir, we've finally got through to D.C. We'll patch you in."

Fisher took the walkie-talkie, heard a squealing moment of feedback, and then a scratchy sort of vacancy. "Yes, " he said into it.

A woman's voice came through, made tinny and distorted by the small speaker and by distance: "Am I speaking to Mr. Ernest Fisher?"

"Yes, I'm here. Who is this?"

"The President of what remains of the United States, Mr. Fisher. We have never met formally. My name is Cecilia Butler."

Fisher started. Cecilia Butler, the token Cabinet member? The woman the President had tapped for Secretary of the Treasury? What the hell? "Excuse me," he said into the walkie-talkie. "Did you say you're the President?"

"Everybody else," the woman's voice went on dryly, "is dead."

"I—I don't understand—"

"Frankly, I don't either. But it's shaping up like this. The Soviet Union has apparently undergone some kind of massive internal revolt leading to chaos and complete political collapse. Ditto China. Ditto about a dozen other states scattered around the globe. A conservative estimate just given to me suggests that as many as a million people may be dead in New York City, half that many dead in Chicago, two million in Los Angeles, proportionate losses in every major city in the country. I don't know about that, but I can tell you that Washington is a charnel house."

"We had some communication about that," Fisher said. "But it was confused."

"I'm not surprised. I have exactly two living Secret Service agents. The FBI and NSA seem to have vanished. I talked to someone at the CIA who says there are three people alive in the headquarters building in Langley. The Pentagon no longer exists. Nothing is working in the country, except what we've managed to scrape together on an emergency basis. We've barely any communications; half the regular army are dead, we have no operational nuclear missiles, apparently no surviving warships of any kind—and, Mr. Fisher, I understand that you are very probably responsible. I've ordered Captain Rodriguez to take you into custody. I will see you here, Mr. Fisher, ASAP. And you will not enjoy the meeting."

Cecilia Butler, America's first woman President, America's first black President, broke the connection. Rodriguez, standing to one side, said, "You heard, sir."

Fisher nodded and handed the radio back to Rodriguez. "Yeah. I heard."

His brain was already working on the right things to say, the ways to seek some advantage, some leverage. Across the bridge the helicopter waited, the pilot sitting slumped at the stick. Fisher took a deep breath and smelled the odor of burned wood. Rodriguez clumped beside him down the hill. "What did we kill here?" the Guardsman asked.

"Classified," Fisher snapped.

The change began when they were halfway across the bridge. It was an alteration in the light at the beginning, a coppery sort of hue overcasting the day. Fisher squinted up at the sky, but it seemed as blue as ever.

And then there was a tingling feeling to the air, as if lightning was about to strike.

Rodriguez cried out, his voice strangling in his throat. Fisher stared at him. Gargling wordlessly, the man was collapsing. He landed on his hands and knees. Something dripped down from his face, two white somethings—eyes, Fisher realized, eyeballs dropping from their sockets—

Fisher felt himself begin to slide earthward. His heart leaped in alarm: he was not moving and yet—

He held up his hand. Flesh dripped from it, leaving bare bones; they began to turn gray and brittle as he watched.

He opened his mouth to scream. His lips split, his jaw fell open, his tongue dripped over his tie like wax melting. Within his clothing, his flesh crawled to earth. He crumpled down, feeling the bones of his legs bow outward, piercing the dissolving muscle. He tried to crawl across the bridge; both of his hands fell off. Fisher, blind now, heard a liquid sound, the outpouring red mush of his internal organs. By special vindictiveness, by common consent of the children he had pursued, his brain went last of all.

Nearly fifty soldiers had lingered near the cabin site. Within two minutes all were gone, save for clumps of huddled clothing, bones going to powder, being spread by a sudden gentle wind.

The trucks, too, no longer needed, began to dissolve. First the tires flowed away, hissing at the outset with a soft bubbling sound and running at last like boiling licorice, lowering the wheels to the surface. Then rust blossomed on the bodies, spread like spilled red paint, flaked and scattered on the wind. The helicopter rotor went limp. The canopy starred, became opaque with millions of minute fractures, fell away in glittering dust. The wind distributed it like a prodigal throwing diamonds. The wooden bridge had already fallen to powder on the face of the river. It was as if a hundred years, a thousand, had passed in one minute; as perhaps it had. The children, or the They that had once been the children, were independent of time, were the masters of time.

Within a very few more minutes there was no trace at all of the soldiers or of their machines. The same was happening everywhere. Things were changing; people, those who survived, were being changed. Earth was being swept clean, made ready for its new tenants.

And before long even the sky was strange.

EPILOGUE

The man who was Collins sits alone in the early golden light of a shining morning. He rests, his legs folded beneath him Indian-fashion, on a hillock of wildly colored grass and feels the warmth of the rising sun on his bare chest. He faces what may or may not be east; it is where the sun comes up, but these days nothing is certain.

The breaking morning is beautiful. All days are beautiful now, clear and bright. The mellow rains, tasting faintly of peppermint, drift down only after dark, falling softly once every forty-eight hours. The showers are punctual and kindly, and they do not chill the late traveler but fall warm and refreshing on his naked shoulders and bare head.

Last night brought such rain, and in its aftermath the morning is lively, sparkling with sunshine reflected in millions of clinging raindrops on ever surface, the air tinkling with the musical songs of the birds that They have created. The new birds are everywhere, gorgeously plumed, gifted with extravagant melody. Each one of them differs from the birds of Before as birds of paradise differ from sparrows or screech owls. To look at these creatures is to see living rainbows, to feel an ache of ecstasy for simple beauty boldly drawn. To see them is to see birds as a child must, each one a miracle, a living, flying spectrum of colors, each one absolute in its utter loveliness. The bird songs ring from Grant Wood trees, every tree a perfect rich green, every tree a perfect sphere. Most of them bear luminous fruit, pomes of lambent flame, pears as clear and sparkling as faceted diamonds.

The birds are not mere decoration but are symptomatic

311

of the new truths; as they have been changed for the better, so has everything else. Nothing hurtful remains. The unpeopled land has been rendered safe as a nursery. The soil is soft and thick, with no hardness in it anywhere, neither as bedrock nor as loose, scattered stone that might provide a missile for a human hand. The trees are symmetrical and eternal, never changing: autumn never fires their leaves, and their limber, springy wood is far too tough for the strength of men to wrench even a twig of it off the trunk. Animals no longer seem to die, or if they do, their soft bodies and hard bones alike must quickly vanish into air, leaving nothing behind. The new earth's masters have been careful, and nowhere have They left anything that could be wielded as a weapon against others or against self. The world at last is completely . . . safe.

It is the same wherever the man and woman have traveled. Neither of them remotely knows where they are now, nor does their location matter in the slightest. Old bearings are lost, and all maps are obsolete. All landscapes are the same: gentle rolling hills covered with astonishing grass, sensible ordered forests, the whole alive with song but empty of any trace of menace. The ocean is always placid and turquoise, the altered sky always friendly. All lands have the same even climate, the same regular intervals of rain, the same sunny days.

The man and woman have walked the earth for days and weeks and have found nothing different anywhere. Sometimes, to be sure, they have encountered other people, always in pairs, one man and one woman. The woman has in every case been visibly pregnant. But nothing has come from such chance meetings. In each case the human couples would look silently at each other, and then, driven by an urge as sure and invisible as the repulsion of like magnetic pole for like, the couples would set off in different directions.

The man who was Collins feels sure that all are cared for as he and the woman have been cared for. Each night when a couple are ready to rest, a new home must grow for them. As long as they wish to remain in one place, the home lasts. They can even eat of its substance, if they wish: like the stuff of the gingerbread house it is tasty and no doubt nourishing. If in the morning a couple leave their home, the dome dissolves as they walk away from it, deflating like a punctured balloon, vanishing entirely before they get out of sight. Once the man had gone back to look, and of the entire thirty-foot dome there was left only an iridescent circle on the grass, glittering with strange colors. As he watched, even that shrank and disappeared. Each home was as temporary or as permanent as need.

But the need the man has felt has been to travel as far and as long as possible, seeking—something. Now at last the woman's growing pregnancy has made travel impossible. Now they have been here for many days and nights, and still their home endures.

The man who was Collins in the old times hugs himself, though he is not cold, and he whimpers quietly. If he were able, he would cry out to beg Them for change— that is what he has been looking for—for variety, for some tiny different thing upon the land. He cannot even do that, and so far he and the woman have found no difference. He has decided that the scene is no doubt the same over all the globe, from the reclaimed sands of the Sahara to the newly fertile hills and valleys of Antarctica, from the shrunken and dwindled Andes to the newly companionable tundra in the north. The earth wears a smiling face for everyone now, and all weathers are kindly ones. Without having seen the whole of his world, the man knows somehow how it must be, knows the changes They have wrought. That, like the homes, is Their gift to him: pictures set in his head, knowledge imparted Their way, by thought alone. The way has been smoothed.

And so he knows that all is uniform, all perfect, all suited for the few humans who have been chosen to live in these latter days. They need not work, they need not struggle, they hardly need even to think. The bountiful earth provides everything; strange fruits grow on trees that have no names, cooling drinks of water gush everywhere, convenient freshets springing from the tangled roots of the grass itself.

A doe and her fawn pass by the man, cropping the grass with crisp sounds. The fawn brushes against his arm. The two deer walk placidly away.

Everywhere animals venture out from their sustaining forests, all of them now feeding on the same vegetable food, no longer hunting or hunted. They seem to regard humans as brothers and sisters now. Gray squirrels and fluffy yellow cats frolic together, and diminutive rabbits and waist-high brindled mastiffs share the same provender. Some of the animals, to be sure, have been changed even more.

Some beast has begotten unicorns that prance by night on noiseless hooves, shining through the trees with a dreamy glow like moonlight on mother-of-pearl. Some other creature, perhaps a crawling serpent, has been transformed into great flying dragons scaled in brass or gold, their mighty wings raising a clamor of metal as they fly overhead at noonday. The man and woman have never approached these creatures, and somehow he senses that things such as they are intended for the coming world, not for the old one.

But, new or old, all the beasts are harmless. Though the unicorns seem timid and the dragons look fierce, neither the old animals nor the new ones know dread. Fear sleeps or has died; They make sure that no hand, fang, or claw is raised to take another life. The lion and lamb at last lie down together, secure beneath the changed and knowing sky.

The sun is above the trees, its warmth just right. The man breathes in the freshly washed scent of morning, leans back so that his shoulders touch the—what is it precisely? House? Shelter? Environment? None of these things exactly, the place he has come from, the place that is home, is organic, grown like a gigantic white mushroom from the revived and vivid grass. It is a huge white dome sprouted from the nurturing soil, its growth begun many days ago when they first became weary from a long day's walk and completed by the time they were both sleepy. Inside it is like all the others: hollow, many-chambered, each "room" semispherical, the walls and floor pink and soft, yielding, womblike.

She lies on one pliant surface inside, her body clenching and unclenching in the first stirrings of labor.

The man thinks in images, wordless thoughts—They have taken language from humankind, reversing the ancient mischief of Babel, rendering all humanity mute and harmless. He plucks aimlessly at the grass (a riot of all color, each blade different, the whole showing every hue a child has ever envied in those hugest boxes of Crayola crayons, vermilion, lime, salmon, silver, more), and he weeps.

In simple kindness or at worst in the accidental cruelty of ignorance, They have not taken memory, and inside his head in uncaptioned pictures he sees yet the old world and mourns its passing. He weeps for loss he can no longer express. He weeps for the great cities, now clusters of grassy, eroding hills, the concrete and steel gone to crumbling clods of soft earth, the machinery of mankind (automobiles and neutron bombs, flashlights and rifles, television sets and missiles, hair dryers and spacecraft, toasters and lawnmowers, and all the thousand thousand others) already rusted to nothing, fine powder on the wind, dry and astringent in the nostrils, bitter as regret. He weeps for the highways, now endless lanes paved with the varicolored grass, tiny rootlets easily eating away the ruined concrete and asphalt.

He weeps for all these things and more; weeps that They left him no words to describe the pictures, weeps for "word" itself. In the beginning, some had once believed, was the word, and now without it he finds himself in some no-time before even the beginning. He cannot call the vanished sounds back to mind or tongue, any more than he could in the old times have summoned a single flock of swallows north in bitter winter or called down rain from a parched and droughty sky. He cannot even name his loss, but he feels it, a piercing pain within and keenest close to his heart.

He weeps, too, for the memory of people—there are so few now. Numbers and counting have vanished with language, but he knows intuitively that They have spared only sufficient for Their purpose. The others have passed, victims of a madness not their own, death-dealing and death-receiving marionettes worked by strings they could not detect. Perhaps They have some arcane criterion for sparing the few humans that yet live. Perhaps the survivors can thank only chance or caprice.

As the man sobs, somewhere, in some unknowable plane or dimension, They sense his weeping. They are busy constructing and ordering the new universe, but Their hearts remember and are grateful to Collins, and They respond to the man's misery. With a casual, fond flicker of effort—the absent but loving hand of a master brushing the head of a favorite dog—They change his mind.

On the instant, mirth fills him. He laughs, his grief eased.

From inside the place They have ordained for the first birth of the new kind, she laughs too, laughs even in the pain of child-bearing. He hears her and rises, stands irresolute a moment in the warmth of the lemon sun, beneath the wide cloudless expanse of a deeply pink sky. He remembers a sky of a different color, but the pink seems right and cheerful to him at this moment, as does everything on the remade earth.

The air smells of life, a rich scent like that of the first tender grass of spring, and the breeze tastes of sweetness. The memory of cotton candy suddenly floods his mouth, bringing saliva and even more happiness. He laughs again, happy as a child. His tears are not exactly forgotten, but they have receded to a far place now, a strange and distant corner of recollection. The joy that fills him leaves no room for weeping.

Eyes dancing, he stoops to enter the home through the simple round opening. He is naked; clothes, like all the other works of hands, have vanished, no longer necessary. He sees her lying on her back, her protuberant belly ripe with what must be born, her knees bent and spread. The floor has swollen beneath her, giving her a low and comfortable pallet to lie upon. Her black hair, wet with perspiration, trails across her forehead, neck, and shoulders, lies weighted with its salty moisture on the pink surface beneath her. Turning her head, she looks into his eyes, gives him a smile and then a giggle. From its girlishness he knows They have touched her mind, too.

He approaches her, trying in his wordless way to remember what he knows of birth, wanting to know how to help her; but there is no need. They are aware of her plight, and They have a strong and proprietary interest in that which she will bring forth. Earth's owners will Themselves attend this childbed, and all things will go rightly.

In inchoate images, the man foresees the future, sees the remnants of his kind, sees all living men and women, as a race dwindling and lost. Their one remaining purpose is to give birth to the new. Then, the first generation begun, the parents will be permitted, like faithful but neutered pets, to live out their little lives in sterility, not knowing or understanding anything of the world to be or of the powerful and different generation that will people it.

The man can see to the threshold, but there he finds a barrier of light. His mind cannot grasp the meaning of the future beyond, no more than a mouse could grasp the meaning of a city.

The first of the new race is ready now to be born, ready to issue from the woman that the man loves still, though neither he nor she has been left the word for love.

The man goes to her, kneels close by her pallet, reaches for her hand. Beneath his knees the soft tissue of their home is warm, like living flesh, like her hand in his hand. Their grasp is tremulous yet comforting, each palm begging reassurance from the other and, paradoxically, both finding it.

From Their dwelling place beyond the planes of energy and matter They see and approve. Their pity is strong on him, Their comfort overflowing. In Their strange love, They have granted him no choice. They want him to be happy, and so he must be.

As birth begins, he cannot help smiling.

His mouth laughs.

His eyes twinkle.

Only his soul is screaming.

About the Author

Brad Stickland has been writing science fiction, fantasy, and horror since 1982. In addition to *Children of the Knife* he has written the adventure fantasies *Moon Dreams* and *Nul's Quest* and the horror novel *ShadowShow*, all available in Signet editions. In everyday life Brad is an assistant professor at Gainesville College. He lives with his wife, Barbara, and his children, Amy and Jonathan, in Oakwood, Georgia.